Letting Misery Go

JAN 2012

CH

Letting Misery Go

Michelle Larks

www.urbanchristianonline.com

Urban Books, LLC
78 East Industry Court
Deer Park, NY 11729

Letting Misery Go Copyright © 2011 Michelle Larks

ISBN 13: 978-1-60162-811-4
ISBN 10: 1-60162-811-0

First Printing December 2011
Printed in the United States of America

10 9 8 7 6 5 4 3 2 1

Distributed by Kensington Corp.
Submit Wholesale Orders to:
Kensington Publishing Corp.
C/O Penguin Group (USA) Inc.
Attention: Order Processing
405 Murray Hill Parkway
East Rutherford, NJ 07073-2316
Phone: 1-800-526-0275
Fax: 1-800-227-9604

Letting Misery Go

A Novel

by

Michelle Larks

This book is dedicated to the memory of my friend Mary LaFran Flanders; she was truly a warm, caring, classy, beautiful lady.

I'm going to miss you, RIP.
The book is also dedicated to the readers who bought and enjoyed *Keeping Misery Company*.

You asked for a sequel, and here it is! I hope you enjoy it. . . .

Acknowledgments

First, and foremost, I have to give thanks to my Father above. He continues to make a way out of no way and directs my path. Most of all, He gives me strength to keep going when I don't think I could take another step. I thank my Father for the many blessings He's bestowed upon me.

I'd like to send a big shout-out to my mothers: Mary and Jean. You have nurtured me and provided an ear when I needed someone to talk to. My mothers have been there for me emotionally, much like a safe haven during life's storms. I thank God for mothers who are able to love their children unconditionally.

My father and stepmother, I.H. and Carole, I love you.

To my daughters, Keisha and Genesse, I try to emulate my mothers and love you unconditionally. Know that I love you.

My sisters, Patrice, Sabrina, Adrienne, Donna, Catherine, and Rolanda—there's nothing like sister love, and I love all of you very much!

My brothers, Jackie, Marcus, Darryl, Wayne, Michael, and Rodney—I am so proud to be your sister. Much love to you!

Brothers Roland and Trey, I miss you so much, RIP.

To all my nieces and nephews: I'm proud of you all.

To my friends Kelley, Mina, and both Cynthia's, I've been MIA. You are always in my thoughts, even if we don't talk as much as we used to.

Acknowledgments

A special shout-out to my sister/friend authors: Sheila P. Miller, Dr. Linda Beed, Nikita Nichols, Dyanne Davis, Nicole Rouse, and Pat Simmons. Thank you, ladies, for the help you've provided to me over the years, and checking on me from time to time.

Special thanks to Joylnn Jossel, my editor, and Tee C. Royal, my agent. I don't know where I would be without either of you. You are both phenomenal women. Thank you for all your support and guidance.

Marina Woods, thank you for always stepping in and helping a sista out, when I need it.

Tera' Carter and Shelia Ross, thank you for encouraging me when times became crazy at school; and I didn't know how I was going to make it. Your words of encouragement were greatly appreciated. Can't wait to walk across that stage together.

A heartfelt shout-out to Greta Brown, owner of Paradise Web and Digital Designs. Thank you for revamping my Web site. I appreciate and needed it. Check her out. Thank you, Ghostwriter Extraordinaire, for the wonderful book trailers you've created over the years.

Kudos to the wonderful book reviewers for taking time out of their busy schedules to read and review my books. I appreciate it; you know who you are. I don't want to leave any one out.

I appreciate the book clubs, which have supported me over the years, and invited me to their meetings. I had a blast. I also want to thank the librarians who have invited me to their book fairs, and the bookstore managers and owners who allowed me to sign at their establishments.

Most of all, I have to thank the readers, old and new, who have purchased my books, and sent me encouraging e-mails. You've given me incentive to continue writing.

Acknowledgments

Last but not least, much love to my husband, Fredrick, who has walked beside me during this literary journey. I may not say it all the time, but I love and appreciate all your effort. Much love and thanks to my #1 fan.

Peace & Blessings!
Michelle Larks

Chapter One

Reverend Ruth Wilcox was in the throes of a deep sleep, tucked inside the master bedroom of her seven-room apartment. She resided in the Chatham Community, on the South Side of Chicago. She lay in the middle of a dark wood four-poster bed, wearing a sleeveless white cotton nightgown, trimmed with red eyelets. The garment was bunched over her thighs, and her left arm was tucked neatly under her head.

At five o'clock, the silver cordless telephone on the nightstand next to the bed sounded loudly. Ruth shuddered as she swam into consciousness. She turned toward the nightstand, squinted at the clock, and groped for the phone before voice mail kicked in.

"Hi, Momma," her youngest daughter, Naomi, whispered. Naomi was conversing quietly like she was inside the room too. "Are you awake?"

"Hello, Naomi. I wasn't awake, but I am now. Is something wrong?" Ruth asked fearfully. She clutched the telephone so tightly, her knuckles swelled and whitened.

"Well, Sarah called me late last night, to tell me some news about Daddy. I couldn't sleep a wink and apologize for calling you so early. I want to share it with you. . . ." Naomi's voice trailed off then. Wearing a peach-colored nightgown and bathrobe, with matching slippers on her feet, Naomi paced the airy bedroom of her three-bedroom town house in Edwardsville, Illinois. It was located on the outskirts of Southern Illinois University. Naomi had transferred to the Edwardsville campus following her freshman year at the Carbondale campus.

Ruth couldn't breathe for a moment as she forced out, "Is Danny, I mean, Daniel okay? What's wrong?"

Naomi's voice rose conspiratorially. "Lenora has finally left Daddy," she announced triumphantly, a smile touching her lips.

Sitting up straight, Ruth pulled the wrap scarf off her head, ran her fingers through her hair, and sighed heavily. "You don't think this call could've waited until later in the day?" she asked, chiding her child.

"Momma," Naomi replied, eyes widening, "I thought you'd want to be the first to know. Come on, you might put on a content façade for the rest of the world, but trust me, I know that you still love Daddy. I assumed the news would be the answer to your prayers," she added smugly.

"Well, you're wrong, Nay," Ruth replied grumpily after stifling a yawn. "I can't say that I've spent a lot of time praying for the demise of your father's marriage. Matrimony is a holy ritual, and as a Christian, you should feel a sense of sadness when any union comes to an end. Anyway, Lenora has left your father more than a few times over the past years. Why is this time any different?" she asked intently as she lay back down in the bed.

"You must not have talked to Sarah yesterday," Naomi remarked as she sat on the edge of the bed, pulled her robe down over her thighs, and crossed her shapely legs. "What's different this time is that Lenora served Daddy with divorce papers the day after she left. She left him five days ago." Her voice and eyebrows rose dramatically. "And guess what? She left the boys with

Daddy. Stepmother Dearest has flown the coop, and left the chicks with the rooster. Daddy should've left her years ago," Naomi stated with a snort. "I'm surprised the marriage lasted as long as it did. All I have to say is that both of them got what was coming."

"That wasn't a nice thing to say. I'm sure your father must be devastated. Poor Daniel." Ruth's heartbeat accelerated. Then she mentally berated herself. It seemed like she'd been trying to justify Daniel's actions to his children and grandchildren since their divorce seven years ago, and even years before that. Unbeknowst to Ruth, Lenora was pregnant before the Wilcox's divorce was finalized. Daniel married Lenora before the ink was dry on the decree, just days later. Ruth's best friend, Alice, warned her about breaking away from old habits. Alice also reminded Ruth that her children were more than old enough to form their own opinions of their father.

"I never understood why you insist on defending him," Naomi complained, as if reading her mother's mind. "If the shoe was on the other foot, I doubt that he'd do the same for you," she remarked candidly. She wasn't shy about speaking her mind.

Ruth stifled a chuckle. "I'm not concerned about Daniel Wilcox. My focus is on being the best person that I can be. He's still your father, though," she said forcefully.

"You mean my grandfather," Naomi threw in snidely. Then she felt a twinge of shame. "I'm sorry, Momma. I didn't mean that the way it sounded."

Seven years had elapsed since the truth of Naomi's biological parents had been divulged. Naomi found out in the worst way that her older sister, Sarah, and Sarah's husband, Brian, were her biological parents. To the rest of the world, the Wilcox family had maintained the status quo that Ruth and Daniel were her parents. Naomi had not taken the news well, causing Ruth and Daniel to spend a pretty penny for the services of a Christian psychologist for Naomi. Naomi was now twenty-seven years old and had adjusted well from her tumultuous teen years. Sarah was forty-three, and DJ, Ruth and Daniel's son, was forty-one.

Lenora was not happy about Naomi's counseling expense coming out of her household budget. Spending money for anything concerning the offspring from her husband's first wife had been a bone of contention between the married pair.

"I know," Ruth replied. "It's all right. Maybe we need to do something about that. Perhaps it's time for us to come clean to the world, or at least to the church and our immediate family and friends, about what really happened years ago. I know you said before that you weren't ready. Have you changed your mind?" She held her breath in anticipation of Naomi's answer.

"I don't know. Sometimes I think I'm ready, and other times, I just want to be Daddy's and your baby," Naomi admitted wistfully.

Clad in pajamas, Naomi's boyfriend, Montgomery, walked into the bedroom after he adjusted the thermostat in the living room. He eased his tall, gangly frame into bed. He lay on his back, with his hands clasped behind his head, and watched Naomi as she talked to her mother.

He admired her beautiful caramel face and curvaceous body. Naomi was at the peak of her beauty. Her legs were very shapely, and they supported her plus-size body. She was amazed at the rush of love that spurted from her heart when she beheld Montgomery's chiseled, dimpled chin. Locks of unruly brown hair covered his forehead, along with longer hair on the sides. Montgomery's eyes were cornflower blue, and the silver wire-framed glasses he wore, giving him a nerdy look, belied his thirty-five years of age. Those bright colored orbs endeared him to Naomi.

"Well, that's something we can discuss the next time you come to Chicago. When do you think you'll come home?" Ruth felt a keen longing to see her youngest daughter's face.

Naomi wrinkled her nose and tugged at the ends of her hair, which had escaped the scarf, along the back of her neck. Naomi like her mother wore a scarf during the night, to keep her hairdo do fresh.

"Sarah wants me to come home this weekend. She thinks Daddy is incapable of taking care of the boys. She thinks we should have a family meeting to discuss what can be done to help him. Sarah stayed at Daddy's house last night. Daddy finally broke down and told her what was going on. She says the boys are a mess. When Sarah called, she said the twins had almost been crying nonstop since Lenora left," Naomi said.

Daniel and Lenora's oldest son, Damon, was eight years old, and the twins would be seven years old later that year.

Ruth thought it was strange that Sarah hadn't called her yesterday. Mother and daughter talked regularly several times a day, and now she knew the reason for the silence.

"Sarah is doing the right thing. In times like this, one must look to family for help. So I hope you'll do all you can to help your father during his trying time," Ruth said.

"Mom, do you have to be so sanctimonious all the time? If you were any other ex-wife, you'd be crowing how your rival is finally out of the love of your life's life. Instead, you sound like Reverend Ruth instead of the former Mrs. Daniel Wilcox."

Ruth's cheeks reddened as she opened and closed her mouth. "Your father and I were over and done with a long time ago. We've gone our separate ways, Naomi. I know most kids, despite their age, hope their parents will get back together one day. But that won't be the case for your father and me. That's a reality you'll have to face, if you're harboring that misconception," she told Naomi, in no uncertain terms.

Naomi shook her head, as if admonishing an unruly child. Then she replied loftily, "If thinking that helps you make it through the day, Momma, then you're deceiving yourself."

"Let's continue this discussion another time," Ruth suggested. She felt like she was on treacherous water. "It's early, I'm tired, and I need to get up soon to wake up Alice." She glanced at the blue LED display on her alarm clock, which illuminated the room.

"You're right," Naomi said contritely. She sat on the edge of the bed and appeared unsettled. Montgomery scooted behind her and began massaging her tight shoulders. "I'm sorry, Momma. I didn't mean to upset you."

"Apology accepted, and I wasn't trying to minimize your feelings either. We'll talk later today. I promise. I'll talk to Sarah and see what's going on with Daniel and Lenora."

"Okay, Momma. Have a good day. Tell Aunt Alice I said hello. Love you, Momma."

"I love you too," Ruth replied as she relaxed her body against the headboard.

The women said good-bye and hung up the phones.

Though Ruth had a matter-of-fact demeanor when she was talking to Naomi, learning that Daniel was going to be a free man caused her heart rate to accelerate. Growing up a preacher's kid, she had always been taught that marriage was a till-death-do-us-part proposition. And when she stood at the altar at The Temple and married Daniel Wilcox, there was no doubt their marriage would be one of those long-lasting partnerships.

Still, she was old and wise enough to realize that life threw curveballs from time to time, and that life didn't always go according to script. Ruth lay back against the pillows and felt incredulous; she couldn't wrap her mind around the fact that Daniel and Lenora were breaking up. Her mind shied away from the possibility that the couple's breakup would affect her life in any way.

Ruth readjusted her head wrap and stretched out her body on the bed. She pulled the sheet around her waist. Within a few minutes, she fell back asleep.

Montgomery smiled at Naomi after she lay in the bed when she hung up the phone. She snuggled close to him. "There always seems to be a high level of tension that surrounds you when you talk to your mother and other family members," he observed. "The tension fills the room like a pumped can of air freshener."

"Lately that's been the case," Naomi replied, with a faraway look in her eyes. "It wasn't always like that. Momma has changed so much since the divorce, and after she was ordained as a minister. I remember when my siblings and, most of all, my father were the center of her life, and I ran a close second. Now all that has changed." She shrugged her shoulders.

"You know what I think? It's time I met your family," Montgomery said casually. "I know that you said we needed to give our relationship time, and I think we've survived the test of time. We've been together for four years. What's the problem? Are you ashamed of me or something?"

Naomi leaned over and hugged Montgomery. "Never that," she said fiercely. Then she kissed him. She shifted her body and laid her head on her pillow. "The timing has just been lousy. There always seems to be some drama going on in my family."

"I know, or at least that's what you tell me, Naomi." Montgomery's deep bass voice, with his English accent, sent chills down her spine. "I love you and we're engaged. Not having met your family in all this time bothers me."

A chill of fear crisscrossed Naomi's body. She looked into Montgomery's blue eyes and put her hand on her heart. "I promise you that I'll talk to the family. Just give me a little more time," she said solemnly. Then she took his hand in her own. "I agree with you; I've been remiss in not saying anything to the family about you before now. I promise you that by my graduation, you will meet the Wilcox family, en masse, and that's only a few months away."

"Okay, Ms. Wilcox, you have two months to get it together." He got out of the bed and headed to the adjoining bathroom.

Naomi watched him walk away as she gnawed on a hangnail. She wasn't sure if her family would understand her marrying outside her race, or how her lover was more than a few years older than she was. Though Noami didn't think the age difference significant, she knew her mother would.

Ruth had always proclaimed that God's children came in different shades. But Naomi wasn't sure if her mother, now in her early sixties, would accept an older white man as her daughter's future husband. To complicate matters, Montgomery was from England,

and a member of the Anglican Church. Naomi was sure her mother would be scandalized to learn that she was "shacking up" with a man, as her mother and Alice called it.

Naomi also had yet to inform her family that she planned to remain in Edwardsville to work after her graduation. They were under the impression she would be returning to Chicago, and would be employed as a CPA at a prestigious accounting firm in the downtown Chicago area. Butterflies fluttered in her stomach at the thought of telling her family what her real plans were.

Montgomery exited the bathroom, returned to the bed, and lay beside Naomi. They leaned over and turned off the lamps on their nightstands. Montgomery's arms lay possessively around Naomi's waist. The couple was quiet and lost in their own thoughts of the Wilcox family. Montgomery thought Naomi was ashamed of him and his race. Naomi obsessed over the family's acceptance of Montgomery, and she also pondered Daniel's situation. She debated going home for the weekend. Finally sleep claimed the couple. The answers to their questions would be revealed soon enough. Though Naomi had convinced herself that it didn't matter if her family liked or accepted Montgomery, she cared deep down inside. Like most daughters who share a close bond with their mothers, Naomi craved her mother's approval.

Chapter Two

Several hours later, Ruth leaned to her right and laid her Bible on the nightstand. She had completed reading her morning scripture, and was finishing saying a prayer aloud.

"Thank you, God, for the many blessings you have bestowed upon me and my family. And, Lord, take care of Daniel, Lenora, and their family during this moment of crisis. I know that there isn't any problem you can't solve. Lord, bless the world, its leaders, and all your children here on earth. Lord, bless my church family. Amen."

She opened her eyes and peered at the clock, noting that it was almost six-thirty in the morning. She was supposed to call Alice at seven o'clock, to ensure that her best friend was awake in time to attend a doctor's appointment scheduled for later that morning.

Ruth was worried because Alice hadn't been herself lately. Ruth was aware her friend's energy level had dipped. Ruth recited scripture to stop her mind from focusing on worst-case scenarios.

Ruth's eyes trailed across the off-white room to the deeply polished dark cherrywood armoire, which was opposite her bed. Her gaze settled on the pictures lovingly arranged atop the dresser. Early morning was "me time" for Ruth. Before she began the hustle and bustle of the day, her thoughts, as always, centered on her family.

Bishop, Ruth's father, peered at her with an enigmatic smile. His face was enclosed by an eight-by-ten silver frame, and he was clad in a black robe, with an immaculate white ministerial collar around his neck. Bishop was the first picture that caught Ruth's attention, as it did every morning. The twinkle in her father's eyes caused a tear to trickle down her honey brown face.

Five years had elapsed since Ruth's beloved brother, Ezra, had made his transition home, and Bishop followed him two years ago. She took comfort in knowing her father and brother had mended their fractured relationship. She knew they were in heaven, keeping an eye on the family.

She reached upward and rubbed a wet spot from her check. Then her brown orbs traveled to another picture, inside a five-by-seven ornate picture frame. Ezra, her beloved brother, was playing the organ at The Temple. His head was bowed, and he was enthralled in his one passion in life. Though Ruth fully realized the Lord didn't put more on a person than they could bear, nonetheless, she wasn't quite ready to admit to anyone how overwhelming life had become because of family and church issues.

Ruth swung her legs back into the bed. Her lips curved into a smile as she leaned back against the fluffy white pillows and took stock of her family. Her thoughts, as always, seemed to be attuned to Naomi, who was scheduled to receive a master's degree in accounting in May. Ruth was so proud of Naomi.

She leaned across the bed, pulled open the top drawer of the nightstand, and removed Naomi's graduation announcement. Just seeing Naomi Patrice Wilcox in the lovely script filled Ruth's heart with happiness.

"Thank you, Father," she whispered.

One of the best decisions Ruth had made was to hire a good Christian pediatric therapist to work with Naomi. With Dr. Brown's help, Naomi eventually was able to find peace, despite the choices her relatives had made in the past that had affected her life so crucially.

After changing her major in college multiple times, and elongating her undergraduate college experience, Naomi eventually decided on accounting for her future career goal. Sarah and Daniel Jr., also known as DJ, often joked that Naomi was going to be a career student. It had taken Naomi three years to complete her studies for a master's degree. During that time, Ruth continued supporting her daughter financially.

"You showed everyone," Ruth said to herself, smiling. She could hardly wait for her baby girl to return home.

The only dark cloud hanging over Ruth's life was the possibility of the change in the dynamics of the relationship between Naomi and Sarah. She often pondered whether it might be time for her to step back and allow the mother-daughter bond between the two women to flourish. She found herself at such odds with that theory, and prayed many a night for God to show her the way. She tried putting herself in Sarah's footsteps. Family secrets had haunted the Wilcox and Clayton families for so long, in an adverse way.

As part of her post Daniel life, Ruth and Alice had purchased a redbrick six-flat apartment building, in need of serious rehabilitation, for a song and dance. The friends had the building gutted and rehabbed. The apartment building was located fairly close to Ruth and Daniel's former residence, which Ruth had presented to Sarah and Brian. Ruth and Alice lived in the first-floor apartments, across the hall from each other, and rented out the second- and third-floor apartments.

"Lord, take care of and bless us all." Ruth closed her eyes, and said, "We are just your imperfect children, trying to lead a Christian life, to make it into your kingdom. Father, be with Alice today when she goes to her doctor appointment. I wanted to go with her, but she has told me she prefers to go by herself. Take care of my best friend, no, Alice is really my sister. We just had different parents"

She glanced at the clock again; the time was a quarter to seven. She stretched her arms over her head. Then she pulled her wrap scarf off her head and ran her fingers through her close-cropped short silver-gray hair. A web of lines intersected her face, giving her character and strength. She was one of those women who became more attractive during the aging process.

When she and Alice moved into the building, they began an exercise regimen together, and Ruth had managed to keep most unwanted pounds from her body. She maintained a perfect size-sixteen figure.

Ruth folded the scarf into a triangle and placed it on the nightstand. She then opened the drawer again and laid Naomi's graduation announcement on top of a pile of papers. She shuffled through the papers until she reached the bottom of the stack. She pulled out a Polaroid of her and Daniel from their wedding day. She traced Daniels's face, and then dropped the picture back into the drawer. She covered it with the papers and firmly closed the drawer. The photo was the one relic of the past that Ruth kept to remind herself of happier times with the first love of her life.

She swung her legs over the side of the bed and took the cordless phone from its base. Ruth couldn't keep her thoughts from straying to her ex-husband, and the humiliation she'd suffered when he chose to end their marriage of thirty-plus years. Daniel had been her first and only love, and he occupied a secret place in her heart that had never been relinquished to another man.

There's an old saying, "What goes around comes around." Daniel married a much younger woman before the ink was barely dry on his and Ruth's divorce decree, and he was definitely a beneficiary of the other tried-and-true saying, "You reap what you sow." From what Sarah had told Ruth over the years, Daniel and Lenora shared what could best be described as a rocky marriage.

Daniel hadn't wanted any other children after his and Ruth's son, DJ, was born, and he had been reluctant to adopt Naomi. Now, he was the father of three little boys, age eight and under. He had suffered a debilitating heart attack years ago, and his health hadn't been the same since then. Hours of rehabilitation therapy had been successful to a certain point, leaving Ruth's ex-husband a mere shell of his former outspoken and opinionated self.

Ruth shook her head, as if to clear it of the cobwebs of memories, and quickly picked up the cordless phone and punched in Alice's telephone number.

"Hello, Ruth. How are you this morning?" Alice asked, answering her phone on the second ring, after glancing at the caller ID. She pressed a button, switched the phone to speaker mode, and clipped the phone's earpiece to her earlobe. She then pulled and twirled the gray twists around her head and walked into the kitchen.

"I'm good. How are you feeling this morning?" Ruth answered her friend tentatively. She changed the phone to her other ear. At the thought of Alice being seriously ill, Ruth felt her heart race like a NASCAR driver.

"I'm blessed," Alice reassured Ruth, ever mindful of her friend's concern. "Now, Ruth, I don't want you worrying about me. God has this situation under control. You have enough on your plate right now, dealing with Queen's health issues."

"Humph, that's true. But I can always make time for you. I really wish you'd reconsider and let me go with you to your appointment today. I'm going to be a nervous wreck all day until I talk to you. I still don't understand why you're being so secretive," Ruth crossly informed her friend. She absently scratched her scalp.

"You will be fine. Anyway, it's Monday, your day to spend with Queen. I think you should go ahead with your plans and we'll talk this evening," Alice said firmly. She knew Ruth was grouchy because she refused to share with her the nature of her appointment.

"I don't think it would be a major loss if I don't visit Queen today. It's not like she knows who I am most of the time." It hurt Ruth to say those words. She scowled and her lips tightened.

"You're right," Alice shot back. "That's why it's important for you to go. This could be one of Queen's good days. You and your mother have worked so long and hard to improve your relationship. So enjoy the time you have left. Tomorrow is not promised."

Ruth swallowed hard as a feeling of uneasiness sky-rocketed through her body. "You aren't trying to tell me something, are you?"

"Of course not," Alice answered quickly. "I only meant that Queen is getting older, and you should savor every day you have with her. Let me clarify that, I speak as a person who has lost both parents." She tried to quell Ruth's fears.

Ruth's body sagged with relief. "Okay, I'll go visit Mother today. But you and I have a dinner date, and I'm going to cook. Deal?"

"Definitely, you don't have to cook anything fancy, though." Alice smiled.

She checked the coffee, which was brewing, and returned to her bedroom. Alice opened the closet door and removed a turquoise-colored tunic pantsuit, which she laid on the bed. She opened her dresser drawer and took lingerie and hosiery from it, putting them on the bed too. Then she walked back to the kitchen.

"What's new with you?" she asked Ruth as she reached into the cabinet and took a cup out of it.

"Nothing much. After I visit Mother, I'll probably come home and work on the church budget, to prepare for the finance meeting scheduled for next Friday. Offerings are down. I know the economy has hurt a lot of people. The loss of money has impacted the church, and I'm hoping I won't have to take a hard stance and shut down some of our outreach programs," Ruth confessed.

"I know what you mean. When I visited my childhood church last Sunday, I noticed attendance was lighter than normal. The high gas prices don't help. My cousin, Mark, was saying that my family's church is facing many challenges too," Alice said.

"He's right. You know, I always feel like I have to be as good a leader as Bishop was, and I think I put more pressure on myself when things don't go as I plan." Ruth opened up to Alice about some misgivings she'd been feeling.

"I understand, but, trust me, these times would even challenge Bishop. The economy is in the toilet. Gas prices are on the rise, and we live in Cook County, which has the highest tax rate of all the counties in the United States. The only bright star is that the stock market is still stable, but how long can that last? People are losing jobs left and right. A lot of people are questioning their faith in God," Alice pronounced.

"I know," Ruth said glumly. "Sister Willa Mae, a mother of the church, called me last week and she was insistent the world was coming to an end, and how we're living in times that were described in the Book of Revelation."

"Well, that had to be an interesting conversation. What did you tell her?" Alice was sincerely curious. She poured herself a cup of coffee and sat at the table. She glanced at the clock and saw that it was nearly time for her to begin dressing for her appointment. She had been up since six o'clock. She had only asked Ruth to call her because she knew her friend wanted to help.

"I managed to soothe her nerves, but it took much longer than I anticipated it would. I told her what we are experiencing is an enormous challenge, and how Christians must rise to the task, and be more prayerful and helpful when they can. I told her that I don't pretend to know the future, and how we must be vigilant and steadfast in leaning on our faith. I also suggested we trust in God's unchanging hand. Eventually she calmed down. I was on the phone with her for so long that I nearly missed a counseling meeting with Miles and Lisa Dennison," Ruth said.

"Save that thought," Alice said. "I have got to get going. I'll see you this evening, and don't worry. Everything is going to work out fine."

"I'll try not to," Ruth replied. "See you later."

The women hung up, and Alice returned to her room and began dressing for her appointment, while Ruth showered and dressed. Afterward, Ruth walked into her kitchen to prepare breakfast. Before long, she was ready to depart.

Ruth was turning the key in the lock to secure the front door when she heard her telephone ring. She debated going back inside the apartment, but then she heard the answering machine activate. She walked outside to the garage and got into her black Cadillac CTS.

She pressed the remote unit and the garage door began lifting. Ruth leaned over to the passenger seat, reached inside her purse, and removed her cell phone. She put the Bluetooth device into her ear and started the car.

She had driven to the end of the alley when her cell phone chirped. She activated the Bluetooth device and answered the call.

"Momma," Sarah said frantically. "Where are you? I called the house, and the phone just rang." Sarah was sitting inside her cubicle at ComEd Electric Company. After years of being a customer service representative, she had finally been promoted to a manager, and she loved her job.

"I'm headed out to see Queen," Ruth answered. "Why, what's wrong?" Everyone; children, grandchildren, friends alike called the former first lady of The Temple Queen.

"I meant to call you yesterday and tell you about Daddy. I was at his house all yesterday." She smothered a yawn. "I should've taken off work today. I'm so tired. Lenora left him and the boys, and the whole situation has been a mess," she said anxiously as she untwisted the tangled phone cord.

"Naomi called me this morning and told me about Daniel's latest drama. What happened?" Ruth managed to ask it calmly, though her insides had turned to mush. She pulled the car around the corner, slid into an empty parking spot, and turned off the car.

"Lenora pretty much said she's tired of being married to an old man. Can you believe that's what she called Daddy? She ran off with another man to Nevada. She called Daddy last night, and told him to forget the divorce papers she served him, because she plans to get a quickie divorce in Reno. And to make matters even worse, Lenora cleared out her and Daddy's bank account." Sarah's eyes stole a look outside her cubicle, making sure no one was listening to her conversation.

"I'm sorry to hear that." Ruth tried to impart sympathy into her voice as she massaged her left temple.

"Not only did she leave Daddy, she left the boys with him." Sarah's voice rose dramatically and her eyes widened. Then she remembered she was at work, and she lowered her tone. "What kind of mother just ups and leaves her children?"

"We don't know what demons drove Lenora to do the things she has. The situation is terrible, and I'm sorry to hear about it." Ruth silently asked God to forgive her for that little white lie she had just told. A part of Ruth rejoiced upon hearing the news of Daniel's marital woes. She just wasn't about to reveal that fact to anyone.

"Daddy barely raised us, so he doesn't have a clue as to how significantly his life is about to change. I don't know how he's going to cope with three little boys with very minimal home training. Poor Daddy," Sarah observed. She looked up to see a coworker walking inside her office, pointing to her watch. "Momma, I've got to go. I'll call you back later when I have more news."

"Okay, sweetie. I'll talk to you later. I'm sure everything will work out for your dad." Ruth clicked off her cell phone and sat in her parked car for a few minutes.

She knew that it wasn't her business what happened in Daniel and Lenora's household. Still, she twisted her lips into a wry smile, because she had been waiting a long time to hear those words. Everyone with eyes knew it was only a matter of time before Daniel and Lenora split up.

Ruth was loath to talk bad about anyone, but she couldn't help reflecting on how Lenora had been her nemesis for so long. Her ex-husband's wife was condescending to her when they saw each other at family functions. Lenora always had to be the center of attention. She had even requested that Ruth change her surname back to her maiden name, and she actually had acted offended when Ruth refused to comply with her request.

Ruth wasn't sure if Daniel's split from his wife would affect her life or not. After all, she had moved on. At least that's what she told herself in the still of the night, when she felt most lonely, and missed Daniel more than she could have ever imagined.

Still, Sarah's news was joyous to Ruth's ears. She knew firsthand that one didn't always know what the Lord had in store for them. *Maybe, just maybe,* she mused as she shook her head from side to side, clearing cobwebs from her mind.

Chapter Three

Ruth put on her turn signal and moved to the left lane, entering the Dan Ryan Expressway, heading north. The distribution from Bishop's life insurance policy afforded Queen Esther residence at Sunrise Senior Living, located in Lincoln Park, on the North Side of the city. It was one of the best assisted-living facilities in the Chicago area.

One of the hardest decisions Ruth had made, besides her divorce, was placing her mother in Sunrise. She had prayed long and hard for guidance from God before moving her mother to the facility. Queen Esther had actually lived with Ruth for a year, before Ruth relinquished her mother's care to the nursing home. As time elapsed, Queen Esther grew frailer and more forgetful. She often thought Ruth was her own deceased mother, Lady Mona. She'd left her house, wandered off, and had gotten lost more than a few times. Ruth had to call the police to find her mother. Ruth had hired a nurse to stay with her mother. After six nurses had quit in seven months, she knew it was time for her to explore other options.

Ruth and Alice had visited many facilities before they decided on Sunrise. When Ruth took Queen Esther to the facility and left her there, it was a heartbreaking experience. It still haunted her.

Ruth pushed open the door and entered Sunrise. Emily, the receptionist, greeted her warmly. "Reverend

Wilcox, how are you doing this morning?" the perky young woman asked.

"Blessed—I'm simply blessed. I'm grateful to God for allowing me to see another day," Ruth replied. She stood at the desk and scrawled her name on the visitor sheet.

"Amen, then," Emily said. "You're always so cheer-ful. I don't think you've ever come here and said you were sad or depressed," she observed.

"That's how life is when you acknowledge the Father above as the head of your life. You trust Him to direct your path," Ruth replied optimistically.

"Do white people go to your church?" Emily asked. Her peaches-and-cream complexion and long, curly red hair proclaimed her Irish ethnicity. "Maybe one day I'll visit."

Ruth's eyes widened with surprise at the bluntness of Emily's question. Then she smiled and shifted her purse from one arm to the other. "We have a few white members. What we all have in common is that we are all God's children. We simply come in different colors, and from different walks in life."

"Fascinating," Emily murmured as she handed Ruth a badge with Queen's room number on it. "I will see you later, Reverend."

"Okay," Ruth replied.

She pinned the badge on her jacket and headed down the hallway to the elevator. Before Ruth removed her hand from the up button, the elevator doors opened, and she walked inside. Her stomach felt queasy, and Ruth prayed today would be one of Queen's better days.

The bell chimed, indicating the elevator was about to stop on the fifth floor. When the doors opened, Ruth greeted several medical personnel, who manned the floor at all times. A security guard greeted Ruth and checked her badge. Ruth turned to her left and walked down the hall to room 512. The door was slightly ajar, and she strode inside the room.

Queen was sitting on a rocking chair, facing a window. She didn't turn around when Ruth entered the room.

Ruth walked over to her mother, placed her arms around her thin shoulders, and kissed her cheek. "Hello. How are you feeling today?"

"Fair to middling," Queen answered in a quavery voice. She looked at Ruth suspiciously. "Who are you?" Her left heavily veined hand clutched the gold cross on a chain around her neck.

"I'm your daughter, Ruth," she replied in a thickened, emotional voice. She walked across the room, took a chair from the kitchen table, and sat down next to Queen at the window. She took her mother's shaking hand in her own.

"Oh, Ruth," Queen Esther cackled. "I know you." She looked toward the door. "Where are your father and Ezra? Why didn't they come with you?" She looked at Ruth accusingly.

"They're . . ." Ruth gulped hard. Queen Esther's doctor had advised her to tell her the truth; her husband and son were deceased. "Mother, they're gone. Daddy and Ezra are dead."

Queen Esther's hands flew to her mouth. She moaned. "No, that's not true." Then she straightened her shoulders and said, "Bishop will be here to see me later. You just wait and see."

Though Ruth reminded her mother of Bishop's and Ezra's deaths many times, it still hurt her heart to hear her mother ask about her father and brother.

"I thought I'd make lunch for us and read to you. What do you think about that, Mother?"

"That's fine, but who did you say you were again?" Queen Esther squinted at her daughter as she repeated her question. Then she turned her attention back at the window.

"I'm your daughter, Ruth, and I'm going to fix us lunch." She stood and walked to the kitchenette area. She turned on the radio to a gospel station. There were a few dishes in the sink, and she quickly washed them. After Ruth completed that task, she looked inside the refrigerator and removed bread, a package of sliced turkey, mayo, lettuce, and a tomato. She prepared sandwiches, with a few salt-free chips on the side for them, along with glasses of iced tea.

After Ruth set the plates on the table, she went to her mother and led her to the bright, cheery yellow kitchenette, where they sat together. Ruth blessed the food, and the two women ate.

"So, Mother, did you participate in any of the activities this week?" Ruth asked, taking a bite of her sandwich and peering at her mother.

"Huh?" Queen Esther took the top slice of bread off her sandwich and removed the lettuce. "You know I don't like this green stuff," she said huffily, setting the lettuce on the side of her plate.

Ruth popped up from her seat, removed a paper towel from the rack on the counter, walked back to the table, and put the pieces of lettuce on it.

"I'm sorry," Ruth apologized. "You ate lettuce last week. I fixed you a sandwich and some soup. Do you remember?"

Queen Esther shrugged her shoulders. "I don't remember." She pushed her plate away from her, saying, "I'm not hungry now. I'll eat it later." She peered at Ruth's face intently. "I know who you are. You're my daughter, Ruth."

"That's right, Mother. I'm your daughter," Ruth replied. She felt a sense of relief that Queen recalled who she was.

"How are Sarah, Nay, and the other children? My great-grandchildren?" Queen Esther asked Ruth. She grabbed her cane, stood up, and walked slowly to the living-room area, where she picked up a picture of Sarah, Brian, and their children from the end table. "See, these are the children I'm talking about." She showed the picture to Ruth.

"Everybody is doing fine. They told me to tell you hello, and to give you a kiss for them," Ruth informed her mother. She stood up from the table and walked into the living room, where the two women sat together on the couch.

"How come they didn't come to see me?" Queen Esther asked as she smoothed her dress over her thighs.

"Sarah's at work, and Maggie, Joshua and Naomi are at school. Today is Monday; it's a work and school day. They will come see you over the weekend," Ruth said.

"I miss seeing them," Queen Esther said. "Ruth, would you be a good girl and get my tea for me? I'm thirsty."

Ruth's cell phone buzzed from her purse. She stood up, went into the kitchen and took her bag off the counter. "Excuse me, Mother, that might be someone from the church." She looked at the caller ID unit and then flipped open her cell phone. "Hello, Naomi. How are you doing, dear?" she asked her daughter.

"Hi, Momma, I'm doing fine. Sarah just called me. She said she filled you in on Daddy and the witch."

"Now, Naomi, that wasn't a very nice thing to say. As I told you earlier, the whole thing is sad. We'll have to keep the entire family in our prayers."

"Momma, please," Naomi scolded her mother. "You need to drop the prayer thing. We're talking about your ex-husband." She rolled her eyes; then she smiled. "I almost feel like one of the Munchkins from *The Wizard Of Oz*. I danced around the room singing 'Ding-Dong! The Witch Is Dead' when I heard the news."

Ruth suppressed a smile. She said sternly, "Naomi, now you know you aren't right. Lenora is your father's wife, your stepmother, and you have to respect her for that."

"No, Momma, that's your take on life. Daddy will be better off without her. She just brought him down. I remember when Daddy was a young-acting, vibrant man. Now he acts like he has no reason to live. If only he hadn't married Lenora." Naomi seemed to run out of steam.

"Well, nonetheless, we should keep them in our prayers. I'm visiting Queen. Would you like to speak to her?" Ruth asked her daughter.

"Does she know who you are today?" Naomi asked her mother uneasily.

"Praise God, she does today. Hold on. I'm going to give her the phone." Ruth passed the phone to her mother.

She watched while Queen Esther chatted with Naomi; and when Queen Esther was done, she gave the telephone back to Ruth. Ruth told her daughter that she'd talk to her later. She turned her attention back to her mother after she disconnected the call.

"Are you tired, Queen? Would you like to take a nap?"

"No, girl, I feel okay. When is Naomi coming home? I miss her. It seems like she's been in school for a long time. Now, when is she graduating again?" Queen Esther asked her daughter.

"She might come home this weekend. She has one degree already, a bachelor's degree. She's getting a master's degree in May, and then Naomi will be done with school," Ruth told her mother proudly.

Queen Esther's eyes bucked. "For real? Naomi is going to get another degree? What is she going to do when she finishes school?"

"She's going to come back to Chicago and work as an accountant."

Queen Esther rolled her eyes. "An accountant? Naomi likes numbers? I didn't think she was smart enough to do that. Why does she want to do that?"

"Naomi was smarter than we thought she was." Ruth laughed. "I guess the tutoring sessions Daniel and I paid for when she was in high school paid off. After Naomi passes the CPA certification exam, she can earn a nice salary. Plus, she'll have options. She can open her own company or work for one."

"That doesn't make any sense to me," Queen Esther muttered querulously, with a confused look on her face. She shook her head and picked up the remote from the cocktail table. She turned on the television to CBS, and they watched the antics of the defendants and plaintiffs for a while on *Judge Judy*.

Ruth glanced at the clock on top of the entertainment center that housed the 32-inch high-definition television. It was nearly three o'clock, close to rush hour, and if she wanted to beat that crowd, she knew it was best she leave now.

She stood and walked back to the kitchenette and put the plates she had just washed into the cabinet and the clean utensils inside the drawer. Then Ruth wiped off the counters and kitchen table. When she was done with those chores, she walked back into the living room and removed her coat from the closet. "Mother, I'm going home now. I have some things I need to work on for the church," Ruth informed her mother as she donned her coat.

"Do you have to leave now?" Queen Esther's eyes darted between Ruth and the television.

"Yes, traffic can get heavy on Lake Shore Drive. I'll be back on Thursday," she said, wrapping a scarf around her head. Although it was March twenty-fifth, in the "Windy City," and officially a new season, spring weather had yet to make an appearance. Ruth said to her mother, "I was thinking, maybe I'll give your doctor a call in the morning and see if you can stay with me this weekend, since Naomi may be home. I'll have the family over for dinner. What do you think about that?"

Queen Esther shrugged her shoulders and replied, "I guess so."

Ruth walked over to the couch and sat down next to Queen Esther. "It's time we had a family get-together. So I'll probably see you on Thursday, and I'll call you tonight before you go to sleep. Okay?"

Queen Esther seemed to morph into senility right before Ruth's eyes. She looked at Ruth suspiciously, and then she nodded her head.

Ruth leaned over and hugged her mother. She stood and walked to the door. "Good-bye, Mother."

"Bye." Queen Esther waved and turned her attention back to the television.

Ruth rode the elevator to the first floor. As she was leaving the building, she heard someone call her name. It was Emily.

"How was your visit with your mother today?" the young woman asked Ruth as she buttoned her lightweight tweed coat. The women exited the building together and walked down the street.

"Not bad at all." Ruth nodded. "We had a rough patch when I arrived. She wasn't sure who I was. My mother has a tendency to mix me up with her mother. This was one of her good days, and she eventually remembered who I was. Overall, we had a good visit." Ruth smiled.

"I'm glad to hear that," Emily said approvingly. "So many older people are brought to Sunshine to live out their last days, and family members rarely visit them. It lifts my heart to see you, or a member of your family, visit Mrs. Clayton as often as you do. That's so important to the well-being of the residents after they move in here."

"Oh, that's no problem. I'm lucky that my daughter Sarah visits, as well as my friend Alice. And we can depend on my son-in-law, Brian, to stop by here also."

Emily pointed to a dark blue Ford Escape . "That's my car. Have a great evening, Reverend Wilcox."

"Thank you, Emily, you do the same," Ruth replied as she walked down the street.

Emily got into her vehicle and beeped her horn as she passed Ruth, who had nearly reached her car.

Ruth entered her auto and started it up. Soon she was on the expressway, on her way back to the South Side of Chicago.

An hour later, after Ruth had stopped at the grocery store, she was standing inside her gray-and-white wallpapered kitchen, with splashes of maroon, preparing dinner. She decided to bake chicken breasts and prepare wild rice and a tossed salad. She turned on the oven to a low setting. Then she took a package of home-made rolls out of the stainless-steel refrigerator.

Before long, the water was boiling in a pot, and the aroma from the baked chicken filled the room. The onions and mushrooms that Ruth had seasoned the chicken with were wreaking havoc inside her stomach. She glanced at the wall clock and thought about calling

Alice, but she didn't want her to feel pressured. She decided, instead, to wait until Alice put in an appearance.

She turned down the burner under the rice. She walked over to the counter and picked up the cordless white phone. She checked the caller ID and called The Temple to check her messages. She wrote a couple of names and numbers on the notepad next to the telephone. A young couple in the church, Nolan and Patrice Lindsey, had called and left an urgent message for her to call them back.

Brother Clarence Parker, the chairman of the finance committee, had also called, requesting a callback. Ruth snapped to attention when she heard the last message. She didn't recognize the cheerful, melodic male voice. The caller was Aron Reynolds, the father of one of the members of her congregation, Monet Caldwell.

Ruth heard a knock on the front door, and then a key turning in the lock. She walked to the hallway, between the kitchen and living room, and waited for Alice.

Alice walked inside the living room. "Hey, how are you doing? It smells good in here."

Ruth scanned Alice's face and noted her friend seemed tired. "I'm good. My visit with Queen went well, overall. Dinner is just about done. "

The friends walked into the kitchen. Alice went over to the table and sat on one of the chrome-backed padded chairs, while Ruth walked to an oak cabinet, opened it, took plates out, and set them on the table. She opened the oven and poked the chicken with a long-handled fork. She told Alice the food would be ready in five minutes. Then she sat down across from Alice.

Ruth studied her friend's face. She clasped her shaking hands together. Her throat was dry as a desert. Ruth swallowed hard a couple of times, and then croaked out, "What happened at the doctor's office?"

Chapter Four

"Why don't we discuss my visit with the doctor after dinner?" Alice asked Ruth after taking a sip of the sweetened tea that Ruth had just poured. She set her glass on the table.

"Girl, you know, keeping me in suspense is going to kill me," Ruth said half jokingly.

She stood up and turned off the jets under the pots, then removed the pan of chicken from the oven. Ruth put portions of food onto the plates, while Alice bustled around the kitchen, removing eating utensils from the drawer.

"Now, Ruth, you know that we haven't been *girls* in how many years?" Alice held up her hands and opened and closed them six times. "Shall I stop there?" She smiled at her friend.

"Let's not go there at all," Ruth warned, placing colorful floral paper napkins on the table. She looked around the kitchen, checking to see if she had forgotten anything else.

The women sat down at the table and clasped hands, while Ruth blessed the food. Then they picked up forks and knives and began eating.

"The meat tastes good," Alice remarked after she chewed and swallowed a sliver of chicken.

"Thank you," Ruth replied. "Since you don't care to tell me what happened with your doctor, I have some news of my own to tell you. There's been drama in the

Wilcox family." She looked at Alice with a mischievous look on her face.

"With whom? Don't tell me, it was Naomi." Alice wiped her mouth with the napkin.

"Not this time," Ruth said serenely. "Lenora left Daniel." After dropping that bombshell, she scooped rice onto her fork and into her mouth.

"Oh, my God! You've got to be kidding." Alice's mouth sagged open, and her fork clattered to the table.

"I kid you not," Ruth replied smugly. "And while you're at it, pick your mouth up off the table," she laughingly instructed her friend. "Naomi called me in the wee hours of the morning, and Sarah gave me another update before I went to visit Queen."

"That's some news." Alice cut her eyes quickly at Ruth. She picked up her fork and laid it on the side of her plate. "How do you feel about that?" she queried her friend.

"I don't feel anything," Ruth answered quickly. Her eyes dropped to the table, then back at Alice. "I'm going to tell you as I told Naomi—we have to keep Daniel and Lenora in our prayers."

"*Pleeze.*" Alice held her hand up. "Don't get holier-than-thou on me. Hello? This is Alice you're talking to." She pursed her lips together. "I repeat, what are you really thinking?"

"Truthfully, I'm thinking Daniel has his work cut out for him. Not only did Lenora leave him, but she left the children with him. So now Daniel has to raise those children alone. It's a sad state of affairs. Sarah said Lenora nearly cleaned out all their joint bank accounts." Ruth shook her head from side to side, looking pensive. She cut another piece of chicken and ate it.

"You got that right." Alice nodded her head, agreeing with Ruth. "It's not like he did the best job in the world with your three. Are you sure you don't feel a small sense of redemption? We all knew that marriage was doomed from the start. That is, everyone except for Daniel," she remarked candidly. She put another forkful of food into her mouth.

"You're right. I think we all knew that, but Daniel didn't. One part of me believes that Daniel knew he was in over his head when he married her. And, God forgive me, I feel like telling Daniel, 'I told you so.' But, most of all, I'm stunned that Lenora left the children with him. What in God's name was she thinking?"

"She probably got tired of taking care of an older man," Alice remarked candidly. "God don't like ugly, and Daniel Wilcox has done some terrible things to people over the years." She picked up and bit into the homemade roll.

"Be that as it may, God still forgives all of us, and that includes Daniel," Ruth said in her Sunday pulpit voice.

The women burst into loud laughter together. Their bodies shook with glee. Tears streamed down Ruth's face. Alice handed her a napkin. They shared a moment of silence.

Alice cleared her throat. "Tell me you aren't going to do something foolish, like try and get back with Daniel?" She looked at her friend somberly.

Ruth's cheeks warmed as she waved her hand airily. "Now, you know I'm not the one who goes back to former loves. I have no interest whatsoever in Daniel Wilcox, other than where it concerns our children. I promise you, we are over." She put her hand over her heart.

"We'll see." Alice sighed. She then looked across the table at Ruth, and fear flashed momentarily across her face. "Anyway, the reason for my appointment with Dr. Shapiro was because I found a lump in my breast last month. I had a second mammogram performed this morning, and the results were the same. There's definitely a growth. I just don't know if it's cancerous yet." She folded her trembling hands together.

"Alice! Oh, no," Ruth wailed. "What happens next? How are you feeling? Oh, Lord, this is too much."

"Well, he wants to do a biopsy. Dr. Shapiro seems to feel it's a benign tumor, because postmenopausal women are prone to benign tumors. He's a little concerned that breast cancer runs in my family. Since I had a mammogram done six months ago, he thinks this situation would qualify as early detection. I'm going to Christ Hospital in a few days to have the biopsy done, and we'll take it from there," Alice said.

Ruth's brain quickly processed all the information Alice had imparted. "Well, I agree with Dr. Shapiro, the signs are good. Thank God, you get your mammograms done yearly. I wish you had told me what was going on, Alice. You didn't have to suffer alone. I would have been there for you." She glared at Alice.

Alice looked chastened. "I know, Ruth, and I apologize for not telling you sooner. I just didn't want to worry you needlessly. I was praying the second mammogram would be normal, but that wasn't the case."

"How are you feeling? Are you in any pain?" Ruth inquired solicitously.

"Actually, I'm not in any pain. Girl, finding that lump scared me to death." Alice shook her head. "I think I was in denial for a day or two. Then my brain kicked in, and I decided to go see Dr. Shapiro."

"I'm glad you did. I'll forgive you for not telling me what was going on with you. But I'm accompanying you to the hospital, that's not up for debate," Ruth proclaimed staunchly.

"I wouldn't have it any other way." Alice nodded as Ruth reached across the table and clasped her friend's hand in her own. "My appointment is at ten o'clock Wednesday morning at Christ Hospital. If you can't get away from work, I can go by myself, or call my cousin Phyllis and ask her to go with me."

"Are you crazy?" Ruth's feelings were hurt. "Of course, I'm going with you. I will check my calendar tonight. I think I have a meeting with Brother Duncan. If so, I'll reschedule it," she said firmly as she folded her arms across her chest.

"I figured you'd say that. And, of course, I want you to come with me."

"How are you feeling? Are you having any symptoms?"

"The suspense is killing me . . . just kidding." She smiled at Ruth. "Overall, I feel good, sometimes a little tired. Then I remind myself that I'm a woman in my sixties, and I'm entitled to feel a little tired sometimes."

"You're right." Ruth bobbed her head up and down. "Sometimes when I come home, my feet hurt and my bones ache. Like you, I attribute my aches and pains to aging."

"How did your visit with Queen go? I know you said earlier it went well, overall," Alice inquired. She stood up and put the dishes and silverware in the sink, and then she began rinsing them off.

Ruth stood, walked to the cabinet, took out a few bowls, and put the leftover food inside them. "Today was one of Queen's good days. I was fearful of how she would be when I arrived. When I walked inside her apartment, I knew immediately that she didn't know who I was. Again, she thought I was her mother. But later she realized who I was. It really breaks my heart when that happens."

"I know it does. But she's still here, and you have a parent alive, unlike quite a few of us baby boomers." Alice tried to comfort Ruth. She took a paper towel from the holder and dried her hands.

Ruth crinkled her nose, then walked to the refrigerator and opened it up. She put the bowls inside.

"Queen asked for Daddy and Ezra. It always breaks my heart when she asks for them. Again, I had to explain how they had passed." She pointed to the counter. "Do you want dessert? I bought a low-fat pound cake."

"I'll take a teeny, tiny piece," Alice answered. She sat back on the chair.

"I'll get it. I have coffee left from this morning, if you don't mind it being warmed up." Ruth turned on the coffeemaker.

"That's fine with me. I'm not choosy," Alice quipped back. "It seems like we have a lot going on in our lives. Did you have a chance to speak to Queen's doctor about changing her medication?"

Ruth sliced two pieces of cake. She slid them onto saucers and put them on the table. She took two forks out of the drawer and set them on the table.

"He wasn't available today. If Naomi comes home this weekend, then I'm going to request a weekend pass for Queen. I'll also talk to the doctor then," Ruth said.

"So, do you think Daniel will call you?" Alice asked Ruth after her friend sat back down on her chair.

"Not really, I don't see why he would. Our communication has been limited to family matters only. We didn't become chummy friends after the divorce. Daniel and I see each other on some holidays, and that's about it. I can't think of a single reason for him to call me," Ruth said.

"I'm going to play devil's advocate and ask what you would do if he did call you. What if Daniel wants to get back with you?"Alice remarked after she finished eating a bite of cake.

"It's nothing that I would waste my time considering," Ruth replied evasively. Her eyes dropped to the saucer, where she had cut the slice of cake into square pieces. "I mean, a part of me had a fantasy where he'd declare his undying love and ask if we could reunite. But, realistically, I know that's not going to happen. And, for your information, if he asked me, the answer would be no. Daniel put me through hoops that no woman should have to go through."

"Good answer. Both of us are what you could call 'over-the-hill.' Sharing life with a companion could be a good thing," Alice mused. She stood up. "Since you're eating, I'll pour the coffee."

"I agree. I miss male companionship sometimes," Ruth admitted. "If that's what God has chosen for me, then I'm okay with it. Both of us have been married, and the only difference between us is that I had children whom I gratefully share with you. Overall, despite the highs and lows of life, I think both of us have had good ones."

"I agree with you." Alice passed Ruth a cup of coffee. "Not that I'm looking for a husband or anything, but I think knowing I might have cancer has forced me to take stock of my life."

"That's normal under the circumstances," Ruth said. "Every year after January first, I try to take stock of my life, and focus on what I call areas of improvement. I think it was two years after Daniel and I divorced that I gave up the fantasy that we would ever reconcile. It finally sank into my brain that he was Lenora's husband, and no longer mine."

"I think I was so traumatized by my marriage to Martin that I never entertained the idea of marrying again. Male companionship is good, if you can find the right man. Every now and then, Phyllis will set me up on a blind date. But nothing good comes of it," Alice said, looking down at the table. She didn't want Ruth to see her reddened face. "I just hope that my life isn't almost over, because I haven't been able to accomplish a few more things that I'd like to."

"Don't talk like that," Ruth chided Alice. "God has got this situation, and you know that. I wouldn't be me if I couldn't try to comfort you with a scripture. What comes to mind is Isaiah 58:11, 'The Lord will guide you always; He will satisfy your needs in a sun-scorched land and will strengthen your frame. You will be like a well-watered garden, like a spring whose waters never fail.'"

"I appreciate the scripture. I will be okay. Just bear with me," Alice implored her friend.

Ruth took Alice's hands in her own. The women bowed their heads. Ruth prayed, "Father on high, I ask you to stop by here tonight, because someone needs you. My sister Alice is in need of your reassurance. She is facing the unknown. I delight in knowing that you will heal my sister and stand by her side. You promised never to leave us, Father, and I know that you won't. You are with us always, and you will be with us during Alice's procedure. Give us strength, Lord, to face the outcome, and I know you will. I have faith that you will make it all right. Amen."

"Thank you, Ruth. I know you meant every word of that prayer, and I appreciate you praying for me. I think I'm ready to call it a day, so I'm going to head home," Alice said, rising from the chair.

Ruth stood up and followed her friend to the foyer. She hugged Alice before she opened the door. "If you need me for anything, I'll be here. Or you can spend the night, if you feel that you don't want to be alone," Ruth said.

"I'm good," Alice said as she walked out the door. "Do you want to drive to the hospital Wednesday?"

"Of course, I will. That's no problem. Don't worry, and hold on to your faith. God will see you through."

"I know, girl. I don't want you to worry either. Have a good evening. I'll see you tomorrow."

Ruth watched Alice walk to her apartment next door. When she heard Alice lock her door, she did the same. Then she walked into her living room, on trembling legs, and sat heavily upon the sofa, where she reflected on Alice's plight.

Minutes later, Ruth dimmed the lights; then she returned to the sofa and meditated. She closed her eyes, bowed her head and spoke. "Father, from whom all blessings flow, thank you for allowing me to rise and greet another day. I hope everything that I did was pleasing in your sight. It seems like a lot is happening with Alice and Daniel. I also feel like something is going on with Naomi. She's keeping something from me, although I don't have a clue as to what yet. Father, how could I be a minister and not ask for blessings for Daniel? Hold him and comfort him in his hour of need.

"Lord, please give me strength to help Alice through her medical dilemma. I know she will be just fine, and if she isn't"—Ruth's body trembled and her voice broke—"then I know it's your will and I have to accept it. If cancer is in Alice's body, Lord, I ask that you heal her. She is like a sister to me, and I can't imagine her not being with me." Ruth wiped a tear from her eye.

Later she arose from the sofa and went into her bedroom, where she quickly stripped off her clothes and headed to the shower. When she was done showering,

Ruth put on a caftan and sat on the edge of the bed, rechecking the messages from the answering machine.

There was another message from Aron Reynolds. *I wonder what he wants,* Ruth thought as she wrote down his telephone number. There were several other messages, and she wrote down the names and phone numbers.

After she finished writing down her messages, Ruth glanced at the clock on the nightstand. It was eight-thirty, so she decided to call Aron the following day.

The thought of calling Daniel flitted through her mind. Upon further thought, she couldn't think of a good reason to justify calling her ex-husband. She checked the front and back doors, making sure they were locked. Then Ruth set the burglar alarm system.

She left the light on over the stove, returned to her bedroom, and retired for the night. After she read her Bible, she said another prayer for Alice. Her theory was that one could never pray enough.

Chapter Five

While Ruth and Alice had been sharing dinner, Ruth's biological daughter, Sarah, was at her father's house, attempting to help him put the pieces of his life back together.

Sarah, Brian, and their children, Joshua and Magdalene, known as "Maggie," had arrived at Daniel's house after Sarah and Brian finished their workday. After stopping at their house briefly to pick up their children, Sarah prepared dinner for the two families at her dad's house. Shortly after dining, Brian and the children departed for home.

Daniel and Lenora's oldest son, Damon, had been acting out since Sarah and her family arrived at Daniel's house. Much to Sarah's chagrin, Daniel never disciplined his sons.

Darnell, the younger twin by five minutes, had cried off and on most of the day, only stopping when he plopped his thumb in his mouth.He sucked his thumb as a child, the habit returned after Lenora abandoned her family. His twin, David, was silent. He kept looking at the door, as if expecting his mother to swoop through it any minute.

Sarah and Brian tried to comfort the boys by explaining their mother had gone on a trip. Sarah reassured her half brothers that their dad would be there for them, along with her and her family. Darnell whined and asked if his mother was coming home tomorrow.

Sarah put on a bright face and explained his mother wouldn't be gone too long.

After the boys had finally fallen asleep, Sarah returned to the kitchen and turned off the light. Then she walked into the living room and sat down on the forest green suede chair, while her father sat on the couch.

"Dad, you look so tired," Sarah observed.

Daniel's face was filled with gray stubble, since he hadn't shaved in a few days. Bags circled his droopy eyes. He ran his trembling hand over his nearly gray head of hair.

"I'm okay," Daniel said, his voice dripping with fatigue. His body sagged as he leaned against the back of the couch.

"I guess you need to make some decisions about what you want to do." Sarah peered at her father absorbedly. "I can take a week off, two tops, to help," she said.

Daniel rubbed his eyes. "I can't believe Noree walked out on me." His voice sounded as if he was in a daze.

"Daddy, I'm so sorry about what happened to you, but there are three little boys upstairs in their rooms, and they don't understand why their world has been turned upside down. They need a strong parent to lean on right now. I would hate for them to suffer even more behind Lenora's leaving."

"What about me?" Daniel asked his daughter irritably. "I can't believe she did this to me, considering how good I was to her."

Sarah snapped her fingers, and the noise rented the air. Daniel's head swerved toward his daughter. "Here's a news flash for you, Daddy, those three little boys need you like they've never needed you before. You've got to be there for them. Their mother leaving is a devastating blow for them, along with lifelong ramifications, if she doesn't return home. This is not about you. It's about being a good father, and making amends for what you couldn't do for your older children."

Daniel scowled. "That was low of you, Sarah. Of course, I'm concerned about the boys. But I take Lenora's leaving personal. She has shamed me, and I don't take that lightly," he spat out furiously. "And she cleaned out our bank accounts. I'm broke."

"Oh Lord," Sarah muttered as she folded her arms across her chest. "I'm sorry about the money. You'll have to figure out how to live off your pension. You do get monthly payments, don't you? I remember you saying you were going to set up your pension disbursements that way, instead of a lump-sum payment."

"Well, yes, I still get my pension, but I cashed in several annuities and a couple of the IRAs that I was able to keep after your mother and I divorced. Lenora thought it made sense to use most of the money as a down payment on the house. My pension alone is not nearly enough for the upkeep on this house. Lenora contributed the majority of her salary to the household expenses." Daniel dropped his head, feeling disgraced.

"Daddy, you didn't keep any of your money for yourself? That doesn't sound like you." Sarah poked her nose in her father's business.

"I got a little money put away. Sarah, what if we get put out? Where would I go?" Panic filled Daniel's eyes. He remembered when he left Ruth, and how he had to go live with his brother, Fred.

"Then we'll cross that bridge when we get to it," Sarah said calmly, though her insides churned. *This situation gets worse every day,* she thought. *Lord, help us.* "You've got a lot going on. Let's just focus on each issue individually. I think it would be best for all concerned if you could focus on the boys right now. Have you heard from Lenora's sister or her parents? You need to make decisions about getting someone to help you with the children," she said.

"I'm not well," Daniel groused. "I can't be expected to make any decisions about the children. I have enough to cope with, as far as my health is concerned." His deadened eyes met Sarah's flashing ones.

"Daddy, you had the heart attack years ago, and it was a minor one at that," Sarah reminded her father as she tried to keep impatience out of her voice. "You have to work with what God gives you, and your minor children are your first priority, believe me." She rubbed the area between her eyes and suppressed a yawn. She felt tired. She had started work at seven o'clock that morning, and it was now after eight in the evening.

The doorbell sounded, and both Daniel and Sarah looked toward the door. Sarah popped out of her seat. "I'll get it," she said, strolling toward the door.

Daniel looked hopefully at the door, licking his lips. He prayed Lenora would be standing on the other side, apologizing for leaving him the way she had, and begging him to allow her to return home. His pride was fractured, and he couldn't wait to tell Lenora to get stepping.

Instead of his wife's petite figure at the door, Daniel saw his in-laws crossing the threshold into the stately Olympia Fields home that he and Lenora shared until a few days ago.

Daniel closed his eyes to block out the expression of hurt and confusion on the faces of his mother-in-law, Glenda, and his sister-in-law, Felicia. Ernest, Lenora's father, looked irate, while Felicia's husband, Reggie, looked concerned.

Ernest walked over to the recliner and pointed his finger at Daniel. "I trusted you with my Nora, and look what happened. You couldn't be a man to her and keep her at home. You good-for-nothing, son of a—"

Glenda strode quickly to the couch and pulled her husband's arm. "Ernest, this is not the time for all that. I'm sure Daniel is feeling as bad as we are. After all, it was his wife who left him."

"We should have made him take a physical when he married Nora. It ain't our fault he couldn't keep up with his wife. Maybe she would still be here if he was in better shape." Ernest twisted his lips into a sneer.

"Maybe you should have taught her to be a faithful wife," Daniel retorted, bristling.

Sarah held out her arms. "Let's try to keep our heads, and focus on the children. Why don't you all have a seat, and maybe we can discuss this situation like adults."

"That's a good idea," Felicia remarked. Reggie nodded his head approvingly.

"Why don't we go sit in the dining room," Sarah suggested. "There's more room in there."

"I agree," Felicia answered.

Everyone walked into the dining room and sat around the large marble-and-glass table.

"I'm going to check on the boys," Glenda announced as she took off her jacket and placed it on the back of one of the chairs. "I'll be back in a moment." She left the room and proceeded upstairs to the bedrooms.

Ernest sat unceremoniously on one of the chairs. He sneered at Daniel, who had just walked into the dining room and had sat on the chair at the head of the table.

"So, Daniel, what exactly did Lenora say?" Felicia wasted no time in her interrogation of her brother-in-law.

"She left me a note saying that she was leaving me for another man. And that she was going to Reno to get a quickie divorce, and that she would be in touch with me later. She doesn't want custody of the boys.

She feels they would be better off with me since they are males. What kind of woman does that?" Daniel couldn't keep the loathing he felt for Lenora from teeming in his voice.

"A woman who don't want no part of an old man," Ernest growled. "I can't blame her. I swear you done fell off, man. I wouldn't want no part of you either."

"Mr. Johnson, that was uncalled for," Sarah said, with fire in her eyes. "I hope you aren't here to place blame. I could say the same thing about Lenora. What mother just ups and leaves without her children?"

Ernest banged his hand on the table. His voice rose as he said, "I know you ain't trying to turn this around and blame this mess on my daughter. Yo' daddy should have left her alone years ago, and none of this would have happened."

"Ernest Johnson," Glenda said as she returned to the dining room from checking on the boys, who were upstairs sleeping. "Would you keep your voice down? The boys are asleep. I know they're missing their mother. So keep it down." She cut her eyes at her husband as she sat on the chair next to him. "Now, what wuz y'all saying?"

"Lenora left Daniel a note." Felicia brought her mother up to date. "Knowing Lenora as I do, I bet she's moved on with her life."

Glenda dropped her head; then she looked up. "I didn't raise Lenora that way. I can't believe she would even entertain the thought of leaving those precious babies behind. She didn't mention any problems to me. Felicia, did she say anything to you?"

Felicia shook her head no.

"Well, she *did* leave me, and Lenora knows I'm not well. I can't understand why she would do that," Daniel whined.

"Man, quit acting like a sissy," Ernest said. His voice betrayed the animosity he felt for his son-in-law, who was almost the same age as he was. "You need to man up. You shoulda handled your business."

"My father will take care of the boys. You don't need to worry about that," Sarah said adamantly. "I was hoping we could all come together, and come up with a plan to make life easier for Daddy and the boys."

"Ain't nobody trying to help Daniel." Ernest's eyes glowed with malice. "We only here cuz of the boys. Forget Daniel."

"Daniel is the boys' father. So he has the final say-so regarding them. Ernest, you're wrong, and Lenora was wrong for walking out on the boys," Glenda stated. "Whatever was going on in the marriage is between Daniel and Nora. We're here for my grandsons."

"Thank you, Mrs. Johnson," Sarah said as her body slackened against the back of the chair.

"Reggie and I will do what we can to help. What do you want to do, Daniel?" Felicia turned and asked her brother-in-law.

"I'm not sure. I know that I'm not up to keeping three little boys. My health isn't that good," Daniel proclaimed.

"Daddy, you're not on a death watch, nor are you disabled," Sarah stated, reproving her father. She folded her shaking hands together. "If you get someone to help you with the boys during the day, I think you'll be okay. Being without Lenora will be an adjustment, but you'll survive it."

"What are you saying, Daniel? You don't want the boys?" Felicia looked at him with eyes as round as saucers.

Daniel rubbed his prickly chin. "I really don't know. I mean, I don't think I can handle them. Maybe it would

be best if someone else kept them. I'm too old for this.
. . ." His voice trailed off.

"Daddy, you don't want to make that kind of decision
in an emotional state of mind. You need to think about
it more. Things will look better in the morning." Sarah
urged her father not to make any decisions he might
later regret.

"I agree with Sarah," Felicia said. "You need more
time to think about what you want to do. If you didn't
keep the boys, they would feel even more abandoned.
They need to stay put and with you for the time being."

"I told Daddy that I could take at least a week off
work and stay with him and help him with the boys,"
Sarah stated. "Then after that, he needs to make some
permanent changes. I'm praying he'll do the right
thing and keep his family together," she shared with
the group. "Would anyone like coffee or something to
drink?"

"I'd like a soda," Glenda said. "A Pepsi."

Everyone else, with the exception of Ernest, requested soft drinks. He walked downstairs to the basement
to the wet bar and returned with a bottle of Tanqueray.
On his way back to the dining room, he stopped in the
kitchen and asked Sarah to bring him a glass of water
with ice. Sarah looked at his retreating back disapprovingly. She imagined saying to Ernest, *There's nothing
wrong with your hands, get it yourself.*" Instead, she
said, "Sure."

Sarah looked in a bottom cabinet in the kitchen and
found a silver tray, which she set on the kitchen table.
She removed cold drinks from the refrigerator and
placed them on the tray. Then she turned on the faucet
and filled a small glass with water, and added a few ice
cubes from the freezer to it. Sarah returned to the dining room and put the tray on the table.

"Thank you, sweetie," Glenda said. She reached for a Pepsi, popped it open, and gulped down a few sips. "Daniel, what happened to Ms. Lewis, the nanny Nora hired for the boys? Is she still around?"

"No, we had to let her go a few months ago. Lenora's clients were having financial difficulties and money became tight," he answered tiredly.

Lenora was self-employed and owned a bookkeeping business.

"Aren't the boys in school during the day?" Felicia asked.

"Yeah, I guess so," Daniel responded despondently, sounding as if he didn't really know the answer to the question.

"Then you would only have to be bothered with them after school. Man, where is your head?" Ernest yelled. "If you don't want them, we'll take them. I'm sure Lenora has money put aside for the boys. You could pay me and Glenda, and we'll take care of them."

"Speak for yourself," Glenda shot at Ernest. "I done raised my kids, and I ain't looking to bring up no more." She quickly backed down, and said, "Unless I have to."

"There ain't no money," Daniel announced. "Lenora took most of our money when she left."

"I wouldn't mind keeping the boys," Felicia offered, sneaking a peek at Reggie. He nodded his head in approval.

The couple was the parents of two children, a boy, who was the same age as the twins, and a four-year-old daughter. They often had their nephew Kente, Lenora and Felicia's youngest sister LaQuita's son, and Lenora's three sons over for weekend stays.

"I don't think we should make any final decision today, until Daddy has time to explore all his options," Sarah announced. "I think if we all pitch in, Daddy would still be able to care for his sons. I plan to stay here the rest of the week. Why don't we meet Friday evening? Hopefully, by that time, Daddy will have adjusted to Lenora's leaving, and his focus will be on the boys."

"That sounds like a good idea to me." Glenda burped, and she covered her mouth. "I ain't working, so I could come by during the day. Or I could pick the boys up from school and come over here and cook or clean up." She looked around the room. "Too bad Nora didn't get a smaller house. That would have made life easier."

"Thank you, Mrs. Johnson. I think between the two of us, we can handle things until the end of the week. By then, Daddy should be able to make some final decisions." Sarah smiled. "Does that sound fair to you, Felicia?"

"Yes, it does. If you need me to do anything, Sarah, Daniel has my number," Felicia said.

Everyone chatted for about another half hour. Then they heard a cry from upstairs. Darnell was yelling for his mother. The women flew up the stairs to see about him. Daniel, Ernest and Reggie remained at the table.

"You know you a sorry excuse for a man," Ernest hissed at Daniel. "I hate the day that Lenora ever decided to hook up with you."

Daniel shrugged his shoulders. "I hate that day too."

"I know you ain't talking 'bout my daughter!" Ernest jumped up from his seat and walked menacingly toward Daniel.

"Pops, sit down. You don't want to do this." Reggie rose from his chair and restrained the older man.

"I'ma let it go for now cuz of the ladies. Don't let me catch you outside, Daniel Wilcox. I'll get to working on you like a bee in a honeycomb." Ernest balled up his fist at his son-in-law.

Daniel was still caught up in a state of self-pity; he barely reacted to his father-in-law's outburst.

Ernest continued muttering to himself. He drank shots of the gin, while he hurled verbal insults toward Daniel.

Finally the women returned to the room and took their seats.

"What took so long?" Reggie turned and asked his wife.

"By the time we got upstairs, all the boys were crying. Damon tried to hold it in, but he couldn't, so we had to comfort all the boys. It took a while to settle them down," Felicia told him.

Glenda looked at her husband. "It's time for us to go. Ernest, I think you've had a little bit too much to drink. Sarah, I'll talk to you tomorrow."

The Johnson clan stood up, put on their jackets and departed.

After Sarah locked the front door, her cell phone rang. She removed it from her pants pocket and looked at the caller ID. "That's Brian," she told Daniel. "I'm going to take this call in the kitchen." She walked into the other room.

Daniel's body was slumped over as he rubbed his temples. He thought, *How the heck did this happen to me? And what possessed my wife to leave me for another man?* Daniel bemoaned the fact that he was an elderly retired man stuck with raising three small children, with an albatross of a mortgage around his neck like a noose. The situation was like a role reversal for him, much like women had faced when they divorced and were left to cope with the broken pieces of their former lives.

Questions without answers, and fear of the unknown, swirled around in Daniel's head. He sat at the table, with his head dropped into his hands, paralyzed by a bout of inertia. He sat that way until the sound of the doorbell shook him out of his musings.

"I wonder who that is," Daniel muttered to himself.

Chapter Six

Daniel rose from the chair and shuffled to the front door. He peered out the peephole and saw his brother, Fred, on the other side. *Man, I don't feel like dealing with him tonight after the Johnsons*, he thought wearily.

Fred pressed the doorbell again and squinted into the peephole. "I know you in there, Danny. Let me in."

Sarah raced from the kitchen to the door with her cell phone in hand. "Dad, what are you doing? Are you trying to wake the boys? Open the door."

Daniel reluctantly turned the lock on the door, opened it, and then unlocked the screen door. He stood to the side to allow his brother inside the house.

"Shoot, what took you so long to answer the door? I know you weren't asleep." Fred smirked at his brother. "Then again, you might have been. I swear you done turned into an old man." He walked into the house and took his cap off his head. The two brothers eyed each other warily.

"How you doing, Danny? Sarah called and told me what happened with Nora. I guess that's rough for you." Fred's eyes swept over his seemingly elderly brother, who was younger than him by five years. He was shocked at his brother's appearance.

"I swear women can't hold water. Whatever they know, they gonna call another woman and tell the story. I just finished dealing with the Johnsons, so excuse me for being a little tired. We might as well sit in there," Daniel said, walking into the living room.

Sarah came into the room. She walked to Fred and hugged him. Then she sat down on the sofa. "Uncle Fred, how are you doing? Though I've talked to you on the telephone from time to time, I haven't seen you in a while." She smiled at her uncle.

"I'm doing good, girl. You look good, Sarah." Fred's eyes landed back on his brother. "I stop by and see your daddy every now and then. He doesn't seem to want my company as much as he used to. How are Brian and the kids?"

"They're doing well. Joshua is playing basketball for Whitney Young High School, and Maggie will be graduating from elementary school in June. We have two graduations this spring, Maggie and Naomi," Sarah said.

"That's good. I'm glad to hear everyone is doing fine. How are DJ and his family?"

"They're good. DJ has been assigned to a military base in Atlanta, and he's making great strides with his rehabilitation."

"That's good. I was sorry to hear about his foot injury in Afganistan. I felt even worse when I heard about his foot being amputated. When they brought him back to the States, I told Danny he should go see him. But you know my brother—he has turned into a knucklehead," Fred said affectionately.

"Aw, man, see you didn't have to go there." Daniel smacked his lips.

"You're right about everything, Uncle Fred. Look, I'm going to spend the night with Daddy, so I'm going to turn in. I have to get up early to get the boys ready for school. I'll see you next time. Don't be a stranger." She rose from the chair, walked around the table, and kissed her father and uncle. Then she walked upstairs.

"She's a wonderful woman, Danny. Sarah dropped everything and came to be by your side. It don't get no better than that," Fred said.

"Sounds like you done got soft in your older years, my brother," Daniel remarked.

"Nope, I ain't gonna say all of that. But sometimes you gotta grow up and do the right thing. Now tell me what happened with Nora," Fred said.

Fred poured two shots of gin and passed a glass to his brother as Daniel spilled his guts. Fred was Daniel's hero when they were growing up. They had been raised by their hell-raising grandmother. She was an alcoholic, who was emotionally absent from their lives. The men had become somewhat estranged after Daniel married Lenora. She wasn't crazy about her brother-in-law, because she felt his allegiance was toward Ruth and Daniel's family.

An hour had elapsed before Daniel finished telling his tale. "So that's where I am. Time flies, and before you know it, I'll be seventy years old. Now I'm stuck raising three little boys. If anyone had told me this would've happened to me, I never would have believed it. I still can't believe Nora left me," he said.

"You know what they say, bro, stuff happens." Fred nodded as he waved his hand in the air. "You gotta pick up the pieces and keep moving on. Are you gonna be able to keep this house? I never understood why you two needed such a big place to live." Fred sipped a little gin.

"Because Nora was determined to keep up with the Joneses. I used money from annuities and IRAs for the down payment on the house, so the mortgage isn't too bad. But she didn't leave me a lot of money after she cleaned out our accounts. I'll be lucky if I can cover the living expenses for the next few months with just my pension. But I don't think I want to stay here; there are too many bad memories in this house." Daniel flung his hand and sighed. "I know stuff happens, but it wasn't supposed to happen to me. I feel like I've lost control of my life. What do I really know about raising kids? Shoot, Ruthie raised our kids, and me and Nora had a nanny for the boys until the economy got bad. Fred, I don't think Nora's coming back," he lamented, looking sorrowful.

"What makes you think that?" Fred questioned. "Maybe she'll miss the boys and come to her senses?"

"That's all she would be coming back to. I wouldn't take her back if someone paid me a million dollars. She didn't think I knew, but she had been messing around on me with a man much younger than her. Game knows game. But my pride wouldn't let me confront her. I didn't want to have to raise the boys alone. I wanted her to stay." Daniel shook his head in disbelief. "Look how things have turned out. She left me, anyway. And dang it, if I ain't married to a cougar!"

Fred threw back his head and laughed gustily. "Do you have any chips?"

Daniel told him there were some in the kitchen.

When Fred returned to the dining room with chips in hand, Daniel continued speaking. "So I wasn't surprised when she up and left, even though I told the Johnsons that I was. What happens in this house isn't really their business. Lenora had been staying out all hours of the night, and too cheerful, all happy, singing and stuff. Know what I mean?"

"Man, I can't believe she played you like that." Fred couldn't believe Daniel's revelations. "You know what I wanna say, but I'll leave it for another day. So what you gonna do?"

"I think I should give the boys to Felicia or Glenda, and let them raise 'em," Daniel answered. He took a tiny sip of gin and swallowed.

"I don't think you want them to go with Glenda and Ernest. The boys ain't used to that kind of life. You want better for the boys, not worse."

"I know what you mean, Fred, but I don't have the energy to raise a family by myself," Daniel confessed candidly.

"There's still some life left in you, Danny boy. Think about the boys, and leave your pride out of it," Fred advised.

Daniel shrugged his shoulders. "The man Nora left me for is barely legal. When I say a lot younger, I mean he's only in his twenties. Shoot, Nora's only a few years younger than Sarah. She's old enough to be his mother. I don't know what she was thinking. And to marry him, she must be out of her mind."

"Ain't Ernest and Glenda still living in that same apartment they was living in when you met them all those years ago?"

"Yep." Daniel nodded. "They still live in South Shore on Colfax Avenue."

"How you gonna let them boys move from Olympia Fields to the South Side of Chicago? We ain't talking about one of the better neighborhoods. You want them to end up like them twin brothers of Lenora? What's their names? Jumbo and Jimbo?"

Daniel laughed. "Their names are Jabari and Jamal." Then the laughter left his eyes. "You're right. I don't want them to turn out like them bangers."

"Then why would you even think of sending the boys there? That ain't gonna work, man."

"You right. I guess I need to think about this some more," Daniel said morosely.

"Darn right, you do," Fred fussed at his brother.

Fred was still outspoken, and said what was on his mind. He had not gained an ounce of weight over the years. His signature single braid was now entwined with gray. Lines crossed his face, but his eyes were twinkling and clear. Fred's mind was as sharp as ever. He had matured over the years after watching his younger brother make a debacle of his life. Fred had even settled down to just admiring one woman, turning in his player's card. The brothers had become estranged over the past few years due to Lenora's feeling that Fred was closer to Daniel's first family. Fred had never told Daniel about his change of lifestyle. Sarah called Fred and explained Daniel's dilemma, and Fred made it his business to see his brother and show his support.

"If you had to send them away, Felicia and Reggie would be the better choice. You know all Ernest wants to do is get his hands on some money," Fred mused.

"That's the truth. For somebody who barely got a pot to pee in, he always had high aspirations for someone else's dollar." Daniel chuckled.

"Yes, he did. Glenda is okay, but she'll do what her old man wants. Have you talked to Naomi lately?" Fred changed the subject. His chin rested on the palm of one of his hands.

"Yeah, she called today, sounding all fake and stuff, trying to get the story out of me. She even said she might come home over the weekend. Since she moved to Edwardsville she don't come home much. And when she comes to Chicago, she don't come to see me," Daniel said.

"If she calls, that means she still has feelings for you. Nay ain't been right since she found out Sarah and Brian are her parents," Fred observed.

"Naw, the truth is, Nay ain't had much use for me since Ruth and I divorced. Nay called just to get in my business. We wasn't never close, like me and Sarah are. Nay calls me on my birthday, and we see each other about once a year. She couldn't stand Lenora, so she wouldn't come to this house."

"Count your blessings, Danny. At least she's still a part of your life. I hope you've been trying to mend your relationship with DJ?" Fred shifted his body on the chair.

"Nope, things are about the same with me and DJ. I can't get through to him. But I will think about doing what's best for the boys. Sarah said the same things you're saying. But I don't think I can be there for them, man, I'm old."

"Ain't nothing old about you but your mind. The doctor told you years ago to resume your life. You act like you had a heart attack yesterday. It happened a long time ago, and it was from you taking Viagra when you didn't need to. I think Lenora leaving might be the best thing that happened to you. At least you can work on getting the old Danny back, and making good with all your children," Fred pronounced.

"You sure you haven't been talking to Ruth?" Daniel guffawed. Then he became sober. "You haven't, have you?" he asked his brother suspiciously.

"I talk to Ruth sometimes, and visit The Temple every now and again," Fred admitted.

"Dang, I feel like I'm in that movie *Invasion of the Body Snatchers,* and someone done got my big brother," Daniel told Fred disapprovingly.

"Nope, that ain't what happened. Little brother, I done grew up. I visit with my kids and grandkids. We ain't getting old, we just getting mellow. It's time we get it together before our time is up."

"I swear, having this conversation with you is becoming more and more like talking to the Claytons, my former in-laws." He lightly tapped Fred's wrist. "Where is my brother? Fred, come on out."

"You got jokes, huh? I realize I didn't raise you right, and didn't give you the right advice when it came to women. I accept the responsibility. But now you gotta step up and be there for them boys. They ain't asked to come here, and you gotta do right by them," Fred said.

"Seriously, Fred, I don't think them living with me would be the best for them. I'm old enough to be their grandfather. Heck, great-grandfather in some parts of the world."

"You might be old enough to be their great-granddaddy, but you ain't. You the daddy, so you gotta act like one. Shoot, I'm older than you, but I'll help you. I realize now that nothing comes before the love of family. I ain't got much, but I'll do what I can," Fred offered. He looked up to see a tear trickle down Daniel's face, and he looked at his brother with astonishment. He got up from his seat and walked over to Daniel. "Man, one thing hasn't changed over the years. We still brothers, and I got your back." He leaned down and clasped his arm around Daniel's shoulder.

Daniel quickly wiped his face and sniffed loudly. "Thanks, Fred, I needed that. I really missed talking to you. I'm just scared. I didn't really raise Sarah, DJ, and Naomi. What if I mess up with the boys?"

"You got too many people helping you to mess up this time. As much as we make fun of the Johnsons, we know that family is important to Glenda and Felicia. Sarah has always been on your side. She's a good woman, like her mother. You ain't got to go through this alone. Just don't make any snap judgments you might regret. You got a chance to make a difference in them boy's lives."

"I know you right. I just need time to figure out how I'm gonna pull everything together."

Fred looked at his watch. "Look, I gotta go. I'ma come back tomorrow, and we'll talk some more. I just don't want you to give up on life and yourself. There's still a whole lot of life to be lived." He stood up and put his White Sox cap on his head.

The men walked to the foyer and said farewell. Daniel locked the door and turned the light off in the dining room. He sat on the couch and decided he didn't want to sleep in his and Lenora's bedroom, at least not tonight.

He walked to the foyer, flipped on the light, and took a blanket from the closet. He shuffled to the couch, lay down on it, and pulled the blanket over his shoulders. He chuckled as he thought how Lenora would have a fit if she knew he was laying on the couch.

Daniel felt a burst of nostalgia. He wondered what Ruth would have to say about the changes in his life. He shook his head, musing on how messy his life had become. Daniel missed his life with Ruth and his other children. He loved his young sons, but there was an order to his life with Ruth, which he'd missed during his marriage to Lenora.

Daniel hit the side of his head. He thought he must be crazy to care what Ruth would think. He shied away from the thought that he still had feelings for Ruth. A smile softened Daniel's features as he dreamed about his past life with his ex-wife.

Chapter Seven

On Wednesday, Ruth awakened at six o'clock in the morning. She had dressed and eaten breakfast, and was sitting at the kitchen table, although Alice's appointment was many hours away. Ruth felt a spirit of anxiety, mainly because she had tossed and turned the night before. She kept trying to quell her fears about Alice's procedure, but she wasn't quite able to swat away the butterflies fluttering inside her stomach.

The Bible on Ruth's nightstand kept calling out to her. She walked into her bedroom and sat on the side of the neatly made bed. She picked up the Word and turned to Joshua 1:9.

Have not I commanded thee? Be strong and of a good courage; be not afraid, neither be thou dismayed: for the LORD thy God is with thee whithersoever thou goest.

She closed her eyes and bowed her head and prayed. Ruth spent the next hour meditating on God's Word, and preparing for what lay ahead. When she was done, she turned the radio to her favorite gospel station. The telephone rang.

"Hello, this is Reverend Wilcox. How may I help you?"

"Good morning, Reverend Wilcox, this is Aron Reynolds. I hope I haven't awakened you. I'm an early riser, and I thought you might be too. I've been trying to get in touch with you for a couple of days," he said.

"Mr. Reynolds, how are you doing? I planned to call you later today. What can I do for you?" Ruth asked Aron, glancing at her watch.

"I'm doing fine. Look, the reason I called you was because Monet told me there was a position open at the church for a janitor, and I wanted to apply for the job."

"Oh, okay. Yes, there is an open position, but I'm not sure if it will be a paying one yet. Church funds are tight. But are you sure you're up to the task? Oh, my, I didn't mean that the way it sounded," Ruth apologized, feeling flustered.

Aron laughed aloud. "No harm taken. I may be up in age, but I'm stronger than I look. I have a lot of free time on my hands, and need something to do to fill that time. I'm certainly capable of sweeping, mopping, and any other tasks the job calls for."

"Well, I don't know." Ruth was at a loss for words. "I had planned to ask for volunteers for the upkeep of the church, at least temporarily."

"Reverend Wilcox, I have so much free time on my hands that it wouldn't be a problem for me to volunteer for whatever needs to be done. Why don't you let me try on a trial basis, and see how it goes?" Aron requested.

"Um, that seems fair. Why don't I give you a call tomorrow or the next day? I have a meeting scheduled with the finance committee next Friday. I need to concentrate all my energies on the meeting. And after the meeting, I'll be able to let you know if the job will be a paying one or not. I apologize for not getting back to you when you called."

"Fair enough. I'll be waiting for your call, Reverend Wilcox. I also wanted to tell you that I find you to be a phenomenal woman. You are truly an inspiration to the church." Aron cleared his throat, as if he was going to continue speaking but didn't.

"Thank you, Mr. Reynolds. God knows I try to lead by example. It's nice to know that church members appreciate my efforts," Ruth replied with a smile in her voice.

"Well, I know that you inspire Monet and Marcus. They're always singing your praises."

Ruth asked how the Caldwell family was doing, and Aron told her everyone was fine.

"Monet told me how she has her hands full raising the twin boys," Ruth added, enjoying her conversation with Aron.

"That's the truth. Marcus and Micah are busy little fellas. Faith loves being a big sister. Her personality reminds me so much of my late wife, Gay," Aron remarked of his grandchildren.

"Faith is certainly an old soul. As people used to say back in the day, she's been here before," Ruth replied, nodding her head.

"I won't take up any more of your time, Reverend Wilcox. I'll talk to you later this week. Enjoy your day. I presume even ministers are allowed to do that?" Aron teasingly asked Ruth.

"Thank you, you do the same. And yes, Mr. Reynolds, ministers are allowed to enjoy themselves. We are not always stuffy, upright religious people in a suit with white collars, sprouting scriptures all the time. A good many of us are married with children, and we face everyday problems like everyone else." Ruth's face warmed with embarrassment. "I'm sorry, I didn't mean to come off self-righteous or anything."

"I enjoyed talking with you, Reverend Wilcox. I like what I'm hearing, and at my age, believe me, I know no one is immune from problems in life."

Ruth was surprised that Aron grasped the meaning of her words. She had a feeling he knew exactly what she was saying.

"Have a blessed day, Mr. Reynolds," Ruth said as she began ending the call.

"Please call me Aron. I hope one day I can call you Ruth. Good-bye."

Ruth still held the telephone to her ear. The strident recorded message of "If you'd like to make a call" sounded in her ear. With a puzzled look on her face, she hastily put the phone back into the cradle and stroked her chin. She had a strong feeling that Aron Reynolds had attempted to put the moves on her. A sense of giddiness filled Ruth's body. Then like a switch had been thrown, the feeling dissipated.

"What am I thinking?" Ruth scolded herself aloud. "I'm way too old for that kind of foolishness. I'm a grandmother. There's no way I can have a relationship with another man as long as I still have feelings for Daniel."

She abruptly closed her lips and sat heavily on the bed as she waited for Alice to call her. Alice knocked lightly on Ruth's front door a few minutes later. When Ruth opened the door, she noted her friend looked peaceful.

Ruth greeted her. "You're early, I was supposed to pick you up. How are you feeling? Are you ready to go?" Her eyes searched Alice's face.

"I'm okay. I am just impatient and ready to get the appointment over with. So I came here instead of you coming next door. Anyway, I prayed for good news this morning, and God does answer prayer. How are you feeling?" Alice's face was drawn. She looked tired, as if she hadn't gotten much sleep.

"I'm good. I just need to get my sweater, and then we can get out of here." Ruth opened the closet and pulled a lightweight cardigan out of it.

She locked the front door; then she and Alice exited from the back door. The property included a multicar garage, which the women entered. Minutes later they were on the way to the hospital.

Ruth noticed Alice staring at her out of the corner of her eye, licking her lips. She glanced at Alice. "Is there something you want to say?" she asked.

"Uh, yes, there is. I should have told you this yesterday, but I chickened out." Alice's face dropped, and she clasped her trembling hands together. "Well, I've kind of been seeing someone, and he might be at the hospital."

"Girl, you been holding out on me? Is he someone I know?" Ruth glanced in the rearview mirror and then at Alice. She laid on her horn as a car cut her off.

"I prefer for you to see him for yourself. He's someone I've, I mean, we've known for a long time. We met for coffee about a year ago, one thing led to another, and we've been seeing each other socially for a while." Alice felt like a kid. She wished she had mentioned her friend sooner.

"Why haven't you shared that with me? Are you ashamed of him or something?" Ruth slowed down to turn on Ninety-fifth Street.

"No, that's not it. It didn't start with us dating. We were just two friends who would meet sometimes for coffee or lunch. Then we became closer. I never envisioned we would take the relationship to another level. So I didn't bother to say anything. It was just a casual thing."

"Are you saying that you're in love with him?" Ruth's mouth gaped open. She peeped at Alice, then back out the windshield.

"I'm not saying that. I enjoy his company, and I'm comfortable; and yes, I have strong feelings for him. We are opposites in personality, and that makes for interesting conversation. He opens my eyes to other possibilities in life." Alice's face had a spark of happiness to it.

"If he makes you happy, then I'm pleased for you. God knows we weren't meant to live alone. I hope he's there for you today," Ruth replied fervently.

"Thanks, Ruth. You don't know how good that makes me feel," Alice gushed. Then she sighed with momentary relief.

Ruth had many questions she wanted to ask Alice, but decided to hold her peace, for the time being. It would be a different ball game after Alice's procedure. She began formulating questions in her head.

"Speaking of opposites attracting, one of the men from church called me twice, yesterday and this morning. If I didn't know any better, I'd think he was trying to flirt with me." Ruth's cheeks flamed at the thought.

"Get outta here," Alice ribbed Ruth. "Maybe this will be our year, and we'll both have male companionship. Lord knows our wells have been dry for a long time."

"You're crazy, Alice. Aron Reynolds, Monet Caldwell's father, called me. I was so surprised that you could have knocked me over with a feather." Ruth switched to the left lane. She wasn't far from the hospital. "You do know, though, that he's an ex-con, and I don't know about seeing someone with a criminal past."

Alice nodded her head. "I remember him. He's not bad-looking, for an older guy." After a pause, Alice continued, "So you're sitting in the judgment seat. You couldn't date someone with a criminal past, even if he's paid his debt to society? I have to admit this is deep," she observed.

"I'm not sitting in the judgment seat. He hasn't even asked me out or anything like that. It was a feeling I had, like he wanted to ask me out," Ruth said, correcting Alice, and then pursed her lips tightly together. "He actually called about the janitor position at The Temple."

"All I can say is people change if they want to, and Mr. Reynolds has paid his dues. In the long run, you have to please yourself and not other people."

"That would be easier to do if I wasn't a minister. I'm held to different standards by my members. I have my hands full leading the church, dealing with the financial crisis, and trying to balance the budget. I'm committed to doing what is pleasing in God's sight."

"Okay, I hear you. But if he or any other man asks you out, you should at least consider the possibility. That's all I have to say for now. I'm sure you'll come to the right decision about what to do."Alice dipped her head toward the hospital. "We're here already? The ride didn't take long," Alice said as Ruth steered her car into the hospital parking lot.

Ruth parked the car and turned it off. She twisted her body and faced Alice. "Yes, the traffic was light, so it didn't take any time at all. Shall we pray?"

Alice nodded, and they held hands.

"Lord, I ask that you stop by Christ Hospital today. Heal and comfort the sick and shut-ins, and their families today. Lay your healing hands on them and my sister Alice. Lord, you said we only have to ask and it will be given. I come before you, Lord, and ask you to take care of my sister, and when we leave here today, all will be well in her world. These blessings I ask in Jesus' name. Amen."

"Amen," Alice echoed. "I'm sure everything will be all right, and if it isn't, God is able and He will surely fix it. Let's go get this over with."

The women got out of the car and walked toward the hospital entrance. Once inside the building, they took the elevator to Alice's doctor's office.

When they walked inside the door, Ruth did a double take. Fred, Daniel's brother, was sitting in the waiting room. He stood and walked toward them.

He leaned over and kissed Alice's check. "Good morning, ladies. How are you doing this morning?"

Ruth's hands flew to her mouth, and she stepped back. "Is he your mystery man?" She looked over at Alice, and then back at Fred.

"Yes, Fred is the one," Alice said nervously as she watched the surprise on Ruth's face.

"I don't believe it! You were talking about my brother-in-law, Fred, the player? The one who taught Daniel everything he knows?" Ruth exclaimed, her eyes darting between Alice and Fred. They were the most unlikely pair she could imagine.

Alice's caramel face was flushed. "I've got to go sign in. I'll be back in a moment." She strolled across the room to the reception window.

Fred pointed to the seats, and he said to Ruth, "Why don't we sit down?"

"That's a good idea," Ruth replied tartly. "I need to sit down before I fall down."

They sat on beige-colored chairs, near the back of the waiting area.

"I'm almost speechless, Fred." Ruth turned and looked at her former brother-in-law, who looked down at the floor, abashed, and then up at her.

Ruth admitted that Fred still cast a fine figure in his older years. He was always suave and handsome, and also wore a sardonic expression on his smiling face.

He and Ruth looked up as Alice sat down on the seat between them.

"You two have some explaining to do," Ruth announced in a mockingly stern voice. "God, I sound like someone's mother, don't I?" she asked pitifully.

"I would say so." Alice laughed nervously as she twisted her hands together. "Fred attended one of the concerts I host for the Chicago public schools. Fred's granddaughter, Whitney, is one of my students. So when we'd see each other at her recitals from time to time, we'd go out for coffee, and the rest is history."

"That's all well and good," Ruth interjected as she looked away from Alice to Fred. "But when did you turn into a couple? I can't believe you didn't say anything to me. When did this start?" Her eyebrows arched with amazement.

"Ruthie, we started out as friends," Fred explained. "I've been trying to make up with my children, especially Tamara. When she told me Whitney was taking piano lessons and invited me to Whit's concert, and I saw Alice was her teacher, you could've bowled me over with a feather. Alice and I began talking. You know I always thought you and she were the smartest women that I know. So I asked Alice what I could do to be a better father and grandfather to my children."

"And let me guess, that's when one thing led to another." Ruth's voice rose with amazement. "You know what? I'm happy for you two; you're both adults. But, Fred, let me warn you. If you hurt my friend, I will haunt you until the day you die." She gently punched him in the arm. "Just kidding," she added. "Please treat her right. She deserves some happiness."

"Woman, I ain't gonna do nothing to hurt Alice." Fred looked hurt that Ruth would even suggest such an idea. "She's good people. That's why I'm here today. I want everything to work out for her today, so I can keep being a part of her life. We ain't talking marriage or nothing, we're just good friends."

"Friends with benefits?" Ruth probed. Her head was cocked to the side as she looked at Alice and then Fred.

They all burst out laughing. Then the door to the waiting room opened, and a nurse in blue scrubs, with her hair pulled back into a ponytail, walked inside the room. She glanced down at the chart she was holding and said, "Alice Collins."

Alice stood up on trembling legs. "Hold that thought, and, Ruth, keep cranking out those prayers."

Ruth and Fred rose from their seats. Ruth pulled Alice into her arms and said, "God got this, and everything will be just fine. I love you, girl."

Alice nodded; and when Ruth released her body, she turned to Fred, and he engulfed her in a big bear hug. He whispered, "I'm gonna join Reverend Ruth and send up a prayer or two of my own. We know you're gonna be all right."

Alice stepped away from Fred. She smiled at both of them. Then she waved before she went into the examination area. Ruth and Fred sat back down.

Ruth stared at the closed door, and suddenly she was filled with a sense of dismay. She thought, *Lord, take care of my friend. Please, I beg of you.*

Fred didn't miss the look of angst on Ruth's face. He stood up and sat on the chair that Alice had just vacated. He took Ruth's quivering hand, and held it in his calloused one.

"She'll be fine, don't worry. We just have to hold on to that faith you're always talking about," he said.

Ruth let out a loud roar. "Who would have thought you would be telling me that!" She removed her hand from Fred's, took off her sweater, and put it on the back of her chair. She wore denim jeans and an ash-colored angora sweater, along with short brown boots. Her gray hair shone, and she wore a light smattering of lip gloss.

"You're looking good," Fred observed. "Life must be treating you right."

"I can't complain, and where would it get me, anyway?" Ruth quipped. She folded her left leg atop her right one, and settled erectly against the back of the seat.

"I hear you. Sarah told me everyone is doing okay. I'm glad to hear that. I been meaning to call you to see how you were doing, but got busy," Fred added smoothly.

"Yes, everyone is doing well. We're just waiting for Nay and Maggie's graduations. I can't believe my baby is getting another degree," Ruth bragged. She took a copy of the graduation invitation out of her purse and handed it to Fred.

"One thing I have to give you credit for is how you never gave up on Naomi. She's grown into a fine woman. Daniel told me that she's gonna open an office after she gets her new degree."

"That's right. I can hardly wait for her to move back to Chicago," Ruth said.

"You done good by all your children, Ruthie. I just hope I can do the same with my grandchildren. It hasn't been easy for me. Tammy and Freddie Jr. gave me a hard time, but I'm hanging in there."

"That's good, Fred. Every child should know his or her parents and grandparents." Ruth nodded. She took a deep breath. "Sarah told me about Danny. How is he holding up?" She exhaled.

"I ain't gonna lie to you, he's in a bad way. I ain't never seen him this bad off. It's like he's thrown in the towel and given up on life. I stopped by to see him last night, and I broke up his pity party. I told him, he needs to get up off his butt and take care of them boys."

"Hmm, you are right. The boys need him more than ever before," Ruth said as her heart rate increased threefold.

Fred frowned. "Try telling him that. The Johnsons were at his house before I got there, and from what I heard, old Ernie let Danny have it. I thought that might have lit a fire under his tail, but it didn't, not really. I tell you that durn Lenora was like a vampire; she sucked all the life out of my brother."

"I will definitely pray for Daniel and his family. Hopefully, he will get it together and things will work out."

"I hope so. I think he lost his confidence, because Lenora left him for a boy. At least that's what I call him. He ain't but twenty-something years old." Fred shook his head disgustedly. Trevor was actually twenty-three years old.

"Oh, my!" Ruth exclaimed. "That is so sad." She tried to suppress a smug smile that wanted to creep on her face.

"Are you thirsty?" Fred asked. "There's a vending machine downstairs. I need to stretch my legs." He stood up.

"Yes, bring me a black decaffeinated coffee." Ruth reached for her purse.

"No, I got it. I'll be right back." Fred walked away.

The waiting room had become more crowded as people arrived for appointments. Ruth couldn't help but notice the terror on some of the patients' faces. She said a quick silent prayer for all of them. She glanced at her watch, and an hour had elapsed since Alice had left the waiting room. That worried her. She wondered what could be taking so long.

Ten minutes later, the nurse who had called Alice into the patient area returned to the waiting room. "Is there a Ruth and Fred Wilcox here?" she asked.

Ruth nearly jumped out of her seat and rushed over to the nurse. "I'm Ruth Wilcox. Is something wrong?" She nervously ran her hands along her upper arms.

"Mrs. Collins would like you and Mr. Wilcox to join her in the doctor's office," the nurse said.

A trembling began from the soles of Ruth's feet, to the top of her head. "Mr. Wilcox went to get coffee. He should be back momentarily," she said.

Fred walked up. "I'm here. Is something wrong?"

The nurse said once again, "Mrs. Collins would like for y'all to join her in the doctor's office. Please follow me."

Ruth's legs felt heavy; it was like she was wading through sand. She and Fred followed the nurse around the corner and down the hallway to the doctor's office. *Lord, give strength for what lies ahead,* Ruth prayed silently.

Chapter Eight

Ruth walked stiffly, futilely trying to stop her body from shaking like she was naked in the middle of an Antarctica desert. Fred put his arm across her back, to impart strength to her inner being. They walked into Dr. Shapiro's office, where they found Alice sitting on a chair across from the doctor's untidy, glossy dark mahogany desk.

Memories of visits to Ezra's, Bishop's, and, lastly, Queen's doctors blanketed Ruth's mind. She shook her head slightly, to erase those memories.

Alice's eyes were reddened and puffy. She clutched a pink tissue in one hand. Ruth slid into the empty seat to the right of her friend. Fred stood by, helpless, until the nurse brought an extra chair into the office. He then sat on the other side of Alice, who still looked dazed.

After the nurse departed the room, with a sinking feeling in the pit of her stomach, Ruth frantically asked Alice, "What did he say?" She knew the answer before she asked the question.

Alice sniffed, and could only shake her head sadly.

Dr. Shapiro walked into the room. He had a full head of thick, wavy salt-and-pepper hair. He was dressed in dark trousers, a red tie, and an immaculately pressed white shirt, covered by a blue jacket, signaling his physician status. He walked to his desk, carrying Alice's folder under his arm.

After he laid the folder on his desk, Dr. Shapiro put his spectacles on his face, extended his hand, and asked Ruth, "You are?"

"I'm Ruth Wilcox, Alice's best friend." She nervously clasped her shaking hands together after she shook the doctor's hand.

The doctor turned to Fred, and repeated the process. "And you are, sir?"

"I'm a close friend of Alice's. My name is Fred Wilcox." He nervously crossed and uncrossed his legs.

"Are you two married?" the doctor inquired after he sat down on his leather swivel chair.

"No. Ruth was married to my brother and they're divorced," Fred answered. He glanced over at Alice, and could see the misery that was transparent on her face. He grabbed one hand, while Ruth took the other.

"Mrs. Collins has requested your presence during our consultation. To bring you up to speed, Mrs. Collins has a mass in her breast. Since she's genetically predisposed to the disease, I put a priority on Alice's test, and I had the tissues sample analyzed immediately after the procedure. And I'm sorry to say we did find traces of carcinoma. Since Mrs. Collins has been diligent in having mammograms performed over the years, I believe we caught the cancer in time to treat it successfully. Of course, we have to run more tests, and determine the best course of therapy for her." Dr. Shapiro paused to let his words sink in.

Alice looked and felt devastated, and two tears trickled down her face. Dr. Shapiro handed her another tissue. The one she held was shredded. Ruth sat back; her face was crumpled with sorrow. Fred grimaced like someone had punched him in his abdomen.

His voice was thick with emotion as he asked the doctor, "Are you sure about the results? Couldn't there be a mistake?"

"Mrs. Collins is more than welcome to seek a second opinion, but I stand by our lab results. We have a state-of-the-art laboratory facility here at Christ Hospital, one of the best in the city. I know most people feel that receiving confirmation of cancer is akin to a death sentence, but new techniques are available today for successfully treating cancer. Our cure rate is among the highest in the nation. So I don't want you to feel like this is the end for Mrs. Collins," Dr. Shapiro explained in a calming tenor voice. He possessed an excellent bedside manner.

Hope began to stir in Ruth's chest as she listened to the doctor talk.

"I have found that patients with a good support system have a higher survival rate than those who don't. She told me that you two are her support system, and from what I can see, she was correct. That's why I suggested Mrs. Collins ask you to join us during the consultation."

Ruth cleared her throat. "Without a doubt. Alice is my sister in every way, except blood. No, I take that back." She shook her head. "We stuck a pin in our fingers when we were ten years old, and smeared blood with each other. So, whatever you need me to do, and I think I can speak for Fred, we're here."

Fred nodded his head as Alice blew her nose into the tissue.

Dr. Shapiro took a sheet of paper out of the folder on his desk. He handed it to Alice and said, "This is a list of the oncologists on staff here at Christ. You're free to seek another doctor if you so choose. I've highlighted those that I have referred patients to, and gotten good feedback from. They are all excellent, so feel free to call several before you make a final decision. I would suggest you do so as soon as possible."

Alice took the paper, folded it up, and placed it inside her purse. She turned her attention back to Dr. Shapiro.

"After you select an oncologist, please call my nurse, so she can get him your medical history information. Hopefully, by the end of next week, depending on how quickly your tests can be scheduled, he would have come up with a recommendation for treatment," Dr. Shapiro said.

Alice nodded. "Do you think I'll have to have chemotherapy or radiation treatments?" Her body shivered as she asked the question. She pulled at her purse straps, something to do to steady her body and mind.

"It's too soon to say what course of therapy will be effective, until you see the oncologist, Mrs. Collins," Dr. Shapiro answered kindly. "Do either of you have any questions?" He peered at Ruth and Fred.

Fred shook his head. Ruth did the same.

"Alice?" the doctor asked, looking compassionately at his patient.

"Not at the moment, but I'm sure by the time I return, I'll have more questions." Her voice trembled.

"Okay, then. Alice, please call my nurse as soon as you can. Mr. and Mrs. Wilcox, it was a pleasure meeting you." Dr. Shapiro extended his hand again.

He walked toward the door and opened it. Ruth, Alice, and Fred trailed somberly behind him. Dr. Shapiro started to say "have a good day," but nixed the idea. He nodded at them respectfully. Then he headed to the receptionist desk, to find out which examination room his next appointment was in.

While Alice and Fred waited at the nurse's desk to get further information, Ruth asked the nurse where the ladies' room was located. She pointed down the hall. Ruth told Alice and Fred she would meet them in the waiting room.

When Ruth locked the door to the restroom, she turned down the seat on the toilet, sat on it, and rocked back and forth, sobbing silently. She felt crushed, but she tried to compose her frazzled nerves.

She threw her hands in the air and said, "Oh, Lord, God in heaven, please don't take my friend from me. There are so many things we planned to do. Please let her stay here with me many more years."

She sobbed a few minutes more, then stood up and peered at her face in the mirror. She was shaken, but she knew she needed to pull it together to comfort her friend. Ruth turned on the faucet and rubbed cold water on her face. Then she bowed her head.

"Lord, forgive my selfishness. You are in charge, and I don't really have to worry, because you will take care of my friend and cure her of this horrible disease. Lord, you brought her here six months after her last mammogram, which is a blessing. You were on the case back then. Give me strength, Lord, to help Alice, as she would help me."

Ruth tried to paste a brave expression on her face, but she couldn't stop her lips from trembling. She twisted the lock on the door and walked to the waiting room.

Alice was leaning against Fred, who spoke softly to her. Ruth walked over to her friends.

Alice cast water-filled eyes at Ruth and asked, "Would you mind if Fred drove me home?"

Ruth's cell phone vibrated against her hip. Since she was inside the hospital, she let the call go to voice mail. Ruth checked the caller ID and said, "I need to return this call. I'll be right back." She walked to the double doors and headed outside the hospital. She fumbled as she dialed June's cell phone number.

When her secretary answered the call, Ruth asked, "Hi, June, what's happening?"

"Reverend Wilcox, one of the pipes in the church has burst. James can't come in; he said he has a family emergency. I've tried calling some plumbers in the area, but no one can get here for at least a few hours. I don't know what to do," June cried helplessly. She watched water accumulate in the children's church.

"Okay, let me think about who I can call. Why wasn't James available?"

"Faye became ill, and James is on the way to the hospital. We need another janitor pronto," June answered, moaning.

"I was just leaving the hospital, so I'll be there as soon as I can. Keep trying to find a plumber," Ruth advised her secretary.

"Okay, Pastor Ruth, I'll see you shortly," June replied.

After Ruth told June farewell, she dialed her home number to retrieve her voice mails. Luckily, she had saved Aron's telephone number. She wrote it down on a piece of paper and quickly called him.

She felt relieved after Aron answered the telephone. She explained the situation at the church, and Aron reassured her that he was more than happy to assist in any way he could.

Ruth sighed gratefully, secure in the knowledge that God provides resources when most needed. She thought how she needed to apply the same principle to Alice's situation, and not to panic when a curveball came her way. *Who better than I,* Ruth thought, *knows how kind and loving the God I serve is.*

She walked back inside the hospital to explain to Alice and Fred the crisis at the church. She promised to stop by and see Alice later. She realized that Fred being at the hospital that morning was a bonus, and she knew that Alice was in good hands.

Ruth hurried to her car, ready to tackle the next item on her "to do" list. She made it to The Temple in twenty minutes flat. Luckily, she wasn't delayed by many stoplights, as if the Lord ensured she would arrive at the church in a timely fashion. She locked her car door with the keyless remote and walked into The Temple.

When she entered, June was waiting for her at the door. "I saw you drive into the parking lot. Aron Reynolds arrived about twenty minutes ago, he's downstairs now," she informed her boss as they walked toward the stairway leading to the basement of the church.

The heels of Ruth's boots clattered as she walked down the metal staircase. June walked behind her. The lights were dim in the basement, so Ruth and June squinted as they strolled into the large boiler room.

"Mr. Reynolds," Ruth called while she looked at the ceiling at the pipes to see if a leak had sprung from there. From what she could see, everything looked normal.

Aron emerged from the shadow of an opened door, wiping his hands on a rag. "Hello, Reverend Wilcox," he greeted Ruth.

"Please tell me you were able to find the source of the leak?" she asked anxiously as she peered at Aron. Her expression telegraphed, *"Please have good news for me."*

Aron nodded. "Yes, I did. One of the washers had worn out. I turned off, for now, the main water source in the church. After I replace the washer, I'll turn it back on. I'll go to a hardware store and pick up the parts. I should be able to replace it easily enough."

"Great." Ruth exhaled and smiled. She opened her purse and took out her leather wallet. "How much will the washer cost?" she asked.

"No more than ten dollars," Aron informed her as he set the soiled rag on a table.

Ruth was struck by how fit he looked, considering his age. He cut a dashing figure, even though he was in his seventies. His full head of gray hair was combed back on his head. The jeans he wore, along with a checkered flannel shirt, clung to his body.

Ruth handed Aron the money.

"Luckily, the leak wasn't bad. It didn't appear anything was damaged in the children's church. There is just water that has to be removed. It looks like June caught things in time. Do you have a wet vacuum? If so, I can clean up the water after I fix the leak," Aron said.

"There's an equipment closet outside the room, around the corner. June can give you the key to it. I believe there's a wet vac in there. Thank you, Aron," Ruth gushed. "I guess it could have been worse." They walked back upstairs.

June told Aron she would have the key available for him when he returned from the hardware store. She then headed back to the office.

"Thank God you discovered the leak when you did, June," she told the church secretary. "What made you go downstairs to the children's church?"

"I had ordered pamphlets for Sunday School, and they came in the mail today, so I took them downstairs. I was shocked to see the water down there," June informed Ruth. She laid the key to the closet on top of her desk.

"Praise God. Once again He was taking care of The Temple." Ruth nodded, then sighed. "The building is old and definitely in need of repairs. James planned to retire at the end of the month, and I suspect Faye's illness might push up his date. Sometimes, when it rains, it pours. Thank God Mr. Reynolds was available, or we'd probably have a small lake in the children's church. The condition of the building is one of the topics I'll address with the finance committee." She took a pad of paper from June's desk and wrote a note to herself to mention the leak at the meeting.

"Can I get you a cup of coffee, boss? You look like you've had a rough morning," June offered.

She stood and walked over to the coffee machine on a counter opposite her desk. She poured the brown liquid into a cup, added a dollop of cream, and handed it to Ruth.

When she returned to her desk, June handed Ruth a batch of pink message slips. "I put them in order by importance, and did what I could to divert some of the calls. The utility bills came in the mail, and you need to look at them ASAP."

"Thank you, June. Sometimes I feel you can read my mind, and today has been one of those days."

Ruth walked into her office and set the coffee and messages on her desk. She took her purse off her shoulder and put it on her desk. She unlocked her desk and placed her purse in the bottom drawer. Ruth sat back and massaged her temples.

She still couldn't get over the fact that Alice and Fred had been seeing each other. *Stranger things have happened,* she thought. Her thoughts turned to Aron. Then she shook her head and began going through the messages June had given her.

By the time Ruth had returned several calls, and given June several letters to mail, Aron had returned from the hardware store, had replaced the washer, and had just about completed the cleanup of the children's church. It was close to five o'clock in the evening.

June walked into Ruth's office, wearing a sweater and carrying her purse and tote bag in both hands. "I'm going to leave, unless you need me to hang around for something," she said.

Ruth shook her head and laid the paper, which she had been reading, on her desk.

"How did things go at the hospital with Miss Alice?" June asked.

When Ruth rescheduled her appointments for the
day, she confided in June that she was going to the hospital to support Alice. After working with Ruth for over
five years, June knew Ruth, her moods, and her expressions well. She knew the sad versus the concerned
looks that Ruth wore on her face at times. June assumed correctly that the sadness she saw on her boss's
face was due to Alice's hospital appointment.

"Not too good," Ruth answered. She swallowed hard.
"She has another round of testing to go through."

"I'll keep her in my prayers then. Miss Alice is a
wonderful musician. She brings the church much happiness with her musical ministry. Well, I'm out of here,
Reverend Wilcox. I will see you in the morning," June
said.

"Thank you, June, have a good evening," Ruth told
her.

Ruth glanced at the clock and turned her chair toward the window. She laid her arm on the side of her
chair and propped her chin inside her hand. She sighed
heavily as she thought of Alice battling cancer, Queen
fighting dementia, her son, DJ, adjusting to life without his left foot. Her spirit felt heavily laden.

"Ruth crooned softy, the words to the song, I'm a
soldier in the army of the Lord. She closed her eyes.
"Lord, I feel so overwhelmed sometimes, but I know,
like everything else in life, I must turn my burdens over
to you. With all I have going on, I have to remember
you're in control. Daddy used to always say, 'There is
no secret what God can do,' and I know that's right."

She wiped tears from her eyes and turned her chair
back to her desk. She looked up to see Aron looking at
her with compassion smoldering in his eyes as he stood
at the door to her office. Ruth assumed he'd come to
discuss the condition of the children's church. Ruth
prayed the news wasn't too bad.

Chapter Nine

"How is the lower level of the church?" Ruth greeted Aron a bit awkwardly. She ran her hand over her head and tried to put a bright smile on her face, which didn't quite reach her eyes. She felt flustered as she picked up and then set down a piece of paper on her desk.

"May I come in?" Aron asked, with a compassionate expression on his face.

"Sure, I'm sorry. I forgot my manners for a minute. Have a seat." She swept her hand to the chair placed in front of her desk.

"The children's church is fine. There wasn't any serious damage done. I managed to get the water off the floor and replace the washer. The water is back on, so all is well," Aron answered after he sat across from Ruth.

"Praise God! That is good news. I'm so glad you were available and able to come here today to help out." Ruth smiled.

"It was my pleasure. I'm glad I was able to help. I'm hoping this might score me some brownie points in trying to obtain the job," Aron admitted candidly. "I feel useless sometimes, and need something to do to pass the time."

"Hmm," Ruth pondered as she dipped her head. "I can understand that. I thought Monet told me that your skill is gardening. Lord knows, we may have to let the crew that tends to the grounds go. If there's a choice of the upkeep of the inside or the outside, then I'd say the inside is the priority."

"I'd say that you've found the right man. I can do both, and I'd still like to try on a trial basis, if you'd allow me, until you make the position permanent."

Aron's eyes roamed the room, looking at the heavy wood desk with matching cabinets and burgundy wingback leather chairs. An oil painting of the Clayton family, when Ezra and Ruth were teenagers, was lovingly placed on one of the walls, along with other ministerial relatives and family. Hundreds of leather-bound books, interspersed with paperbacks, filled the floor-to-ceiling bookshelves. The walls in the office were painted a soft cream color.

"This is a homey office. The woodwork is excellent, a work of art. You don't see work like this anymore. Truthfully, I would have expected an office a bit more feminine for a woman minister," Aron said.

Ruth threw back her head and laughed. "This office belonged to my father, Bishop. I inherited it when he passed away. You're right, it was a bit dark for my taste. My friend Alice and I decided to at least paint the walls brighter, and to change the window treatments."

"I'm glad I was able to bring a smile to your face. You looked sad when I came to talk to you," Aron observed.

"You're right. I've been indulging in a mini pity party most of the day," Ruth acknowledged. "My best friend, Alice, was diagnosed with cancer today. She and I have been friends since we were in elementary school. As a minister, I know that God will see us through this dilemma, but sometimes the human side of me comes out. And sometimes, but not often, I tend to worry needlessly about things I have no control over."

"I would imagine that's a trait that makes you effective as a minister, retaining your human side," Aron complimented Ruth. He cleared his throat. "I'm not an expert on these types of matters. Still, I sense a presence of goodness about you."

Ruth smiled, and it was the smile that transformed her face from plain to beautiful.

"Thank you, Aron. I think I needed to hear that today. I just need to turn my burden over to God, and let Him handle it. Alice is like a sister to me, and my family seems to be shrinking rapidly. My brother and father have passed, my mother has Alzheimer's disease, and I just don't think I could bear if something happens to Alice." Ruth sniffled and covered her eyes. "Please forgive me," she said.

"I understand what you mean. I felt the same way when my wife, Gayvelle, passed. I'm ashamed to say that I treated her badly for most of our marriage. Still, she forgave me time and time again. That gave me the motivation, along with meditating on the events in my life, to lead me to seek God. I used to ponder how Gayvelle could forgive me after all the wrong I did to her. When I eventually came to terms with everything I'd done, and sought forgiveness from God, I knew it was time for me to change. I managed to do that while I was in prison. My first order of business was reconnecting with my children, which, in turn, led me to The Temple," Aron said.

"Monet has told me your story, and what a blessing from God that you were able to reconcile with your children. God always gives us chances to right wrongs. I could sense how Monet always wanted a father figure in her life, especially after her mother passed. I think you've done a wonderful job of establishing a relationship with her and the boys. I know whatever God has in store for Alice, I will be there for her, as she has been for me in the past."

"Wiser words were never spoken," Aron quipped, lightening the moment between the two. "I'm not keeping you from anything, am I?" he inquired, stretching his legs out in front of the desk.

"No," Ruth replied with a sigh. "There is always work to be done. You coming here is a welcome reprieve from my gloomy thoughts, and I'm sure you guessed you earned the janitor spot on a trial basis. When can you start?"

Aron thrust out his hand, and Ruth gave him hers. "Thank you, Reverend Ruth, you won't be disappointed. I can start tomorrow, just say the word."

Ruth was surprised by the tingly, warm feeling that emanated from Aron's hand to her own, and then coursed through her body. She shook her head almost unconsciously, trying to figure the root cause. Her other hand flew nervously to her forehead, and she finger combed her bangs. "Why don't you come on Friday, so James can begin training you," she suggested.

Aron nodded. "I will. Um, I hope I'm not stepping out of bounds," Aron said after he cleared his throat. "I asked Monet if you were dating." He chuckled. "That word sounds so old-fashioned."

Ruth nodded as she stared into Aron's hypnotic hazel-colored eyes. "My grandchildren say I should be hip to the new sayings, and they tell me 'dating' is now called 'hanging out' or 'kicking it.' I guess the word 'dating' has become a thing of the past, like a lava lamp."

"Whatever that is, it's obviously something I missed while I was away." Aron cocked his head to the side. Aron has been incarcerated since the mid seventies. His sentence was thirty years to life.

As her mind darted between the possibilities of what Aron would say next, Ruth explained what a lava lamp was.

He nodded. "Reverend Wilcox, may I call you Ruth?"

She stared at him with an indecisive expression, as if debating how she should respond to Aron's request. Then a smile broke over her face. Ruth nodded.

"Whew." He wiped his brow, rolled his eyes upward and sighed as Ruth giggled at his antics. "Ruth sounds better than Reverend or Pastor Wilcox. Anyway, Ruth, you are simply an amazing woman. I don't know any other way to put this, except I find you an attractive woman, and I'd love to get to know you better." He peered at Ruth and saw that he held her undivided attention. He waved his hand casually. "Don't get me wrong. I've lived long enough to know that relation-ships aren't based on outward looks, but what's inside a person's heart, instead. I have watched you in various settings at the church since I've been in Chicago, and I must say I'm impressed by what I've seen."

"Wow." Ruth's eyes dropped to her desk, and her body trembled. It had been a long time since a man had expressed admiration for her. She blinked back tears. "Aron, thank you. That's the nicest thing I've heard from a member of the opposite sex in a long time." She blushed and chastised herself for using the word "sex" in The Temple.

"I mean it, Ruth," Aron replied forcefully. "I found you attractive the day that Monet introduced us, when I first visited your church. And it doesn't hurt that you preach sermons that everyone can relate to. You're an inspirational speaker. What really impressed me was Pastor's Day last year, and how the members paid homage to you. The stories they told about your visit-ing the sick and the shut-ins, comforting them when they lost a loved one, or during hardships in their lives. And I know firsthand what you did for my Monet."

Ruth blushed and shook her head. "That's what ministers do. It's part of my job."

"You're right." Aron nodded. "But what I felt was the love and admiration the church has for you. Like the MasterCard commercial says, the program was 'priceless.'"

The two shared a laugh as dusk cloaked the city.

"Thank you. If I were a different woman, my head would swell." Ruth grinned, and just as suddenly, the corners of her mouth drooped. "But I don't date. I'm not good at it, and I've been burned—no, make that singed—by my former husband."

"I understand. But once you reach our age, you have experienced some of the bumps and bruises associated with this thing called life. We don't know what God has planned for us, unless we take a chance and enjoy life to its fullest." Aron leaned forward as he pressed on with his case.

Ruth felt shaky, and she laughed almost tensely. She began stacking folders on her desk to keep busy.

"Did I say something wrong?" Aron glanced at her worriedly.

"No. Actually, I was thinking about Alice. I don't usually talk about someone outside my inner circle about personal situations in my life, Aron. But for some reason, I feel comfortable talking to you." Ruth relaxed and melted her back into her chair.

"That's good. That's what I was hoping to hear." He nodded. "Now tell me about Alice."

Ruth explained how finding out about Alice having cancer had thrown her for a loop, though she'd tried to prepare herself for the worst. She explained how devastated she felt when the doctor confirmed Alice's disease.

Aron told Ruth he could relate to her feelings, since he had felt the same way when he heard of his wife's demise.

Ruth went on to say how matters were complicated for her, when she found her former brother-in-law, Fred, at the hospital. She told Aron how she felt disappointed that Alice hadn't mentioned that she and Fred were dating.

Aron dipped his head at intervals. When Ruth finished talking, he asked, "Are you upset because Alice didn't tell you about her relationship? Or are you having a problem with her dating your ex-husband's brother?"

"I think a little bit of both," Ruth confessed. "Fred is the last person in the world that I would expect Alice to see socially. They have very little in common, and Fred is a womanizer," she spat out. "I don't want Alice to be hurt, and I don't see Fred being the type of person to be there for her during her illness, and I mean a major illness. It takes a special person to take care and be there for someone with cancer. The Fred I know was too self-centered to be concerned about another person's feelings, much less their health."

"Did you consider the possibility that maybe he's changed?" Aron interjected. "If you know Alice as well as you say you do, then I don't see her putting herself in a situation that would hurt her. Opposites have been known to attract."

"I've told myself that same thing since I left the hospital. You're right. Alice wouldn't deliberately put herself in harm's way. Maybe I'm holding on to the past, and that's something I never want to do."

"Then maybe you should talk to her before you jump to any conclusions," Aron suggested gently.

"I know that you're right, and the reason Alice probably hasn't confided in me is because she knows I wouldn't approve, at least not of the guy Fred was in the past."

"I suggest you reserve judgment. How is your relationship with Fred?"

"We talk every now and then. We talked more today at the hospital than we had in a long time. I think he always knew I harbored resentment against him for my husband's—I mean, ex-husband's—behavior for many years." Ruth had a faraway look on her face, and then she looked down at her desk, feeling embarrassed. She looked up at Aron. He dipped his head encouragingly, and she continued speaking. "Fred is my ex-husband's older brother and his hero. If Fred said something, then it was the gospel truth to Daniel." She licked her dry lips. "Daniel always liked to brag about how Fred taught him everything he knew regarding women. I think something went awry when it came to me."

Aron leaned across Ruth's desk and handed her a tissue. He could sense from her luminous eyes that she was having a moment. "I'm sure whatever your brother-in-law taught your ex happened when they were young bucks. Your husband had plenty of time to get it right. He didn't, and he lost. Believe me, his loss will be a better man's gain."

Ruth wiped her eyes. "I know what you're saying is right. I just need time for it to soak into my brain. When Daniel and I split, I didn't think I'd ever function again. In fact, I took to my bed for a couple of weeks, until my dad came to rescue me. He told me to do what was best for me regarding my marriage. Whereas, my mother wanted me to preserve my marriage by any means necessary, and that included putting up with a cheating spouse."

"That had to be a difficult time for you," Aron murmured. "But you got through it, and you'll be wiser the next time you decide to entrust your heart to a man. We all make mistakes in our youth, and hope to God that we learn from them and don't repeat them as we become older."

"I'd better be careful," Ruth joked. "You're sounding more like a minister than I do."

"That's because I've traveled on this highway of life, and learned my life lessons," Aron volleyed back. "Most of them, I learned the hard way, but I'd like to feel I'm a better person at this stage of my life."

Ruth's telephone rang. She looked at it. "I'd better get this," she told Aron. She picked up the phone and greeted the caller. She listened for a few minutes, and then put the call on hold. She looked across her desk at Aron. "I really need to take this call." She and Aron stood up. "Thank you for spending time with me this afternoon, and for helping resolve the mishap in the basement. I'll see you on Friday," she said.

"How about we go to lunch after my workday on Friday and we discuss the position in more detail?" Aron asked boldly. He could see the indecision on her face.

"Okay," Ruth answered, exhaling. "I'll see you Friday at noon."

"Thank you, Ruth. I think you'll enjoy yourself. I'll see myself out. I hope things go well with you and Alice. Listen to her, and I'll bet things have changed with Fred."

"I will." Ruth nodded. "Now I've got to take this call."

Aron walked to the door. He stopped when he got to the entrance, and then he turned and waved to Ruth.

She raised a trembling hand in return. She was still overcome with emotion, and she was surprised that she had opened up so candidly to Aron about her feelings. Then she sat back on her chair and pressed the button on the phone to resume her call. "Sister Lucas, how may I help you?" she asked.

After Ruth finished the call, she turned her chair toward the window and stared out of it. Her mind processed her conversation with Aron. He appeared to be articulate and caring. Then her mind wandered to Daniel. The two men, Aron and her ex-husband, were different as day and night. She longed to call Alice and get her friend's opinion about Aron's lunch invitation.

The telephone rang again. "Hello, this is Reverend Wilcox. How might I help you?"

"Hi, Momma. Are you busy?" Sarah asked her mother as she peered out of the kitchen, hoping one of her half brothers wouldn't come to her with yet another complaint.

"Never too busy for you, dear. How are you feeling this morning?" Ruth replied.

"I'm good. Well, a little tired." Sarah's shoulders slumped like they were weighed down. "I've been at Dad's house since yesterday, tending to his rug rats, and Damon is a handful. I swear that boy has had me running like crazy all morning."

"What's wrong? Is he sick or something?" Ruth asked solicitously.

"I heard him crying in the middle of the night. When I went to see what was wrong, he said he didn't feel good. So he stayed home with Dad and me today. I'm trying to be sympathetic about Lenora leaving, but his behavior makes it difficult sometimes. When they're all home, as they are now, they can be even harder to handle. I'm waiting for the next crisis"—Sarah looked down at her watch—"any minute."

"Just hang in there. I'm sure you'll be just fine." Ruth tried to soothe her daughter's frazzled nerves. "Didn't the boys have a nanny? What happened to her?"

"Daddy had to let her go. I don't know what they were paying her for. The boys, with the exception of Darnell, are out of control. Apparently, Lenora didn't believe in discipline, and Daddy is totally useless. I almost hate volunteering to stay with him this week," Sarah whined. She sat in the kitchen, folding clothes that she had washed and dried.

"Doesn't your father help?" Ruth couldn't stop herself from asking.

"Not much," Sarah responded grumpily. "The boys run rings around him."

"Try to be patient," Ruth advised. "Their mother has left, and I'm sure the boys are just acting out."

"I guess," Sarah said dubiously. "How was the rest of your day?"

Ruth explained about the catastrophe at church, and how Aron Reynolds came to her rescue.

"Hmm, that's Monet's father. She told me he's been looking for work," Sarah said as she folded a red-and-blue striped shirt.

"Yes, he is. So he's going to work at the church on a trial/volunteer basis as the janitor, since James is leaving at the end of the month," Ruth replied smoothly. She wasn't quite ready to share with her daughter all the details of her conversation with Aron.

"I'm glad he was able to lend a hand. I called Queen this morning, but she didn't answer the phone. I called the nursing staff on her floor, and they said she was doing okay. She told them she just didn't feel like talking to anyone."

"That sounds like my mother." Ruth sighed. "I'll try to swing by there tomorrow."

"I know you have a lot going on with the finance meeting coming up. I need a break from here. So I think tomorrow, after the boys go to school, I'll go visit Queen."

"That's a great idea. How are Maggie, Josh, and Brian doing?" Ruth opened a folder that June had set on her desk. She quickly scanned it.

"They're all fine. I called them this morning. Brian had things under control." Sarah yawned.

"I'm glad to hear that. Thank God your children are older and self-sufficient. That makes Brian's job easier."

"That's the truth," Sarah agreed.

She had finished folding the clothes and had separated them into piles of what she perceived belonged to each of her young half brothers. She hoped her father knew which clothes belonged to what boy, but she didn't hold out much hope.

"How did Aunt Alice's appointment go?" Sarah finally asked.

"Not good," Ruth replied guardedly. "You know Alice; she's putting on a brave face."

"I know Jesus will work it out, and that His grace and mercy will fall on Aunt Alice, and she will be all right. I'm surprised you aren't home with her, instead of at church." Sarah frowned.

"Amen to all of the above. The Lord has my sister in His hands. Actually, Alice had a male friend accompany her to the hospital."

"You're kidding!" Sarah exclaimed. "Was it anyone that we know? Was it a deacon from the church?"

"Not quite," Ruth announced drily. "It was your uncle Fred."

"Uncle Fred?" Sarah shrieked. Her eyes widened. "You've got to be kidding. How long has that been going on?"

"Your guess is as good as mine," Ruth said matter-of-factly. "This is the first I've heard of the two of them seeing each other. I'm sure Alice will fill in the blanks when I see her later. Fred took her home."

"I can't picture Aunt Alice and Uncle Fred dating. Their personalities are different as night and day. I remember some of their heated discussions when I was a kid." Sarah shook her head wonderingly.

"Stranger things have happened," Ruth said, thinking about Aron. She heard a long thud and then a yowl of pain in the background.

"Momma, I've got to go. Shoot, I wish Daddy would get involved with his sons. I'll call you back because I want the 411 on Aunt Alice and Uncle Fred," Sarah said.

"Bye, Sarah, I'll talk to you later."

Ruth closed the folder and laid it on the side of her desk. Then she pulled the folder labeled *Monthly Finance/Expenses* and set the thick folder in front of her. She dragged her reading glasses from the top of her head and placed them on her face. She sighed, opened the folder, and began skimming through invoices, hoping the church's expenses hadn't risen higher than the previous month.

Ruth's hope was short-lived. Not only was the heating bill higher, but there was a red notice included with the invoice, stating the bill was overdue. The letter further stated that if payment wasn't received in five days, the heat would be shut off.

Ruth rubbed her forehead and plowed on through the notes June had left her before leaving work.

Chapter Ten

Sarah ran into the kitchen to find Damon, with the twins in tow, standing beside the kitchen table. David stared at his twin, horrified, as Darnell ran his hands over his wet face. Damon stared at his brother and the floor as if hypnotized. Sarah had been busy all day picking up behind the boys and chastising them in the next breath, and she was at the breaking point. Sarah had forgotten to put the glass pitcher of orange juice into the refrigerator after lunch. The orange liquid was spreading on the floor, mixed with shards of glass.

She looked at Damon and asked him, trying to keep her voice even, "What happened here?"

"I didn't mean to. It was an accident." Damon shrugged his shoulders and answered his half sister, with an angelic expression on his face. His appearance was remarkably like his mother's. His hair was a golden sandy brown, like Lenora's, and he had her catlike eyes.

"Well, how did juice get on your brother?" Sarah narrowed her eyes, and placed her hands on her hips.

"Well, I was trying to pour me some juice. Darnell got in the way, and it kinda spilled on him," Damon explained innocently. His thin, restless body leaned against the kitchen table.

Sarah pointed to the door. "Damon, go to your room and wait there until I come and get you." She walked to Darnell and took him by the hand. "You come to the bathroom with me, so I can clean you up."

"Why I gotta go to my room?" Damon asked argu-mentatively. "It was only an accident."

Sarah glared at him. "Because I said so. Now go to your room, like I told you to." She dropped Darnell's hand and folded her arms across her chest.

David watched the exchange and strolled over to his twin and took his hand. Damon poked out his lips and stalked out of the room.

"I hate you!" Damon yelled vehemently over his shoulder as he stomped up the stairs to his room.

"That's too bad," she said to his retreating back as she and the twins walked to the bathroom. *Daddy, why can't you control your house, and most of all these boys?* Sarah thought as she walked Darnell into the bathroom. The upper part of his body, including his hair, was drenched in juice. His body quivered, and tears spilled down his cheeks.

Sarah put down the top to the toilet seat. She placed a towel on the seat, lifted the sticky boy in her arms, and carefully placed him on the seat.

After she bathed him, Sarah vowed to have a long talk with her father about the boys' behavior, and his seeming lack of interest in his sons. She surmised that if Daniel wasn't careful, his son would turn out like Le-nora's brothers, who'd spent more time locked up than on the outside.

Sarah was very disturbed by Damon's behavior. Af-ter spending a couple of days at Daniel's house, she was also aware of the control the older boy exerted over his younger siblings. For her father's sake, she truly hoped that Damon wasn't a young thug in the making. She thought if her father thought he couldn't cope with the boys now, what would he do later when they grew up? Sarah prayed she could get through to Daniel.

By the time Sarah had finished bathing Darnell, lecturing Damon, preparing and giving the boys their dinner, she felt exhausted. Later that evening, after the boys retired for the night, Sarah went to Damon's room to check on him after she had checked on the twins. Damon had fallen asleep. As she stood at the bedroom door, she thought how much he looked like his mother. She walked to the bed, bent over, and placed Damon's sneakers in the corner of his room. Then she pulled the comforter over his waist and walked downstairs.

She walked into the living room and found her father sitting in his favorite burgundy leather recliner. Sarah fumed as she watched his head loll against the back of the chair. A sliver of drool snaked down his cheek.

Sarah sat on the sofa and meditated on the untidy mess that seemed to have consumed her father's life. The Daniel of old was a snazzy dresser. Since she'd been staying with her father over the past days, he seemed to wear the same clothes over and over. He had on a pair of dark denim jeans, which looked as if they hadn't been washed in months. He wore a dingy white-collared T-shirt under a long-sleeved cotton pullover. Sarah shook her head.

She exhaled, and then said, "Daddy."

Daniel didn't respond. His breathing made a whistling sound.

Sarah called him again; and when Daniel didn't respond, she stood up, walked over to the chair, and poked her father's arm.

"Huh?" Daniel sat upright. "Oh, it's you." His eyes dimmed. He was hoping Lenora had returned home, to rescue him from the chaos his life had become.

"Daddy, didn't you hear the boys making a mess in the kitchen earlier?" Sarah walked back to the matching burgundy couch, adjacent to the chair, and sat down. She reached over and turned on an ornate Tiffany lamp. "It's much too dark in here," she said.

"Naw, I didn't hear them. What have they done now?" Daniel asked in a bored tone of voice. His eyes darted around, landing outside the window.

Sarah debated talking to her father about the state of the household, and finally decided to forge ahead, thinking there's no time like the present.

"I'm sorry I didn't visit you more, Daddy," she murmured in a conciliatory tone of voice. "It was just hard for me to see you living happily with a woman other than Momma."

Daniel made a snorting noise. "I don't know if this house has been happy for a while. I missed you, Princess, and Nay, DJ, and the grandchildren—all of you. It seems like life with Lenora was better when we were on the down low."

She kept a stoic expression on her face, to encourage her father to open up to her.

"That's too bad," she remarked casually. "But, Daddy, you know that life changes, it never stays the same, and you can't feel sorry for yourself. You have to move on, and deal with the issues at hand. I'm sorry about you and Lenora. I know you're hurt by her leaving, but the boys need to be your first priority. You need to comfort and work with them before they get out of control, especially Damon." Sarah's nose crinkled. "Sometimes they act like children who haven't ever been disciplined, and I find that hard to believe, because I know you didn't think twice about spanking the three of us when we were children. What happened?" She leaned forward on her seat.

Daniel shrugged his shoulders helplessly. "I guess Noree was a new-school mom. She didn't believe in hitting the children." His eyes dropped to his lap, and then he looked back at Sarah. He held out his hand. "She thought time-outs were more effective. But she didn't stick to her guns, and the boys ran over her like syrup on waffles," he replied, embarrassed.

Sarah snickered at her father's description of Lenora's antics with the boys. Then Daniel joined her. The two shared a hearty laugh. Sarah reached up and swiped a tear from the corner of her eye.

"I think today is the first day I've laughed or smiled in a long time," Daniel admitted gravely.

"There will be more smiles in the future, Daddy. You just need to get it together. Damon is a handful, and I think he needs a man's touch. I know firsthand raising boys can be tough. Though Joshua was nothing like the imps running around here." Sarah shook her head in disbelief.

"I know," Daniel said. "By Damon being our oldest child, Noree and her family spoiled him rotten. I tried to stop her from letting him have his way so much, but she wasn't having it," he remarked as he ran his hand over his spiky gray hair.

"Well, that explains why he acts the way he does. Still, you've got to do something before his actions spiral out of control." Sarah felt saddened that her father, whom she'd looked up to most of her life, had been reduced to sitting in the living room, allowing life to pass him by. "What are you going to do in the long run if Lenora doesn't come back?" She didn't miss the look of consternation that filled her father's face.

"I don't know. I haven't thought that far ahead," Daniel admitted.

"Daddy, you need to think about it. You and the boys can't remain in this unsettled state. It's not healthy," Sarah said. She folded her hands together and put them in her lap.

"I hear you, Princess, but what can I do? My health isn't great, and sometimes the boys are too much for me. Maybe I should let them stay with Felicia. I know she'll take good care of them."

"Daddy, do you hear yourself?" Sarah asked him, clearly appalled. "Why would you give up your sons? You're not incapacitated, merely older. I can't believe what I'm hearing." Her head swung from side to side in disbelief.

"I know it doesn't sound good, but it's the truth. I'm trying to do what's best for the boys. Perhaps they need the firmer hand of younger parents," Daniel said dejectedly. His body slumped, and he dropped his head and rubbed his eyes.

"I think that's a lousy idea," Sarah responded resolutely. "What those boys need most of all is a parent, and they need love. Don't tell me you forgot how to do that?" She couldn't keep a note of rancor from dripping from her voice.

Daniel flinched from the anger that emanated from his daughter. "Maybe I have forgotten. All I know is that I'm so tired," he muttered, his voice dropping despairingly.

"Daddy, we all get tired. I get tired myself a lot of times." Sarah waved her hand dismissively. "But children don't ask to be born. You and Lenora made them, and you both can't desert them. This is the time for you to step up." She glanced down at the thin gold watch on her wrist. "Looks like it's time for your medicine," she said.

Daniel nodded. "Why don't you get it for me." He held his hand out for his heart medication, with a hangdog look on his face.

Sarah wanted to say, *"No, you need the exercise, get it yourself!"* She opened her mouth and closed it.

Instead, she strode into the lilac-colored bathroom, off the kitchen, and removed a vial of pills from the medicine chest. Then she took a paper cup from the dispenser on the wall and filled it with water. She returned to the living room and handed Daniel the pills and water.

He swallowed the pills and took a few sips of water. When he was done with that, Daniel balled up the cup and laid it on the TV tray next to his chair, while Sarah returned to the couch and sat down.

"You know I wouldn't admit this to anyone except for you," Daniel remarked, looking at Sarah.

"What would that be?" Sarah asked her father quizzically.

"I made a big mistake when I married Lenora. I always felt in the back of my mind that her picking me was too good to be true." Daniel looked back out the window, refusing to meet his daughter's eyes.

Stunned by her father's confession, Sarah's mouth gaped open. All she could manage to say at first was "Wow." Then she composed herself. "Oh, Daddy, that's too bad. I wish you had thought about that before you tore our family apart," she lamented.

"There are so many things I wish I had done differently. I remember talking to my doctor before I married Noree. He said something to the effect about 'there's no fool like an old fool.' I know what he meant. I get it now. Many a night I pondered his words, especially when I lay up in the hospital, not sure if I was going to live or die. But you know what kept me going?"

Sarah shook her head, and continued listening to her father. She had a feeling that he needed to verbalize his thoughts and to get some things off his chest.

"I don't know if your mother told you this or not." Daniel cracked his knuckles. "When I was in the hospital, wondering if I was going to live or die, Ruth came to check on me a few times. She always encouraged me to do what the doctors told me to do so I would get better. She would tell me how it wasn't time for me to go yet, that I still had some things I needed to do."

"I didn't know that," Sarah admitted. "Momma never said a word. But I'm not surprised, that's Momma. She always puts other people's feelings before her own."

"I know I had a good thing and I blew it. I may never get a chance to tell her that," Daniel said in a strangled voice, with a haunted expression on his face.

"No one knows the future but the Lord, Daddy. So you never know what might happen." Sarah wondered if through all the madness her father was experiencing, if her parents might find their way back to each other. Her face gave no hint of what she was feeling. "What you need to concentrate on is what you're going to do with the boys."

Daniel nodded his head. "As I said, I really feel like I should sign them over to Felicia and her husband. Their children are better behaved than my rascals. I'm not a young man anymore, so perhaps that would be best for them."

Both Daniel and Sarah looked toward the entrance of the room as Damon came running into the room. He looked almost deranged with fury.

He ran to his father and began beating him in the chest with his small fists. "I don't want to stay with Aunt Fee!" he yelled. "I want my mommy! Why did you make my mommy leave? I hate you!"

Daniel was aghast at his son's behavior. He mumbled encouraging words to his son, which fell on deaf ears. "Come on now, Damon, that's no way to act." He tried to grab Damon and hold him in his arms, but he was squirming and wouldn't be still.

Sarah looked on helplessly. Her first inclination was to help her father. Then she dismissed that idea. Too many people had been helping Daniel his entire life, starting with her uncle Fred, and then her mother. Sarah thought it was time for her father to step up to the plate and handle his own business.

Damon hit at Daniel. Daniel deflected the blows and grabbed Damon's wrists and held them in his hands. The little boy ranted about how he hated his father. He screamed for his mother at the top of his lungs, until the fight had left his little body. Daniel let go of Damon's wrists, and the boy collapsed on the floor at his father's feet, with his head dangling between his legs. His shoulders shook as tremors racked his small body.

Pick him up and hold him in your arms, Sarah silently implored her father, but to no avail. Her body was tense as she sat on the edge of the sofa. Her hand clutched the edge of the sofa, like she was holding the side of a life raft.

Daniel clumsily patted his son's head and, with tear-stained eyes, looked to Sarah for help. She stood and walked over to her half brother and pulled his trembling, inert body from the floor. She shot a look of revulsion at her father as she took Damon by the hand and led him to the couch.

Damon's face was a picture of abject misery. His matted hair framed his reddened face, and tears continued to dribble from his eyes. He hiccupped and ran his hand across his dripping nose.

Sarah took him in her arms and murmured softly, "It's going to be okay, Damon. I know it doesn't seem like it now, but I promise you that everything is going to work out."

"No, it's not," Damon protested, shaking his head. "My mommy is gone, and me and my brothers are alone. And Pops don't like or want us." He looked at Daniel accusingly, and then he began wailing again.

Daniel felt as if an arrow had pierced his heart, and his hand flew to his chest as tears streamed from his eyes.

"You are not alone," Sarah corrected Damon. "You have your daddy, and he does care for you. He's just been sick. You have me and my family, your grandmother, grandfather, and aunts and uncles. I promise you that we're going to take care of you and your brothers."

Damon pressed his body against Sarah's and began sobbing again. By that time, the twins had awakened from the clamor. The little boys stood in the doorway and stared at their family. Daniel's head was buried in his hands, while their older brother sobbed as Sarah patted his back. The twins' eyes were wide circles as they walked tentatively into the living room. Their eyes traveled to their father, and then to Sarah and their big brother.

David walked over to Damon and Sarah. He stood in front of his brother and patted Damon's arm. "Don't cry, brubber," he crooned over and over with a lisp, and tears trickling down his face.

Darnell walked over to his father and poked Daniel in the shoulder. "Daddy, don't cry," he begged Daniel in a timid voice. Daniel groaned and then scooped Darnell into his lap. He cradled his son tightly to his chest, like he never wanted him to go.

Lord, stop by here, Sarah prayed silently, closing her eyes. *My family is in need of your healing touch. My daddy is a good man at heart. He just doesn't know how to express his feelings sometimes. Father, stay with these children as they transcend into what may be a new way of life. We don't understand why things happen in life the way they do sometimes, and we just have to trust in your grace and receive your mercy. Lord, I beseech you in the name of the Father, help and heal my family today.*

With that prayer, Sarah released the Wilcoxes' burdens over to God. She couldn't help but wonder what was to become of her father's family. The boys were motherless, and her father seemed to be stuck in an indecisive mode. Sarah knew with God all things were possible, and that He would deliver them from this seemingly hopeless dilemma.

She also wished she could consult with Ruth, to make sure she was doing the right thing. She hoped that she hadn't spoken too harshly to her father, and that she had given the boys a small measure of comfort.

Momma, what are you doing right now? I need you, Sarah thought. Her cell phone rang from the kitchen. Laying Damon on the sofa, and telling him that she would be back, Sarah rose and went to the kitchen to answer her cell phone. She glanced at the caller ID and saw Naomi's number on it. She clicked on the telephone and said, "Hello?"

"Hi, Sarah, what's going on? Is this a bad time? Can you talk?" Naomi asked.

"Well, your timing isn't great. There's a crisis brewing here at Daddy's house. But I can talk for a few minutes," Sarah said.

"Okay, should I call you back later? I have something I want to talk to you about," Naomi announced breathlessly.

"Why don't you ever ask how Daddy and the boys are doing?" Sarah asked pointedly. She peeked into the living room, and everyone was the same as she'd left them.

Naomi sucked her teeth loudly and rolled her eyes. "How are Daddy and the boys?" she asked.

"Not too good. I think it just really has set in for the boys that Lenora is gone, that she may not come back, and they are struggling."

"That's too bad," Naomi replied with a false tone of voice. Truth be told, she could care less. Daniel had brought everything that had happened to his second family upon himself.

"Nay, these kids didn't ask to be brought into the world. And life as they know it has ended, so try to have some sympathy for them," Sarah chastised Naomi.

"You're right," Naomi sighed, tugging on her other earlobe. "They didn't ask to come here. I imagine this has to be a tough time for them. Still, you would think Daddy and Lenora would be more responsible. She has some nerve running out on Daddy, and then leaving her children behind. What kind of mother does that?"

"Apparently, one interested in her own self-gratification. Legally, the boys are Daddy's too, so Lenora didn't break any laws," Sarah added.

"But she's their mother. How could she just abandon them? . . ." Naomi's voice trailed off. "I didn't mean anything toward you by my comment," she said, apologizing. "Your situation and Lenora's are different."

"No harm taken." Sarah tried to reply imperturbably, though a sliver of guilt rang in her voice.

She reflected on the intricate scheme she'd concocted over twenty-five years ago, and she still prayed for forgiveness daily.

Sarah was actually Naomi's biological mother, but to the world the two were sisters. Sarah had become pregnant as a young teenager, at the age of fifteen. She became a mother for the first time at sixteen years old. In reality, she had been impregnated by her now-husband, Brian. Too scared to face the music, and being the granddaughter of a prominent Chicago minister, Sarah followed Queen's urging and led the family to believe she was sexually assaulted. Sarah was whisked away to stay with a relative, and Ruth and Daniel adopted the baby.

After the truth of Naomi's parentage was divulged, Ruth was fearful of Sarah stepping up and taking on the role of Naomi's mother. Sarah privately yearned for a maternal relationship with her sister/daughter, and was relieved just to be a part of Naomi's life, even if their relationship had to be one of siblings. Since Sarah's secret was exposed, the family wasn't sure how to deal with Naomi. So they kept her at arm's length, like she did with most of them.

"So, do you still plan on coming home this weekend?" Sarah asked Naomi, holding her breath, then exhaling loudly. "I know that Daddy would be thrilled to see you, and Queen also, not to mention Momma."

"I am coming home, but I'll be there next weekend instead of this one," Naomi murmured. "That's the reason I called you. I wanted to know what you'd think about me bringing a friend home with me. I wanted your opinion before I talk to Momma."

"Is it a male friend?" Sarah asked nosily.

"Uh, y-yes," Naomi stuttered.

"That's great," Sarah said, her voice overflowed with enthusiasm. "I don't think you've ever brought anyone home with you in all the years you've been away. You must admit, Nay, you've been away from Chicago a long time."

"That's true. I like the warmer weather and small-town feel of Edwardsville, so it has become home. I have to admit, I would like to see Queen. Momma hasn't said so, but I get the feeling her health is deteriorating."

"It is. Speaking of health issues, did Momma tell you about Aunt Alice?"

"No." Naomi felt her stomach drop to her feet. "What about Aunt Alice? Is something wrong with her?"

"She found a lump in her breast a few weeks ago and had a mammogram done. The radiologist saw something he didn't like on the film, so Aunt Alice had another mammogram with the same results. She went back to the hospital today, her doctor ordered a biopsy. The lab analyzed the tissue sample while she was at the hospital. Momma went with her, and the doctor confirmed she does indeed have breast cancer." Sarah felt miserable; Alice was like a second mother to her and her siblings.

"Oh, my God," Naomi moaned as her body sank against the back of the chair she was sitting in. If she had been standing, her legs would have given out. "Momma told me she was going to the doctor with Aunt Alice, but she never said there was anything seriously wrong with Aunt Alice."

"In Momma's defense, she probably didn't want to worry anyone until she knew something definite. And knowing Aunt Alice, she probably didn't give Momma any details until the last minute."

"You're probably right. So it's more imperative than ever that I come home as soon as possible. Why is there always so much drama in our lives? Lenora has left Daddy, Queen is drifting heavily into senility, and now Aunt Alice has cancer. This is too much," Naomi lamented.

"Well, I'm glad you're coming home soon. I can't wait to see you. I love you, Nay," Sarah said caringly.

"I love you too. Sarah, I'll call Momma tonight and tell her I'm bringing a guest home. Tell Daddy I said hello, and I'll see you next weekend," Naomi said.

The two women hung up the phone and Sarah returned to the living room. She was shocked to see that her father had moved from his permanent residential chair. He was now sitting on the couch, talking to the boys, who were huddled on both sides of him.

Sarah smiled with satisfaction and tiptoed back into the kitchen. She sat at the kitchen table and bowed her head in silent prayer. *Gracious Father, thank you for helping Daddy to see the light. Continue to give him strength and guidance. In Jesus' name, I pray.*

After praying, she was so overjoyed, she had an overwhelming urge to talk to her children, to see how they had been faring without her presence for the past few days. She picked up her cell phone and called home. Brian informed her that he was holding down the fort, and he advised her to relax.

She could hardly wait to talk to Ruth and tell her of the initial changes at Daniel's house, and how she hoped her father was coming out of his funk.

Tears sprang to Sarah's eyes as she thought about how God was good, and how He supplied her every need.

Later after everyone retired to bed, Sarah's thoughts wandered to Naomi, her oldest child whom she didn't claim publicly. How she wished that she could. She had to keep her emotions in check, especially when she was around her other children. Every year, the deception became harder for Sarah to perpetrate.

A part of Sarah wanted to reach out and try to establish a mother-daughter relationship with Naomi. But she couldn't, because there was one person stopping her—her own mother, Ruth. She knew Ruth had invested too much love, energy, and time to relinquish the maternal bond with Naomi willingly. Still, those facts didn't stop Sarah from wishing the true nature of Naomi's parentage could be revealed. Sarah sighed. She picked up her cell phone from the nightstand and called Brian again. She had an urge to hear his voice, tell him that she loved him, and say good night. After her conversation with her husband had ended, Sarah settled into the bed. Her thoughts shifted to her children. She wondered how Maggie and Josh would react to learning Naomi was their sister.

Chapter Eleven

When Ruth arrived home late Wednesday evening, worry lines navigated a path across her forehead as she turned off the engine of her car. She walked hurriedly toward the apartment building as rain sprinkled the air. She noted Fred's car parked down the street. Ruth's day hadn't improved as it progressed; instead, it had become more grueling. June had left work early for an appointment, and the telephone had rung nonstop. June had warned Ruth to set the telephone system to voice mail, but Ruth hadn't heeded her advice.

She had received many calls from parishioners, worried about the state of the church's finances and their solutions. An elderly member had passed, and Ruth consoled the family and promised to visit them later that evening. Tonight there was a prayer meeting at the church, and Ruth had breathed a sigh of relief when Reverend Bowden suggested he preside over the service in her place. She had made a mental note to delegate that task to him until the church budget was passed. Ruth needed to dedicate as much time as possible to work on the finances.

Much to Ruth's dismay, she hadn't been able to make as much headway working on the church budget as she would have liked. When she had finally put down her pencil, she felt disheartened. It seemed no matter how many times she added or subtracted the numbers, they still came back with the same disheartening results. The church faced a massive shortfall in offerings due to the dismal economy. She was also dismayed to learn that many of the utility bills for the church had not been paid. The church's emergency fund was nearly depleted after Ruth paid those tardy bills. She would need a miracle to pay the utilities for the upcoming month.

After removing the mail from her mailbox, Ruth walked up a few stairs to her apartment. Usually when Ruth arrived home, Alice's door was open, and pleasing aromas would be wafting through the stairwell. Ruth would stop at Alice's apartment so they could discuss the ups and downs of the day. But that evening, Alice's door was closed. Ruth felt sad, and tears gathered in her eyes as she fumbled to unlock her door.

The tenants who occupied the apartments on the second and third floors didn't usually arrive home until late in the evening. One of the tenants who lived on the third floor planned to move by the end of the following month, so Ruth planned to ask for Sarah's help in finding a new tenant to rent the apartment.

Ruth put her umbrella in the oak rack near the matching coatrack. Then she placed her tote bag on the floor, and her alligator purse atop the cherrywood console table in the foyer. After she removed her jacket and hung it in the closet, she took the mail and set it next to her on the navy-blue-and-white striped sofa. She kicked off her shoes. Her head lolled along the back of the sofa, and she closed her eyes.

Heavenly Father, thank you for delivering me home safely one more day. Tomorrow is never promised, so I give thanks to you for allowing me to see another day to give you the praises and glory, she prayed silently.

Lord, I ask that you look favorably upon the members of The Temple. Keep them safe and sound as they

*make their way home from work. Lord, please take
care of my family; keep them in your watchful eye.
Lord, please heal Alice. She has a tough road ahead,
and nothing but your grace and mercy can help her.
Lord, thank you for sending Aron to The Temple today to help out. Thank you for putting a desire to fill
the maintenance position in Aron's heart. He was a
blessing for me and for the church today. Thank you,
Father.*

Ruth thought about Alice, and she brushed a tear
away from her cheek. "Let it go," she reprimanded herself aloud and stretched her arms upright. "Turn it over
to the Master," she told herself.

She opened her eyes and rose from the sofa. She then
walked into the kitchen and put on a kettle to brew
some tea. Her stomach growled, hungry from the salad
she'd had for lunch many hours ago. After she turned
the flame to low under the kettle, Ruth went back to the
living room. She sat on the sofa and sorted the mail.
The doorbell sounded, and she nearly leaped from the
sofa to the door. Her legs screamed to slow down. She
opened the door to find Alice standing on the other
side; there was a Mona Lisa smile upon her face.

"Well, come on in," Ruth said, pulling her friend's
arm and leading her inside the apartment. "Is Fred still
at your house? I saw his car when I came in," she whispered, as though Fred could hear through the walls.

"No," Alice replied, "he left thirty minutes ago. I tried
to wait for you to come home, but I dozed off. If you
haven't started dinner, I thought we'd send out for Chinese. What do you think about that, sister-girl?"

"I think that's a good idea. My stomach is yelling at
me to feed it." Ruth laughed. "Hold that thought, I'll be
right back. I need to turn off the teakettle."

"Good," Alice said, walking into the living room. "I already placed the order and the deliveryman should be here"—she paused and looked at her watch—"in half an hour." She sat down on a wingback chair, and Ruth made her way to the sofa. "So how was your day?"

"Not too bad. A pipe burst in the church and water spilled into the children's church. Luckily, I was able to get in touch with Aron Reynolds. He came to the church and replaced a washer in one of the pipes and cleaned up the mess."

"Ouch, that had to be ugly," Alice replied. She tugged on one of the twists in her hair. Her natural reddish hair was now completely gray, but the color was complementary to her face. A few more wrinkles had taken permanent occupancy on her still-plump face.

The women talked about the biopsy procedure until their meal was delivered. Ruth took the bags to the kitchen, while Alice paid the deliveryman.

When Alice walked into the kitchen, Ruth had set the table. Alice removed glasses from the cabinet. Finally the women sat down, and they bowed their heads and closed their eyes.

"Gracious Father, thank you for the food that has been prepared for the nourishment of our bodies. Through Christ, we pray. Amen," Alice recited.

The delectable aromas of garlic chicken for Ruth, and orange chicken for Alice, along with noodles, fried rice, and egg rolls, drifted through the air.

"Um, that smells good," Ruth observed as she ladled a generous portion of rice on her plate. The women dug into the food with gusto.

Several minutes later, they had finished eating and returned to the living room and sat on the sofa to converse.

Alice crossed her feet at the ankle and cleared her throat. "Ruth, I want to apologize for not telling you sooner about Fred. When we began having coffee together, I never imagined we would start dating and develop a relationship. I just couldn't find the words to tell you that I was dating your former brother-in-law." Alice looked down, clearly abashed. Then she looked back up at Ruth.

Ruth couldn't help but notice the glow in her friend's eyes. "I accept your apology. I just can't believe you two are in a relationship and didn't say a word about it to me, your best sister/friend in the world. Girl, we like this." She pointed her fingers at Alice's eyes, then at her own. Alice burst out laughing.

"I hear you," Alice chortled. "Fred told me over and over again that I should tell you. How could I tell you that I was beginning to have feelings for the man we had labeled 'the biggest womanizer in Chicago'?"

"I think we called him 'the biggest dog in the Midwest,'" Ruth quipped drily. "I can see why you would be hesitant. I guess you just didn't want to hear my mouth."

"That too. Truthfully, I wanted to give it time to see what would happen, and I didn't want to hear you say that you told me so, if things didn't work out between us," Alice declared.

"I can understand that," Ruth said. "Does he make you happy?" She searched Alice's face carefully, although she knew the answer; it was written all over her friend's face.

"Ruth, he makes me so very happy. Sometimes I can't believe it. Fred said seeing Daniel lying in the hospital after his heart attack was a wake-up call for him. He knew it was time to change his ways; and from what I can tell, he has."

"You know Queen and your mother used to tell us how a leopard never changes his spots, and you know how strongly we believed them."

Alice nodded, and a faraway look gleamed in her eyes. "They sure did, but what they failed to mention was that people can change if they truly want. It's because they really want to make a change in their lives for the better, and they find the strength to do just that."

"Let's hope that Fred's womanizing wasn't an addiction then," Ruth remarked. "We wouldn't want him to backslide." She leaned back on the couch and folded her arms across her chest.

"I don't think that he will. I can sense his sincerity when he talks about how he turned his life around. You know what he feels really bad about? It is how Daniel's life turned out. He knows that he played a big part in Daniel's behavior toward women."

"I know that's right." Ruth bobbed her head up and down. "All I used to hear from Daniel back in the day is what Fred said. Like Fred was the be-all and end-all expert in life."

"A lot of it was just a younger brother who hero-worshipped his older brother," Alice observed, nodding her head.

"That's true. And, girl, if he makes you happy, then who am I to interfere? I just hope your relationship with Fred won't come between our relationship." Ruth looked down at her lap, clearly troubled.

Alice reached over and grabbed Ruth's pinkie finger with her own. "Remember we made pinkie promises when we were little girls?" she asked. Ruth nodded. Alice continued to speak. "How nothing—especially a man—will ever come between the friendship, sisterhood, and love we share."

The women entwined their fingers together and pulled; then they hugged each other.

"It seems like you've been keeping more than your relationship with Fred away from me," Ruth stated firmly. "How could you not tell me about your illness earlier?"

"I wanted to talk to you so many times. But if I had to verbalize what I was going through, then I couldn't stay in denial. Denial was a good place to be, because I didn't have to deal with reality, illnesses, heartache, or pain."

"But, Allie, I could have helped you cope with what you were going through," Ruth objected. "That's what friends, especially best friends, are for. We help and encourage each other through the bumps and bruises of life."

"You are so right." Alice nodded. "I goofed." Her head dropped with shame.

"I'll let you slide this time," Ruth said. "But from here on out, I expect to be a part of your life, and be there for you through the good times and bad."

"You will." Alice held up her hand like she was a Girl Scout. "So how do you really feel about the possibility of Daniel becoming a free man?" Alice probed gently.

"I don't know what to think." Ruth looked away. She was never a good liar.

"This is your BFF you're talking to. I know you still have feelings for Daniel; so therefore, you must have had some reaction to the news. What are you thinking? You can tell me."

Ruth inhaled and then exhaled slowly. "You're right, you do know me. A part of me has never stopped loving Daniel, and I do believe wedding vows are forever or until a spouse passes. So the news excites me in a way. But on the other hand, I'm ashamed that I still have feelings for a man who couldn't be faithful to me."

"I understand what you mean, and I would never judge you. If it's meant to be, God will bring the two of you back together. So tell me about Aron Reynolds. I couldn't help but notice how your eyes lit up like candles when you spoke of him."

"I believe Mr. Reynolds was flirting with me. I mean, I know he was. He asked me out on a date," Ruth replied modestly, lowering her eyes.

"Get out of here." Alice's eyebrows rose. "What did you say?"

"I told him that I'd have lunch with him on Friday," Ruth announced.

"Wow. Good for you. It's about time someone got you out of that shell you've inhabited since your divorce." Alice's toothy grin beamed her approval.

"Are you forgetting that I'm the minister of a church, and that Aron Reynolds served a lengthy sentence in prison for murder?" Ruth shot back. Aron was convicted of felony first degree murder. He couldn't afford a criminal attorney and was at the mercy of a public defender. His case was complicated by his history of burglaries.

"And?" Alice lobbed back a challenge with her eyes.

"What do you mean by 'and'?" Ruth looked at Alice like she was talking to a child. "I'm a minister, and my members expect me to carry myself with a sense of decorum. I'm the head of the flock. I don't think the church board would approve of me dating a murderer. They might even try to vote me out of the church, or something."

"Well, bravo." Alice clapped her hands together. "Have you been practicing the speech you're going to present to Aron Reynolds when you tell him that you can't see him anymore? Just like you did with the other men you've dated, who just didn't measure up to Daniel."

"That was hitting a little below the belt, don't you think?" With a pained expression on her face, Ruth looked at Alice.

"I think you like the man, but you're too afraid to admit it, or to let yourself become involved with a man, because Daniel hurt you too badly."

"Allie, he murdered someone. There's a good possibility that someone in my congregation won't approve of me dating him. Still, I admit I felt an attraction to him, and that's why I accepted his lunch invitation."

"I'm sure your congregation has studied the Bible, and has listened to you and Bishop preach over the years about how Christians aren't perfect. Wasn't King David a murderer? Didn't the apostle Paul spend time in prison? Didn't God have good things in store for those men? The key is asking for forgiveness for our sins, and owning up to our faults and trying to do better."

"I know you're not trying to debate theology with me?" Ruth's eyebrows rose in disbelief.

"Well, you know I'm not lying. Most of the people you read about in the Bible were flawed. But through faith, repentance, and much prayer, they were able to fulfill the destiny that God had in store for them. Even Cain, after murdering his brother, was forgiven by God. I don't know Aron personally. I've seen him around church, and he seems to have taken responsibility for his shortcomings, and made the most of life. He's cute for an older guy," Alice said innocently.

"I'm attracted to him, and that scares me. I've only been that attracted to one other man in my life, and where did it get me? I'll tell you—divorced by the time I hit my fifties, discarded like an old mare, and abandoned for a younger woman." Ruth shrugged her shoulders helplessly.

"You've got to let those feelings go and live your life, girl. We both know you're a good person. Just breathe, and then you'll be okay." Alice waved her hand in the air and exhaled loudly. "Who would have thought that in our sixties, we'd be talking like this about men, like we did as preteens?" She giggled, picking up her can of 7UP, and then sipped.

"You got that right," Ruth agreed. There was a moment of comfortable silence between the two friends. "I'm really struggling with the church budget," Ruth confessed. "We truly need more money to keep some of the ministries afloat."

"I'm sorry to hear that," Alice remarked. "What do you plan to do?"

"I'm not sure. My mind tells me that I'm going to have to shut down a few of the outreach programs until the economy picks up. And only God knows when that's going to be. I have been praying and fasting over the matter."

"You know it's all going to work out in the long run, don't you? There have always been times when the economy has slowed down, and despite that, the world continues to function."

"I know in my heart that the high unemployment rate in Chicago, has contributed to offerings being down. Chicago TransitAuthority has raised bus fares. People are having a hard time just trying to survive," Ruth responded.

"You're right. But God takes care of His own, and you and Bishop have done so many good things for The Temple. I don't think God will let you down now."

"I thought about asking the members to increase their offerings and tithes, but it doesn't sit well with me in this tough economic time. For the first time in many years, our food pantry is running low on supplies. I've been supplementing the food from my own pocket."

"What has the finance committee suggested?" Alice asked.

"That we cut some programs and maybe combine services to save on utilities. The Temple is old, and the upkeep can be costly at times. I'm torn about what to do," Ruth admitted.

"Stay prayerful and listen to God's direction. He will never steer you wrong." Alice yawned. "I'm a little tired, so why don't we do scripture and pray now? I have a student I'm going to tutor at Fort Dearborn School tomorrow, so I'd like to get some rest." She leaned her back against her seat.

"Are you sure you're up for tutoring? Maybe you should rest tomorrow," Ruth suggested, a concerned tone in her voice.

"That's why I'm going to bed early. If I'm not up to it in the morning, then I'll cancel. Right now, I plan to go."

"Okay." Ruth hopped up from the sofa, went to the dining room, and removed the Bible from the buffet. She thumbed through the pages of the Bible. "I'm going to read from Deuteronomy 31:8. 'And the Lord, he is it that doth go before thee; he will be with thee, he will not fail thee, neither forsake thee: fear not, neither be dismayed.' The second scripture is from Joshua 1:9. 'Be strong and courageous. Do not be terrified; do not be discouraged, for the Lord your God will be with you wherever you go.'"

"I like those verses, good choices, Ruth. Amen," Alice said, and closed her eyes.

Ruth laid the Bible on the cocktail table, and then she and Alice joined hands. Ruth closed her eyes tightly and prayed fervently.

"Amen," Alice said, waving her hands in the air when Ruth was done. She turned to her friend and said, "Well done. Sometimes I'm going to need you to be a friend, and then at other times my pastor. You'll know when I need you to step into either role. I'm not going to worry about what tomorrow brings, and I don't want you to either, because God has this. He is our Redeemer, our bright and morning star, and He will never leave us."

Alice and Ruth hugged each other tightly. Then they stood and walked to Ruth's front door.

"See you in the morning," Alice said to Ruth, winking, after she unlocked the door.

"Yes, see you then," Ruth said, and waved.

After Alice locked her door, Ruth did the same. She walked back into the living room and took the glasses she and Alice had drunk from to the kitchen and loaded them along with the other dishes into the dishwasher. She returned to the living room, and then she sat on the sofa and meditated.

A few hours later, Ruth retired for the night. She turned off the light on the nightstand, but she was too keyed up to sleep. She rose midway off the bed and turned on the light again. She turned on the CD player and resumed listening to the Smokie Norful CD that she'd been listening to before she left the house that morning. The song "God Is Able" flooded the room. She leaned against the pillow, closed her eyes, and listened to the music. As she let the music soothe her spirit, the telephone rang. She peered at the phone anxiously.

Ruth picked up the receiver from the cradle and tentatively said, "Hello." Her stomach muscles clenched at the thought of yet another crisis to be faced. Her first thoughts flitted on Alice, and then her children. *Please, Lord, let all be well.*

Chapter Twelve

"Momma, are you still up?" Sarah asked. She sat on the edge of the bed inside the ash-gray-and-mauve striped guest bedroom of Daniel's house. Her laptop was placed on the other side of the bed, booted up, and she was logged on to her e-mail account at her job.

With the receiver cradled in her neck, Ruth sat up in the bed and reached over to turn off the CD player. "I am. I'm just lying in the bed listening to Smokie Norful's *Nothing Without You* CD. How are you feeling?"

"I'm good. I love that CD. I picked up Mary Mary's new CD for you. I think you'll like it. I just wanted to see how things went today with Aunt Alice. We really didn't get a chance to talk earlier. How is she feeling, and how are you doing?"

"We're both a little tired." Ruth sighed. "It's been a long day. Alice is doing as well as can be expected under the circumstances."

"Good," Sarah commented. "Aunt Alice is one of the strongest women I know, and I'm sure she's ready to face the disease head-on and beat it."

"How was your day?" Ruth asked, shifting in the bed to get more comfortable.

"Not too bad. The boys are little demons sometimes. I was ready to pull out my hair, until I realized they're trying to cope with the abandonment of their mother, as well as an indifferent father. Looking at it from that perspective has given me patience."

"It's good you're there, because they need a stable influence right now," Ruth said.

"I had a talk with Daddy, and I pretty much told him he has to get it together. He lets the boys run roughshod over him and the house. He just sits on that chair by the window and stares outside, while the boys are wreaking havoc inside. He's been wearing the same clothes every day, and he's beginning to smell." Sarah's nose wrinkled, as if she smelled a dead rat.

"Hmm, it sounds like Daniel is suffering from depression. That happens sometimes in situations like this," Ruth observed. She kicked the bedcoverings off her body and crossed her feet.

"If he's suffering from depression, he's been doing that for a while, from what Felicia told me. She and her husband offered to take the boys home with them. I asked them to give me a little time with Daddy; and if that didn't work out, then I'd give her a call. Then today Daddy had the nerve to say that maybe he should give the boys to Felicia and her husband."

Ruth could feel the crossness in her daughter's voice from that idea. "Daniel must really feel overwhelmed to have said something like that. Well, I'm glad you're there to help him, Sarah. I know he appreciates your presence, even if he doesn't say so."

"I think I had a major breakthrough with him this afternoon about the state of his family and his behavior. I basically told Daddy that it was time for him to grow up. The boys are the children, not him; and I emphasized how much they need him, with Lenora not being here. I'm hoping he'll become more understanding about his sons' needs," Sarah shared with her mother. She reached over and clicked to save an e-mail she had been working on before she called Ruth.

"Good for you," Ruth responded. "I know God put the right words in your heart to get through to your father."

"Oh, I'm pretty sure I did," Sarah observed. "Daddy broke down and cried after we talked. I don't ever remember him crying my entire life. He admitted that he was ashamed of how he handled some things in his life."

Ruth's breath seemed to be caught in her chest. Her interest was piqued. She wanted to ask Sarah if Daniel had said anything about her, but she quickly dismissed the idea. "That's even better," she managed to reply smoothly. "There comes a time when one has to admit their failings and sins, and take responsibility for the outcome of the hurt their actions might have caused. Good for Daniel. We'll keep praying for him, and God will make it right for him and the boys."

"I also talked to Naomi this afternoon, and she's not coming home this weekend, but next Friday, instead," Sarah informed her mother.

"Well, that's good to hear," Ruth replied enthusiastically as a smile filled her face. "It seems like it's been ages since we've seen her. Too bad it's not this weekend, but at least she's coming home. How is she doing?"

"Looking forward to graduation. And she asked me the oddest question," Sarah told her mother.

"What was that?" Ruth was immediately alarmed. "Naomi isn't ill or anything, is she?"

Sarah laughed out loud. "No, nothing like that. She asked me what I thought about her bringing a friend home with her."

"That's different," Ruth mused as she unloosened the wrap scarf on her head. "I don't remember her ever asking about bringing someone home with her."

"I didn't tell her, but I was surprised too. I asked Naomi if her friend was male or female, and it's a man."

"Oh, my." Ruth sat upright in the bed. "Do you think she plans to get married or something? I don't know what to think."

"I think you're jumping the gun, Momma. I don't think anything is wrong. Naomi is almost thirty years old. It's time she settled down. I think it's good that she's bringing a man with her," Sarah said, voicing her opinion.

"Goodness, where will the two of them stay? Did she say?" Ruth's head was spinning with thoughts.

"No, but they can always stay with me if they like. There's a little bit more room at my house," Sarah hastily added. "Not that there's anything wrong with your place."

"I have a futon that can be converted to a bed, if needed," Ruth said, defending her space.

"That's fine, Mom, I didn't mean anything. I'm just saying they're welcome to stay here. She'll be here next Friday. I was thinking of having the Saturday dinner, when Nay comes home, here at my house for the family. Are you okay with that?"

"That sounds like a plan. My meeting with the finance committee is scheduled for next Friday evening, and there's no telling what time I'll get out of there. Sunday is the first Sunday, and we have Communion. So Saturday sounds good. Just let me know what you want me to bring."

Ruth debated mentioning her date with Aron. Then she decided not to mention it, and felt a flash of guilt. Ruth always shared her news with Sarah. She justified her actions by telling herself that it wasn't worth mentioning, anyway, since she wasn't sure she would see Aron again socially after Friday. Ruth hadn't yet come to terms with her congregation's possible reaction.

"What else is new?" Sarah asked Ruth.

Ruth talked about the plumbing problem at church and how Aron had come to the rescue.

"That's another good man. I'm surprised some woman hasn't snatched him up at church. I see the mothers, and a few of the younger women, congregating around him after church. Monet and I had a conversation about that a few weeks ago," Sarah told her mother.

"Hmm. I didn't know he was that popular. I just assumed people judged him by his past deeds."

Sarah waved her hand, dismissing her mother's comments. "Momma, that was years ago. Mr. Reynolds has paid his debt to society. And I think he has proven his worth to the church. Did you know that he attended Brian's mentoring group two weeks ago and had a talk with the young men about the consequences of committing crimes? The session went really well. Joshua attended, and I decided to tag along. Quite a few parents were in attendance, and the feedback that Brian received afterward was very positive. He plans to talk to Mr. Reynolds about joining the committee."

"You never told me that," Ruth said. She thought she had her finger on every facet of the church.

"I thought I did. But you've been so busy with the financial crisis, I sometimes don't think you hear a word I say. After Mr. Reynolds spoke, Marcus Caldwell talked to the boys and made himself available for questions too. I think the two made a good pair. The boys were simply spellbound by the lectures. Brian and Marcus plan to sponsor a career fair at the church, which I think is a good idea."

Ruth chided herself for not paying closer attention when Sarah talked to her about church activities.

"I meant to tell you earlier, if you hire Mr. Reynolds, then you're going to have to present his application to the board of directors," Sarah advised.

"Why is that?" Ruth asked. "I thought applications had to be presented for salaried positions. Aron has volunteered for the time being. Although I feel bad about the lack of payment, since the church is so enormous."

"You're right," Sarah commented. "If the position is on a volunteer basis, then it's up to your discretion. If you decide to hire him after the trial, then you'll have to present his application to the committee. If you have time, mention it at the meeting."

"That's a good idea." Ruth picked up the notepad on her nightstand and wrote herself a note. She planned to ask Aron to fill out an employment application on Friday during their lunch.

"Momma, I've got to go. I'm logged on to my e-mail account at work, and I need to find a document to attach to an e-mail from one of the managers. Luckily, I e-mailed myself a copy and saved it. Have a good night, and I'll talk to you tomorrow. Love you."

"Love you too, Sarah." Ruth hung up the telephone and pulled the covers back on her legs.

She was simply astonished to learn that Aron played a bigger part in the church than she suspected. Perhaps she had been overreacting about her congregation's response to dating him. Then her mind roamed to Daniel. What if he was beginning to change, as Sarah suspected? What if he decided he wanted her back? Ruth couldn't imagine herself ever being the object of desire between two men. She married Daniel when she was barely out of her teens, and she didn't have any points of reference regarding other men.

She admitted to herself, if she could pass the hurdle with the church and they had no problems with her dating an ex-convict, then maybe she could see Aron socially if they clicked. All of Ruth's anxieties regarding her date with Aron were for naught. As it turned out, she ended up canceling her date with Aron. One of the church members had emergency surgery and Ruth had to go to the hospital.

When she called and told Aron about her change of plans, Aron was gallant and asked for a rain check for the following week. Ruth told him definitely, and that she was looking forward to having lunch with him. After hanging up, she smiled prettily to herself. She really was looking forward to it.

Chapter Thirteen

The second week of April, spring showers pounded unmercifully on the city of Chicago. The Wilcox family eagerly awaited and prepared for Naomi's weekend visit.

Sarah and Ruth's houses were spick-and-span clean. Both women anxiously anticipated Naomi's visit, as well as meeting her friend. Sarah and Ruth had talked on the phone during the week, wondering about Naomi's friend. They promised to do everything in their power to make the weekend a memorable one for Naomi and her guest. It was a big deal to the Wilcox family—their baby girl Naomi was bringing a man home.

Naomi and Montgomery had booked a reservation at the Hilton Hotel in Oak Lawn, a suburb of Chicago, for the duration of their visit.

By midmorning, Naomi and Montgomery were on their way to Chicago. She looked attractive in a pair of stonewashed jeans, with a beige-and-cream sweater and a tan leather jacket, with a matching cap lying jauntily on her head. Naomi still liked to pamper herself as she did as a teen, so her toenails and fingernails were painted a burnt sienna color, which matched her lipstick. She had given up weaves, and her hair was styled in a precise blunt cut with a hint of red highlights. Montgomery wore a pair of dark jeans, with a gray pullover shirt. He had on a black leather jacket.

The couple traveled on I-55, and they were about two hundred miles south of Chicago. Montgomery put on his turn signal and easily moved to the left lane masterfully, steering his sleek and powerful silver platinum Jaguar XJR. The automobile was Montgomery's pride and joy.

He peered at the GPS unit on the dashboard, saying, "We should be in Chicago in another three hours, give or take a few minutes." Then he looked over at Naomi, who was engrossed in a paperback book. "Babe, how much have you told your family about me?" He flipped on the turn signal again and returned to the right lane.

"Um," Naomi fumbled for words, "I haven't told them too much about you. I thought it would be easier to introduce you, and then take it from there." Her face was flushed.

"So who do they think I am?" Montgomery asked. "Would you hand me a bottle of water?"

Naomi reached into a small cooler on the backseat, took out a bottle of water, twisted it open, and handed it to Montgomery. He gulped down a couple of swigs, and then put the bottle in the cup holder.

"Monty," Naomi said nervously as she bit her lower lip, "in all the years I've been at SIU, I've never brought a man home. So the fact that you're with me will speak volumes to my family."

"I would have liked it better had your family at least known my name, and you had clarified our relationship. Honesty is the best policy, Nay."

"You're right," she admitted, sighing. "But, as I've told you, things are still kind of strained between me and my family, and I haven't really shared a lot of my personal business with them. They hid secrets from me for so long." She turned and looked out the window.

Montgomery said tenderly, "I understand, babe. I know you've had issues with your parents, but that stuff happened in the past." Montgomery was in the dark regarding the depth of Naomi's issues. He continued speaking. "You've just got to let it go to make room for the future we have planned together." He looked at her hand. "You're not wearing my ring?" he asked disbelievingly as his lips tightened.

"Well, um, until I have a chance to talk to everyone," Naomi fudged, "I'd prefer to keep that between us." She knew Montgomery wasn't going to be happy with the way she presented him to her family. Still, she preferred to do things her way.

"I think you're making a mistake," Montgomery observed, cutting his eyes over at her. "I feel like I'm a dirty secret or something." He turned off the CD player.

"Of course, you aren't," Naomi protested, leaning over and kissing Montgomery's cheek. "I love you, but I have to do this my way. Trust me, my family will love you. This is the best way to do things; just spring it on them during the weekend."

"If I were your parents, I don't think I'd appreciate you doing it that way. I have already introduced you to my mum and my sister, Elizabeth. I thought their reaction to the news was admirable. They love you."

Naomi rolled her eyes. "Let's keep it real. I admit they were polite when they first met me, but it took them a while to come around to accepting me as your girlfriend. Everyone is not like that, and racial prejudice is a tad bit more prevalent in the United States."

"Prejudice exists everywhere, in some shape, form, or fashion. I wish you'd handled the situation differently. But my coming with you this weekend is a big step in the right direction." He reached over and grabbed her hand with his free hand.

"Slavery is what makes prejudice different here in the United States. There are still ramifications that I don't think we'll ever be able to overcome," Naomi said.

"Prejudice unfortunately has existed in all parts of the world. Great Britain practiced that peculiar institution, and many Irish people have no love for England," Montgomery observed. They passed a sign that stated: *Chicago 125 miles.*

"That's true, but what's different is that slavery took place right here on our continent, in the United States. There were more slaves in other countries than there were in England," Naomi retorted.

"Okay, you got me there," Montgomery conceded. "You know you could tell your family." Montgomery began saying, but Naomi held up a finger and pressed it across his lips.

"No, we'll be okay. I know what I'm doing, and everything will work out just fine," Naomi replied.

She picked up her book, which had fallen to the floor, and resumed reading. They would be in Chicago soon. She couldn't help feeling a little apprehensive about what lay ahead. She knew her family, and she had no doubt that they would treat Montgomery with the utmost respect. She turned the page, and wished she could skirt the part of the trip where her family met Montgomery. If only the visit could be just like the page she had finished reading, over and done with.

As Naomi and Montgomery were completing the last leg of their journey, Sarah was at home in a tizzy, completing the last of her household chores. Sarah decided to postpone the family meeting one week so that Naomi could attend. Sarah, with Glenda's help, had been holding down the fort at Daniel's house. The meeting was scheduled for five o'clock that evening at Daniel's home. Sarah had decided to keep the meal simple for Naomi and Montgomery. Her menu consisted of a pasta salad, macaroni and cheese, baked beans and green beans, rotisserie and fried chicken, with corn bread and rolls. Maggie had baked cupcakes and brownies. She planned to take leftovers to Daniel's house.

Sarah's kitchen had a homespun feel to it. The tiled flooring was rust, while the walls were painted an apricot, contrasting with white appliances. Amber-and-white curtains hung at the window over the sink. The cabinets were a brown wood, and there was a matching table with six chairs.

The back door opened and Brian walked into the house, carrying bags of soft drinks. "Hmm, it smells good in here," he said, putting the bags on the counter. Then he took off his jacket and laid it on the back of one of the kitchen chairs. He walked to the refrigerator and began putting two-liter bottles of Pepsi, 7UP, and fruit drinks inside it.

Sarah looked around the kitchen. "I hope I haven't forgotten anything," she murmured. "I feel like I've forgotten something, but I don't know what it is."

"You always say that," Brian noted, chuckling. "I'll go back out if necessary." He walked to the stove and peeled back the aluminum foil from the chicken. He picked up a wing, and smiled sheepishly at his wife.

"Go ahead," Sarah said.

She took off the apron tied around her waist. She wore a pair of jeans, which clung to her size-twelve figure, with a red cable-knit sweater and matching red flats. Time had been good to Sarah. Though she was in her early forties, she maintained her cover girl looks. She pushed her bangs off her forehead and ran her fingers through her bobbed hair.

"I forgot to put on jewelry. I'll be right back." She rushed to the bedroom and returned a few minutes later, fastening the back on an earring.

"You look beautiful, Sarah," Brian said appreciatively.

Brian was handsome himself, and in his middle years. He was still trim and played basketball with his son. His hair had grayed a bit at the temples, and he sported salt-and-pepper sideburns and a thin mustache.

"Thank you," she said, preening. "You look pretty good yourself."

"Are you nervous?" Brian stood up and put the chicken bones in the garbage can, then he sat back down at the table.

"A little," Sarah admitted. "I never know what to expect from Naomi, and she's bringing a friend, a man. And this is a first for her. I wonder if she's serious about him." She tugged nervously on her earlobe.

"Hon, the fact that Nay is bringing a man home is a sure sign that she has feelings for him. Let's face it, her bringing someone home was bound to happen one day. Let's just be glad that she's going to introduce us to him. There had to be other men over the years that she never even bothered to bring home."

"I guess you're right." Sarah sighed. She reached into the sink, removed the dish towel, and ran it over the table and stove one more time.

Brian walked over to his wife, took the dishrag from her hand, and put it back inside the sink. Then he put his arm around her waist. "The kitchen, like the rest of the house, looks fine." He led her to a chair and gestured for her to sit down. He stood behind the seat, massaged her shoulders, and said, "Why don't you relax for a moment." His eyes darted to the apple-shaped clock hanging on the wall. "They should be here soon."

Sarah purred in delight from Brian's fingers gently kneading her shoulder. Suddenly her eyes zoomed to the dining room. "Did you remember to get ice?" she asked. She put a finger on the side of her face. "Maybe we should use the good china? I don't remember the last time I cleaned it. Lord, help me." Sarah was nervous about Naomi's visit and her sister bringing a male guest home.

"Sarah, calm down. You're overdoing it. We're having baked beans and chicken. I don't think that calls for the good china. This is just a casual meal. I think the Chinet paper plates are in order. We can break out the good stuff for the family dinner tomorrow."

"You're right, I definitely need to calm down," Sarah said, fanning her face. "I just want things perfect for Nay and her friend." Then she switched gears, saying, "I wonder how Momma is doing. She's been kind of stressed-out all week about the finance committee meeting this evening. If Nay wasn't coming home, I'd go to the church myself and offer her moral support."

"I'm sure Mother Ruth is and will be fine. Between her and Brother Clarence, they will get the church finances under control. Why don't you fix yourself a cup of tea and chill out for a minute?"

"That's a good idea." Sarah nodded. She stood and walked over to the butcher-block countertop and picked up a silver kettle, filled it with water, placed the kettle on the stove, and turned on the jet.

The couple turned as they heard the front door opening. "Oh, Lord," Sarah said, "do you think that's Nay and her friend already?" She twisted the end of her hair nervously.

As they began walking toward the foyer, they heard the thump of a basketball. They stopped in their tracks, looked at each other, and said simultaneously, "That's Joshua!"

"I forgot he had a half day of school today." Sarah lightly smacked her forehead.

Their son walked into the kitchen, still palming the basketball in his hands. "What's up?" he asked his parents.

Joshua was a handsome young man, with his father's height and boyish good looks. He wore his hair cut short, and his luminous smile and large doe-shaped brown eyes, in his honey-colored face, was pure Sarah. Joshua had been fending off the girls since he was twelve years old. He twirled the basketball on his finger, and then rolled it into a corner of the room. Joshua walked to the refrigerator, opened it, and pulled out a carton of orange juice. After he finished drinking the juice, he placed the glass inside the sink. Joshua closed the carton and put it back into the refrigerator. "What time will Auntie Nay be here?" he asked his mother.

"Actually, she should be here any minute, unless she and her friend ran into heavy traffic," Sarah answered.

The chimed doorbell rang. The Monroe family stood paralyzed for a moment. "I guess one of us should get the door," Sarah commented as she moved toward the doorway.

Joshua made a beeline to the living room and was staring out the window. "Hey, it's Auntie Nay and a man," he said.

Sarah felt as if someone was playing racquetball inside her stomach as she stood at the front door. She inhaled deeply, then twisted the bottom lock to the left. With a trembling smile on her face, she slowly opened the door.

As Sarah was opening the door for Naomi and Montgomery, Ruth and Aron were being led to a cozy table at Izola's Restaurant for their luncheon date.

Patrons were lightly scattered throughout the restaurant, and minutes later, Ruth and Aron were seated. Shortly afterward, the waitress brought menus to the table, followed by glasses of water.

"Are you ready to order?" she asked, smacking a piece of gum.

"Why don't you give us a few more minutes?" Aron glanced up at the young woman.

"I'll be back then." With a lively bounce in her step, the waitress bounded away from the table.

Ruth flipped through the pages of the menu. "I think I'll have a bowl of clam chowder and a Caesar salad. If I eat anything heavier, I'll become drowsy. And my big committee meeting is later on, and I need all my wits about me." She closed the menu and placed it near the edge of the table.

Aron closed his menu and set it on top of Ruth's. "Monet and Marcus say the baked chicken here is great. So I'll have that."

The waitress returned to the table and took their orders.

"Good choice. They're right. The chicken is wonderful. I come here sometimes after I leave church and pick up an order to go," Ruth remarked. "How are Monet, Marcus, and the children doing?"

The couple conversed about their children. Aron remarked Faith was a miniature version of her mother, Monet, and the twin boys were growing like weeds and were very mischievous like his son Duane was when he was a baby. Ruth threw back her head and laughed when she heard that. Aron went on to say that his other son, Derek, and his girlfriend, Elise, were getting married in the fall. He told Ruth that Derek would be in touch with her soon about performing the ceremony. He added the family was pleased by the news because everyone assumed his twin sons were confirmed bachelors and wouldn't ever marry. Ruth told Aron how her daughter, Naomi, was coming home for the weekend, and how her family was looking forward to seeing her. Aron asked if Naomi came home often.

Ruth faltered then replied, "Not really. Naomi has dedicated her life to higher education, and will be awarded a master's degree in accounting in May. Maggie, my granddaughter, will be graduating from eighth grade in June."

"I know you must be very proud of both of them," Aron said.

He looked up to see the waitress walking toward their table with plates of food on a tray.

She set the entrees on the table, and asked if they needed anything else. Ruth and Aron told her they were fine.

Ruth bowed her head and briefly blessed the food.

"That was short and sweet," Aron commented. He picked up his knife and fork and began cutting the chicken. He sprinkled salt on the rice and began eating.

"My grandchildren would complain or whine when they were younger if the blessing lasted more than a few seconds. So, since then, anyone praying for the food tries to keep the blessing to a minimum. I think I've gotten the blessing down to a fine science." Ruth put a dash of salt and pepper on her salad. She speared a piece of lettuce, put it in her mouth, and began to chew.

The two continued to talk about various subjects, including Aron's job at the church. They both decided to pass on dessert.

Ruth said wistfully, "I love Izola's peach cobbler, but I need to watch my weight."

Aron's eyes slid over her body. He remarked, "I don't think so. You look just fine."

Smiling and blushing rosily, Ruth excused herself to go to the ladies' room. While she was gone, Aron ordered a small order of peach cobbler to go.

Several minutes later, Ruth returned to the table as the waitress was handing Aron a small white bag and the check. He quickly scanned the tab, took a debit card out of his wallet, and presented it to the waitress. He'd added a generous tip to the total.

They exited the building and returned to Aron's car. He started the engine and headed back to The Temple. Once he arrived, he parked the car near the parking lot entrance and turned to Ruth. "I hope you enjoyed lunch as much as I did. I had a great time. I think there's a vibe between me and you, Ruth Wilcox."

Ruth looked into Aron's eyes and saw admiration and respect.

"The food and the company were marvelous, Aron. Thank you very much."

"So I hope since you enjoyed yourself that we can do this again. Maybe, instead of lunch, I can take you to dinner?" He looked at Ruth hopefully.

Ruth hesitated before she answered. "I would like that." She glimpsed at the clock on the dashboard. "I have got to go. I really need to start preparing for the meeting."

"Okay, I'll let you go this time," Aron teased. "How about I give you a call tomorrow, since you'll be tied up with the meeting and then your family this evening?"

"Sure, you have my number," Ruth said. She picked up the flower Aron had given her earlier when they got inside the car.

"Oh, before you go, I bought a serving of peach cobbler for you. Enjoy it, and when you analyze our lunch later, I hope you'll think of me favorably. I have no ulterior motives, Ruth. I like you, and I've enjoyed your company today," Aron said. He reached into the backseat and gave her the white bag containing the dessert.

Ruth grinned at him. "I think we're both too old for games. And yes, I enjoyed your company too. There's something about you, Aron Reynolds. I'll meditate on it later."

He walked her to the church entrance. Before she went inside the building, he took her hand in his and said, "I will talk to you tomorrow. I don't have to say good luck, because I know God has the situation in control."

"Thank you, Aron. Keep me and the church in your prayers. The committee has a formidable task before us. Enjoy your weekend, and I'll see you at church on Sunday."

Aron opened the door to the church for Ruth. As he returned to his car, there was pep in his step and he was whistling. Ruth walked to her office, and June was nowhere to be found. Ruth found a vase on a shelf in her office. She poured the remains of the bottled water she'd had earlier into the vase and inhaled the rose before she placed it inside the vase. Ruth swerved the chair from the window toward her desk. She was pleased with how the lunch date had gone and looked forward to her upcoming dinner date.

Reluctantly, she returned her thoughts to the meeting that was scheduled to begin in a couple of hours. Matters of a financial nature tended to be stressful for Ruth, and she wasn't looking forward to the meeting, and the tension that she knew would ensue. If the church's ministry was to continue, it was imperative that the committee come up with methods, albeit painful ones, that would preserve The Temple and all that it stood for. Ruth couldn't bear the thought of failing the church and, most of all, her father, Bishop. She had never been more aware than she was at that moment of how tall the boots were that she had to fill.

Chapter Fourteen

Sarah pasted a smile on her face as she opened the front door of her house, where she found Naomi and Montgomery standing at the threshold with smiles on their faces. Sarah's mouth dropped at the sight of Montgomery; then she composed herself and stood back to allow the couple to enter. She closed the door and the two women hugged.

Brian and Joshua stood back in the room and watched the scene unfold. Sarah shot her husband a puzzled look. Father and son walked to the foyer.

Naomi turned toward Montgomery, then back to her family, and said, "Everyone, this is my good friend, Montgomery Brooks. Monty, this is my sister, Sarah, and my brother-in-law, Brian, and my oldest nephew Joshua."

Montgomery frowned for a second when he heard Naomi introduce him as a "friend." He plastered a neutral expression on his face and responded, "Pleased to meet you all. Naomi has told me a lot about all of you." His voice sounded cheery as he shook hands with everyone.

Sarah led everyone to the living room, and they made small talk about the drive from Edwardsville. Then the doorbell chimed, and Sarah leaped from her seat, saying, "Excuse me."

She opened the door to find Maggie. She was wearing a denim jacket and jeans, with a backpack in tow.

When Maggie saw her aunt, she screamed, "Auntie Nay, you're home!" She ran to Naomi, who rose from her seat, and threw herself into Naomi's arms.

"Hey, girl, you've grown so much," Naomi said after the two parted.

Maggie looked at Montgomery inquisitively, and then asked Naomi, "Who is he?"

"He's a good friend of mine from Edwardsville, and his name is Montgomery." Naomi introduced the pair.

"Hello," Maggie said, staring at Montgomery.

Montgomery stood up and shook her hand. "You look like a younger version of Naomi," he commented.

"That's what everyone says." Maggie giggled. She took a chair from the dining room and brought it into the living room.

"Are you two hungry?" Sarah queried the couple nervously. She had to stop herself from staring at Naomi and Montgomery, who seemed quite comfortable with each other as they sat on the sofa.

"We are. We didn't stop for lunch and drove straight through," Naomi replied. She fluffed her hair, and then set her purse on the floor on the side of the sofa. Montgomery asked where the loo was located.

"What's a loo?" Maggie asked him, with a baffled expression on her face.

"I'm sorry, that's what we call the restroom in England. I slip up sometimes and call it 'the loo.'" Montgomery looked at Naomi. "I think Naomi knows some of my British terms by now."

Brian stood up and said he'd show Montgomery where the bathroom was located. As they walked down the hallway, Brian asked Montgomery about the Jaguar.

Joshua and Maggie asked if they could be excused and go to their rooms. Sarah nodded and they left the room.

"Naomi, will you help me set the food out in the dining room? I thought we'd have a light meal before we go to Daddy's house," Sarah said.

The sisters stood up and strolled to the kitchen. "It looks like you've done some redecorating since I've been here," Naomi observed. "Those look like new curtains in the living room, and you've painted in here and in the living room."

"True. You know I like to spruce up the house from time to time," Sarah replied. She walked to the stove, turned on the oven, and placed the aluminum pan of chicken inside it. She eyed Naomi, and then whispered, "Just how good a friend is Montgomery? You two seem mighty cozy." She handed Naomi the bowl of baked beans and asked her to warm them in the microwave oven.

"We're friends, as well as lovers." Naomi clarified the relationship nonchalantly. She took the glass top off the bowl, placed it on the counter, and put saran wrap around the bowl. Then she opened the microwave door, placed the bowl inside, and set the timer. "What else did you fix?" she asked Sarah, who stood gawking at her with her mouth agape.

"Nay, I don't believe you," Sarah huffed. "What would possess you to bring a man home, and then calmly announce you're having sex with him, and fail to mention that he's white?" She leaned against the counter, with her arms folded over her chest.

"Chill out, Sarah," Naomi said. "I was just messing with you. Montgomery and I are engaged, and have been for a year. He insisted he wanted to meet my family, so here we are." She took a bow.

"You're having premarital sex? I hope you're using protection. Oh, Nay," Sarah said dramatically, "you were raised better than that. Why didn't you wait?"

Nay turned up her nose. "You are hardly one to be preaching to me, Miss 'I Had Sex As A Teen, Had A Baby, And Palmed It Off On Momma And Daddy.' You sound so hypocritical."

"That wasn't a very nice thing to say." Sarah looked pained. The corners of her mouth turned down, and her eyes looked sad.

"I didn't mean it the way it sounded," Nay said contritely. The beeper on the microwave sounded and she removed the beans. "I'm an adult, and have chosen to live my life the way I see fit, just like every other person in this family."

Sarah held out her hand in a gesture of calling a truce. "I understand what you're saying. We have all made mistakes, or done things we wish we could take back. I just don't want you to repeat some of the mistakes that Momma, Queen or I have made." She walked over and kissed Naomi's cheek. "If he makes you happy, then I'm all for him. I hope to get to know him better this weekend. He is nice-looking for a white man, though a bit on the studious side."

Naomi's eyes glowed. "Monty is truly a good guy. He's been there for me, and I love him to pieces."

"Good." Sarah's smile wired her approval. "So where's your ring?"

Naomi pulled a chain from under her sweater, and on it was a marquise-cut five-carat diamond ring.

Sarah put a hand over eyes, as if shielding them. "Goodness. It hurts my eyes to look at it. Congratulations, Nay, I'm happy for you. You'll have to tell Momma and Daddy. They will be glad for you as well."

"I hope Momma likes him, and that she doesn't have a problem with me marrying out of my race. Once Monty has met the family, then I'll put my ring back on my finger, where it belongs." Naomi held up her hand.

"I don't think I've ever heard Momma say anything negative about interracial couples. So she won't be a problem," Sarah remarked as she took a pack of napkins from out of the lower cabinet. "Daddy is so traumatized by Lenora's leaving him, he might not even notice that Montgomery is white." They shared a laugh.

Soon they began taking the food to the dining-room table, which was already set. Brian and Montgomery sat in the living room, chatting and watching the fifty-inch high-definition television mounted on the wall.

Sarah and Naomi stood in the kitchen, glancing around one more time, making sure they hadn't forgotten anything.

Naomi's hands flew to her mouth. "You know who will more than likely give me a hard time about Monty?"

The two women yelled in unison as they grabbed each other's hands. "Queen!" They laughed.

"Bishop had a saying, and it took me a long time to see what he meant. Do you remember?" Sarah asked Naomi.

"Um." Naomi cocked her head to the side and closed her eyes. "I remember." She snapped her fingers. "He said, 'Don't go looking for trouble . . .'" she began.

"'. . . And trouble won't come looking for you,'" Sarah finished, nodding her head. "You got it. I think we better stick to that philosophy until we face the situation head-on."

"You're right," Naomi concurred. She dipped her head and then raised it, looking at Sarah, abashed. "Thank you for supporting me, Sarah. In retrospect, I realize that I shouldn't have sprung Monty on the family without any warning. I kept recalling how Queen would crow about how our bloodline on her and Bishop's sides were pure. The lines hadn't been tainted.

I wasn't sure how you and Momma would react, so I kept my relationship a secret."

"Girl, as light-skinned as Queen is, there had to be some tainting of the bloodlines," Sarah said dismissively as she made quotation marks in the air. "I bet we have relatives who have passed for white that we don't know about."

"You're probably right." Naomi nodded. "Remembering how Queen used to make those statements is what made me hesitate about introducing Monty to the family. And let me tell you," she shared, looking toward the doorway, "Monty was not happy about it either. He kind of gave me an ultimatum."

"So you didn't come just to see Daddy?" Sarah asked, visibly disappointed.

"Not quite. I thought I could kill two birds with one stone," Naomi admitted. Her brow wrinkled. "Do you think Queen will be so out of it that she won't know what's going on, or notice that Monty is white?"

"You wish," Sarah chortled. Then she became sober. "Some days are better than others for her. Momma seems to catch the worst of it, Queen can be cranky. She knows who Brian and I are eighty percent of the time. Sometimes she forgets who Josh and Maggie are." She pointed to the dining room. "For now, that's enough about Queen. Let's get the rest of the food out there before everything gets cold. My stomach is yelling, 'Feed me.'"

Naomi complied, and before long, Brian had blessed the food and they were all breaking bread together. Napkins were spread over laps, and bowls and platters of mouthwatering cuisine were passed back and forth. Conversation ensued as the family quickly demolished the food.

"The meal was great, Sarah, my kudos to the cook," Montgomery said as he wiped his mouth with a napkin.

"That's not all that's on the menu. I hope you left a little room for dessert." She got up and walked to the kitchen, returning with a platter full of the cupcakes and brownies.

Sarah walked around the table so everyone could make a choice of the sweets. She returned to the kitchen, and then came back with a carafe of mocha coffee.

"I thought I was full," Montgomery said after he selected a brownie and put it on the small plate next to his dinner plate. "But I can't resist. Naomi can tell you, I have a wicked sweet tooth." He cut a piece with his fork, placed it in his mouth, and swallowed. Then he said, "This is heavenly. Sarah, you can bake too? You need to go into the catering business."

"I made dessert," Maggie piped up. "I love cooking. Joshua says I should be a chef." She glanced at her brother momentarily, and then back at Montgomery.

"Yeah, Maggie can burn when it comes to food, just like the other women in the family." Joshua praised his sister; then he bit off a piece of a cupcake.

"Aunt Alice showed me how to make red velvet cake, so I've been making red velvet cupcakes too," Maggie said modestly. "I love cooking."

"She may love cooking," Sarah mentioned, "but she doesn't like cleaning up afterward."

"Mom, please," Maggie whined, embarrassed by her mother's comment. She tossed a braid over her shoulder.

Montgomery was correct in his assessment of the resemblance between Maggie and Naomi. Maggie was a little carbon copy of Naomi, and both girls clearly had Daniel's features. Brian often complained he was glad Joshua resembled him, or none of his children would have looked like him at all.

Joshua's cell phone in his pocket chirped. He excused himself to take the call. Maggie, who was staying overnight with a friend, also excused herself so she could pack her overnight bag.

"They are growing up so fast," Naomi mused. "Joshua is a giant, and Maggie is such a young lady now. And she's going into high school. Time is really passing quickly."

"So, Montgomery, tell us more about yourself," Brian urged his guest. He asked Sarah to pass him the carafe of coffee and poured himself half a cup.

"Let's see," Montgomery paused and then said, "I was born in Cheltenham, England. My father was an officer in the military. He retired twelve years ago, and into his second year of retirement, he passed from a brain hemorrhage."

"Our brother, DJ, is in the army. I'm sorry to hear about your father. I know how difficult that must have been," Sarah offered.

"It was a shock, and it happened so suddenly. I spoke to my dad that morning; and by that afternoon, he was gone. My mum and dad had me late in life, so she dotes on me. I have an older sister, Elizabeth. She's married, and has a girl and boy."

Brian cleared his throat. "I'm assuming you and Naomi are in a relationship. How long have you two been dating, and what are your family's feelings about the cultural difference?"

"Sweetie, you sound so politically correct. Cultural differences?" Sarah teased her husband.

Naomi listened to Brian interrogate Montgomery. His questions had a paternal tone, which unsettled Naomi. She shifted and chewed her lower lip, clearly perturbed by Brian's grilling of Montgomery.

"Naomi and I have been together for four years. She has traveled to England with me a few times, and she has met my family. I think the worst we endured from my family was when my niece, Emma, blurted out, 'Mummy, Uncle Monty has a colored girlfriend.'"

"I was taken aback, to say the least!" Naomi exclaimed. She sneaked another cupcake. Then she looked at everyone guiltily. "This will be my last one, Scout's honor." She held up two fingers.

"Knock yourself out," Brian said to her. A wide grin split his face. He raised his coffee cup.

"Naomi conducted herself admirably. My family realized we had a long way to go to change our way of thinking about and treatment of black people. And I think we've come a long way since then. I've never been married, so Naomi will be my first, and only, wife. I own an accounting firm in Edwardsville, and I have an M.B.A. from Southern University. So I'm financially secure," Montgomery said.

"What a minute. Are you saying, what I think you're saying? Just what are your intentions toward my dau . . . I mean, sister-in-law?" Brian questioned sternly.

Naomi and Sarah's faces swiveled toward Brian as their mouths gaped open in amazement. *Dang,* Naomi thought, *I can't believe Brian went there.* She didn't know whether she should cringe from embarrassment, or take pleasure in the knowledge that her biological father cared enough to query Montgomery. Embarrassment won, and a flush of heat rose from her neck to her face.

"Brian, that's not necessary," Naomi stated firmly as she tossed her napkin on the table. "I'm more than capable of looking out for my own interests. I'm a big girl, and I have enough credentials to know how to make my decisions. You are out of line." Her mouth snapped closed.

"I'm sorry if I was out of line. I didn't mean you or Montgomery any harm," Brian said stiffly. He rose from his seat abruptly and walked to the den, near the front of the house.

"What just happened?" Montgomery looked from one sister to the next. When no answer was forthcoming, he dropped his napkin, which had been lying on his lap, on the table and followed Brian to the den.

Sarah and Naomi looked at each other uneasily. Sara spoke first. "I'm sure Brian didn't mean anything. I think he just got caught up in the moment. Like he said, he didn't mean any harm."

"I wish he had just let it go. I haven't exactly been honest with Monty about you and Brian being my biological parents," Naomi said, exasperated.

"Nay, why not? If you're marrying this man, then you need to come clean with him about your past," Sarah said, feeling disappointed with her.

"I don't know . . . I mean," Naomi said, confused and gulping. She held out her hand entreatingly. "I plan to tell him, and I will before we get married. I just don't want him to think I'm bringing a lot of drama to the relationship. His mother, sister and her family are so proper." She paused. "Or maybe 'stuffy' is the word I'm looking for. I don't want Monty to think I'm not good enough for him. He's even related to royalty, on his father's side."

"You can't start off a relationship with secrets and without trust. You know firsthand how secrets have affected our family. If Montgomery loves you, then he'll accept you regardless who your parents are," Sarah advised, although personally her feelings were hurt. She felt like Naomi was ashamed of her and Brian.

"I will talk to him," Naomi said weakly. "Give me time. Anyway, give me the 411 on Daddy and Lenora.

What's happening with them? Have you talked to DJ and Chelsea lately? How is D3? Hold that thought, I'm going to get a bottle of water." She rose and walked to the kitchen.

Sarah turned the face of her watch over and noted the time. It was nearly time for the finance committee meeting to commence. She bowed her head and said a quick prayer for her mother and the finance committee. Then she turned her attention to Naomi, who had returned to her seat. She told Naomi that she and Glenda had been caring for Daniel's little boys. Sarah mentioned Daniel was finally showing signs of life, taking an interest in his sons. Though her tone was light and she was thrilled to be with Naomi, Sarah couldn't keep her thoughts from wandering to Ruth, and what she was sure would be a spirited meeting at The Temple.

Chapter Fifteen

Ruth and Clarence sat at the round table inside her office, under bright fluorescent lights, trying to crunch numbers as they had been doing for the past hour. The committee meeting was scheduled to begin momentarily at seven o'clock. June was in the office at the Xerox copier, printing off the financial reports for the committee members.

Clarence, a short, fastidious man, with a pencil thin mustache, was dressed in a dark suit, white shirt and tie. Half-moon, gold-rimmed glasses were perched on the edge of his nose. He pushed the glasses snugly against his nose as he made a notation on a pad of paper.

"Ruth, the good news, or blessing in this, is that while offerings are down, attendance hasn't slackened. So we can definitely attribute the financial shortfall to the economy," he reassured her.

Ruth rubbed her temples and smiled morosely. "I kind of figured that, and given the state of the economy, that's believable. Still, I feel like I've let the church down."

"There is nothing you or Bishop could've done differently. We aren't in serious trouble yet, but we do need to make adjustments so that we don't have any problems in the near future," Clarence said.

"I understand what you're saying." Ruth nodded. "But the programs here at The Temple serve a great purpose, not only to our members, but to the community at large. It's going to be hard to choose which ones should be discontinued."

She leafed through a pile of papers cluttered on the table in front of her. Finally she found the list of social programs. The Temple offered many ministries, which included after-school tutoring, scholarship search services, the boys-at-risk program, and teen parenting classes, to name a few. The preschool classes, babysitting services, food pantry, senior breakfast, and the outings were near and dear to Ruth's heart.

Before the financial crisis arose, the church had begun exploratory research on establishing an elementary school at The Temple. Now Ruth felt like every milestone she and Bishop had accomplished was in jeopardy.

Clarence couldn't help but notice the glum expression that overtook her face. "Cheer up, Ruth, the Lord will make a way." He winked at Ruth. "I have a few tricks up my sleeve. We may not be able to save every single program, but we will give it our best shot. The Lord works in mysterious ways, His wonders to behold."

"You're right, Clarence." Ruth began straightening the table. "My motto is, 'when the majority come together and are on the same page, much can be accomplished.' So I'm going to leave this matter in God's hand and allow Him to guide us." She patted her Bible, which was in front of her on the table.

"Good choice." Clarence nodded approvingly as he laid his pencil down on the table. "With that philosophy, you can't go wrong." He glanced down at his watch. "Well, we have a little time before the meeting convenes, so let's continue to go over our plan."

June walked into Ruth's office thirty minutes later. "Reverend Ruth, the committee members have started to arrive," she apprised. "They are in the meeting room, and I'm going to the kitchen to get coffee, cookies, and scones."

"Thank you, June." Ruth and Clarence straightened the papers into a tidy batch and stood up.

"Let's do this," Clarence said. He squeezed Ruth's arm. "We're going to be fine."

Ruth nodded, saying, "I'm ready. God will be with us."

She and Clarence greeted the committee members as they filed into the room. Ruth took her seat at the head of the table, with Clarence to her left, and June to her right. Then she greeted the finance committee, which was made up of six men and six women.

After the men and women sat down at the table, Ruth said, "Thank you for coming out this evening." She made eye contact with each member. "We have an enormous task ahead of us. But with God's mercy and guidance, I think when we leave here tonight, we will have made great inroads into our financial dilemma. Shall we pray?"

The members joined hands around the high-gloss dark wood square table. Ruth bowed her head. "Heavenly Father, I thank you for waking us up this morning, allowing us to see another day. Bless the members of The Temple and your children all over the world. Lord, bless the people gathered here today at this table. Help us to find the ways and means to help our fellow brothers and sisters as we explore options to keep our ministry programs operational so that we can help your children. These blessings I humbly ask in your son's name. Amen," she said ardently.

Resilient choruses of "Amen" echoed in the room.

Closely following Robert's Rules of Order, June duly
noted there was a quorum in attendance. She made a
motion for the meeting to begin, which was seconded
by Clarence. June passed out the document, and Clarence asked the committee to open it to page two. After
speaking on the projected budget for 2003, and the
shortfall the church faced, Clarence turned the meeting
over to Ruth.

"I hope everyone has been reading the e-mails that
June has been sending you over the past month. As
Clarence mentioned, The Temple is facing a financial
shortfall. Clarence and I," she said, with her eyes darting to her left, "have been working very closely over the
past two months to monitor the situation."

Brother Nelson raised his hand and stroked his
beard. "May I speak?" he asked Clarence, who technically presided over the meeting. Clarence nodded his
head. "How much of a shortfall are we talking about?"

"Our operating expenditures on a monthly basis are
close to one hundred thousand dollars. In the past, we
have usually collected about two hundred thousand a
month. So we had a pretty good cushion. But with the
economy failing, we've been collecting between one
hundred and one hundred fifty thousand a month. So
we are barely breaking even, and therein lies the problem," Clarence concluded briefly.

"Oh, my," Sister Kathleen Long said, placing her
hand on her neck. The bangles on her wrist jangled. "I
assume that you and Reverend Ruth have verified that
attendance isn't down? Are you sure that a decline in
attendance is not the major factor contributing to our
shortfall?"

Clarence nodded as he held up the document. "We
had the membership committee pull the data for the
past two quarters, and that's not the case. We have in-

cluded a chart of attendance, which is exhibit A in your handout."

"Are we bringing in any new members?" Sister Patrice Henry asked. She was a modest woman, but sharp as a tack. She was employed as a financial planner for one of the top banks in the Chicago area. "In the past, new members have usually equated with more money for the church."

"That was true in the past," Ruth interjected. "We've been averaging twenty-five new members monthly for the past quarter. None have committed to tithing, and they've been giving what I assume to be in accordance with their financial means."

"Isn't tithing on the agenda of the sessions that new members are required to attend?" Brother Macio Brown asked.

"Yes, it is," Ruth confirmed. "But you can't force people to tithe. Let's face it, times are hard. People have been losing jobs, gas prices skyrocketed, although the prices have seemed to level off somewhat. The economy has impacted many sectors of life, and, of course, that, in turn, affects the church."

"That's true," Sister Denise Burnett added. "So I suspect our job here tonight is to come up with suggestions on how to save money?" she asked gloomily.

"That is correct." Ruth's head dipped up and down. She was about to discuss the utility expense shortfall, when there was a knock at the door. Everyone looked toward it.

Ruth asked, "Who's there?"

The door opened, and one of the older members of the church, Brother Eddie Duncan, walked slowly inside the room. His shining white cane was grasped tightly in his hand. "Good evening, Reverend Wilcox. I know the finance committee is meeting now, but I have something I want to give to you."

Brothers Whiting and Layton looked at the man disapprovingly. Then Brother Collins stood up and said, "Brother Duncan, what are you doing here? I know that you're aware this meeting is closed to church members. We will present our findings to the church at a later date. Why don't you come back another time?"

The older man's body stiffened as he looked at Brother Collins, obviously affronted. "I'm here because I think I may have something that may help the church."

Brother Whiting looked at Brother Duncan with a superior expression on his face. "Sir, I don't think you'd be much help here. I have an M.B.A. from the University of Chicago. So trust me when I say that neither I nor any committee member needs your help."

The look Brother Layton gave the older man telegraphed: *"There's nothing here for you, old man. Your time has come and gone. We can handle this."*

"But I don't think you understand," Brother Duncan objected. "I have some crucial information. . . ."

June stood up and walked over to the elderly man. She took his arm, to lead him out of the room. "The meeting is closed, like Brother Whiting stated. Why don't you give me the information, or you can make an appointment to see Reverend Wilcox next week, all right? I'm sure she'd be more than happy to see you."

"See, that's the problem with young people, you don't want to listen to your elders," the old man said in a thin querulous voice. "I have information that can help Reverend Ruth." Brother Duncan planted his feet and refused to move.

"Brother Duncan, please come with me," June said firmly as she led the man from the room. "I'll be right back," she told the committee as she pulled the door shut.

"Perhaps I should listen to him," Ruth mused aloud, looking at the closed door. "After all, he was the committee chairperson during my father's tenure. He obviously had something he considered important to tell us."

Clarence disagreed. "I beg to differ. If Brother Duncan was head of this committee at one time, then he knows the meeting protocol, and how it's closed to the members. He shouldn't have come barging in. Let June handle the matter."

June returned to the room minutes later. "I apologize for the interruption. Reverend Ruth, Brother Duncan says that he'll call you soon. He kept insisting that it's imperative that he talk to you." She walked to her seat and sat down.

"Okay, where were we?" Ruth asked Clarence.

"I think we should set up another meeting two weeks from today. That will give the committee members time to brainstorm on the issues, and to think of realistic ways we can cut expenses at the church. We have to keep an open mind to the possibility of cutting programs."

"It's my prayer that it doesn't come to that," Ruth told the committee. Passion resonated in her voice. "With all these bright minds at the table, as Brother Layton so eloquently pointed out, I know we can come up with some long-term solutions to our problem."

"I have a suggestion before the meeting ends," Clarence said. "I'd like for three of you to volunteer to form a subgroup, and contact the chairperson or president of each committee and talk with them to see what type of minimal cuts could be made. Or suggest ways to improve the organizations with less money."

"One of the biggest drains on the church finances is the musical ministry. They are paid salaries. Perhaps we could get them to volunteer their services one Sunday a month. Otherwise, I can see massive cuts being made there. Do we really need so many musicians? We've got to work smarter with what we have," Brother Layton said.

"I would be careful there. The cornerstone of every Baptist church is the musical staff. We must not be hasty about anything without the research first." Sister Cox looked at Brother Layton scornfully. "We have to be very careful."

"I disagree," Brother Layton interjected. "We have organists, pianists, the choir director, and the praise dance team director. Perhaps we need to merge some of those positions and save money there."

"Then you're talking about cutting jobs. Until we have a full understanding of the ministries, and the costs associated with the upkeep of them, it's premature to talk about cuts that could affect the staff's jobs. We're trying to save money, not cause people to lose their jobs," Sister Cox countered.

The meeting became heated for a few minutes, before Clarence asked for order. He designated the subcommittee members, and asked that they report their findings in two weeks. He mentioned there were two other items on the agenda to discuss.

Before long, the remaining agenda items were duly discussed and noted. Clarence opened the floor for new business. Ruth informed the committee that she had hired Aron on a temporary basis for James's position of chief custodian. She also mentioned the building needing repairs.

"With all due respect, Reverend Wilcox, we are possibly facing a deficit. Perhaps you were a bit hasty," Brother Layton said respectfully. He looked at Brother Whiting and shook his head, as if to say, *"Sometimes women don't get it."*

"I'm the senior minister of this church, Brother Layton, and I'm aware of the rules and bylaws that govern this church. I would hardly put the church in a precarious position, knowing we're facing a budget shortfall. Mr. Reynolds plans to volunteer his time on a trial basis, so we don't have to worry about a salary yet. But if he works out, then I will submit his application to the committee for approval," Ruth responded tersely.

"I apologize if I sounded out of line." Brother Layton backed down. "Well, maybe if Mr. Reynolds works out, then we can offer him the position with a salary reduction. That would save money." He removed his suit coat off the back of his chair and slipped it on.

"We'll cross that bridge when we get to it. I plan to talk to James before he leaves, and get an estimate on his monthly expenditures," Ruth said.

"If there isn't any other new business, then I make a motion that the meeting be adjourned," Clarence said. June seconded the motion.

Ruth said a quick prayer for everyone to make it home safely. Then the newly formed subcommittee members chatted among themselves for a while, while the other members gathered their handouts, bade each other good-bye, and dispersed from the room. Twenty minutes later, the room was empty, save for Ruth, Clarence, and June.

The secretary removed paper cups and napkins from the table, and put them into the garbage bin in the corner of the room.

Clarence put his papers into his briefcase, while Ruth put the cap on her fountain pen.

"I think the meeting went well, Ruth, considering the task before us," Clarence commented as he put on his suit jacket.

"I agree to a certain extent. I felt some of the members presented good ideas. Meanwhile, we're still in a holding pattern and we have a long way to go," Ruth lamented. She picked up her stack of documents and held them in the crook of her arm.

"I'm going to straighten up in here and then I'm going home," June announced. "I'll see you Sunday, Reverend."

"Have a blessed weekend, June. Thank you for your help tonight. I really appreciate it."

"No problem," June said.

"All things in time, Ruth," Clarence said, patting her arm. "Budgetary decisions are always stressful. Overall, the meeting went as I expected it would. The committee is up to the task of making and implementing methods that will benefit the church. I think once we have the information we need and it's compiled, we'll be in a position to make educated decisions about what our next step will be. It wouldn't be a bad idea if you mentioned the church's economic issues to the church members," he said.

"You don't think that would be jumping the gun?" Ruth stared at Clarence dubiously. Then they walked toward the door; Ruth turned off the light in the room. She locked the office, and they walked to Ruth's office.

"I don't mean to start a panic, but give them a heads-up of what's going on. Who knows? We may get some good suggestions from them too," Clarence said.

"I'll think about it." She walked into her office and retrieved her briefcase. She turned off the light in her office and returned to the foyer. "I can't believe it's already a quarter to nine," she said to Clarence. "I planned to stop at Sarah's house on my way home to see Naomi. She came home for the weekend. Maybe, instead, I'll just wait and see her tomorrow."

Before long, Ruth and Clarence were inside their vehicles and exiting the parking lot. Clarence was heading east and Ruth west.

As Ruth drove home, she mused on the meeting.
She wholeheartedly prayed the finance meeting would
come up with creative methods to keep the church's
budget from sinking into the red. She didn't think she
could bear downsizing some of the critical ministries,
like the musical one. Ruth felt a moment of regret that
she didn't mention the utility dilemma. She planned to
resolve that issue on her own. Even if she had to pay
the bills out of her personal funds, and use her love
offering temporarily. A love offering is given to the
pastor for their personal use. Failure wasn't in Ruth's
vocabulary, and she vowed the church would operate at
full steam during her watch.

Chapter Sixteen

A few hours later following dinner at Sarah and Brian's house, the women packed food to take to Daniel's house. Following the meeting, Ruth called Naomi to tell her that she would see her the following day. Brian and Montgomery opted to stay at the house to watch Friday night basketball, which would be airing on ESPN. The Chicago Bulls and Miami Heat were playing in a game that was sure to be a preview of an Eastern Conference play-off game.

As Sarah took her jacket out of the hall closet, she told Brian that she and Naomi wouldn't be gone too long, and she warned him to take it easy on Montgomery.

Naomi kissed Montgomery's cheek, and she asked him if he felt comfortable staying with Brian while she was gone. He told her that he would be fine. She reminded him that they still needed to check into the hotel.

Brian said that he and Montgomery would take Maggie to her friend's house for a sleepover and then go to the Hilton. Then they would return to the house to catch the remainder of the game.

"Good idea," Sarah said. "Then we don't have to rush back if things get crazy at Daddy's house."

Maggie came downstairs, carrying her overnight bag. "Daddy, I'm ready," she said.

Sarah hugged her daughter and told her to be good, and that she'd pick her up in the morning. Joshua had departed earlier to hang out at a friend's house.

Brian clicked off the television with the remote control. He and Montgomery stood up.

"I guess I'm stuck with chauffeuring duties tonight. Luckily, the house that Maggie is going to isn't far from here, and the Hilton isn't far from here either," Brian said.

Everyone ended up leaving at the same time.

Naomi and Sarah got inside Sarah's Ford Escape SUV, and before long, Sarah merged into traffic. Sarah said, "I know before the weekend is out, Brian is going to angle for a ride in the Jag. Montgomery has a nice ride."

"It runs pretty smoothly. So what's happening with Momma? She told me a little about the meeting," Naomi said.

They chatted away and soon they were in Olympia Fields. Sarah parked her vehicle in Daniel's circular driveway.

"The size of this house is amazing," Naomi observed. She clicked off her seat belt. "Who needs to live in a house this size? I bet heating costs are astronomical."

"Daddy might not be living here for long. And you're right, I think the house is too pretentious," Sarah added.

They exited the car and walked to the front door. Sarah pulled out her key and opened the door. Naomi noticed a gold-plated sign on the right side of the gray brick house: *The Wilcox Family*. She rolled her eyes.

"It's awfully quiet. I hope nothing has happened. Daddy?" Sarah called out as they stood in the foyer.

To her surprise, Daniel strode into the foyer, and she noticed there was a little pep in his step, which had been missing. The boys were hot on his heels.

"Sarah!" the twins shouted as they ran and encircled her waist.

"Hi, boys," she greeted. "Were you good boys for Daddy?"

David and Darnell bobbed their heads, and then flashed a snaggletoothed smile at their older sibling. "Kind of," David replied.

Damon hung back and stood near Daniel's side. Naomi walked to her dad and gave him a lackluster hug. Sarah was carrying the bag of food, she took it into the kitchen.

"Hey, Daddy, how are you feeling?" she asked him.

She looked at the little boys, who were dressed in jeans and striped polo shirts.

When Sarah returned to the living room, she bade Damon to come and give her some love, and she held out her arms. He begrudgingly gave her a quick hug. Then Sarah turned to Daniel and gave him a warm hug. "Daddy, you look much better," she complimented him.

"Thanks, I've been trying to take the advice you've been giving me. So I thought I'd freshen up and spend some time with the boys when they came home from school."

Sarah noticed a bandage on one of Daniel's hands. "What happened?" she asked, concerned.

"I baked fish sticks for the boys for a snack after they came home from school. I used the dish towel instead of that other thingie." He snapped his fingers. "You know what I mean," he said sheepishly as he shrugged his shoulders.

"You mean the oven mitt?" Naomi asked wryly. The straps of her purse were slung over her shoulder, and she folded her hands across her chest.

"Who is she?" Damon asked Sarah, pointing at Naomi. He peered at her suspiciously.

"That's your other big sister, Naomi," Daniel told his son.

"How come we ain't seen her before?" David asked his father, looking at him with widened eyes. He looked back at Naomi with a puzzled look on his face.

"She's been away at school. Isn't it nice that she came by to see us today?" Daniel nodded at his boys. They looked at their father dubiously, and then they tentatively nodded their heads. "Let's go to the den," he said. Everyone followed him to the rear of the house, into the den.

Damon walked over to the heavy wood cocktail table and picked up the remote for the television. He turned on the TV and flipped through the channels. A violent movie came on HBO and he stopped channel surfing. Damon and his brothers were transfixed by the gruesome images on the television screen.

Sarah sat on one end of the sofa, and Naomi sat to her right. Daniel was planted on a chair, adjacent to the sofa. Sarah leaned toward her father and whispered, "Daddy, I don't think that movie is appropriate for the boys."

"Damon, find something else for you and your brothers to watch, or bring the remote to me and I'll find something myself," Daniel ordered the boy.

Damon ignored his father until Daniel repeated his request again.

"No, Mom lets us watch this channel. I've seen this movie before," Damon replied. His eyes never left the television set.

"Boy, I know you didn't tell me 'no.'" Daniel's eyes were bulging out of his sockets. "Bring me that remote control, and bring it now!" he ordered.

Damon turned around and looked at Daniel. The boy twisted his lips and rolled his eyes, visibly exasperated by his father's request. He stood up, slammed the remote on the table, shook his fists, and ran from the room.

Sarah and Naomi watched the display. If Naomi hadn't been so glad to see Daniel get his comeuppance, she, too, would have been just as appalled as Sarah at the young boy's behavior. The Daniel Wilcox of old would never have tolerated his children behaving the way Damon had. Naomi held her breath to see how her father responded.

"Damon, come back here!" Daniel bellowed. The boy didn't return.

The twins never turned away from the television, like nothing out of the ordinary had occurred. Sarah reached for the remote and turned the channel to the Cartoon Network. The twins twisted their heads and looked at Sarah, who then turned the channel to a Garfield movie that was airing.

Daniel slumped down and rubbed his eyes. Naomi held her tongue and didn't say a word.

Sarah whispered heatedly, "Daddy, I know you're not going to let that boy get away with talking to you like that."

"What can I do?" he asked. He felt humiliated because he knew what Sarah said was true.

"You can go and tan his little butt. I can't believe you. He needs to be put in his place. It seems like he's gotten away with too much over the years." Sarah's lips narrowed into a thin line.

Daniel hunched his shoulders defensively; then he said, "I left the discipline of the boys to Nora."

"If you let Damon continue to act out and talk to you that way, the younger boys will do the same. Then all

three of them will be out of control. What are you going
to do then?" Sarah tried to keep her voice even, but the
emotion she felt was evident.

"I guess I'll cross that bridge when I get to it," Daniel
said tiredly.

"That's not acceptable, Daddy," Sarah proclaimed,
waving her hand in the air dismissively. She sat up and
leaned forward.

"Sarah, I don't appreciate your talking to me like
that. I've never told you how to raise your children, and
I expect the same respect from you." Daniel glanced
over at Naomi, who had a sneer on her face, and was
shaking her head at the back-and-forth banter between
father and daughter. "I know you're not being critical
of me," he said to Naomi. "You don't even have kids."

Naomi's temper flared, and she wanted to lash out at
Daniel. Instead, she mentally counted to ten and held
her peace. "I haven't said a word. And you're right—I
don't have children. But I did take psychology classes,
so I know about children and their behavior. As you
said, those boys are yours, so do your thing, Daddy."

Daniel stood up; then he said, with a pained expression on his face, "Excuse me, I'll be back in a few minutes." He left the room in search of Damon.

Sarah looked at Naomi and asked her if she was
thirsty. Naomi almost said no. Then she realized her
sister wanted to talk to her in private. The women left
the room and walked into the kitchen. They removed
the food from the bag and put it on the counter.

Naomi's eyes roamed the room, taking in the décor
of the house. She had to admit Lenora had good taste.
The house was a definite showplace from what she
could see. However, she concluded it didn't have the
homey feeling of the house where she had grown up.

"I can't believe Daddy? Can you?" Sarah asked Naomi, rolling her eyes upward and twisting her lips. "I've been telling him all week that he needs to step up and be a father to those boys, even if it means hurting their feelings."

"And what does he say?" Naomi inquired, leaning against the side of the island in the kitchen. She was impressed with the silver refrigerator, oven/range, and washer and dryer in a utility room off the spacious kitchen, which was sage green and cream.

"He says that the boys are acting out because Lenora left so abruptly," Sarah explained, wringing her hands in frustration.

"He does have a point there. However, he still needs to maintain control over the boys. You were right; if he doesn't nip their behavior in the bud, it will lead to serious consequences later in life," Naomi declared.

"I thought after I talked to him, Daddy might try to make a better effort." Sarah shook her head. "Those three little boys could end up like Lenora's twin brothers."

"Well, if Lenora doesn't come back, perhaps Daddy will consider counseling for them," Naomi suggested. "Maybe I could talk to him about it."

"He might listen to you," Sarah said thoughtfully. "Nay, do I detect a thawing of your feelings for Daddy?" she queried in a half-teasing voice.

"Not really. I feel sorry for the boys. But I will never forgive Daddy for breaking up our family," Naomi said in a tone that let Sarah know that she was quite serious, and still bore some residual scars from their parents' divorce.

"Never say never," Sarah advised, patting Naomi's arm. "Since you've never come to visit Daddy here, how about I take you on a tour of the house? Then we can go back into the den and see what the little 'munchkins' are up to."

Naomi followed Sarah and she was simply amazed by the opulence of the residence. She was in awe of Lenora's collection of African art, and eclectic paintings by contemporary artists, such as Annie Lee, Alonzo Adams, and Brenda Joysmith, hung on the walls. She walked over to a bookshelf filled with African-American fiction by notable authors.

They returned to the den, finding the boys still watching television. The sisters returned to their seats on the sofa, and Naomi half listened to Sarah's prattle. Daniel returned to the room with Damon in tow; the young boy's eyes were swollen and red. Daniel returned to the recliner seat, and Damon walked over to Sarah and Naomi and mumbled he was sorry. They graciously accepted his apology.

"Daddy, I brought a few leftovers from my house for you and the boys for later this weekend, along with snacks for the family meeting. Maggie made cookies especially for the boys, so they can have them now. We had an early dinner at my house." She peered at her watch. It was after seven o'clock. "Everyone should be here shortly."

Daniel nodded, indicating the suggestion was all right with him. Naomi and Sarah went to the kitchen and took out the containers of food they had brought. Sarah put them into the freezer. She also took ice trays out and put the cubes into an ice bucket.

Her sister had put the snacks into bowls when the doorbell rang.

"Why don't you get that for me," Sarah suggested to Naomi.

"Sure." Naomi wiped her hands on a dish towel.

"I'll get it," Daniel yelled. He walked to the door.

Naomi took the foil paper off the cookies that Maggie had made.

"Had Brian planned on coming to the meeting?" Naomi asked. She took a plastic bag of paper plates from the wrapper and stacked them neatly into a pile on the table.

"No, he decided to pass this time." Sarah blew her bangs out of her face and smiled at Naomi. "After he found out you were bringing a male friend home, he said he'd hang out with Montgomery."

"Well, that was nice of him." Naomi sat as she took serving utensils out of the drawer.

"Trust me," Sarah said, shaking her head from side to side. "Brian would rather go to or watch a basketball game. It's Friday, which means doubleheader night on ESPN. The first one started early. Brian would rather watch the games than deal with drama."

After greeting the boys, Glenda and Felicia went into the kitchen. Glenda asked the women sassily, "What drama?"

"Hi, Glenda and Felicia," Sarah greeted the women airily. "Naomi and I were just talking about my husband, Brian, and Sarah's friend Montgomery, and sports drama. How are you doing?"

"We'll be better when decisions have been made about the boys," Felicia threw in. "I know where Nora's stashes are. I need a drink." She walked to a cabinet, bent down and removed a bottle of wine. She took a glass out of the dish drainer and filled it with wine.

"I'm sorry. I don't think you've met my sister, Naomi. Nay, this is Lenora's mother, Mrs. Johnson, and her sister, Felicia." Sarah made introductions.

"Oh, you must be the daughter who never came to visit Daniel and Lenora," Felicia observed smugly. "Lenora told me all about you."

Naomi's hackles were raised. She wanted to wipe that smug expression off Felicia's face. She knew whatever gossip Lenora had shared with her sister couldn't be good. As far as Naomi was concerned, Lenora couldn't tell anyone about her, since the two women had never shared a conversation.

"Pleased to meet you," Naomi said insincerely. But inside, she was fuming, and she wondered if Lenora was anything like her sister. If that was the case, Naomi wasn't impressed.

"Nay and I just finished warming up the food, and we're just about done. I thought we'd sit in the dining room, since it's large," Sarah told the women.

"That's fine with me," Glenda replied. She and Felicia headed to that room.

Sarah and Naomi made exaggerated faces at each other as the doorbell chimed again. Sarah said, "I'll get it."

After letting Reggie in the house, Sarah returned to the kitchen and said to Naomi, "Well, let's start taking this food into the dining room and get the meeting started." Sarah picked up the pan of beans.

Naomi had just finished putting the dessert on a platter, so she followed Sarah. When they entered the dining room, Fred had arrived. He walked over to his nieces, and after they set the dishes on the table, he gave them a big hug. "Nay, it's good to see you. It's been a long time. You're looking good, all grown up." Fred's eyes twinkled with merriment. He held up a bag containing a six-pack of beer. "Is it okay if I put this in the refrigerator?" he asked Daniel, who nodded. "Anybody want a can of beer before I put this in the fridge?" he asked. Glenda nodded that she wanted one.

Felicia went downstairs to the laundry room, and returned with TV trays, which she took into the den.

Then she and Glenda prepared plates of food for the boys.

Fred set two cans of beer on coasters on the table, and then he went to the kitchen and put the remaining cans of beer inside the refrigerator. He sat down on one of the twelve rattan-and-wood chairs at the dining-room table. Ernest stood in the media room in front of a dark cherrywood bar tucked into the corner of the room. The top of the bar was filled with bottles of alcohol. Ernest removed a crystal snifter from behind the bar and filled the glass halfway with Courvoisier. He walked into the dining room and sat down.

Ernest looked at Naomi and asked curiously, "Who are you?"

"I'm Daniel's youngest daughter, Naomi. Who might you be?" Her eyes flickered over Ernest's big belly, which made him look as though he was pregnant. Then she looked upward to the stern demeanor on his bearded face.

"I'm Lenora's father, Ernest Johnson." He sipped the amber alcohol and set the snifter on the table.

Naomi refused to say "pleased to meet you" to the unkemptly dressed man. Instead, she nodded. When Glenda and Felicia returned to the room, Naomi furtively studied her father's in-laws.

"The boys seem to be doing better today than the last time I saw them," Glenda told Daniel as she picked up the can of beer from the table. She popped the lid and sipped the foamy brew.

"Yeah, they are," Daniel admitted. "Sarah being here was a big help." He flashed a grateful look at his daughter.

"Why don't we go ahead and eat, then we can talk," Sarah proposed. Everyone agreed. After everyone was seated, Sarah blessed the food, and everyone began eating.

Before everyone had almost finished, Naomi went into the kitchen and brought out the dessert and put it on the table.

"The dessert was good, Sarah," Felicia said as she took a second red velvet cupcake and placed it on a paper plate.

"Thank you. My daughter made them." Sarah smiled.

Ernest poured himself another snifter of cognac. He took a sip, looked at Daniel, and asked, "So whatcha gonna do, old man?"

Daniel looked pensive; then he answered. "I think I'm going to keep the boys with me. I haven't figured out how I'm going to do it. I just think its best that the three D's," his voice choked, "stay with me."

Thank you, Lord. Sarah's face radiated approval at her father's decision. She clasped her hands together tightly in her lap.

"Are you sure you're up to keeping them boys?" Ernest asked. He looked disgruntled by Daniel's decision. "You ain't no spring chicken."

"Neither are you," Daniel shot back. "And yes, I'm one hundred percent sure about my decision. They need to be with one parent; and since Lenora has seen fit to remove herself from being a wife and a mother, I guess I'm it."

"Daniel," Felicia began. Her eyes flew to her husband, and then back to her brother-in-law. "Reggie and I really don't mind keeping the boys. Are you sure you don't want to reconsider your decision? You seemed so indecisive about keeping them when we talked about it the last time we were here." She dabbed at her mouth with a napkin.

"I've had some time to think about it, and I know keeping them with me is the right decision. I'm just hoping you all will be around for support when I need it." Daniel dipped his head humbly.

"Shoot, man, you can barely walk, and I'm supposed to think you can chase behind them boys. You on some bs. I think you just trying to get paid. I know Nora left plenty of money to take care of the boys." Ernest drained the glass of cognac and stared at Daniel contemptuously. His lips curled into a sneer. Glenda looked at him warningly and shook her head.

"There isn't anything left for me to get paid with," Daniel admitted, agonized. "Nora took most of the money with her when she went to Nevada. At least I think that's where the money went." He looked down at his plate sitting before him.

The boys came running into the room and ran over to Glenda. "Grammy, we're thirsty. Can we have something to drink?" Damon asked.

Glenda picked up a can of unopened Pepsi and began to open it.

"I don't think they need caffeine this late in the evening," Sarah began. "They'll be bouncing off the walls later. I'll get them some milk." She stood up and walked toward the kitchen.

"I don't see nothing wrong with them drinking some pop. That's what they used to," Glenda objected. "Shoot, Nora used to give it to 'em all the time. And if they momma did, then it's okay with me."

"Grammy," Damon whined, "I don't want milk. I want pop! Mommy gave us pop." He screwed up his face.

Sarah stopped in her tracks and turned back to the living room. "Daddy, what do you think?" she asked sweetly.

"Milk it is," he declared. Sarah continued walking into the kitchen.

"I don't want milk!" Damon shrieked, and his brothers joined him in his outburst. They all began stomping their feet.

"Stop that noise," Daniel ordered his sons harshly. The boys ignored him, and they kept on yelling at the top of their lungs.

"I said stop it!" Daniel banged on the top of the table. His sons stared at him wide-eyed and stopped yelling.

Glenda and Felicia leaped from their seats. Glenda hugged Damon, while Felicia did likewise to the twins.

"Do you have to be so hard on them?" Glenda railed.

"Please, I don't want you trying to undermine my authority when I'm disciplining the boys, Glenda," Daniel said through clenched teeth.

"I know you ain't trying to tell me what to do." Glenda rolled her eyes at Daniel as she patted Damon's back.

"Yeah," Ernest retorted, stumbling a bit as he jumped up from his chair, "don't talk to my wife like that." He pointed his finger at Daniel.

"I don't think we should be acting like this in front of the children," Sarah pleaded with the Johnsons. "We should be showing them a united front." She turned her attention to her scowling half brothers. "Now, boys, your choices are milk or water. Which one do you want?" She put three plastic cups on the table.

The twins looked at Damon, who said, "We'll take milk." Sarah filled the cups with milk. The boys drained the glasses, and then began running down the hallway to the den.

Sarah called out, "No running in the house. . . ." Her voice trailed off behind them.

With amused expressions on their faces, Naomi and Fred had watched the interaction among Daniel, the children, and his in-laws. Fred winked at his niece. Naomi bit her lip to keep from laughing aloud.

"Ernest, I'm ready to go home," Glenda asserted. "Obviously, we aren't needed here." She sniffed like her feelings were hurt.

"Yeah, I'm ready to blow this joint too." Ernest stood up and tottered before regaining his balance. "I guess you gonna have to drive home, Glen," he told his wife, fumbling in his pocket for the car keys.

"Y'all got some food left over?" Glenda asked, shooting Daniel a surly look.

"There's a little bit left. You're more than welcome to it," Sarah said amiably. "Follow me to the kitchen."

"I'm going to the bathroom," Ernest said as he stumbled to the powder room off the kitchen.

"I guess we'll be leaving too. I'm sorry about the way my parents acted," Felicia had the grace to say as she rose from her seat. "They're just upset about Nora's leaving, and don't know how to express themselves. I think you're making the right decision. If you need Reggie and me to help you in any way, just give me a call. In fact, I'm keeping Kente tomorrow night; Quita has to work. The boys are more than welcome to join us."

"Thank you, Felicia," Daniel remarked. "I appreciate your offer, and I may take you up on it. I'll give you a call tomorrow morning."

Reggie stood up too. "Take care of yourself, Daniel." Then he headed toward the door.

Felicia told Fred it was nice seeing him again. Glenda and Ernest returned from the bathroom and kitchen; after telling the boys good-bye, the Johnson family departed.

"I don't think that went too bad," Daniel said, looking at his family sitting around the table.

"You think?" Naomi replied derisively. She got up from her chair and began clearing the table.

Daniel shrugged. "It could have been worse. Ernest is nothing pretty."

"You're right about that." Naomi laughed. Everyone joined her, and the mood lightened in the dining room.

"Daddy, if you decide to let the boys go to Felicia's house tomorrow, you can join us for dinner tomorrow at my house." She held out her hand, and then pointed to Fred. "Uncle Fred, if you aren't busy, you're more than welcome to come too," Sarah said.

"Naw, I couldn't do that." Daniel shook his head from side to side.

"I don't see why not. It will just be the family and Aunt Alice," Sarah informed him.

"We'll see." Daniel rubbed his chin thoughtfully as a lightbulb went on inside his head. "Maybe I will."

Chapter Seventeen

While the Wilcox and Johnson families were departing from Daniel's house, Alice and Ruth were sitting in Alice's breakfast nook, rehashing the happenings of their day. Ruth filled Alice in about the financing meeting.

"You know, Sarah and Naomi are at Daniel's house participating in the family meeting," Ruth commented. "Sarah has been working on Daniel all week, trying to persuade him to keep custody of the boys."

"I know. Fred went there too, to give Daniel moral support," Alice replied. They had just finished the dinner Ruth had prepared. Stir-fry chicken and a baked potato for herself, and chicken soup for Alice. They were sipping on sweetened raspberry tea.

"I brought fresh strawberries for dessert, if you can keep them down. I know the medication you're taking sometimes makes you nauseous," Ruth said, rubbing her hands together. She stood up and removed the strawberries from the refrigerator. She put some inside a bowl, sprinkled sugar on them, and poured a little milk on them. "Do you need anything?" she asked.

"No, I'm good," Alice replied. "You told me all about the meeting at church, but you didn't say anything about your lunch date with Aron. What are you waiting for? Give me the gossip, girl."

Alice's remark caused Ruth to throw back her head and laugh. Alice sounded just like she did when the two were teenagers. Ruth put a strawberry in her mouth, chewed, and swallowed it.

"Well, it's not too much to tell you," Ruth said artlessly as she laid her fork on the side of the plate.

"You've been grinning like the cat that ate the canary since you got here. So don't even try to insult my intelligence by saying there's nothing to tell me," Alice twitted her friend.

"I had a really good time, Allie. Aron is a true gentleman. He was gallant, opening and closing the car door for me, and pulling out my chair when we went inside Izola's. The conversation was good, like it always is. I enjoyed myself," Ruth confessed. "Listen to me, I sound like a young girl."

"No," Alice corrected her friend, "you sound like someone who is long overdue in meeting someone who treats you nicely."

"It's a bit early for you to say that." Ruth picked up another strawberry and popped it into her mouth.

"Girl, please. You know you want to see that man. Who are you trying to fool?"

"You're right." Ruth exhaled loudly. "I'm not fooling anyone except myself. On the one hand, it feels weird, seeing and talking to another man, after being with Daniel for more than half my life. And then on the other hand, I am truly enjoying myself. Aron and I talk on the telephone almost every evening, so we're really getting to know each other."

"You need to discard the last piece of your emotional baggage," Alice advised. "Take it to the Salvation Army and leave it there. Daniel moved on, and it's time you did the same."

"My head knows what you're saying is right, but my heart is scared." Ruth looked at Alice with a frightened look on her face.

Alice grinned and patted her friend's hand. "It's going to be all right. From what you told me, Aron sounds intriguing."

"He is. Did I tell you he brought me a yellow rose? He said it was to cement our growing friendship."

"He sounds like a keeper," Alice observed. "Just what you need to help you erase that scar Daniel left on your heart. I think you should give Aron a chance, and please don't make the mistake of comparing him to Daniel. God broke the mold when he created Daniel Wilcox Sr."

The laughter of the women filled the air. Ruth wiped her eyes. "Thank God for that favor."

"Amen to that. I'm really glad you're giving Aron a chance. He can't be any worse than those guys you've dated in the past."

"He's much better. We click on some level. We have a vibe going on."

"That's great, Ruth. Just give the relationship time, and, most of all, enjoy yourself, because tomorrow is not promised."

"Is that the advice you gave yourself when you decided to see Fred?" Ruth probed.

"I didn't really have to. Fred is good people, and I could immediately sense the change in his attitude from when we were younger."

"Good for you. You've always been a strong person, much stronger than me."

Alice threw back her head and laughed. "You're just a late bloomer. You're going to be fine. So, are you picking up Queen tomorrow for dinner? Do you want me to ride to the home with you?"

"Yes, to all of the above. Her doctor approved my request for an overnight stay. So she'll spend the night with me. Oh, I forgot to mention Brother Duncan crashed the finance meeting. Calvin Layton was beside himself. He felt Brother Duncan didn't observe the proper protocol."

"What did Brother Duncan want?" Alice asked.

"I'm not sure," Ruth replied thoughtfully. "He implied something to the effect that he had something to give me or tell me that could help the church's finances."

"What did you tell him?" Alice asked after she sipped from her cup of tea.

"June shuffled him out of the meeting so quickly that I barely had a chance to respond to what he was trying to tell me. June said she was going to set up an appointment for him to come and see me next week."

"So, did Sarah give you the 411 on Naomi's friend? What did she think of him?" Alice asked eagerly.

"Naomi left me a voice mail, telling me they had arrived safely in Chicago. I thought about stopping over at Sarah's house after the meeting at church; but when I called, Brian told me they had left to go to Daniel's house. So I don't know anything, I'm clueless. But I guess I'll find out tomorrow."

"If Nay has found a good man, then I'll tell her, like I tell you, more power to her." Alice picked up her glass and indicated she wanted Ruth to do the same. They clinked their glasses together. "Who knows, this may be a breakout year for Nay, you, and me."

"We'll see," Ruth said evasively. "I think I'm going to head home. I need to make a pot of greens for Sarah's house tomorrow, and I want to get started on them tonight."

"You could have brought them over, and I would have helped you pick them," Alice said.

"That's okay. I thought Fred might be coming over here."

"Actually, he should be here soon. He said he was going to stop by after he left Daniel's house. You can bring the greens over here, and we can both get the info on what happened at the big family meeting."

"You know what, I don't know if I even want to know what happened at Daniel's house. I offered up a prayer for him and his family before I left church, and that's all I feel obligated to do," Ruth said emphatically as she stood up.

The doorbell rang.

"I'll get that," Ruth said. "I bet that's Fred. I'm going to head home, and I'll see you in the morning. I plan to leave for the North Side around noon."

Alice protested that she didn't have to go. Still, Ruth walked to the foyer and opened the door. She wasn't surprised to see Fred standing before her.

"Hey, sister," he greeted Ruth, and then gave her a hug.

"Hi, Fred. How are you doing?" she asked.

"Not bad. Are you running off so soon? You don't have to leave on my account," he said.

"I know, but I have some things I need to do before I go to bed tonight. Queen will be home for an overnight visit tomorrow. So I need to change the linen in my guest bedroom, along with other chores."

"How is she doing?" Fred asked politely. He shifted his weight from one leg to the other. He was dressed casually in denim jeans and a red-and-blue Bulls sweatshirt.

"About the same. She has good days and bad," Ruth told him.

"You have a good evening. Oh, I saw Nay at Daniel's house. She looked really good. It's funny how much she looks like Daniel," Fred said.

"She always did." Ruth nodded. "Alice!" she yelled. "I'll see you tomorrow."

Alice walked from the kitchen into the foyer. "You know that you can hang out with us if you want to," she told Ruth.

Ruth didn't miss the doting look the couple exchanged. Ever since Ruth knew the true nature of their relationship, Alice and Fred had looked relaxed and happier.

She shook her head. "I'm good. I have things I need to do," she told them. "You guys be good." She walked outside the door and across the hallway to her apartment. Alice closed her door when she heard Ruth lock her door.

Ruth walked into the kitchen, where she checked her telephone messages and flipped through the mail. She sighed heavily, trying hard not to feel jealous of Alice and Fred's relationship. She went into her bedroom to change clothes, when her telephone rang. She turned around and snatched the phone off the nightstand and clicked it on.

"Hello," she said. Her lips curved into a smile.

"Hello, Ruth. Did I catch you at a bad time?" Aron asked. "I know I said I wouldn't call you tonight, but my day wouldn't be complete without talking to you one more time."

"Not at all," Ruth replied. She sat on the side of the bed and removed an earring from her ear. She swung her legs onto the bed, and then talked to Aron for two hours. When they finished the conversation, Ruth had a satisfied expression on her face, and Aron had accomplished his goal. Ruth had agreed to a date with him the following Friday evening. Ruth yawned and decided to prepare the greens on early Saturday.

Ruth rose from her bed early the following morning, knelt next to it, and prayed earnestly that the day would go well for her family, and that Queen Esther would be in a coherent state of mind. She also asked the Savior to bless the finance committee to come up with ideas that wouldn't be too painful to the church's ministry. She put the meat into a pot to cook with the greens. Then she picked and washed the greens. Before long, the vegetable was cooking.

She dressed casually in jeans, and a royal blue T-shirt that read *Crusader for Christ* in gold letters. It was a relic from a fund-raiser that one of the clubs at The Temple had sponsored. Ruth walked out of her bedroom to the spare bedroom down the hall and worked out on her treadmill.

After she had showered and changed into her clothes for the day, Ruth checked her appointment book. She saw that she had an appointment with her hairstylist at nine o'clock that morning, which she had forgotten about. She went into the kitchen and turned on her coffeemaker. While the java was brewing, she put a pot of water on the stove to boil.

She sat on a chair and ate a container of key lime yogurt and drank a cup of coffee. When the water began to boil, Ruth put smoked meat inside the pot. She wiped her hands on a dishrag, and took the cordless phone off the base and dialed Sarah's number.

"Hi, Momma. How are you feeling this morning?" Sarah asked after she answered the telephone.

"Blessed to see another day. How are you feeling?" Ruth replied.

"I'm doing good. I'm looking forward to the family dinner evening. All that's missing is DJ and his family. I talked to him and Chelsea this morning."

"I take it they're doing well?" Ruth inquired.

"Yes, they are. I told DJ since the weather has broken, maybe Brian, the kids, and I will drive to Atlanta to visit them for a weekend."

"That was a nice gesture. I'm sure they will appreciate it."

"How did the finance committee meeting go?" Sarah asked.

"We didn't get as much accomplished as I would have liked. So we're going to meet in another week or so, with recommendations from the committee," Ruth admitted.

"Sometimes progress is slow. But as long as the end result is good, we just have to be patient."

"You're right. So what's new with you?" Ruth asked her daughter.

Sarah scratched the side of her head. "We had a good dinner with Naomi and her friend. His name is Montgomery. I think you're going to be surprised when you meet him."

"Why? Is something wrong with him?" Ruth asked tensely. Her maternal instincts had kicked in, like antennae had sprouted from her head.

"No, he's a very nice man," Sarah reassured her mother. "I'm pretty sure you'll like him. While Naomi and I went to Daddy's house, Brian hung out with Montgomery, and Brian had good things to say about him after I got home."

"That's good. Naomi bringing home a man is a first. I can't wait to meet him. So, did things go well at your father's house?" Ruth couldn't stop herself from asking.

"God does answer prayer. Dad decided to keep the boys. Praise the Lord. He still needs to work out some logistics. Felicia called me this morning and asked if Brian and I would help her and Reggie pay for Ms. Lewis, the nanny, to come back and help Daddy. He had to let her go when Lenora left."

"That was generous of her, as well as a good suggestion," Ruth said.

"Trust me, it was, because Felicia could have easily suggested her mother help Daddy. I don't think Glenda and Ernest are going to be pleased with Felicia's suggestion. She seems to be the only one with sense in that family. When you're together with all of them, they are a trip," Sarah went on. "That's the God's honest truth."

"I know Daniel was glad that you and Naomi came to his house for moral support. Fred came by Alice's last night, and I'm sure she'll call or come over later to give me the juicy details."

"Uncle Fred has been to see Daddy a couple of times. I'm glad he and Daddy are mending their relationship. I have a feeling, with Lenora out of the picture, things may settle down more normally. How was your lunch date with Mr. Reynolds?" Sarah asked.

"It went very well. I had a great time. He called me yesterday and asked if I would have dinner with him Friday, and I told him that I would. Aron seems to be such a good guy, I just couldn't say no to him. His motives seemed so sincere and complimentary. But I'm still a little shaky about how the church would perceive my relationship with him."

"Well, good for you," Sarah said enthusiastically. "It's about time you had a good time on a date. It's been too long."

"We had lunch at Izola's Restaurant, and I enjoyed myself so much that I was almost late coming back to The Temple," Ruth admitted, her face glowing with happiness.

She took a fork from a drawer and poked at the smoked meat, which was just about done. She would add the greens when she got off the phone.

"That's good. Mr. Reynolds is all right with me. What do you like about him?" Sarah couldn't stop herself from asking the question.

She didn't have many happy memories of her mother and father's marriage. When Daniel philandered, he always stayed away either Friday or Saturday night, and would return at all hours of the morning.

"What I like about Aron"—Ruth's words seemed to stream from her mouth—"is that he's comfortable to be with, like lying against a father's chest as he reads you a story. And he makes me laugh. Aron has such a droll sense of humor. Most of all, he sees me as a woman, and finds me attractive. Something I haven't felt secure about for a long time."

If Sarah was shocked by her mother's admission, she didn't let on. She loved her mother dearly, and only she and Alice knew how much Ruth had suffered when Daniel left her for Lenora. Before Bishop had visited Ruth to comfort his daughter, Sarah had feared for her mother's sanity. Then Ruth brought her brother, Ezra, home to stay with her before he died, and the bond with the siblings was reestablished, and Ezra did much to restore his sister's self-esteem. No one was happier than Sarah and Alice when Ruth received her calling.

Sarah giggled when she thought about how shocked her father would be to learn he had competition. Sarah didn't miss how he drilled her about her mother so many times; she knew her father missed her mother, but he was too proud or stubborn to admit it.

"Momma, I'm happy for you. I just hope you won't let what people might say interfere with a possible relationship. Mr. Reynolds paid his debt to society, enough said," Sarah proclaimed.

"I wish everyone were as open-minded as you are," Ruth told her daughter.

"I think more people are than you think. Just don't think so much, and go with the flow," Sarah advised. "So what time do you think you'll be over?"

"The greens are cooking. When they're done, I'm going to get my hair done and then pick up Queen. After that, I'll head your way," Ruth replied.

"Brian or I can pick up Queen if you like. Saturdays are usually busy at hair salons, so who knows what time you'll get out of there? Oh, I invited Uncle Fred to dinner. He said he may stop by," Sarah informed Ruth. She didn't mention that she had invited Daniel, because she assumed he didn't plan to attend.

"That would be a big help for me if you can pick up Queen. Your inviting Fred to dinner is no problem."

"Okay, Momma, I'll see you later. If anything changes, I'll let you know."

"Thank you, Sarah. I appreciate you picking up Queen, and I'll see you later."

When Ruth estimated the greens were done, she took a fork and tasted them. They were perfect. She let them cool off, and then she poured them inside a bowl. She lined the top of the bowl with foil paper and put it inside a large plastic bag; then she placed the bag in the refrigerator. Afterward, she rushed from the house to the garage, heading to the hair salon. Ruth's spirits were high; she hummed as she drove. She could hardly wait to see Naomi and meet her beau.

The weather was sunny and mild in Chicago for April. The temperature was in the high fifties, without a cloud in sight. It was one o'clock in the afternoon, and Naomi and Montgomery were sitting in a restaurant in Oak Lawn by the window, admiring the weather while enjoying cups of espresso. Naomi had gone to a local salon for a manicure and pedicure earlier, and the couple had gone shopping afterward.

"That's one thing I like about Edwardsville," Naomi remarked as she set her teacup in the saucer. "The weather is much milder than it is here. I have to admit I don't miss Chicago winters at all."

Montgomery was perusing the *Chicago Tribune* newspaper, and he looked up at Naomi and said, "Huh?"

"I was just saying how nice the weather is today," Naomi replied.

"It is. I mean, I hear you talk all the time about the Chicago winters, and how spring is nonexistent, but it doesn't seem bad here at all."

"Trust me, we got lucky. It will probably be snowing here next week."

The waiter returned to the table and asked if he could get them anything else. Montgomery requested another cup of tea. The waiter returned to the table a few minutes later.

"So, do I need to be concerned about any of your relatives? Will there be anyone at dinner that could be deemed overly racist?" he asked, looking at Naomi.

Naomi's eyes dropped to the table. She took a deep breath. "Well, one person comes to mind, my grandmother, Queen Esther."

Montgomery's eyebrows rose. "Queen Esther? Is that a family name?" He put two teaspoons of sugar into the cup and stirred it.

"Not really. It's more like a Southern name. She is quite the character," Naomi confessed as she held up her hand. "I can't be responsible for anything that might come out of her mouth."

"Then I have to make sure I'm on my best behavior around her, won't I?" Montgomery said jokingly. He lifted his cup and sipped from it.

"Queen is the most complex woman I've ever known in my life. She's an attractive woman, and she has always been concerned about how people perceive her and my family. Her attitude caused me a great deal of angst when I was younger. I was brought up to believe my family was perfect." Naomi wrinkled her nose. "Everyone that is, except for my father. I have managed to accept him for who he is."

"I know," Montgomery murmured. "You've told me about your dad. I know you've had issues with him."

Naomi nodded contemplatively. Issues didn't even begin to describe her rocky relationship with Daniel.

"I just wish you had told your folks that I'm white," Montgomery commented.

"Looking back in retrospect, I wish I had too. But it's too late now. They'll just have to deal with it. I'm sure everyone will be cordial. I can't speak for Queen, though. Anything might come out of her mouth."

"Brian and Sarah seem like good people. I enjoyed my time with them yesterday. I thought Brian was a wee bit overprotective of you, though. Your niece and nephew are wonderful kids. Brian showed me tapes of Josh playing basketball, and I must say he has skills."

"He takes after Brian," Naomi said. "Brian used to play basketball in high school. He was truly a jock. Had he not injured his leg his first year of college, he might have played at the professional level."

"It's good he can share that love for sports with his son."

"As far as Brian being overprotective, there is a reason for that, and I probably should have told you before today." Naomi began fidgeting; her hands shook slightly. She clasped them together.

"What's that?" Montgomery closed the newspaper, folded it in half, and gave Naomi his full attention. He had a neutral expression on his face.

"Do you remember commenting on how much Maggie and I look alike?" Naomi ventured. She couldn't get her conversation with Sarah about keeping secrets from Montgomery off her mind. Naomi agreed Sarah was correct, so she decided to reveal her most painful secret with her fiancé before dinner. Another factor was Queen Esther's senility. Naomi shuddered to think what might come out of her mouth.

Montgomery nodded and he pushed the cup and saucer away from him.

"Well, there's a reason for that. You see, Sarah and Brian are my biological parents. Ruth and Daniel, my grandparents, raised me." Naomi felt mortified, but also a sense of relief at the same time.

Montgomery's eyes searched Naomi's face and then fell back down to the table. He opened and closed his mouth; then he licked his lips. "I didn't expect you to say that. I'm speechless. How did that happen?" He didn't miss the expression of misery that coated Naomi's face. He reached across the table and grabbed her hands.

"The usual way," Naomi quipped, on edge. She tapped her foot nervously on the floor under the table. "Sarah and Brian have liked each other since elementary school. Then when my mom and dad started having problems, Sarah began sneaking around to meet Brian. Then she became pregnant, and at Queen's urging, Sarah said she'd been raped. I know that situation doesn't show my family in a good light; still, everyone is cool, and Queen, well, she's just Queen."

Montgomery shook his head in disbelief. "What kind of person tells a child to do something like that?"

"It's hard to explain. She's an older person from a different era, who was a minister's wife, and primarily concerned about what other people thought. I don't condone what Queen did. You have to know her, that's all I can say. She means well, but her execution is poor sometimes. The only person who could keep her in check was her husband, Bishop, and he barely could. Sadly, he passed years ago. He was a great man."

"That's unbelievable. How did you feel when you found out the truth? You don't appear to have a maternal relationship with Sarah. Is that by design?"

Naomi exhaled loudly; she felt almost giddy with relief. She had told Montgomery the truth about her parents, and he hadn't run from the table, appalled.

"I think Sarah would like us to have one, but Ruth is the mother who raised me and took care of me. She loves me unconditionally. I think it would kill her if she had to step back and assume the role of grandmother. I'm very close to her, and I will always think of her as my mother," Naomi said bluntly.

"That's good, and I'm glad you told me the truth. I guess Sarah must suffer because you don't acknowledge her as your mother?"

"She does, but that's the way it is. We were closer when I was younger, although I was always jealous of her. She was what I considered the perfect daughter. I will always love her as my big sister. And before you ask, Joshua and Maggie don't know about me being their biological sister. Sarah and Brian decided to wait and tell them when they get older."

"I hope they don't wait too long. Those types of situations have a way of blowing up in one's face," Montgomery murmured. He still wore a dazed expression on his face. He felt like he had been caught up in a whirlwind, and he still hadn't met Ruth or Daniel yet. "You know this doesn't change how I feel about you," he reassured Naomi.

She leaned across the table and kissed Montgomery softly on the lips. "I was praying to God that it wouldn't. I thank God every day for sending you into my life, Monty."

"I may not have been raised a preacher's kid, as you call it, Nay, but I think we were meant to be together. Call it karma or fate." Montgomery's British accent was so apparent.

"No, hon, our meeting was a blessing from God," Naomi said softly.

The waiter walked to the table and laid the check on top of it. He told them to have a good day.

Naomi looked at the thin gold watch on her wrist. "We need to get back to the hotel, I'd like to relax before we go to Sarah's house. I promise you this dinner will be one of those times that you won't ever forget," she informed her fiancé.

"That's assuming I survive it," he said. Montgomery reached into his pants pocket, took out his wallet, and removed an American Express card.

He helped Naomi put on her jacket and then put on his own. They walked to the cashier and Montgomery paid the check. After the bill was settled, they exited the restaurant and walked two blocks to his Jaguar.

Later on, when the couple departed for Sarah's house, Naomi was very nervous. It felt like someone was playing tennis inside her stomach. Her legs jiggled during the drive in the car.

Montgomery looked somber; a worry line creased his forehead. He knew he was in for yet another round of familial interrogations. He hoped the rest of the family would go easy on him. Most of all, Montgomery hoped that Naomi's mum wouldn't be too shocked when she met him. And more than that, that she approved of him.

Chapter Eighteen

Ruth and Sarah were transporting bowls and platters of food from the kitchen to the sideboard in Sarah's dining room. Maggie had just finished setting the table. The young girl put out the china that Sarah received as a wedding gift many years ago. She retrieved the gold silverware from the bottom of the buffet, along with crystal glasses from the cabinet. Occasionally Sarah liked preparing formal meals. Wilcox family dinners tended to run five to six hours.

The kitchen was warm, and the aromas mouthwatering. Sarah had baked a ham, along with roast chicken and stuffing. She'd also made green beans with white potatoes, and that, along with Ruth's mixed greens, and corn on the cob were her vegetable dishes. Maggie had prepared a casserole of multicheese macaroni and cheese and baked homemade rolls. Several pitchers of iced tea and lemonade were chilling in the refrigerator. Brian had put bottles of water in the cooler on the kitchen floor.

"Nana," Maggie said happily, "today feels like a holiday. We almost never have Sunday dinner on Saturday." She surveyed the table, and pulled down the corner of one of the linen napkins.

"Good job, Maggie," Ruth praised her granddaughter. "The table looks very nice." She took off the apron covering a black pantsuit and mustard-colored blouse. She wore an onyx bracelet on her wrist, which matched her earrings.

Alice and Fred sat in the living room, entertaining Queen Esther; Brian and Joshua were in the den watching a rare Bulls Saturday basketball game.

The house was full of life, much the way it had been when Ruth lived there.

The doorbell rang. "I'll get it," Maggie shouted. "I bet that's Nay and Montgomery." Her eyes shone in anticipation of seeing Naomi. Maggie's microbraids swung from side to side as she hurried from the room. The dark pants with a matching vest, along with a blue cotton top, were slimming on her plump figure.

"Momma, give me the apron so I can put it up," Sarah said, holding out her hand.

Ruth gave her the apron, and Sarah placed it on a clothing hanger inside the pantry. She ran her fingers through her hair as she and Ruth strode out of the kitchen, into the living room.

Naomi and Montgomery stood in the foyer, while Brian closed and locked the door. Maggie chatted happily with the couple. Ruth looked at her daughter and Montgomery, and did a double take. She then glanced to her left at Sarah, who wore an enigmatic smile on her face as she greeted the couple. Ruth shot Sarah a look that said, *"You could have told me."* Sarah shrugged her shoulders and telegraphed back, *"I'm sorry."*

Ruth regained her composure and walked over to Naomi. She put her arms around her daughter's body, and Naomi's arms snaked around her mother's upper arms.

Ruth pulled away and said, "Naomi, you look simply radiant" She turned to Montgomery. "And who is this young man?"

Naomi felt reassured by Ruth's reaction to her fiancé. She grabbed Montgomery's hand, and he walked up to Ruth. Naomi announced, "Momma, this is my fiancé, Montgomery Brooks."

"Hello, Mrs. Wilcox. I've heard nothing but good things about you from Naomi." He held out his hand and Ruth shook it. Her eyes swept over Montgomery.

"Hi, Montgomery, I wish I could say that Naomi had told me some things about you. I'm pleased to meet you," Ruth replied.

"Naomi could have handled things better," Montgomery agreed, nodding his head. "I just hope moving forward, we can get to know each other better."

The family moved from the foyer into the living room. Ruth thought that Naomi never looked lovelier. The cream-colored slacks and burgundy silk blouse complemented her figure.

"Where are Queen and Aunt Alice?" Naomi asked Sarah. She and Montgomery leaned comfortably against the back of the love seat.

As if on cue, Queen Esther walked into the room, flanked by Alice and Fred. The elderly woman leaned on Fred's arm, while walking with her mahogany cane. Her mouth curved into a smile as she spied Naomi.

She held out her arms and said, "Come here, baby girl, and give Queen a kiss."

Naomi sprang up from the love seat and walked over to Queen. She leaned down and enveloped her tiny grandmother in her arms and planted a big kiss on Queen's cheek.

"You look good, Naomi. Look like your momma isn't the only one who lost weight. I think you've lost a few pounds too," Queen said, admiring her granddaughter.

Naomi greeted Alice and Fred with hugs. Brian hurried to the basement and returned with folding chairs. Alice and Fred sat on the dining-room chairs, while Brian helped Queen Esther sit down on the sofa. He sat next to her.

Queen Esther looked around the room at her family members. "Bishop would be so proud that we're all dining here this evening. I wish he were here." She sniffled.

"He's here in spirit," Sarah pronounced. "Both he and Uncle Ezra."

Queen Esther noticed Montgomery and became agitated. She pointed her bony finger with her wedding ring at him. "Who is he?" She looked at Sarah and Brian. "Why is there a white man here? Is he a doctor? Is he here for me?"

Naomi shook her head. "No, Queen, that's my friend from school. His name is Montgomery. He came from Edwardsville with me to meet the family."

"A white man?" Queen spat. Her eyebrows knitted together in a flat line. "I don't know what you mean. Are you saying that you're friends with a white man? What kind of friends? I know your momma taught you better. I'm not having it." She stomped her cane on the floor.

"He's my—my fiancé. And he's a very nice man." Naomi's voice faltered. "He doesn't mean anyone any harm."

Ruth's breath caught in her throat when Naomi referred to Montgomery as her fiancé. The family barely knew the man, who, Ruth could see, was somewhat older than her daughter.

"Humph, he's white, isn't he? White men always mean harm to black women. Girl, he'll use you and toss you in the garbage like a dirty tissue." Queen Esther thumped her cane again.

"Queen, that's not true. We have been together for a long time. We love each other, and we're going to get married." Naomi's voice gathered strength.

"What have you got to say for yourself, young man?" Queen Esther asked Montgomery. "Did you ask Naomi's father for her hand in marriage like Bishop asked my papa? Can you support my granddaughter? How much money do you make?" She glared at Montgomery.

"No, ma'am. . . ." Montgomery's voice simply trailed off. He was taken aback by the furious rate at which the questions spewed from Queen's lips. "I didn't think it was necessary to ask for Naomi's hand in marriage, because today is a different era. Women tend to make those decisions for themselves. I will certainly talk to her father, if that's what Naomi wants me to do. I assure you, Madam Queen, that I'm in love with your granddaughter, and I can take care of her quite well. I own my own accounting firm." Montgomery answered her questions, one by one; Naomi sat beside him, petrified.

"Goodness gracious." Queen put her hand over her heart. "You talk funny too. Where are you from? Do you have a thing for black women? You couldn't find a white woman to marry?"

"I am from the U.K., I mean England." Montgomery's face burned a fiery red. The other family members looked on in amusement. "Yes, I could find a white woman, if I wanted. I do have a thing for one black woman, and that is Naomi Wilcox. I love her, and I plan to make her my wife."

Queen Esther's attention had drifted to Joshua. She said to him, with a hint of disdain in her voice, "Next thing we know, Josh will be bringing a Chinese girl home for his parents to meet." She lost her train of thought and snapped her lips shut. Her eyes became glazed. She looked at Naomi, confused, and said, "Ruth Ann? What have you done to yourself?"

Ruth stood up and walked over to her mother. "Queen, that's Naomi. I'm Ruth. It's all right."

Queen pointed at Naomi and said with a quavering voice, "But she looks like my Ruth Ann. I want Bishop. Where is he? Why isn't he here?" Tears sprinkled down her wrinkled cheeks.

Ruth made comforting noises as she talked to her mother.

"Perhaps we should eat," Sarah suggested helplessly. She shot Naomi and Montgomery a sympathetic look.

"That's a good idea," Brian seconded his wife. "I'll take the chairs back into the dining room and we can get started."

Brian and Fred returned the chairs to the dining room. When Fred returned to the living room, he whispered to Alice, "Some things never change. It's never a dull moment when this family gets together. You gotta love it."

Alice poked him in his ribs and whispered, "Be quiet." Her lips quivered as merriment danced in her eyes.

The family sat around the table. Brian sat at the head, and Sarah on the other end, with everyone else in between.

"Mother Ruth, would you bless the food?" Brian asked his mother-in-law.

Everyone grabbed the hand of the person sitting next to them.

"Gracious Father, we thank you for waking us up this morning and allowing us to see another day. Where would we be without your grace and mercy? We give thanks that on this day you have allowed our family to come together once again and spend time with one another. Thank you, Father, for bringing Naomi and Montgomery from Edwardsville to Chicago safely, and we ask that you grant them a safe journey home.

Lord, thank you for the food we are able to receive for the nourishment of our bodies through Christ. Father, bless the cooks. Amen."

The food sat on a long folding table placed on a wall in the dining room. Sterno heaters under the aluminum pans kept the food warm. The family rose from their seats and formed a line on either side of the table, where they ladled food onto their plates.

Ruth sat next to Queen and tried to coax her to eat, but Queen refused, saying the food was poisoned. Ruth explained that only family members had prepared the food, but the elderly woman wasn't having it.

"The food is exquisite," Montgomery remarked, pushing his chair away from the table. "My hat goes off to all the cooks in this family." After spying the desserts on top of the buffet, he smiled like he was in culinary heaven.

"We can all cook, except for Nay. Nana says Auntie Nay never liked cooking," Maggie piped up.

"I may have to send her back home so she can improve her cooking skills," Montgomery joked. The family laughed, even Naomi.

"Is anyone ready for dessert?" Sarah asked after she saw the empty plates on the table.

"Not yet," Brian groaned, pushing his chair away from the table. "I need time for my food to digest. I am so grateful to Aunt Alice for teaching Maggie to bake, especially red velvet cakes. It's been calling my name all day. And I plan to answer the call soon."

Fred rubbed his hands together. "Red velvet cake sounds good right about now. Why don't you bring me a piece, Sarah?"

"Does anyone else want dessert now?" Sarah inquired. Joshua and Maggie stated they wanted cupcakes, while Naomi and Fred requested cake. Sarah walked into the kitchen.

Maggie hopped up from her seat and said, "I'll go help, Mommy."

They returned from the kitchen minutes later. Maggie carried dessert plates, which she passed out, and Sarah brought a carafe of coffee and set it on the table.

"Queen, Maggie made your favorite, a red velvet cake. She used Alice's recipe. Do you want a piece?" Ruth asked her mother.

"No. Girl, they are trying to poison me at this house. I don't want anything to eat. You shouldn't eat either," Queen advised her daughter. She sipped from the cup of coffee, and her hand trembled.

The doorbell sounded, and Brian got up from his chair to answer it. "I wonder who that could be?" he remarked in a puzzled tone of voice as he strolled from the room.

Sarah peered guiltily at Ruth. "Well, the only other person I invited was Daddy. . . ." She shrugged her shoulders helplessly.

Chapter Nineteen

The sounds of rambunctious voices could be heard from the foyer. Brian returned to the room, with Daniel and his three sons in tow.

Maggie chimed out happily, "It's my little uncles and Gramps." She jumped from her seat and rushed over to them.

Ruth's hand fluttered to her throat. She peered at Daniel, and then down at her plate. Her body stiffened in annoyance, because Sarah forgot to mention Daniel might be attending.

Daniel cleared his throat. "I hope it's okay that we came. Sarah invited me yesterday, and I told her I wasn't sure if we would come or not; then I decided, why not? I haven't seen you all in a while."

Brian helped the boys remove their jackets, while Daniel removed his own.

"Sure, Daddy, you're welcome here anytime," Sarah replied graciously. Her eyes darted to her mother, who didn't look pleased by the new arrivals. "I'll fix a plate for you and the boys." She returned to the kitchen, while Maggie returned to the foyer and hung their jackets in the closet.

Daniel walked over to Naomi, leaned down, and kissed the top of her head. Then he said, "Hey, Alice, Queen, and Ruth, how have you ladies been doing?" His eyes lingered on Ruth's face. He thought she had never looked more attractive.

"Hi, Daniel, long time no see," Alice responded drily. She didn't miss Daniel's glance at Ruth.

Queen leaned over to Ruth and whispered loudly, "Who is that man?"

"That's Daniel, my ex-husband," Ruth whispered back. Clearly flustered, she anxiously tugged the chain of the necklace around her neck. She was surprised to see her ex-husband at the house they used to reside in together. "Hello, Daniel. Good to see you." She raised her eyebrows as he sat down across the table from her, next to Naomi.

"Well, if he's your ex-husband, then what is he doing here?" Queen asked querulously.

"Daniel has every right in the world to be here," Ruth answered her mother serenely. "He's still the father of my children and your grandchildren."

"Oh, he's the one who ran off with that floozy," Queen said, scowling at Daniel.

Damon's ears seemed to perk up when he heard the word "floozy."

"What's a 'floozy,' Pops?" he asked his father innocently. The twins stared at Queen in fascination, as if they had never seen someone that old.

Queen Esther yelled "boo" at them and all three boys jumped. Queen Esther laughed at them.

Sarah interjected quickly, "Josh and Maggie, why don't you take the boys in the kitchen and keep them company while they eat."

Daniel quickly explained to Damon, "That is another word for a funny lady. Go with Maggie and Josh. I bet Sarah has all kinds of good food in her kitchen to eat."

Josh sucked his teeth. He mumbled under his breath, "I always have to leave the room when something interesting happens." Brian shot his son a look that didn't brook any nonsense. Joshua put the napkin on the table; then he and Maggie shepherded the boys to the kitchen.

Naomi introduced Daniel to Montgomery. If he was shocked by her fiancé's race, he didn't let on. He knew in these days and times that interracial couples were more common. He knew it would take a special man to tame his stubborn child.

"Pleased to meet you, man." Daniel gave Montgomery a piercing look. "We'll have to talk later."

Montgomery nodded his head, and his Adam's apple bobbed up and down. Naomi squeezed his hand under the table encouragingly.

"I swear Sarah has the oddest people at her dinner table these days," Queen Esther complained as she looked at Alice. "She's got a white man here, and I know he's a doctor, trying to take me back to that place. And now Ruth's old husband, the biggest dog in Chicago, is here. Alice, don't think I don't miss you and Fredrick making goggle eyes at each other. Why, I swear it feels like the world has turned upside down. You all need prayer. I wish Bishop were here to straighten all of you out. Brian, help me to the bedroom. I'm tired and I want to lie down," she commanded.

Brian complied with her request. He escorted Queen Esther out of the dining room to his and Sarah's bedroom.

"Whew." Daniel's eyes fluttered upward. "I thought Sarah told me that Queen suffers from dementia. I swear, she hasn't missed a beat. Alice, will you cut me a piece of cake? I can see it's your specialty red velvet. I haven't had any in a long time."

Alice smirked. "The last time I checked my last name wasn't Wilcox. I suggest you get it yourself." She rolled her eyes at Daniel and folded her arms across her chest.

From years of being married to Daniel, Ruth almost stood and got a slice of cake for her ex.

Fred wiped his mouth and hands on the napkin and stood up. He walked around the table, picked up a plate, and cut a thin sliver of the cake. He bowed to his brother and handed him the plate.

Daniel smiled sheepishly and shrugged his shoulders helplessly. "Thank you, bro. I guess I could have gotten the cake myself."

"Just add it to my tab," Fred replied good-naturedly.

Alice glared at him; then she leaned over and whispered, "He *could* have gotten it himself."

Daniel polished off the cake quickly, as if he hadn't eaten in years. He laid the fork on the side of the plate and pushed the dish away from him. "Alice, you haven't lost your touch."

"Thank you, Daniel," Alice replied drily. "Give credit to Maggie, she made the cake. I'm surprised you graced us with your presence tonight. It's been what?" She held up her fingers as if counting. "Well, a long time."

"You're right," Daniel said, abashed. "There have been some major changes in my life, and there are some rights I need to wrong." He glanced at Ruth.

"Is that so?" Alice asked snidely. She picked up her glass of tea, with melting ice cubes, and sipped the brown liquid.

"Yes, it is," Daniel replied easily. "I'm working on getting myself together. I just have a lot going on right now."

"Well, do what you have to do," Alice said. She drained the remaining tea out of the glass and set it back on the table. She and Fred decided to relieve Brian from watching Queen Esther so he could enjoy time with the family.

Suddenly there was a ruckus coming from the kitchen. Sarah jumped from her seat and ran to the kitchen, with Daniel trailing behind her.

Damon wore an angelic expression on his face, while Darnell pointed to a broken bowl on the floor next to his brother's chair. "Damon pushed the bowl on the floor. And he did it on purpose," he said, tattling on his brother.

Sarah frowned. "Damon, why did you do that?" The bowl had belonged to Queen's mother, and was a family heirloom.

Maggie looked on, horrified. Joshua began picking up the shards of glass. He removed the broom from the pantry and swept up the tinier pieces.

Damon poked out his lips. "Because I wanted to, and I could," he answered.

"Damon, get your little butt over here!" Daniel roared. He clenched and unclenched his fists. "I swear, I can't take that boy anywhere."

"It's okay, Daddy," Sarah fibbed. She felt awful. Ruth had given her daughters many of Queen Esther's possessions when she was moved from her house to the home.

"Thank you for cleaning up the glass," Sarah told her son. "Why don't you and Maggie take the boys into the den to watch television now."

"Sure," Joshua responded. He put the broom and dustpan away. "Mom, is it okay if I go to Khalil's house later on? We planned to go see a movie."

"Not tonight, son," Sarah replied. "It's family night, and I'd prefer you stay home."

"Okay," Joshua said, swallowing his disappointment. "Come on, boys, let's go watch a DVD."

"Hold it right there, young man." Daniel grabbed Damon's arm. "You and I are going to the washroom for a talk first." He marched Damon to the powder room off the kitchen, and closed the door behind them.

Joshua, Maggie, David, and Darnell returned to the
den, where Joshua put a DVD into the player; the boys
sat, cross-legged, on the floor.

From the dining room, Ruth, Sarah, Brian, Naomi,
and Montgomery could hear Daniel's raised voice from
the powder room. They could also hear Daniel spanking his son, and Damon's yowls of protest.

A few minutes later, Daniel and Damon exited the
bathroom. Daniel warned his son, "Stay out of trouble.
You can go watch television with the other kids."

"I don't know where the room is," Damon replied,
with trembling lips.

"I'll show you," Sarah offered. She rose from her seat
and escorted the upset little boy to her den. She talked
to Damon quietly as they walked together.

Daniel turned his attention to Montgomery and queried him about his background. Naomi would interject
from time to time, and Daniel would inform her that
he was talking to Montgomery and not to her. Ruth
thought the Daniel sitting across the table from her
didn't sound like the old, feeble man Sarah had described to her.

When Daniel finished interrogating Montgomery,
Ruth couldn't help but say, "I thought you were broken
up with all the trouble you had going on in your life?
What brought about the change in your attitude?"

All eyes turned toward Daniel. He made eye contact
with everyone at the table. He wet his lips and spoke
softly. "Naomi, would you go get Alice and Fred? I have
something I need to say to the entire family."

Naomi left the room and returned with Alice and
Fred, who took seats at the table. Queen had fallen
asleep, so she would be okay alone for a short period
of time.

Daniel bit his lower lip, inhaled, exhaled, and then
spoke. "I owe everyone at this table an apology. I've

been a butthead, and I'm sorry for the way I acted. Ruth asked me a good question. What made me change my ways? And I want to answer it. I've had a long time, years to think about how my selfish actions affected my family, and how badly I treated everyone. I hurt all of you sitting around this table when I split up this family. I know that is not what I should have done as a man; and for that, I beg everyone's forgiveness."

Sarah looked at her father approvingly, like she wanted to believe everything he said. Everyone else looked at him skeptically, especially Ruth, like she had been there and done that.

Sarah had to stop herself from clapping and shouting "hallelujah." When she talked to Daniel during the week she had stayed at his house, she told him how important it was to take responsibility for his deeds and to atone for his in discretions by addressing those he had hurt. He sounded like he had taken her words to heart.

"If you're sincere, Daniel, then God will see you through this dilemma, and life will get better for you and your sons," Ruth felt compelled to say.

Daniel nodded at Ruth gratefully. "I hope so. I've taken God for granted, and it's time I stepped up to the plate and do things correctly, like I should have been doing all along."

He continued to speak as everyone listened. His voice would rise and fall emotionally and break at times. Everyone listened intently, drawing their own conclusions as to the change in Daniel Wilcox. There was a period of silence, and then the doorbell sounded. Brian again went to answer the door.

Sarah didn't mention inviting anyone else. All heads turned toward the door with anticipation in their eyes.

Chapter Twenty

Brian called from the foyer, "Sarah, its Monet Caldwell. She has that peach cobbler you asked her to bake for you."

"Coming." Sarah swatted her forehead and smiled apologetically at her relatives. "I've been so busy that I forgot I asked Monet to make a cobbler for dessert. I'll be right back."

Ruth's heart thudded. She wondered if Aron had come with Monet. Then she quickly pushed that thought back into the recesses of her mind. She had mentioned the dinner to Aron, so she assumed he probably wouldn't come with Monet, but she was wrong. Monet walked into the dining room, carrying a brown bag, while Aron trailed behind her, holding Faith by the hand.

"Hello, everyone," Monet said, grinning brightly. "I hope we're not interrupting dinner."

"You're right on time," Brian replied easily as he took the bag from Monet. "We just finished eating the main meal, and most of us are having dessert." He introduced Aron, Monet, and Faith to everyone. When Brian introduced Daniel as his father-in-law, Aron's senses were attuned to the man who used to be Ruth's husband.

Sarah retrieved the bag from Brian and laid the peach cobbler on the buffet with the other desserts. She sniffed deeply and said, "Monet, the cobbler smells heavenly. Would you all like to join us for dinner or dessert?"

Aron looked around the table and noticed how Daniel was staring at him. The men nodded at each other. He glanced at Ruth, as if to ask if he and Monet staying would be all right with her.

Ruth felt tongue-tied. "Hello, Aron," she finally managed to murmur.

With a smirk on her face, Sarah gazed at her mother. Alice had the same expression on her face. Daniel didn't miss the byplay, and his gaze returned to Aron.

"You know what? I think we'll pass on staying, Sarah," Monet answered, feeling awkward. "Marcus is home with the boys, and I know they must be driving him crazy right about now. Those sons of ours can be a handful sometimes." Her eyes flitted on her father.

Faith removed her hand from her grandfather's hand and walked around the table to Ruth. She threw out her arms. "Hi, Pastor Ruth," she said in her high-pitched little-girl voice.

Ruth gathered Faith into her arms and pulled her onto her lap. "How are you doing, young lady? You're getting so big." Ruth kissed her cheek.

"I've been good. I help my daddy take care of the boys, and when school starts in the fall, Mommy says I can go to kindergarten. I go to preschool now." Faith's nose crinkled. Her heart-shaped cinnamon face was all Monet, but her features were a carbon copy of her father, Marcus. She was a thin child, full of nervous energy. Her reddish brown hair was parted in the middle, and her long braids had come loose.

"That's wonderful. I know you can hardly wait to start school. You're such a good girl, helping your mommy and daddy with the boys," Ruth told Faith. "Monet, are you sure you all don't want to stay for dessert? We have plenty, more than enough to go around."

"Well, maybe we can stay for a few minutes," Monet conceded, looking at Aron, who nodded at his daughter.

Maggie walked into the room. "I'm the unofficial hostess, so I'll take your coats." She looked at Faith. "Would you like to come to the den with us kids? We're watching a movie."

"Yes." Faith hopped off Ruth's lap and followed Maggie to the foyer, where she hung up the coats, and then they went into the den.

Monet cut a slice of red velvet cake for herself, and a slice of chocolate cake for her father. Aron sat down next to Ruth.

"Your sermon last Sunday was simply rousing, Pastor Ruth," Monet said, sitting at the table. "We've heard some rumblings that the church is facing financial difficulties. Marcus and I will be more than happy to help in any way we can."

Ruth dipped her head. "Thank you. We're doing okay for now, but we need to make changes before we have problems. Any suggestions would be appreciated."

Monet sliced and chewed a piece of cake. She nodded. "We'll come up with something. A good many people are experiencing tough times."

"So, Mr. Reynolds, what do you do?" Daniel asked Aron. He felt annoyed that Aron was sitting across the table, next to Ruth.

"Actually, I work at the church as the maintenance engineer. And I'm active in my community. I also work part-time with the city, helping communities plant vegetable gardens. What do you do?"

"I'm retired." Daniel instantly dismissed Aron as being the object of Ruth's affections. The Ruth he knew would never date a janitor. Aron could call himself by any fancy title he chose, but the bottom line was that he was just someone who picked up after others.

"If it keeps you busy, then go for it. Like I said, I'm retired from the Chicago Transit Authority, as a bus driver and looking after my youngest boys," Daniel said.

Naomi, who was drinking water, nearly choked. Montgomery thumped her on the back. "Are you okay?" he asked.

Naomi nodded. *Same old Dad,* she thought, *always giving himself more credit than what is due.* She wiped her eyes with a napkin.

"That's good you're actively involved in your sons' lives. More than at any other time, children today need a parent's guidance. How old are your sons, Mr. Wilcox?" Aron asked.

"My oldest is eight, and I have twin sons. They're six. They're little rascals, and they keep me busy." Daniel puffed out his chest, as if to signal how potent he still was.

"My hat goes off to you." Aron dipped his head. "I have grandchildren younger than that, and the little ones can wear me out."

There were sounds of an altercation and then glass breaking from the den. Brian and Daniel jumped from their seats and rushed to the den, with Sarah hot on their trail.

Damon was on the couch and had David in a headlock. The younger boy's face was red and he was gasping. The lamp on one of the cocktail tables lay on the floor, and the bulb from the lamp lay in tiny pieces.

Daniel rushed to separate the boys, while Brian knelt down and picked up the pieces of glass. He glared at Joshua, who was on his cell phone. Joshua told whomever he was talking to that he had to go. He quickly disconnected the call.

"I thought you two were keeping an eye on the boys?" Brian asked his children.

"We were. Everything happened so fast," Maggie said, trying to explain.

"Damon, I thought I told you to behave," Daniel said to his son sternly, pulling the boys apart.

"I was acting good. David started it." Damon scowled at David, as if daring him to dispute his account of what had happened.

Darnell's thumb climbed into his mouth, but he pulled it out. "Pops, I don't feel too good." He promptly vomited on the floor.

Sarah rolled her eyes upward. "Come on, Darnell, let's go to the bathroom." She took his hand and led him out of the den to the powder room.

"Joshua, get some cleaning aids out of the kitchen and clean that up." Brian sucked his breath as he cut himself on a shard of glass.

"Do I have to?" Joshua complained. "I didn't do it. Why doesn't Gramps clean it up? Darnell is his son."

"Did you hear what I said?" Brian said to Joshua firmly and pointedly.

The young man walked out of the room with attitude in his step.

"Pops, I want to go home. I don't like this house, and I don't like these people. Why couldn't we go to Aunt Felicia's house? I didn't want to come here, anyway," Damon cried, sticking out his lip.

Brian took the broken glass to the kitchen, while Joshua returned with a pail of water and a rag. He knelt down on the floor and began cleaning up the vomit.

When Brian returned to the den, Daniel had taken his sons' jackets from the closet. "I think we're going to go home now. The boys are probably tired," he said.

Brian nodded and walked to the dining room with Daniel. Sarah returned to the dining room with Darnell.

"I think this little one has bad nerves. I gave him a bag; so if he feels sick on the way home, he won't mess up your car, Daddy," Sarah said.

"Thank you, Sarah," Daniel replied. "It was nice seeing everyone again," he told the family.

Queen Esther walked into the room, leaning heavily on her cane. "What was all that noise? I woke up and heard kids screaming, and it sounded like something got broken. Sarah, what kind of house are you running? In my day, children were seen and not heard. You might want to take note of that."

"I sure will," Sarah answered. She and Brian walked Daniel and his brood to the door.

Daniel stopped in his tracks and turned around. He said, "Ruth, would it be okay if I call you this week? I have something I want to discuss with you."

"Sure, you know the number at the church. Feel free to give me a call," Ruth replied.

Daniel smiled smugly, giving her a smile that would have melted her insides in the past. She wondered what Daniel wanted to talk about, and why he seemed to be paying her attention like he was romantically interested in her. She didn't miss the admiring glances he'd given her when he thought she wasn't looking.

Fred leaned over and whispered to Alice, "I think my brother is going to have to step up his game."

"I think your brother is out of his mind. There's no way that Ruth would ever contemplate a relationship with him. That ship has sailed," Alice said.

Monet's cell phone chirped. She stood up and went into the kitchen to take the call. When she returned, she remarked, "I think we'd better go too. Marcus has a meeting to go to later on. Sarah, thank you for sharing dessert with Dad and me. Mr. Brooks, it was nice meeting you," she said, glancing at Montgomery. "Naomi, it was nice seeing you again. Congratulations on your upcoming graduation."

Aron and Ruth stood up. "I'll get their coats," Ruth told Sarah. The three walked out of the room to the foyer. Monet stopped in the den to get Faith.

"I hope we didn't impose on private time with your family," Aron told Ruth as he slipped on his jacket.

"Of course not. As you could tell, it can get pretty hectic in my family. Sometimes it's like a three-ring circus," Ruth quipped. "It was good seeing you."

"You too, pretty lady. I look forward to seeing you tomorrow. I'll talk to you later."

Ruth looked down at her wrist. "I should be home in a few hours," she said, yawning. "It's been a long day. My mother is spending the night with me, and I'm taking her back to the home Monday morning. We were lucky; today was a partially good day. I spoke to her doctor a few weeks ago about changing her medication, which he did this week, and she seems to be responding to it very well." She crossed her fingers.

"Great, anything that makes your life easier makes me happy." His caring hazel eyes seemed to hypnotize Ruth. He had to stop his hand from caressing her cheek.

Ruth blushed. Then she noticed Sarah and Monet standing in the living room, chatting, giving them time to talk. They noticed a lull in the conversation and walked toward the foyer.

Monet walked into the den and returned with her daughter. "I wasn't ready to go, Mommy, I'm having a good time. The movie isn't over yet," Faith whined.

Monet put one of Faith's arms into her jacket. "I'll rent it and you can finish watching it at home. Tell Pastor Ruth good-bye," she said.

"Wait a minute," Faith said, "I have to tell everybody else good-bye." She skipped into the dining room, her braids swinging in rhythm, where she courteously told the adults good-bye. Then she went back to the den to say her farewell to Maggie and Joshua.

When she returned to the foyer, she took Aron's hand. "I'm ready, Mommy. Oh, I forgot to tell Pastor Ruth good-bye."

Ruth bent down and hugged and kissed Faith. "Tell Marcus I said hello, and kiss those babies for me," she told Monet.

"I will." Monet and Faith walked outside the door.

Sarah headed back to the dining room, while Aron paused and turned around before he stepped over the threshold. "Take care, Ruth, talk to you later," he said.

"You too," Ruth said, with a smile on her face. She closed the door, locked it, and strolled back into the dining room. All eyes honed in on her. "What?" she asked, returning to her seat. "Why is everyone staring at me?"

Everyone was quiet, until Naomi stood up and did a little cabbage patch dance. "Momma's a player. She got two men after her. You go, girl." She and Sarah exchanged high fives. The room erupted in laughter.

"What does Naomi mean? How is Ruth a player? She can't be a player, or whatever you called her. My girl is a pastor." Queen Esther looked confused.

"Don't worry, Queen, it's all good." Naomi folded her arms across her chest.

Ruth sputtered, "I don't know what you mean. I don't have anyone after me." She held up her hand and shook her head furiously.

"It's all good, Momma. I'm proud of you. It's about time you got your groove on. Mr. Reynolds still got it going on for an older man. He's cute," Naomi said.

"For someone who's about to get their master's degree, you can be silly at times," Ruth said crossly. "Sarah, let's straighten up. I know Queen is probably getting tired, and I want to get her home and settled."

"I'm not tired." Queen's jowls shook as her head flipped from side to side. "What did Naomi mean about you getting your groove on? Ruth Ann, you and I are going to have a talk when we get to your house."

Everyone laughed. Except for Bishop and Ezra not being present, it felt like old times.

Alice stood up. "I'll help you clean up. Then Fred and I are going to go. I had a wonderful time, Sarah. You put on a pretty decent spread, but not as good as me and your mother."

Sarah cracked up and began stacking the plates.

Maggie came into the dining room. "The movie is over. Do you need me to do anything, Mommy?" she asked.

"No, Maggie. You were a big help to me earlier. It's nearly six thirty, Why don't you relax now. I hope you finished your homework."

"I did, but I'll check it again later. I have a history test on Monday, and I'll study some more before the weekend is over." She went upstairs to her bedroom to call one of her friends.

While the men went into the den to see if a sporting event was on television, Sarah, Ruth, Naomi, and Alice quickly and efficiently removed the food from the dining room and began putting the leftovers in bowls.

Naomi scraped the plates and put them in the dishwasher. "So, Momma," she sneaked a peep at Ruth, "what do you think of Montgomery?"

"He seems like a nice man. Of course, I'm going to need time to get to know him better. You could have warned us that he was white. Not that it would have made any difference," Ruth added quickly.

"I didn't think it would." Naomi put detergent into the dishwasher slot.

"I want you to be happy and have a good life, and if Montgomery makes you happy, then I'm happy for you. Somehow, I didn't picture you with an older man from another country. I always assumed you would date men closer to your own age, a year or two age difference."

"I think that's what attracted me to him. He wasn't like the men I'd been dating. He was a refreshing change. We met at the car wash, of all places. He invited me to have a latte with him, and we've been talking since then." She reached inside her blouse and pulled out her engagement ring. She put it on her finger and waved her hand. "Monty and I are engaged. I wanted you to meet him before I told you the news." Naomi looked at Ruth with a beseeching expression. Though she talked a good game, Naomi really craved her mother's sanction of her impending marriage.

The women surrounded Naomi and they all hugged. Ruth's eyes filled with tears.

"You've really been holding out on us, Naomi. Congratulations. I hope you haven't already set a date without talking to us first," Ruth said.

"We haven't. I want to get graduation out of the way, and then we'll visit the topic. Monty doesn't want to wait too long. He's thirty-five years old, and says he doesn't want to be ancient before having children."

Ruth swallowed a lump in her throat, Alice's eyes were moist, and Sarah just took in the scene. Naomi had come so far and seemed to be doing fantastic.

"I'm so proud of you, Naomi. I know Bishop and Ezra would be too." Ruth brushed away a tear from her eye.

"Hear, hear. Ditto that for me. I can't believe you're the same little girl who didn't seem to have much direction in life. Look at you now," Alice added admiringly.

Sarah stood back and watched her mother and Alice heap praise upon Naomi. She knew then in her heart that Naomi was her mother's child, and not her own. The deception had begun years ago, and it would continue the rest of Naomi's life. She felt rancor in her heart for a minute for Queen's misguided direction. Then she thanked God for allowing her to share her sister/daughter's life. Not many women were that lucky or blessed.

She put a smile on her face; then she said amicably, "We'll all help you plan the wedding."

"You'd better." Naomi flashed a smile to Sarah.

Sarah walked over to her and hugged her tightly; Ruth and Alice looked on approvingly. Ruth wiped another tear from her eye.

"Enough of that mushy stuff," Alice remarked. "This is a happy occasion. We're going to have a wedding, and we haven't had one in a long time. This is going to be fun."

The women finished the cleaning chores in no time. Alice and Fred left, and Naomi and Montgomery left shortly afterward. Naomi promised to call her mother before she returned to Edwardsville.

All told, Ruth nodded her head, and her mouth curved into a smile. Today was a good day for the Wilcox family, and they hadn't had one of them in a long time either.

Chapter Twenty-one

By eight o'clock that evening, Queen was asleep in Ruth's guest bedroom, snoring lightly. The day had been a long one; with dinner starting at two o'clock. Ruth sat on the sofa in her den, wearing a comfortable lounging outfit. Her heart was full and she felt content. She thanked God for the blessings He'd bestowed upon her and her family that day.

Naomi was full of exhilaration, and she seemed to be in love with Montgomery. Ruth had noticed Montgomery's Jaguar when he and Naomi departed from Sarah's home. Ruth couldn't deny that the vibe between her and Aron was growing stronger, and she couldn't deny that she was attracted to him.

Alice had Fred, as well as Ruth, to lean on during her medical crisis. Ruth realized, whether she liked it or not, that Fred was a part of Alice's life, and that she had to share her friend, just like she did when Alice married Martin.

Life is good, Ruth mused. Then her thoughts centered on Daniel. She knew her ex-husband as well as she knew herself. Daniel was definitely trying to put the moves on her. And she wasn't sure how she felt about that. She knew they weren't the same people who were stuck in an acrimonious marriage.

Ruth knew she had grown by leaps and bounds spiritually. She personified the term "late bloomer." It took time for Ruth to find and accept herself for who she was. That acceptance included loving all her parts—her flaws and her good traits. She dedicated her life, much like her forefathers, to bringing people to the Christian fold. Ruth loved nothing more than spreading God's Word. She was quite content with her lot in life.

A minuscule part of her psyche wanted Daniel to come crawling back on his knees, begging her to take him back. Then another part of her inner self wanted to explore the possibility of a deeper relationship with Aron. She had never felt so comfortable with another male since she had met Daniel.

The telephone jangled loudly, startling Ruth out of her thoughts. She picked up the cell phone and clicked it on. "Hello?" she said.

"Hello, Ruth. I was just thinking about you, and wondered how you're doing." Aron's caring tone warmed her soul.

"Aron, I'm doing well. I'm sitting in my den, having a conversation with God."

"I'm not interrupting you, am I?" he asked solicitously, his voice deepening.

"Trust me, God isn't going anywhere. I can always continue my conversation with Him later." Ruth relaxed, leaning against the back of the sofa.

"I hear you on that." Aron chuckled. His eyes traveled around the walls of his masculine den. "I hope I wasn't out of place by coming to your daughter's house. I told Monet that I could wait in the car, but she insisted I come inside."

"No, your coming to the house was fine. You had a chance to meet my family en masse. What I meant to say is that you were able to see Naomi. She hadn't been home in such a long time. I realized how much I missed her when I saw her face. Even though we haven't talked about her young man, I have a feeling she's going to stay in Edwardsville after she graduates, instead of coming back to Chicago."

"Would that be such a terrible thing?" Aron asked.

"I guess not." Ruth sighed. "I guess I'm being selfish. My son, DJ, lives in Georgia, and I hate that he lives so far from the family. I guess with daughters it's a little different. I wish Naomi and DJ lived closer, but I realize all three of my children have their own lives to lead—be it in Chicago or elsewhere."

"I can understand that. I love Monet and my sons to death, but I think I'm a little closer to Monet. As close as she was to her mother, she's now become a daddy's girl," Aron said.

"Sarah and I are close too, but at heart she, too, is a daddy's girl. Naomi is a mama's girl, for sure. My son and Daniel don't get along very well. I pray every night that the situation between them will change," Ruth said.

"All good things in their own time," Aron pronounced. "Though I wasn't around him long, your ex-husband seems to have a very forceful personality."

"That he does," Ruth agreed, nodding her head. "Daniel has always craved a lot of attention, whether it be as the life of the party, or flashing dollars or women. He has to be bigger than life."

"I think he still has feelings for you," Aron observed casually.

"Hmm, I don't know about that. We've been divorced for a long time. I don't think either one of us would be inclined to travel down that road again." Ruth's tone of voice was even, although her stomach was performing zigzags.

"You do share a history, and you share children and grandchildren. Sometimes that's a powerful incentive to try to get things right the second go-round."

"That's true, but in our case, the bad times outweighed the good. I won't portray myself as a victim. I did some things wrong that contributed to the end of our union. Still, I know we're both in a better place. He moved on with his life, and he has the household to prove it," Ruth stated with a tremor in her voice.

"But from what you told me, his status has changed. And we learn, 'sometimes the grass is not greener on the other side of the pasture.' That's the vibe I picked up from your ex-husband's demeanor tonight. I hope I'm not speaking out of line here, Ruth. I'm just trying to gauge your feelings for your ex," Aron confessed; then he sighed loudly.

"All you had to do was ask, Aron," she replied gently. "When Daniel left me, I was devastated, and it took me a long time to get over the loss of our marriage. Not to mention, he remarried before the ink was dry on our divorce decree. For many days, I felt like I'd lost my incentive to go on. There were times I didn't think I had the strength to get through another day. I had to pray morning, noon, and night to maintain my sanity. Eventually the hurt went away, and I'm in a much better place than I was years ago." Ruth ran her fingers through her hair and looked upward.

"Great." Aron's face lit up like a hundred-watt bulb. "I like you, Ruth, and I'd like for us to spend more time together, getting to know each other. I've made mistakes in life, and I've learned from them, and I paid my debt to society. I'd like to enjoy the remainder of my years by watching my grandchildren grow, and sharing the companionship of a good woman."

"I know what you mean. I've been blessed. By and large, my family members are doing well. Alice is going through a crisis. God willing, though, she'll be fine. I will have to get used to sharing her. I know that sounds selfish, but Alice and I have been there for each other since we were in elementary school. She's my sister/ friend."

"There's nothing wrong with sharing. Who knows? You may not be as available as you think." Aron smiled.

"Well, Mr. Reynolds," Ruth said coyly, batting her eyes, "I do believe you're flirting with me."

"That I am," he replied smoothly. "I love your smile, and I want to see it on your face as much as possible. It's like a burst of sunshine on a cloudy day."

"Oh, wow, now you're trying to run a Temptation song lyric on me." Ruth threw her head back and laughed.

"I'll do whatever it takes to see or hear you laugh," Aron said in a tender voice.

"Good," Ruth proclaimed. She glanced at the doorway because she heard Queen's petulant voice calling her from the bedroom. "I have to go. My mother is calling." Then she giggled. "I sound like I'm a teenager, don't I?"

"You sound like the caring woman you are. Pleasant dreams, and I'll see you tomorrow," he said, conveying concern.

"Have a good evening," she responded.

"I already have," he said. There was a twinkle in his eyes.

They hung up, and Ruth walked out of the den to the bedroom to tend to Queen. When she settled into bed, Ruth clasped her hands behind her head and pondered the day. What a day it had been: meeting Montgomery for the first time, and Daniel being back in the family fold. Her lips curved into a smile at the thought of how comfortable Aron was with her family. He earned a gold star in the column of positive traits. Ruth sighed; she hoped the church would be as understanding with her decision. Then her personal life would be complete. Ruth put the idea out of her mind. That bridge would be crossed on another day.

Chapter Twenty-two

Daniel stood in front of the ornate brass-framed mirror inside one of the spare bedrooms of his house, where Brian and Sarah had moved his possessions the week after Sarah had stayed with him. After the humiliation of Lenora's leaving him had subsided, he refused to inhabit the room they had shared.

His eyes critically roamed the upper part of his body, which he knew had become flabby after years of sitting and sleeping in the reclining chair, undergoing little physical activity. Daniel's lips twisted sardonically to the side as he spied patches of gray hair sprouting from his head, as well as his upper lip. His eyes looked slightly blurry. *I'm definitely not on top of my game,* he thought. He flexed his sagging muscles, buttoned his pajama top, and walked over to the bed and sat down.

He opened the nightstand drawer and pulled out the letter Lenora had left for him before her defection. Some of the writing was blurred from the tears he had shed while reading the letter, but the contents were seared permanently into his memory bank.

Dan,

There's simply no other way to put this. I have been bored in the marriage since you had your heart attack. The man I loved went away when you stayed in the hospital recuperating, and he never returned. I miss the exciting man I fell in love with. Instead, I got stuck with a dreary old man, who doesn't seem to have any direction or passion in his life. You will always occupy a special place in my heart for the beautiful children we have. One of the happiest days of my life was when Damon was born. Our wedding should be up there along with those fond memories, but all I can remember is barely finishing our vows and how you had to leave to see about that daughter of yours, who's not even your daughter. But enough about the past, it's the future I'm looking forward to.

Dan, I didn't plan to fall in love with Trevor. It sort of just happened, one of those things you can't quite control, kind of like when you and I fell in love. I plan to file for divorce in Reno and marry Trevor. He makes me so happy. I'm not an old woman, so there's no need for me to put my life on hold in hopes of trying to recapture what we once had. I know the boys are going to be upset. Please tell them that I love them, and that I will be back to see them as soon as I can. Trevor plays in a band, so we're on the road frequently. He has gigs in Europe, so we're going there in the fall until the beginning of next year. That's not a life for young children, so it's best they stay with you, at least until they're older. Sometimes I think my attraction to you was the thrill of taking you from your wife. You were so adamant in the beginning of our relationship about how you were not going to ever leave Ruthie. I took that as an insult and a personal challenge. So, to that end, I accomplished what I wanted. The perfect min-

ister's daughter was brought to her feet. What I want, I generally get. You can call me selfish or self-centered or a witch, whatever you prefer. Being with Trevor is as close to perfection as life can get for me. Take care of the boys.

Smooches,
Nora

Every time he read that letter—especially the smooches part—he had an overwhelming urge to smooch Lenora, and he wasn't referring to a kiss. His fists and stomach clenched spasmodically. The letter was cold and calculating, much like Lenora was. He dropped the letter on the bed and bowed his head. He rubbed his forehead. He could hardly believe that Lenora had the audacity to think, much less pen something like that to him. He had been good to her and had treated her like a queen, but look at what it got him: three children whom he wasn't sure that he had the energy to raise.

He'd been silently berating himself for a long time over why he hadn't stayed with Ruth. She kept a clean, beautiful house, although she spent way too much time at The Temple. Her doing so gave him a chance to roam the streets. Back in the day, Ruth had turned a blind eye to his comings and goings most of the time. His children were now grown; and other than Sarah, he didn't have a good relationship with them. Daniel got into the bed, sat with his back against the headboard, and closed his eyes.

He could see Ruth's smile in his mind as she had been at Sarah's house that evening. Her face was thinner, and her silver gray hair, which was styled into a short cut, was very becoming. Daniel could see that his ex-wife had lost weight. She looked good, and it had been a long time since he had been attracted emotionally and physically to her.

Then he frowned as he remembered the old dude who came to Sarah's house with his daughter and granddaughter. The man had the audacity to talk privately with Ruth like she was his woman or something. Daniel poked out his chest. He wasn't having it; Ruth was his. He had been her only husband. She came to him as a virgin, and she had borne his children. That had to count for something, didn't it?

He exhaled loudly, as if his midsection was a balloon and the air was let out. Painful as it was to face, he knew that he had dogged Ruth. The Ruth he was married to bore little resemblance to the self-assured woman sitting at Sarah's dining-room table. If Daniel was honest with himself, he would realize that he didn't know Pastor Ruth Wilcox. He only knew Mrs. Daniel Wilcox, and he'd found her skills as a wife lacking, where it mattered most to a man.

He admitted that although the other man seemed a little older, Aron was in better shape than he was, and that man still possessed good looks.

Daniel's expression hardened. It didn't really matter, because in the long run, he knew Ruth, and she always believed that marriage vows were indeed until death. She also had a forgiving heart. He knew that if he humbled himself and came to her the correct way, more than likely she would return to him.

"I've just got to get myself together and maybe, just maybe, my life will get back in sync," Daniel spoke aloud. He reached over and put the letter back inside the nightstand drawer.

As he closed the drawer, the edge of an envelope was sticking out. Daniel pulled open the drawer and pulled the letter out. It was a statement from the mortgage company stating the house was in the process of foreclosure. He shook his head sorrowfully, because he didn't understand how Lenora could do this to him. The mortgage on the house was high, over $2,000 a month. There was no way Daniel would be able to save the house. He rebuked himself, because he couldn't even provide for his children in the way to which they were accustomed.

He had planned to try to get a lump-sum distribution the first year that his pension payment began, per Lenora's urging. Sarah suggested her father opt for monthly payouts, so he could continue to live comfortably without his money running out. Daniel listened to Sarah. He realized had it not been for his daughter's suggestion, there was no telling where he would be today, especially without Lenora's income from her bookkeeping business.

Life was changing fast, and Daniel felt uncomfortable with the sacrifices he was going to have to make. He felt too old to have to make life-altering adjustments. His children seemed so settled, and look at him. He thought about Naomi's boyfriend and how he seemed to be swimming in dough, but he doubted if she would help him. She still harbored issues about his leaving Ruth for Lenora, and the lie that was perpetrated regarding her birth. So he was going to have to lean heavily on Sarah for support.

He also assumed Ruth was in great shape financially. He knew she was the executor of Queen's financial affairs, and he was more than certain that Bishop would have left the women in his life well provided for after his death. The Temple was a huge church, not a mega-church, but large nonetheless. So on top of that, Ruth had to be pulling in close to six figures as the senior pastor. The apartment building she and Alice owned had to be worth half a million at least.

Then Daniel smiled to himself, thinking, *This old dog still knows some tricks.* He planned to call Ruth the following day. Yes, his ex-wife was looking better and better, the more he thought about her.

He rubbed his hands together and licked his lips. Daniel's expression hardened. It didn't matter to him one whit that the janitor might have designs on Ruth, or that he and Ruth were divorced. Ruth Wilcox was meant to be his wife again, and Daniel planned to do everything in his power to woo Ruth back.

Chapter Twenty-three

By midmorning on Monday, Ruth had returned Queen to the home. During the ride to the North Side, Queen had asked Ruth a couple of times where they were going, and she patiently explained to her mother that it was time for her to return to the home. Queen told Ruth she didn't want to go back there, that she wanted to go back to the house that she shared with Bishop. She pleaded with Ruth to let her stay at her house, and she even shed a few tears. Ruth felt like a dagger had been thrust into her abdomen.

Before the economy had tanked, the finance committee had been looking over a proposal to erect a senior citizen facility, one on a smaller scale than the one Queen resided in. But the project had been tabled until the economy recovered. Had the plan come to fruition, Ruth planned to move Queen Esther closer to home.

Queen Esther refused to acknowledge Ruth's presence when she told her good-bye and that she would return on Wednesday to visit her. Queen just sat on the rocking chair near the window, looking outside.

Ruth's mood was not the best when she stopped by the church. Even though it was her day off, she wanted to check her messages and perform a couple of chores. When she arrived in front of her closed office door, she found a clear crystal vase with a pink rose inside it, and a message taped to the side of the vase.

Ruth bent down and picked up the vase. She sniffed the aroma of the flower, unlocked her office, and walked to her desk. She set the vase on her desk and took off her jacket. She checked her voice mail and jotted down a few names and telephone numbers.

When she was done with that task, she leaned against the back of the chair and opened the folded note. *Ruth, in case you didn't know it, a pink rose symbolizes appreciation and thanks. I want to say thank you from the bottom of my heart for giving me a chance to fill the maintenance position, and for our lunch on Friday. Thank you! Aron.*

Aron's penmanship, Ruth noted, was a lovely, loping script. Her dour mood lifted a smidgen. She diligently returned telephone calls, and received a call from a church member whose mother had passed after a lengthy illness. She also had a message from Elise regarding her wedding to Derek, Aron's son.

Ruth promised to visit later that day the member whose mother had passed. She left a voice mail message for Elise, instructing her to call her back; or if she was busy, they could meet in a couple of days.

There was a knock at the door. Ruth looked up and said, "Come in."

Aron's head popped inside the doorway. "Are you busy? Am I interrupting anything? I thought I heard the front door of the church open and close. I just finished mopping the kitchen."

Ruth gestured for him to enter. "No, I'm not busy. Come on in."

"How was your morning? Did you get your mother safely back to her residence?" Aron asked. He sat down on the chair in front of Ruth's desk. "I see you got my gift," he observed.

"Yes, I did, and thank you. I took Queen back to the center, and she didn't want to stay there. I've had a difficult morning."

"I'm sorry to hear that. I hope your day gets better," Aron replied soothingly, leaning forward on the seat.

"Well, it already has, due to your gift, as you call it. I feel so guilty about leaving Queen at the home. But I can't watch her, and she has a tendency to wander off, if you don't keep a careful watch over her. I feel so torn." Tears sprang to Ruth's eyes. She dropped her gaze and brushed the corner of her eyes.

"I understand." He nodded. "Not that I've experienced what you're going through. Both my parents are deceased, and I know that puts you in a difficult position." He stood up and walked around the desk and took Ruth's hand and rubbed it.

"I feel so helpless, and I know people don't understand why I put my mother in an assisted-living facility. But I did it out of a concern for her well-being and safety. The home is one of the best in Chicago, and they have many activities for seniors. Queen lived with me before I put her in the home, and it just didn't work out."

"You don't have to explain anything to me. Everyone's situation is different, and they have to do what's best for them and their parents," Aron murmured softly.

Ruth removed her hand from Aron's, feeling pleased. "Thank you for listening. Alice is the only person who understands what I go through with Queen, and she doesn't judge me. She went along with me to pick out the home."

"Alice seems like a true friend to you. You're lucky to have her." Aron returned to his chair.

"That I am." Ruth's appearance cheered up. "So how are things going with the job? Has James stopped by to show you the ropes yet? I know he gave you the keys a while ago."

"Yes, James was most helpful. He's been coming in two half days a week to work with me. He's a good guy."

"That he is. The church is planning a retirement party for him next month. He has been a true servant of the Lord, maintaining the church and the grounds. We're going to miss him. He began working here during my father's tenure."

"Well, my work is cut out for me, and I won't let you or the church down," Aron promised. He stood up. "I guess I'll get back to work. Try to relax and enjoy the rest of your day. Is it okay if I call you later?"

"That would be great. I usually don't work on Mondays—it's my day off—but I decided to come by and see how you were getting along."

"Well, I'm a lucky guy, then." Aron looked into Ruth's eyes. "I'll see you later." He walked toward the door; then he turned back and waved.

"See you later," Ruth said as her eyes followed him out of the room.

She reached for a file on the top of her in-box. June had left her a batch of letters to sign. She finished signing the letters, returned a few more calls, and was looking at the church expenditures, when her telephone rang. She picked up the receiver. "This is Pastor Wilcox. How may I help you?"

"Hi, Momma," Naomi said. "I just wanted to let you know that Monty and I made it safely back to Edwardsville. We arrived here about an hour ago."

"Praise God. I'm glad to hear you had a safe trip back to Edwardsville. I was so pleased to see you this weekend, Nay. It had been a long time."

"I agree, Momma. I had a good time, for the most part." Her nose crinkled with distaste. "I could've skipped visiting Daddy. He's still the same old selfish person he's always been. Now he wants pity from everyone because his wife left him. He made his bed; now he's got to lie in it."

"That sounds so harsh, Naomi. He's human and prone to mistakes like most people are," Ruth said.

"That's your take on his predicament. He needs to concentrate on raising those boys of his, and try to make them into more productive and well-mannered children. I was appalled at their behavior. Daddy has his work cut out for him."

"Well, they're still little children. I'm sure their behavior will improve as they get older," Ruth responded.

"We'll see," Naomi replied with a snort. Then her voice became grave. "So, Momma, be truthful with me. Did you like Monty?" She couldn't hide a hint of apprehension in her voice.

"I don't know him that well, because I haven't been around him that much. But from what I could tell, he seemed like a nice man. You know my outlook: if a man treats you well and makes you happy, then I'm happy for you."

"Thank you for saying that, Momma." Naomi exhaled loudly. "I know I should have introduced him to the family sooner. But I just wasn't sure if you all would accept him or not, especially Queen. Queen thinking he was a doctor was kind of funny." Naomi and Ruth shared a laugh.

"Had Monty met her years ago, I know she would've had plenty more to say, and she would've drilled him like a sergeant in the military," Ruth said. They chuckled over that remark.

"You're right about that," Naomi said.

"Sweetie, I hope you don't think the family is prejudiced against people of different colors. I would like to think I raised you better than that," Ruth said carefully. She finger combed the side of her hair back.

"You're right. Truthfully, I was more worried about Queen. You know how vocal she is about expressing her opinion, and I remember her telling me as a child that it was a sin to mix the races," Naomi admitted.

"We both know that Queen has been mistaken at least a time or two in her life," Ruth joked. She spun her chair around and faced the window behind her desk.

"You're right as usual, Momma. Do you think Bishop and Uncle Ezra would have approved of Monty?" Naomi's voice had become wistful; she sounded like she was a young girl again.

"I'm sure they both would have. The two of them pretty much accepted people as they are."

"I miss them, especially Bishop," Naomi said sadly. "Sometimes family gatherings don't feel exactly right without Bishop being there. I can picture Uncle Ezra sitting at the piano at the house, really tickling the ivories. He sure could play."

"You're right, Nay. The void of their passing is still with us as a family. In time, it will become easier, especially when my grandchildren become adults and have children of their own. New memories will be made for our family by the new members."

"That's a good way to look at life, Momma. I never thought about it that way."

"Well, I'm not in my sixties for nothing. I've learned a thing or two along my journey of life."

"Momma, you look so good. Not that you were bad-looking before," Naomi added quickly. "You just have an air about you that screams that you're content with life."

"Thank you, Nay. I am content. I love serving the church. I always did, and still do, even with the challenges I face. The family is doing well, and I'm certain the Lord will heal Alice. All in all, life is pretty good."

"Do you miss being with Daddy?" Naomi couldn't help but ask.

"I miss companionship, but I'm not depressed or feeling needy. God supplies my every need. If He sees fit to bring someone into my life, I won't complain."

"That's good, Momma. I don't want you to grow old alone. Everyone needs someone." Naomi nodded with satisfaction.

"Whoa!" Ruth held up her hand as if Naomi was in the room. "I'm not saying I want to marry again, just that I miss male companionship sometimes. I don't want you to read more into my statement than what I mean."

"I hear you loud and clear. We'll see what the Lord has in store for you, won't we?"

When the call ended, Ruth turned her attention back to her ministerial duties. Two hours later, she stood up and locked her drawer, preparing to leave. When she exited the office, she was startled to see Aron sitting on a bench, apparently waiting for her.

He stood up, saying, "I didn't mean to scare you. I was a little worried about you being here alone. I don't have anything to do for another hour or so. Then I'm babysitting for Monet. She and Elise are going to look at wedding invitations."

"Thank you for staying. Really, I'm all right. I stayed longer than I planned. Naomi called to say she and Monty had made it back to Edwardsville safely. And speaking of Elise, she called to make an appointment to see me about her and Derrick's wedding."

"I don't mind waiting for you, Ruth. These are desperate times we live in. I talked to the store owner across the street, and he said he had a break-in over the weekend. I would be less than a man if I left you here alone. Some people have no respect for anything."

"In that case, thank you. I appreciate your staying. I noticed the window was broken out of the shop, but I didn't know what had happened. I planned to stop by and talk to Mr. Walker when I finished working here. No one was hurt, I hope?" she asked.

"No, it happened overnight. Still, one can't be too careful. I'll walk you to your car, and then I'll be on my way," Aron said.

They walked in comfortable silence to Ruth's Cadillac. When they got to the passenger door, Aron took the keys from Ruth's hand and opened the door for her. He closed the door lightly after she got inside. She rolled the window down.

"Be careful," he told Ruth. "I'll talk to you later." He stepped away from the car.

"I will, and you be careful too. Enjoy your time with the children." Ruth rolled up the window, shifted to drive and pulled out of the parking lot. She honked her horn as she pulled out into traffic.

Aron waved at her; then he glanced at his watch and walked hurriedly to his own car. A minute later, he, too, departed the lot.

Ruth and Aron were unaware that Daniel sat parked across the street, observing their moves. His eyes drooped into slits, and his mouth fell open as he watched Aron open the car door for Ruth and talk to her.

Daniel wasn't an expert at reading lips, but he could have sworn Aron told Ruth he'd talk to her later. His mouth tightened with annoyance. He knew Ruth wouldn't be so hard up that she would accept the courtship of a janitor.

He turned on the ignition and put the car in drive. Daniel thought, *Enjoy yourself, old man, while you can. Ruth is mine; she will always be mine. It's just a matter of time before I resume my rightful position as head of my first family.*

Chapter Twenty-four

When Ruth arrived home, she parked her car in the garage and walked around to the front of the building to get the mail. She glanced up and down the street, and saw Fred's car parked at the end of the block. She opened her mailbox and removed letters, and then checked Alice's box. She opened the storm door and walked up the short flight of stairs to the first-floor landing. She bent over and was putting Alice's mail through the mail slot, when the door swung open. She looked up to find Fred smiling at her.

"How are you doing today, sis-in-law? How was your day?" Fred asked.

"Not bad, Fred. How about yours? How is Alice feeling today?"

"My day was okay. I've been keeping a lookout for you. Alice is not feeling well today, and she wanted you to stop by to see her when you got home."

"She does?" Ruth looked at Fred. "I thought your being here"—she dipped her head toward Alice's door—"would be all that she needed."

Fred stood stiffly, with his arms dangling at his sides. "Now, don't be that way, Ruth. Of course, Alice wants you here with her. Why wouldn't she want you around? I work part-time at night, so I'll be leaving, anyway, in a few minutes to go home to prepare for work. You, as well as anyone, know how important it is for a cancer patient to have"—he scratched the side of his head—"what's that word the doctor used?"

Ruth pushed the strap of her shoulder bag back over her shoulder. "You mean a support group?" she asked, a smile escaping her lips.

She knew then in her heart that Fred truly cared for her friend. How many men would be there for an older woman they weren't married to, who was facing a breast cancer issue?

"You're right, Fred. I was out of line. I couldn't be here this morning because I had to take Queen back to the home. I'm grateful that Alice had you to be with her. Give me a few minutes to take my things into my apartment, and I'll be over there. Truce?" Ruth held out her hand.

Fred pulled her into his arms. They embraced. "We're family! Give me some love, woman. I'll tell Alice you'll be over soon." He turned and went back into Alice's apartment.

Ruth unlocked her door and went inside. She laid her mail on the table in the foyer, hung up her jacket, then walked into the kitchen and put a white paper bag on the counter. Next she went into the bedroom and put her purse in the closet. She went into the bathroom, where she washed her face and hands. Fifteen minutes later, she was knocking on Alice's door.

Fred had on his jacket when Ruth entered the apartment. "Take care of my woman." He winked at Ruth. She smiled back; then she locked the door after he left.

"Alice, where are you?" she called out, walking through the apartment.

"I'm in the sun parlor," Alice replied weakly.

Ruth hurried to the front of the apartment, where she found Alice lying on her side on the floral wicker couch. "What's wrong? Don't you feel good? Do you need to go to the hospital?" She rushed to Alice's side, bent down, and felt her forehead.

"It's that darn radiology therapy, and no, I don't need to go to the hospital." Alice tried to sit up. She began radiology treatment a few days ago.

Ruth grabbed her friend's arm and helped her up into a sitting position. Then she sat on the wicker chair opposite the couch. "What do you need? What can I do for you?" She tried to quell the panicky feelings that invaded her being.

"I just want you to sit with me for a while. My energy level is low, and I've felt tired all day." Alice closed her eyes and leaned her head against the back of the couch.

"Goodness gracious, why don't you lie back down then! Are you hungry? Can I get you something to eat?" Ruth felt helpless. She wanted to do something to put that spark of life back in Alice's face, which now looked ashen and pale.

"You know what, Ruth? I have a taste for minestrone soup from Izola's Restaurant. Isn't that something? It probably won't stay down, anyway." She gave her a pallid smile.

"Well, I guess we had that friend vibe going on today." Ruth nodded. "I stopped at Izola's on my way home from work and bought servings of chicken noodle and minestrone soup, even though I brought leftovers from Sarah's house yesterday."

"Thank you, I appreciate it." Alice opened her eyes and gave Ruth a weak smile. "How was your day?"

"It started off difficult, but got better as the day went on." She told Alice about Queen not wanting to stay at the home.

"I know that has to be hard for you. When I go with you to take her back, she's usually docile. Maybe she felt lonely after being with the family yesterday. What are you planning to do?"

"I don't know, Allie. Of course, I'd love for her to stay with me, but her aversion to the nurses I hired in the past has caused problems. I really don't know what to do." Ruth rubbed her forehead in frustration.

"Why don't you wait and see how she responds to the new medication over the long haul and then reassess your decision," Alice suggested.

"I'll do that. I plan to talk to her doctor when I go there on Wednesday. I'll see what he thinks. Oh, Naomi called me today to see if I approved of her young man."

"What did you tell her?" Alice looked at Ruth, and she seemed to have perked up a tiny iota.

"She wanted that 'momma' stamp of approval, but I told her I needed to get to know Montgomery better. I also asked her why it took her so long to bring him around the family."

"Hmm, what did she say?" Alice picked up the remote and switched the channel to the local news.

"She said she wasn't sure how the family would react, considering Montgomery is white. I told her that our family has never been prejudiced. Then she mentioned Queen; and I have to admit, she had a point."

"Did she mention wedding plans? It's hard to believe our little girl is grown and about to marry. Doesn't that just blow your mind?"

"That it does. It's hard to believe that we're the family elders now. For so long, it was Queen and Bishop and my few aunts and uncles, who are now deceased. Now it's us and my children."

"Well, as they say, time doesn't stand still. So how did it feel yesterday with Aron and Daniel being in the same room? I'm sure you were shocked when Daniel came to Sarah's, and then Aron came with Monet."

"Girl, you could have knocked me over with a feather both times. It was a weird feeling. I thought Daniel's apology to the family was sincere, though those boys of his are something else," Ruth said.

"They are the spawn of Lenora," Alice muttered.

Ruth and Alice cracked up.

"Seriously, though, I think Mr. Wilcox is planning on putting the moves on you. He hasn't considered there's another sheriff in town named Mr. Reynolds."

Ruth looked down at her folded hands, and had the grace to blush. "I think you're reading way too much into this. Daniel is still technically married, but there's no way I'd get back together with him, anyway. Plus, I have to admit, I'm starting to develop deep feelings for Aron. We had a nice chat today and he cheered me up."

"Good. From what I could see of him yesterday, he seems like a good, strong black man. I'm sure everyone with eyes could sense the attraction between you two."

"He would be perfect, if not for that jail record," Ruth mused.

Alice sat up, erect. "I would hate for you to miss out on a good thing because you're concerned about what people might say."

"Now, Alice, you know between us, you were the fiery one, not me. I was, and still am, the compromiser. I tend to go with the flow. I don't deny that I have an attraction to Aron," Ruth said primly. "What do you want to hear?" She stood up and removed the Bible from the bottom shelf of the cocktail table.

"I think I'm in the mood for some verses from Hebrews:13."

"I know just what you mean," Ruth replied. She returned to her seat and opened the Bible to the book of Hebrews, and read the thirteenth chapter.

"Amen." Alice nodded her approval. "There is a lot going on in that scripture that applies to Aron, Daniel, you, and me. Specifically verses four through six. You know the part about whoremongers and adulterers. But the verse that is near and dear to my heart dealing with my health issue is the end of verse five; I will never leave nor forsake thee. What do you think?"

"I don't know what you mean," Ruth replied stiffly, although she knew what Alice was going to say.

"Sure, you do," Alice said triumphantly. "Aron has been imprisoned, and Daniel has been the adulterer. I know whatever God has in store for me regarding my cancer, He will never leave or forsake me. And you, my dear"—she looked gloatingly at Ruth—"you should not fear what man shall do, and that includes your congregation. At some point, we have to come out of that comfort zone and enjoy the blessings God has in store for us."

"Did that scripture tell you anything about Fred, while you were analyzing everyone else?" Ruth asked cattily.

"Now, that just wasn't fair, Pastor Ruth," Alice replied tartly. "I don't like your tone."

"You're right. I just have to give things time on my end."

"I'm sure you will make the right decision. Because, as sure as the sun rises each day, I sense Daniel wants to make a comeback, and I'm not sure his intentions are pure."

"You know what"—Ruth nodded her head—"Naomi pretty much told me the same thing when I talked to her. But I have to take what she says with a grain of salt because of her dislike of Daniel."

"Maybe she sees something that you don't," Alice suggested. "I have faith that you will do the right thing. Now I'm hungry. I think I want some soup. Do you think you can hook a sister up?"

"Coming right up." Ruth went to her apartment and retrieved the bag off the kitchen counter; then she went back to Alice's place. She warmed up the soup, and they sat and talked for another hour or so, until Ruth returned to her apartment to prepare for her visit to one of the neighborhood churches. When she returned home from church, Ruth was not the least bit surprised to see that Aron had called. When she returned his call, he'd wanted to know if she had made it home safely. However, Ruth was astonished to see Daniel's number on caller ID, because she remembered telling him to call her at church. Ruth decided it was too late to call Daniel back; that conversation would be postponed for the time being.

Before Ruth fell asleep, her telephone rang. She noted the caller was Edwina Henderson, Brother Eddie Duncan's daughter. "Hello, Edwina."

"Pastor Wilcox, I hope I'm not calling at a bad time. Daddy suffered a stroke and he's in a coma." Edwina sounded distraught.

"Oh, no. I'm so sorry to hear that!" Ruth exclaimed. "Do you need me to come to the hospital? Is there anything I can do for you?"

"I don't think it's necessary for you to come out tonight. I just ask that you keep Daddy in your prayers. If you could come to the hospital tomorrow, that would be fine."

"I can come tonight. That's not a problem," Ruth assured Edwina.

"Pastor, tomorrow is fine. Just keep our family in your prayers."

After Edwina gave the name of the hospital, the women ended the call. Ruth closed her eyes and said a prayer for Brother Duncan's recovery. She got out of the bed and began quickly dressing. Ruth decided to go to the hospital. She felt remorseful that she hadn't allowed Brother Duncan to have his say at the meeting. Coils of shame consumed Ruth's being. She now feared that she'd never find out what Brother Duncan had wanted to tell her.

Chapter Twenty-five

In early May, Ruth was sitting in her bedroom. She was reading while the television was on. A commercial aired for an art show that was being held at several Chicago hotels. The advertisement caught her attention. Ruth planned to replace several paintings in her living room, and she decided to attend the show. Ruth called Aron and asked him to go with her. He was more than happy to comply with her request.

Ruth had taken Alice's advice, and she and Aron were dating on a regular basis. Ruth was torn about what her congregation might think. The church was still struggling financially, and Ruth felt she couldn't afford to lose any member.

Ruth decided to attend the exhibition at the Oak Brook Marriott. She decided that the location was far enough out of the way that they would not run into any church members.

She and Aron left her house at noon on Saturday and traveled west to Oak Brook.

"I've heard there are several good restaurants in Oak Brook," she remarked to Aron. "So, to thank you for going to the show with me, I'll treat you to lunch."

"Now, you know, that isn't necessary. I'm glad you invited me to come with you," he said meaningfully.

"I'm glad you accepted my invitation." Ruth smiled back.

Before long, they arrived at their destination. Aron parked the car. They exited the vehicle and walked inside the hotel. The warm temperature was an incentive for art lovers to attend the show. The ballroom was crowded.

Ruth and Aron strolled around the room, hand in hand. They circled the ballroom as Ruth tried to decide which oil paintings she wanted to purchase.

After an hour had elapsed, Ruth whispered to Aron, "I need to go to the ladies' room. I'll be right back."

"I'll go with you, and wait outside for you," he said. "I'd hate for us to become separated. It's pretty crowded in here."

Ruth asked one of the hotel attendants where the restroom was located. He pointed toward the bank of elevators for access to the rooms. "The restrooms are around the corner from the elevators. You can't miss it."

When Ruth came out of the restroom, Aron was waiting for her. He asked, "Are you hungry? How much longer do you want to stay?"

The couple had just walked past the elevators, when they heard a voice yell out, "Pastor Ruth!"

Ruth stopped dead in her tracks. Her stomach plummeted to her feet. She turned around to see Brother Thomas Ellis and his wife, Jocelyn, smiling at her.

"Hello, Thomas and Jocelyn. How are you two doing?" Ruth asked politely. Tendrils of dread crisscrossed her stomach because Jocelyn was known to be a gossip.

"We're good," Jocelyn answered. "Well, you're far from home. Aren't you going to introduce us to your friend?" Jocelyn looked at Aron with interest in her beady eyes.

Ruth faltered for a moment. She moistened her lips and said, "This is Aron Reynolds. Aron, this is Brother Thomas Ellis and his wife, Jocelyn."

Jocelyn was unaware that Aron was the custodial engineer for the church. Brother Ellis knew exactly who he was. He smirked as Ruth said his name.

Aron shook hands with the couple. They chatted about the weather.

"Well, Thomas and I came here for brunch. We should be getting along. It was nice seeing you, Pastor Ruth, and meeting you, Mr. Reynolds," Jocelyn added. There was a wicked gleam in her eyes.

"Yes, it was good seeing you, Pastor Ruth," Thomas echoed. "We'll see you in church tomorrow." He took his wife's arm.

"You two, enjoy your meal. I'll see you tomorrow." Ruth watched Thomas and Jocelyn walk away. Jocelyn was leaning toward Thomas, talking animatedly to her husband. The couple glanced back at Ruth and Aron.

"Ruth," Aron asked, concerned, "are you okay? You look pale as a ghost."

"I'm fine. My head is hurting. Do you mind if we go back to Chicago now?"

"That's fine with me, but you didn't buy anything. I thought you wanted to get some paintings for your house."

"You know what? We can do this another time. They have these kinds of shows frequently."

"Okay, if that's what you want to do. I'm sorry you don't feel good. Would you like me to bring the car around to the front of the hotel?"

"No, I can walk," Ruth replied.

The couple strolled quietly to Aron's car. All the gaiety had gone out of their excursion. The drive back to Chicago was equally silent. Ruth closed her eyes and leaned against the headrest.

Before long, Aron was exiting the expressway and driving on Eighty-seventh Street. In a matter of minutes, he parked his car in front of Ruth's building. He got out of the car and opened Ruth's door. They walked into the building and stood outside her door.

Aron grabbed Ruth's hand. "I hope your mood wasn't spoiled because we ran into Mr. and Mrs. Ellis."

"Of course not," Ruth denied hollowly. "My head is killing me."

"Well, I hope it wasn't because you were ashamed of being seen with me." Aron chose his words carefully, though his face was expressionless.

"Of course not," Ruth protested. She knew her voice sounded weak.

Aron kissed her cheek. "I'm not going to pressure you about what happened. Although, I think I can guess why. But we do need to talk about it at some point."

"You're right." Ruth sighed and placed her hand over her brow. "I'm just tired now. Will you call me later?"

"I will," Aron nodded. "Get some rest, and I'll talk to you later." He left after Ruth entered her apartment and locked the door.

Ruth walked into the living room and sat heavily on the sofa. She closed her eyes and massaged her temples. Ruth hoped against hope that Jocelyn would keep her mouth closed about seeing her and Aron that afternoon. She knew realistically that Jocelyn wouldn't.

Ruth would be forced to make a decision. She couldn't keep straddling the fence. She might be forced into revealing the nature of her relationship with Aron, sooner than she had planned.

Chapter Twenty-six

Aron sat on the sofa in his living room. The lights were muted as he listened to music. He hoped the jazz recordings would help lighten his depressed mood. After he and Ruth had returned from Oak Brook, he couldn't seem to shake the feeling of disappointment that had invaded his psyche.

The telephone rang. Aron's eyes scanned the caller ID and he answered it. "Hello, daughter," he greeted Monet.

"Hi, Daddy. What's happening with you?"

"Oh, nothing much. I'm relaxing, listening to music. How are Marcus and the children?"

"Everyone is fine. The kids are in bed. Marcus had to work. Elise stopped by. I'm helping coordinate her and Derek's wedding." A yawn escaped Monet's lips. "Excuse me."

"No harm done," Aron replied.

"I tried to call you about a half hour ago, and your phone just rang. What were you doing?" she asked her father nosily.

"Nothing. I just didn't feel like talking. My date with Ruth was a disaster." Aron told her about running into the Ellises.

"I'm sorry to hear that," Monet said caringly. "Though you haven't said anything to me about Pastor Ruth, I sense you have strong feelings for her. I don't want you to get hurt, Daddy."

"Are you looking inside your crystal ball?" Aron joshed with Monet. "Tell me what you see?"

"That's not it," Monet denied adamantly. "Pastors are different. People expect perfection from them and the people around them. You know I love her, and whatever is meant to be will happen. I debated telling you this, but Sarah mentioned that her father's wife has left him. Sarah always thought Pastor Ruth still had feelings for her ex-husband. Just be careful, Dad," she cautioned.

"Aren't I always? I will admit I have feelings for her, but we're not young children heading to the altar. Love and relationships are different when the parties involved are older."

"I know what you mean. But I couldn't help but notice the looks you were giving Pastor Ruth when we were at Sarah's house. And I don't think her ex-husband missed them either. Come to think of it, both of you were giving Pastor Ruth the eye."

"I think you're reading too much into this, Monet."

"I don't think so, Daddy. I always assumed you were done with that part of life. You're in your seventies." Monet stopped talking, feeling embarrassed. She felt like she was treading in dangerous waters. "That's not how I meant to say that."

"I understand." Aron tried to lighten the now-somber mood. "I'm well over the age of consent. My life is not over; there's still fire left in this old man. I admire Ruth and enjoy her company. I hope we can take our friendship to another level. I want her to accept me for who I am, and not be influenced by what other people think. As for me, there's no need for you to worry. I can handle myself."

Monet felt like she'd offended her father. "Dad, if I was out of line, then I'm sorry. I didn't mean things the

way they came out. You're entitled to your life. I guess
I'm just a little overprotective of you. People can be
so cruel, and I just don't want that for you." Her voice
was emotional and impassioned as she explained her
misgivings.

"I understand, honey, and I appreciate your caring
for me. People are always going to talk, no matter how
a person lives his life. It's the nature of the beast. But
as parents age, that doesn't mean they stop living and
give up on life, waiting for the inevitable, death. I will
be fine."

"Just be careful. Seriously, I'm tickled pink. My favorite woman in the world, who happens to be my pastor,
and my daddy are dating. I didn't see that one coming,"
she deadpanned.

"Well, Ms. Monet, gift or not, you can't always be
privy to everything. Ruth and I have a special friendship for now, and we'll see where it goes from there."

"Okay, I'll see my way out of it. I need to go check on
the children and then call Liz. Love you, Daddy." Liz is
Monet's best friend.

"I love you too, daughter. Kiss the babies for me."

"I will."

Aron's mind began racing. He prayed that Ruth
would see him for the man he had become. Aron didn't
want his sins of the past to interfere with his present.
He knew Ruth reciprocated his feelings. Most of all,
Aron hoped if Ruth had to make a choice between him
and her ex-husband, she would have the courage to follow her heart.

Chapter Twenty-seven

Ruth's favorite season, summer, was around the corner. The family made preparations to drive to Edwardsville to attend Naomi's graduation, scheduled for the second Saturday in May.

Alice was beside herself, since she wouldn't be able to make the trip. She had been receiving radiation treatments, and much to the family's relief, the tumor was shrinking. Brian promised to videotape the ceremony for her.

After some strong coaxing from Sarah, Naomi grudgingly invited Daniel to her graduation. He accepted the invitation. Felicia and Reggie would babysit the boys over the weekend while Daniel attended the ceremony.

Queen Esther also would not be going. Her doctor thought the trip would be too rigorous for a woman of her age. Though Fred was invited to the ceremony, he opted to stay in Chicago to take care of Alice.

On that Saturday, Ruth was inside her apartment when she heard the toot of a car horn. She walked to the living room, peered out the window, and waved. Brian had rented a van for the weekend. The family planned on staying in Edwardsville until Monday morning. Ruth walked into her bedroom and picked up her overnight case. She felt slightly out of sync. Sunday would be the first time she hadn't preached in five years. The last time she missed church service was when Naomi received her bachelor's degree.

She looked at herself in the mirror on the closet door, and she liked what she saw. She looked elegant. She wore an olive-colored suit with a muted gold blouse and matching bronze accessories. She wore bronze pumps on her feet. She placed the strap of her purse on her shoulder, and took her bronze-and-green straw hat off the foyer table. The doorbell rang, and she buzzed the door to admit entry into the building. Seconds later, Brian, clad in a navy suit and pale pink shirt, was standing at her door.

He leaned over and kissed Ruth's cheek. "Don't you look nice today," he complimented his mother-in-law.

"Thank you, Brian," Ruth replied. "I have one bag." She pointed to her overnight bag by the front door. "You can take it down. I'm going to stop at Alice's house for a minute. Then I'll be ready."

"Okay." Brian picked up the overnight bag and headed back outside.

Ruth walked back to the kitchen and verified that the windows were down and the back door locked. She unplugged the small appliances, set the burglar alarm, and exited the apartment. She walked across the hall and tapped lightly on Alice's door.

"It's open," Alice called from inside.

Ruth went inside and found Alice lying on the sofa. She walked over to her best friend, caressed the top of her head, and asked, "How are you feeling today?"

"Not too bad. I had a treatment yesterday, so you know how weak I feel afterward." Alice rubbed her forehead. She sat upright.

"Well, why are you out here? You could have stayed in bed. I just wanted to tell you that I'm headed to Edwardsville." Ruth pulled a sheet of paper out of her purse and handed it to Alice. "This is where we'll be staying and the telephone number to the hotel."

"Ruth, I can always call you on your cell. You look very pretty today. Go ahead and enjoy yourself this weekend. I'll be fine. You're leaving me in good hands. Fred is going to come over today and spend the weekend with me."

Ruth's left eyebrow raised. "Now, don't do anything I wouldn't do," she teased.

"Girl, please. Most of the time, I'm puking my brains out or asleep. You're the one I'm worried about. I have a feeling that Daniel's going to try and put the moves on you," Alice said.

"Humph, I don't think so," Ruth replied. "Look, I've got to go. We're going out to dinner after the ceremony. After breakfast on Monday morning, we'll head back to Chicago. I'll be back before you know it." She leaned down and hugged Alice.

"Oh, I have an envelope for Naomi. It's on the kitchen counter. Make sure you give it to her after she flips that tassel, and tell her how proud of her I am."

Ruth walked to the kitchen and removed the envelope from the counter. She slipped it into her purse. She shook her head when she returned to the room. "I tell you, Alice, you spoil that girl rotten." She put her hand on the side of her face. "I know you, and I know that you've put a check of some obscene amount inside this card. She's getting a second degree, not her first."

"That's all the more reason to give her a little something for her accomplishment." Alice smiled as she walked Ruth to the front door.

"Now, call me if you need anything," Ruth urged her friend.

"And what are you going to do in downstate Illinois? Stop worrying. Like the Allstate commercial says, I'm in good hands. Now go on and enjoy yourself with your family. You need a day off to relax. You've been going at it for a long time."

Ruth hugged her friend one more time before exiting the apartment. She went downstairs and walked in the direction of the van, which was parked a short distance down the street.

To her surprise, Daniel got out of his vehicle and walked toward her.

"Ruth," he said, "you're more than welcome to ride with me." He looked dapper, clad in a charcoal gray suit, with a crisp white shirt and red tie. "I also wanted to thank you for taking time out of your busy schedule to advise me from time to time. I hope I haven't been a pest."

"It was no problem. I would have done the same for anyone in need," Ruth remarked formally as they walked down the street.

Though he felt irked by Ruth's comment, Daniel's expression didn't change. "Anyway, your suggestions for parenting and spending time with the boys have been most helpful. I wish you'd let me take you out to dinner to show my appreciation." Daniel looked over at Ruth hopefully.

Ruth shook her head. "That's not necessary, Daniel. That's what I do as a minister. You don't have to feel obliged to take me to dinner," Ruth said calmly as a pleasant glow spread throughout her body. "I told Sarah that I would ride with her and Brian." She sounded doubtful, and she stopped walking.

"I'm sure they won't mind." Daniel took her arm and steered her toward his SUV. After he opened the door for Ruth, he went to tell Brian and Sarah that Ruth would be riding with him.

As the trip progressed, Daniel was on his best behavior. Eventually he and Ruth conversed easily. "Hey,
do you remember what fun we had when we took the
children to the Grand Canyon for summer vacation?"

"Yes, I do. I was awed by the beauty the Lord had
created."

"Remember my fortieth birthday? You had a surprise party for me."

"Yeah. The kids and I spent months planning it. The
children were so afraid you were going to miss it because you came home late."

"You did a good job. I was definitely surprised. It was
one of the high points of my life. You know I'd never
had a birthday party in my life before I met you," Daniel confessed as his voice choked.

"That's what spouses do for each other," Ruth replied easily. She'd relaxed and gotten into the spirit of
the trip down memory lane.

"You know, Ruthie, I really regret . . ." Daniel started
to say something, but he glanced at Ruth to gauge her
reaction.

"Daniel"—Ruth shook her head firmly—"now is not
the time to talk about what should have been done.
We've both moved on, and I think we should leave
things at that," Ruth said evenly. Inside, she felt an
enormous sense of satisfaction.

"Can I ask you one more question? Are you seeing
anyone?" Daniel asked Ruth.

"That's really not your business," Ruth replied, tight-
lipped. She thought about Aron, grew quiet, and stared
outside the window.

Daniel made several halfhearted attempts to steer
their talk toward more personal matters, but Ruth
firmly led the conversation back to less private conversation.

Daniel felt slightly discouraged. His plan to win back Ruth was hitting a roadblock. Still, he remained hopeful that he'd win her over before the weekend ended. There was no doubt in Daniel's mind that when they returned from Edwardsville, Aron would be permanently out of the picture.

Six and a half hours, and two rest stops later, Brian and Daniel pulled into the Southern Illinois Edwardsville campus. Traffic was severely backed up due to the massive crowd, who'd come together to see their loved ones receive their degree. It took nearly twenty minutes before the men finally found parking spaces. After exiting the vehicles, the family joined the crowd that was entering the grounds where the ceremony would be held.

Ruth tried her best to sit on the end seat, but Brian beat her to it. Sarah sat next to him, with Ruth on her left, and Daniel to Ruth's right. Joshua and Maggie were in the row directly in front of them.

Daniel stood up, took off his jacket and placed it on the back of his chair. He then unloosened his tie. "Nice campus, isn't it?" he remarked to Ruth.

"Yes, it is," she said.

She unsnapped her purse, took out her glasses, and put them on her nose. She quickly flipped open the program book and began reading, to stave off further conversation with Daniel. Ruth quickly turned to the page listing the graduates' names and found Naomi's. She grinned.

Sarah leaned over and asked Ruth if she knew whether or not Montgomery planned to sit with them.

Ruth shrugged her shoulders.

"Do you think we should save the seat for him on the end, next to Joshua, before someone sits there?" Sarah asked.

"It wouldn't hurt," Ruth said. Daniel's eyes roamed the crowd of people.

As if on cue, Montgomery sauntered over to the family, with his video camera dangling from a strap on his shoulder. He welcomed the family to Edwardsville.

After the greetings were exchanged, Ruth asked him if he planned to sit with them. Montgomery declined, saying he had a seat near the stage, so he could videotape the ceremony. "Naomi told me to tell you to meet us at our house after the ceremony, and we're going to have dinner there," he said.

Ruth and Sarah looked at each, and their eyebrows rose simultaneously. Naomi had failed to mention that she lived with Montgomery.

Montgomery pulled a slip of paper out of his pocket with instructions to their house, and handed it to Brian. Brian, in turn, put the paper in his jacket pocket.

"Well, I'd better be getting back," he said, glancing at his watch. "The ceremony should be starting soon. We'll see you afterward."

The classical music, which had been playing softly, intensified in volume as the graduates lined up in the rear area of the grounds. The school band played the opening notes of "Pomp and Circumstance" as the graduates marched to their seats.

Naomi winked at her family as she passed their aisle. Ruth's smile glowed ever so brightly as tears filled her eyes. Maggie waved at Naomi.

As the ceremony progressed, both Ruth and Sarah were filled with emotion. When the president of the university announced Naomi's name and presented her with her degree, tears overflowed from Sarah's eyes. Brian put his arm around his wife. Ruth brushed away a tear from her eye. To her surprise, Daniel took her hand and held it tightly. She looked down at his hand and fought an urge to snatch it back. When Naomi returned to her seat, Ruth gently removed her hand from his.

The ceremony ended ninety minutes later. It took almost another half hour for the family to exit the area and return to their cars. Brian entered Naomi's address into the van's GPS unit, and soon they were on their way.

Montgomery and Naomi's spacious two-story town house was located in an upscale area outside Edwardsville. It was situated on five acres of land. The emerald green lawn was perfectly manicured. Brian whistled as he parked the van in the circular driveway. The front door flew open, and Naomi ran outside to greet her family. Hugs and kisses were exchanged. Brian began snapping pictures.

"I'm so glad you all could make it," Naomi said joyfully.

She looked beautiful, dressed in a cream-colored skirt, with a tan-and-cream striped blouse. Diamond earrings twinkled in her ears, and a gold-and-diamond tennis bracelet dangled from her right wrist. Her body was cloaked in the breezy fragrance of Juicy Couture cologne.

Ruth blinked her eyes a couple of times, as if trying to figure out who the sophisticated young woman standing in front of her was.

After Brian took pictures outside, Naomi said, "Let's go inside. I can hardly wait for you to see my home."

The family followed her inside. If they were amazed by the outdoors, the inside was truly a sight to behold.

"Wow," Maggie said as she peered at the rooms she could see from the foyer, "your house is fly, Naomi. I like it."

The house was formal, yet cozily decorated with warm, earth-toned colors of mocha, burnt orange, cream, and umber. Naomi took her relatives on a tour of the house.

The men retired to the den, while Joshua and Maggie went inside the game room. A billiards table occupied the center of the room, and an Xbox was connected to a flat-screen television. The Wilcox women walked to the room they considered the center of any home, the kitchen.

Ruth remarked, "The house is simply beautiful, Naomi. Is this your house or Montgomery's?" Ruth knew the answer to the question. Still, she wanted to hear confirmation from Naomi as to why she hadn't told the family about her living arrangement.

"It actually belongs to both of us. Montgomery added my name to the deed after I accepted his marriage proposal."

"Good for him," Sarah said, her eyes taking in the high-tech silver appliances in the tangerine-and-white kitchen.

"We were surprised when Montgomery told us we would be coming to your house. How come you didn't tell us that you lived with him?" Ruth asked her daughter.

"I—I don't know," Naomi stammered. "I guess because I thought you all would disapprove, and I feel like I have the right to lead my life as I see fit, like everyone in this family has."

"You're right. I would not have approved, but that would not have stopped me from loving you, or coming to your house," Ruth said carefully.

"Thank you, Momma. I was wrong. I wanted to tell you everything." Her hand swept in the air. "I just didn't know how. I could picture you and Aunt Alice saying, 'Nay, don't tell me that you're shacking up with a man.'"

"You're right, Naomi. That is exactly what we would have said. Anything we say or do is out of love for you," Ruth said.

"It looks like Montgomery makes big bucks," Sarah said. "Is he a millionaire or something?"

"He's very comfortable. His business does well, and he has a trust fund," Naomi said.

The doorbell rang, and Naomi shot up from her seat. "That's probably the caterer. Give me a minute."

She left the room to answer the door, while Ruth and Sarah looked at each other, thinking, *Caterer? We could have just gone out to dinner?*

Naomi and Montgomery returned to the room minutes later, accompanied by three young men who were carrying platters of food. Naomi directed them to put the food on the counters.

Montgomery removed bottles of ale from the refrigerator. "Let us know when the food is ready," he said to Naomi before heading back to the den.

After he left, Sarah couldn't resist saying, "So where's your wait staff? Surely, you hired someone to serve us?"

"Stop teasing me, Sarah." Naomi laughed. "I just thought it would be nice if you guys had dinner here, since this is your first time seeing me and Monty's place. I thought it would take too long to cook, so I ordered dinner. I know you and Momma are going to help me set up the food. Plus, you know I'm not as handy in the kitchen as you two and Miss Maggie."

Maggie wandered into the kitchen. "I love your house, Naomi. It looks like the houses on *MTV Cribs*. Can I come and visit this summer?" She looked at Naomi, with a hopeful spark in her eyes.

"Sure, you can, if it's all right with your mom and dad." She looked at Sarah.

"We'll see," Sarah replied.

"Okay, then. Ladies, can I get your help in setting out dinner? I requested Sterno heaters to keep the food warm, so we just need to set out the plates and utensils."

Naomi gave Sarah and Ruth aprons to put over their outfits. Soon the food had been placed on the dining-room table, and Ruth blessed the food. Naomi had ordered crab cakes, chicken and sun-dried tomato bruschetta, garlic sausage bread, and lamb cannelloni for appetizers. The entrees included baked lasagna, spaghetti and meatballs in marinara sauce, roasted turkey breasts, and slivers of roast beef.

During dinner, Daniel kept glancing at Montgomery, trying to gauge how financially well-off his soon-to-be son-in-law was. He wondered if he could hit him up for some of Naomi's tuition money back. Daniel rubbed his chin thoughtfully; maybe the solution to his financial problem was sitting at the head of the dining-room table.

Chapter Twenty-eight

In Chicago, Fred had just finished fixing Alice a bowl of soup. They were seated in the dining room.

"I wonder how Naomi's gradation was. I sure wish I could have gone," she said to Fred, who sat at the other end of the sofa.

"I'm sure everything went well." He nodded. "It's hard for me to wrap my head around the fact that little Naomi has two college degrees. I know Ruth must be so proud."

"She is. She nearly tore the graduation announcement up from re-reading it. Is there something you want to watch on television?"

"No, the movie you selected is fine. I'm lucky you like action movies and not girlie ones," Fred said.

"Oh, I like them too. I'm just not in the mood for one right now."Alice glanced at Fred. "What made Daniel decide to go to Edwardsville? Ruth told me that Naomi only invited him because it was the proper thing to do. She really didn't expect him to attend."

Fred tore his attention away from the plasma screen and looked at Alice. "I think my baby brother is up to something, but I haven't quite figured out what yet."

"I hope it doesn't involve Ruth. She's finally happy, and I don't want Daniel to bring her any foolishness."

"You know my brother; who knows what he's thinking? We aren't as close as we used to be, but we're working on getting back in order. Lenora really messed up things for everyone. Like a tornado, she left a patch of destruction in her wake."

"You can say that again. It's too bad those boys have to suffer," Alice said. "Well, I'm glad Daniel has pulled himself together, but I hope he didn't do so at the expense of Ruth's happiness. She's been dating a man from the church, and he seems to be good for her."

Alice's comment got Fred's attention. "You mean to tell me the good minister is dating? I hadn't heard anything about that."

"Well, you can't be in on everything that goes on around here. I think for once Ruth is finally experiencing happiness, and I'm glad for her. She's a good woman who has been dogged, and her time has come." A spasm of pain crossed Alice's face.

Fred looked at her with a worried, concerned expression. "What's wrong?" he asked; there was an alarmed note in his voice. "Is something hurting?"

Alice gestured limply to the pail sitting next to the couch, her breathing shallow. "I feel like I'm going to . . ."

Fred jumped up and placed the pail close to Alice so she could have use of it. Her stomach heaved intermittently. Fred went to the bathroom and returned with a wet towel. He put it on Alice's forehead.

When she was finally able to talk, she said weakly, "It's the darn therapy they give me. They say its worse than the disease sometimes."

"I understand," Fred said tenderly as he pushed Alice's thinning twists away from her face.

Minutes later, she drifted off to sleep. Fred returned to the bathroom, where he emptied and rinsed out the pail. He returned to the sun parlor and sat on the end of the sofa, where he kept a careful watch on Alice, who continued to sleep.

Fred stroked his jaw, and became troubled as he thought about his brother. In a way, he was glad that Alice had fallen asleep. He wasn't quite ready to admit yet that Daniel was a completely changed man. Sure, he and his brother had become closer over the past few months, but Fred wasn't picking up on the vibe that Daniel was a changed man yet.

Daniel had called Fred a few weeks ago, to say that Lenora had sent him a divorce decree from Reno, Nevada. Daniel promptly signed and returned it to Lenora. Residency could be established in Nevada within six weeks. The decree stated Daniel would retain custody of the boys. The couple's assets were split. Fred argued with his brother, saying he should have consulted a lawyer before he signed on the dotted line. Daniel retorted that he just wanted to be free of Lenora and move on. Lenora further stated in her letter that she would be in touch with Daniel soon regarding visitation and other matters. No mention was made of child support.

Fred told Daniel that if Lenora had any income, even if it was from her new man, that legally she was supposed to pay him child support. Daniel also told him about the house being in foreclosure status. Fred asked Alice's opinion, not admitting that Daniel was the person of whom he had spoken. Alice mentioned something known as a "short sale." His son-in-law, Vincent, Tamara's husband, was in real estate, so Fred also talked to him. Vincent suggested Fred's friend, aka Daniel, try to refinance the house, or, like Alice had advised, go for a short sale.

Fred told Daniel that he couldn't keep his head buried in the sand forever, and that he needed to take action. Vincent wanted to talk to Fred's friend about his options, but Daniel declined, saying he had a few tricks up his sleeve that he wanted to try first.

Fred was worried that whatever his brother's tricks were, they involved Ruth; and like Alice, he thought his former sister-in-law deserved happiness.

Alice moaned in her sleep. Fred tenderly kissed the top of her head. Then he took her hand. Fred closed his eyes. He hadn't prayed to God in a long time asking for something, but at that moment, he felt compelled to ask God to leave Alice here on earth a little while longer. Fred shook his head and marveled that he and Ruth's sassy friend had developed a relationship, especially a nonsexual one. He smiled as he tightened his grip on Alice's hand. Fred vowed to be there for Alice for the long haul, as long as she needed and wanted him.

In Edwardsville, Brian, Daniel, and Montgomery had gone to the Marriott to check in the family. Ruth, Sarah, and the children were still at Naomi's house. Josh and Maggie were watching television in the den. The women were chatting in the kitchen. Ruth wiped her hands on the napkin and excused herself, announcing that she needed to check her voice mail. When she returned, her shoulders and the corners of her mouth sagged sadly.

"Brother Eddie Duncan was called home this morning. You know he was ill. He suffered a stroke a few days after the finance meeting. And I never got a chance to talk to him about what he wanted that night," she said sadly.

"He was one of Bishop's closest friends, wasn't he?" Naomi asked. She had just brought a tray bearing cups of cappuccino to the table for the women.

"Yes, he was. Brother Duncan was one of the old-timers. Some of the finance committee members looked at him as an irritant, but he was really knowledgeable about The Temple's financial structure. I had to lean on him heavily after I was voted in as senior pastor."

"Don't beat yourself up, Momma. I'm sure he understood how much pressure you've been under," Sarah said comfortingly.

"I know, but I still feel terrible," Ruth said dejectedly.

"Well, you're not a superwoman, and that means some things are going to slip through the cracks from time to time. I know that's happened to me a time or two," Naomi commented. She sipped her cappuccino and set the cup on the table. "I ordered desserts. Whenever you're ready, let me know."

"I'd love some, Naomi. Sweets would go good with the cappuccino." Sarah turned her attention to her mother. "So who else called, Momma? Did you get any good calls?"

Naomi looked at her sister, then her mother. "What am I missing here?"

"Momma's got a boyfriend." Sarah couldn't resist teasing her mother. "He's a hottie for an old man."

"Momma!" Naomi's voice rose shrilly. "You've been holding out on me," she said in a quasi-stern tone of voice. "You told me that you and Mr. Reynolds were just friends." Naomi had missed the byplay at Sarah's house. She was so attuned to Montgomery.

"Well, I wouldn't call Mr. Reynolds a 'boyfriend.' He's a very close friend," Ruth said as a smile crept into her voice. "We go out here and there frequently. I've truly been enjoying my time with Aron. He's an amazing man." Ruth's face lit up with pleasure.

"That's good." Naomi nodded approvingly. "You deserve happiness, even if you're a minister." She couldn't resist teasing her mother.

"That's what I tell her too," Sarah said, crinkling her nose. "She's trying to keep her relationship on the down low, though."

Naomi replied, "Well, I guess when she's ready, she'll let the world know. People will have to trust Momma's judgment. After all she's been through, Momma knows a good man from a bad one."

"Amen to that," Sarah added. "She has our support, and I know Aunt Alice is thrilled for her."

"Stop talking about me like I'm not in the room," Ruth complained. "I called Alice while I was in the other room too. Fred said she's been suffering the effects from the radiation treatment most of the day, but other than that, she's doing well." She opened her purse and presented Naomi with the cards that Queen, Alice, and Fred had sent her, along with her own.

Sarah quickly reached for her purse on the floor and gave her sister a card from her family.

Naomi quickly opened the cards. "Aunt Alice always comes through," she said triumphantly. She waved a check in the air. "It's for a thousand dollars."

She quickly tore open the other envelopes, which also contained checks. She had a nice little stash, close to three thousand dollars.

"Thank you." Naomi jumped out of her seat. "I love all of you. You're the best family in the world." She stood the cards up on the counter and then returned to her seat. "Let's revisit our conversation on these hot old birds!" she whooped. "Who would have thought that Aunt Alice would be dating our playa-playa uncle, and Momma would even be dating, period? I guess, as Bishop used to say, 'you live and learn.'"

"Well, we can't leave you out of the equation, baby girl," Sarah said. "Who would have thought that you would end up engaged to a white Englishman, of all people, and a rich one at that? Now, that truly blows my mind. When are you getting married? Do you plan to marry here or in merry England?"

"Yeah, I guess you're right," Naomi said. "We Wilcox women are just full of surprises. No, we haven't set a date yet, with school and all. We plan to talk about it once the dust settles after my graduation. My first priority is finding a job. I've interviewed at a couple of firms this week. I hope to hear good news from one of them soon."

"I know you'll find something," Sarah consoled her sister.

"You know, this house would make a great setting for a wedding." Ruth stood up and walked to the patio door and looked outside. "The backyard is huge. If you were inclined, you could have your wedding and reception here."

"You know what, that's not a bad idea. I'll keep that in mind. And, of course, I want you and Sarah to help me plan everything. I'll definitely plan it for after Aunt Alice is doing better," Naomi said.

"She would appreciate that, and she'll want to be a part of the planning," Ruth said. "How does Montgomery's family feel about you and him? I mean your being black?"

"If there was any fallout, it wasn't overt. Monty's mother is pure British. She kept a stiff upper lip, as the English say. I met her a few years ago, when Monty and I went to Europe. Of course, I didn't tell you two at the time that I was traveling with a man."

"And all this time, I thought your trip was school related." Ruth shook her head. "You're a sly one, Naomi Patrice Wilcox."

"I did what I had to do to keep the peace." Naomi's chin jutted upward. "Being in Europe was like being in a different world altogether. I enjoyed my time there, but I definitely wouldn't want to live there," she confessed.

"Good," Ruth said approvingly. "It's bad enough that you live six hours away from us now."

"So, obviously, you won't be moving back to Chicago now that you're done with school?" Sarah asked.

"No, I plan to live here, of course. Monty's business is here, and I don't see him relocating to Chicago. Edwardsville is not that bad, and living in a small town has its advantages. The crime rate is lower, and the climate is warmer. I don't miss those Chicago winters at all." Naomi glanced at her sister. "Maggie and Joshua are more than welcome to spend time with us this summer. I would love to have them."

"We'll see," Sarah responded. "Joshua is scheduled for some basketball camps, as well as some campus visits, and Maggie is helping out at the church for Bible School this summer."

"Well, let me know if they have time. The stay could just be a long weekend. I know Joshua is hoping to attend a Big Ten school, like Brian did. It's hard to believe he's almost done with high school." Naomi shook her head.

"That's true. He'll be a junior in September." Sarah sighed. "Time is flying. Momma, I hope the guys come back soon, so we can go to the hotel. I don't know about you, but it's been a long day, and I'm a little tired from the ride."

"You're right, these old bones are tired." Ruth put her hand over her mouth to stifle a yawn.

"Well, now that you've seen our house, perhaps next time you guys could stay with us. We have plenty of room. Since I hadn't mentioned Monty and I were living together, I couldn't ask you to stay with me until you knew my true living arrangements," Naomi said guiltily.

"We understand, and next time we'll see. Goodness, Naomi, the last time all of us were here was for your graduation when you got your bachelor's degree," Ruth said.

"Truthfully, it took me a while to come to terms with everything that happened during my first year of school. I was thrown for a loop. I took a year off school to recover from learning who my biological parents are. I'm happy to say that I've put it behind me."

Ruth smiled happily at her daughter. "I'm so glad to hear that."

The men returned from the hotel, and the women continued to chat. A half hour later, Sarah went to round up the family. Montgomery invited them for brunch at a local restaurant the following morning. The family agreed and planned to spend the afternoon with Naomi. They would then head back to the hotel to rest, to prepare for the long drive back to Chicago.

"Well now that you know where we stay, please feel free to visit us anytime. We would love to have you." Montgomery extended an open invitation to the family.

Twenty minutes later, the Wilcox family was riding the ten miles from Naomi's house to the Marriott Hotel. Before long, they were checked into their rooms.

Ruth called Alice, then Aron. They made plans to meet Monday. She then took a nice hot soak in the tub. She had just finished putting on her nightclothes, and had stretched out on the king-size bed, when there was a knock on the door. She walked across the room and peeked out the peephole. She was surprised to see Daniel standing there. She threw on her robe and slowly opened the door.

"Hi, Daniel. What can I do for you?" she asked, clutching her robe tighter to her body.

"Say, I was wondering if I could talk to you? Can you spare me a few minutes?" Daniel had changed into jeans and a Ralph Lauren striped polo shirt.

"Couldn't we do this another time?" Ruth asked. "I'm tired from the long drive here and the festivities of the day." Her arms snaked around her body.

"We could, but it'll only take a few minutes." Daniel sounded mysterious.

Ruth didn't feel like dealing with Daniel right at that moment. "Why don't you give me a call on Monday? Since I was away from church this weekend, I plan to go to The Temple on Monday. I'm really tired."

"Sure, I'll do that. I'm sorry if I bothered you," Daniel said in a humble tone of voice as he stepped away from the door. He turned to go down the hall, and then he turned back toward Ruth. "Pleasant dreams, Ruth. Sleep tight."

She nodded at him, with a quizzical expression on her face, then closed and locked the door.

Ruth felt agitated after she returned to bed. She wondered what Daniel was up to. Their relationship before the divorce had been contentious at best. It had taken her a long time to discard the feeling of betrayal she felt when he divorced her. To add insult to injury, Daniel married Lenora in a short period of time after the divorce. Ruth was unaware that Lenora was pregnant at the time of the marriage.

Ruth's mind raced a mile a minute. She wasn't sure what Daniel was up to, but she felt in her spirit he was up to something.

Her eyelids fluttered as she fought sleep. She pulled the comforter over her shoulders, and within a few minutes, the television stared at her, instead of the other way around.

Meanwhile, Daniel returned to his room down the hallway. He sat on a chair next to the bed, fuming. He couldn't understand why Ruth wouldn't allow him inside her room to talk. *I must be losing my touch,* he thought. It was bad enough that Lenora had left him for another man. Now Ruth—who, he assumed, still had feelings for him—wouldn't allow him to talk to her. Then just as quickly as those feelings entered his mind, they dissipated. He knew all he had to do was turn up the heat, and Ruth would succumb to his charm.

He had asked Sarah questions about Aron following the family dinner. Sarah informed him that whatever was going on was her mother's business, and not hers to share. Daniel snapped his fingers. Fred had also told him about Aron's background. Daniel stored the information in his memory banks and planned to use it when opportunity presented itself. Daniel felt little remorse at his actions. Ruth deserved better than Aron, and he counted on her doing right by her congregation.

Daniel decided it was time to get the competition out of the way, and he knew just how.

Chapter Twenty-nine

Brian had just returned to his and Sarah's room. They were staying in a two-bedroom suite, and Maggie was in the second bedroom asleep. Joshua had bunked out on the couch in the sitting room, and he, too, was asleep. Brian had gone down the hall to get ice for soft drinks he'd brought from Naomi's house. When he entered the room, Sarah was dozing off.

He quickly woke her up, and when she was coherent, he announced dramatically, "Guess who I saw at your mother's door?"

Sarah quickly became alert. "Who?" she asked.

"Your father." Brian popped open a can of ginger ale and poured it into a plastic cup the hotel had supplied. "Do you want some of this?"

Sarah sat upright in the bed and shook her head. "You're kidding me, right?" Her eyes were glued to Brian, who stood on the other side of the room.

"I kid you not. I couldn't believe what I was seeing."

"Did he go inside Momma's room?"

"I couldn't tell," Brian admitted; he was sipping the gold-colored beverage while they talked. He walked to the bed and sat on the other side of it. "I ducked inside the door to the stairwell. When I thought the coast was clear, I came back to our room. Say, you don't think your parents are going to reconcile, do you?"

"I don't think so," Sarah said decisively. She lay back in bed. "I noticed the two of them holding hands when

Naomi got her diploma." Sarah snapped her fingers. "I bet Daddy was probably trying to hit Momma up for some money when he went to her room. He has this idea in his head that she's loaded. I can tell by some of the comments he's made in the past that that's in his mind. And his finances are pretty tight right now."

"Well, he's right. Momma Ruth does have money. I bet your father's finances are stretched tighter than a rubber band right now. Who in his right mind would have gotten a mini-mansion in an elite suburb at his age?"

"An old man trying to please his young bride," Sarah quipped. "I agree with you, buying that house with Lenora wasn't one of Daddy's smartest moves. He asked me if we would consider taking a loan out on our house for him."

"You didn't tell me that." Brian looked incredulous. "When did he ask you that?"

"Hmm . . ." Sarah closed her eyes, thinking. "It was a couple of weeks ago."

"I hope you told him no." Brian had bought a bag of chips from the vending machine. He opened it and put a few in his mouth.

"Of course, I did," Sarah responded. "I told him that he needed to put the house on the market, and move as soon as he could before he was put out."

"What did he say?"

"That he would think about it. He'd better do more than think. His mortgage is months in arrears."

"How did that happen?" Brian asked.

"Lenora was paying the bills, or so Daddy thought. She was probably taking trips with her boy toy. I loaned him money to pay his utilities until his check comes on the fifteenth."

"Well, how the heck was he able to come here for the weekend? I mean, gas money and pay for the hotel?"

"I loaned him the money for that too." Sarah looked contrite. "I thought about the times in the past when he loaned us money, Brian, and I just couldn't say no."

"I understand. It just would have been nice had you told me before you did it."

"I'm sorry. I planned on telling you this weekend."

Brian nodded. "We need to tighten our belts as far as spending. I didn't mind coming to Edwardsville this weekend. Naomi's graduation is a special event. There have been layoffs at my job, and I just want to make sure we're in a good financial position, should one of us lose our jobs."

"I understand," Sarah murmured. "There have been layoffs at my job too. Luckily, I have seniority, and so far, the last hires have been the ones getting pink slips."

"We have Joshua and Maggie to put through college. Hopefully, with help from the Lord, Joshua will get a sports scholarship, and Maggie will win an academic one."

"That's why I couldn't agree to us taking out a loan against the house. We may need to do that when it's time for the kids to go to college."

"We were blessed that your mother gave us the house when she and Aunt Alice bought the apartment building, and that the mortgage was paid off," Brian remarked.

"You are so right," Sarah concurred. "On another topic, I was so proud of Naomi today. She definitely has her head on straight. Who would've thought that she would have two degrees? She has a sense of poise and sophistication that I could never hope to have. I am so in awe of her."

"You're just fine the way you are, babe." Brian kissed Sarah's cheek. "I'm proud of her too. She seems to have her life mapped out for her. I wish we could have done better by her. Still, in the long run, things turned out well, better than we could have hoped for when you gave birth to her." His voice became hushed. "One day, we're going to have to tell Maggie and Joshua that Naomi is their sister, and not their aunt. Time is passing so quickly, you know, that day may be here sooner that we think," Brian said.

"I know, and I'm not sure how they're going to react." Sarah looked troubled.

"Probably a little confused at first, but they're good kids. They'll be fine," Brian said encouragingly.

"I just hope they don't look at us as hypocrites. We have emphasized so much the importance of waiting to have sex, and then for them to find out I had Naomi at fifteen . . . I don't know." Sarah's voice trailed off.

"I think they'll look at us as being impulsive, and realize that we made a mistake by not waiting to have sex until we were married."

"I hope you're right. But the situation could turn out to be a case of 'do as I say, not as I do.'"

"We'll cross that bridge when we get to it." Brian pulled Sarah into his arms. They snuggled together and continued to talk into the night. Finally Brian dropped off to sleep. Sarah couldn't sleep. She tossed and turned, her body racked with tension. Visions of trying to tell Maggie and Joshua the truth of Naomi's parentage intruded in her thoughts.

Sarah's eyes filled with tears as she imagined a horrible backlash from her children, especially Maggie. The young girl thought the sun rose and fell on her mother. Sarah couldn't bear being imperfect in her daughter's eyes. Finally she nestled against Brian's warm body and settled into a troubled sleep. Nightmares of Maggie pointing an accusing finger at her, yelling, "Mommy, you're a hypocrite," over and over, marred Sarah's rest.

Chapter Thirty

After sharing breakfast in the hotel dining room, the family spent Sunday with Naomi and Montgomery. They all attended a local nondenominational church. Later in the day, Sarah and Ruth prepared Sunday dinner.

Daniel tried several times during the day to engage Ruth in personal conversation. She managed to avoid him like the plague. That evening when the family returned to the hotel, Ruth was relieved there wasn't a knock at her door.

The shrill ring of the telephone awakened Ruth the following morning. She had requested a wake-up call. She rose from the bed and opened her Bible, which lay on the nightstand, and turned to Psalm 118: *O Give thanks unto the LORD; for he is good: because his mercy endureth for ever*. She continued reading the chapter until she came to the twenty-fourth verse. Her lips curved into a smile as she read, *This is the day which the LORD hath made; we will rejoice and be glad in it*. She said her morning prayers. Then she prepared for the day.

Ruth rode back to Chicago with Sarah and Brian. The two older women exchanged worried glances because Maggie was unusually quiet. Her face was pale and her mood withdrawn. Sarah asked Maggie a couple of times if anything was wrong. With her head bowed, Maggie replied that she was tired.

By one o'clock that afternoon, the family had returned safely home to Chicago without incident, and they all went their separate ways. They had decided to leave Edwardsville very early to avoid rush-hour traffic.

After Ruth changed clothes, she went downstairs to collect her mail. Then she went to visit Alice, who was feeling a little better. When Ruth returned to her apartment, she called the home to check on Queen Esther; then she called Aron to tell him that she had made it safely back to Chicago. They made plans to meet later that evening. By midafternoon, Ruth went to visit Brother Duncan's family.

When she arrived at the Duncan home, she found the house filled with his immediate family members, his children, grandchildren, and great-grandchildren. After greetings were warmly exchanged, Ruth and Brother Duncan's three daughters and two sons entered the dining room. Brother Duncan's oldest daughter, Edwina, went into the kitchen to prepare coffee. When she was done, Ruth and the Duncan siblings sat in the dining room to discuss the funeral arrangements.

The wake was set for Saturday morning, with the funeral to follow immediately. Brother's Duncan's middle daughter promised to have the program done no later than Wednesday.

"So, is there anything else I can do for you?" Ruth asked the family. They agreed that was all for now. Ruth prayed for the family and prepared to leave.

Edwina put her hand on Ruth's arm, saying, "Pastor Wilcox, my father had a package he wanted me to give you. Please give me a moment to go to his room and get it for you."

Ruth chatted with the family until Edwina returned to the living room. She handed Ruth a large envelope with her name on it.

"Thank you, Edwina," Ruth said, stuffing the envelope into her bag. "I'll be in touch with you; and if there's anything I or the church can do, please give June a call. The Helping Hands Club will be in touch also. They'd like to assist you with the repast."

"Thank you, Pastor. We've gotten many calls from the church members. They have made our burden a little easier, knowing we have our church family to reach out to."

"Take care, God is in the blessing business, even in the midst of your sorrow," Ruth murmured. She left the house and drove to the North Side to visit her mother.

Queen Esther was not in a very good mood that day. She wasn't talkative, except to say how she wanted to go home with Bishop, and Ruth had to coax her to eat. Ruth stayed with Queen for a few hours and then headed home.

There was an accident on the expressway, which made Ruth's drive home twice as long. By the time she parked her car in the garage and walked inside the apartment building, Ruth was exhausted, mentally and physically. She checked on Alice, who was asleep. Ruth dropped her bag on the floor when she went into her own apartment; she sat on the sofa, crossed her legs, and leaned her head against the back of the sofa, closing her eyes.

She sat that way until her doorbell rang. She got up slowly from the sofa and pressed the intercom button. "Who is it?" she asked.

"It's Daniel."

She reluctantly pressed the buzzer, allowing him entry into the building. She unlocked and opened the front door.

"Daniel," she murmured. Ruth nervously raked her fingers through her hair. "Come in."

They walked to the living room. Ruth sat on a chair across from Daniel, who sat on the couch. He took off his jacket and laid it on the sofa, and then he laid his cap on the cocktail table.

"What can I do for you, Daniel?" Ruth asked him point-blank.

"Thank you for seeing me. I know you told me to call you later today, but I have an urgent problem and need your help."

Ruth was taken aback, her hand fluttered to her neck. She couldn't imagine what Daniel could possibly want, and what she could do to help him. She nodded her head and said, "Go on."

"I'm having a financial situation," Daniel confessed. "And I've lost the house. When I got home today, I had another notice from the mortgage company. This one told me I have thirty days to vacate the premises." He shifted uncomfortably on the couch.

"I'm sorry to hear that. I know the economy has affected a lot of people adversely," Ruth said. Her voice oozed sympathy. "I don't know what I can do to help you."

"Actually, there is something you can do. Sarah told me you have an apartment for rent, and I was wondering if you would consider renting it to me."

Shock blossomed across Ruth's face. "Daniel, I don't think that would be a good idea," she finally blurted out.

"I know it would be a little awkward at first, but I think it could work." Daniel was prepared to present his case.

"First of all, we don't have any children in the building, and that was by design. We prefer to rent to senior citizens, so they can have a quiet place to live. Daniel, you have three boys; and from what I've seen, they're not quiet at all."

"I understand"—Daniel nodded his head—"but this is me, your ex-husband, and I'm in need. I'm begging you to help me," he said humbly.

Ruth had never seen this side of Daniel, and she felt floored, to say the least.

"Aren't there other places you can check into?" Ruth asked. Her eyes searched Daniel's face, trying to find an ulterior motive for his request.

"I've been looking around, and most places want an arm and a leg for enough room for me and the boys. Sarah told me your apartments have two bedrooms, and a sun parlor that could be turned into a third. That would be perfect. It will be an adjustment for the boys, coming from a large house in the suburbs to an apartment in the city. I feel we can make it work, though."

"I understand what you're saying, but here?" Ruth's eyes widened with mistrust. "Maybe you should look for a house to rent. That might be better than an apartment."

"I have." Daniel's voice deepened with emotion and he held out his hand. "I haven't had much luck. I'm on a fixed income. Lenora wasn't paying the bills like she said she was. Most of the bills for the house were in my name, so my credit is shot."

"Oh," Ruth said. Understanding dawned in her eyes. She realized why he had come to her. He needed a place to live.

"I would be good for the money. I just need time to get things together. It wouldn't have to be a long-term lease, just enough time to get back on my feet." Daniel continued to press his case.

"Daniel, I don't know." Ruth twisted her hands together nervously. "The building doesn't belong to me alone. Alice is the co-owner, and she would have to approve as well. Give me time to think about it, and I'll get back to you." Ruth felt extremely uncomfortable with Daniel's request. She wanted the conversation to be over.

Daniel stood up. "That's all I can ask." He put his jacket on and zipped it up. "Wasn't Naomi's graduation great? I'm proud of her. You did a good job raising the kids, Ruth. My hat goes off to you. I was surprised to see Naomi with a white man. It looks like she has done well for herself. Looks like she's about to marry into money." Daniel put his cap on his head.

Ruth didn't miss the veiled challenge that Daniel had thrown at her. She had the feeling that if she didn't go along with his agenda, he would try to hit up Montgomery for money.

"I hope you're not planning on asking Montgomery for money," Ruth said sternly. "He's not your son-in-law yet. And I don't think Naomi would approve, so I wouldn't recommend going that route."

"I will do what I have to do to make sure the boys don't suffer," Daniel remarked casually. "Just give some thought to my request, Ruth. I know you will come to the right decision. Oh, and by the way, your apartment is nice. I like it."

"Thank you." Ruth was visibly upset as she walked Daniel to the front door.

Before he departed, Daniel leaned over and kissed Ruth's cheek. "Thank you for hearing me out, and I'll be looking forward to your call." He then exited the apartment.

Ruth stood at the door with her mouth open. Finally she closed the door and walked to the sofa, where she sat down heavily. "Lord, what should I do now?" she said aloud. "I can't be responsible for those children being out on the street. Guide me, Lord, and show me the way."

Her cell phone rang again. *Now what?* she thought. She clicked the phone on.

"Hello, Ruth, I hope I didn't catch you at a bad time." It was Aron. "I hate to be the bearer of bad news. There is damage on the roof on the south side of the church. Several tiles have fallen loose. I think you need to come here as soon as you can," Aron told her sympathetically.

"Okay, I'm on my way." Ruth exhaled loudly. She went to the bathroom and washed her face; then she headed to The Temple. She hoped the day wouldn't get any worse.

Chapter Thirty-one

Thirty minutes later, Aron led Ruth to the south side of the church, where he pointed out where tiles had come loose from the roof. "It doesn't appear to be very bad, but you may want to have it checked out by a professional. I'm afraid I'm out of my league with roofs," he said.

"Thank you, Aron." Ruth sighed as her eyes traveled along the top of the building. "You may want to give James a call to find out the name and number of the contractor we use. I'm sure I have the information in my office, but James may have it more readily available."

"He gave me a file with vendor information in it. I don't remember seeing a contractor name for roofs. I'll look at it again when I get home."

"I'd appreciate that. The timing is bad, because of the financial crisis."

"You might consider taking bids, or see if a member of the church is a roofer, and he could give you a discounted rate," Aron suggested.

Ruth nodded. "I'll look into that."

They left the balcony and returned to the first floor of the church.

"So how was your visit with your mother?" Aron asked as he walked Ruth to her car.

"It wasn't one of her better days. I think Queen was a bit put out that no one came to visit her this weekend.

She seems to be more manageable with a set pattern. Hopefully, things will get better as the week goes on."

"So, are we still on for this evening?" Aron asked after Ruth had gotten inside her car.

"We definitely are. One of the church members is an author, and she has a book signing at Borders on Ninety-fifth and Western, so I'm going to stop by there. Then we can meet for dinner. How does that sound?"

"Would you like me to go with you to the signing?" Aron asked.

"Not this time, maybe next time," Ruth said. She didn't miss the look of sadness that crossed his face.

She felt bad and knew she had hurt Aron, but Ruth didn't want to run the risk of running into any more church members. As Ruth had feared, Jocelyn had mentioned running into Ruth and Aron to some of her friends. According to the grapevine, Ruth and Aron had rendezvoused at the hotel. Ruth had received a few phone calls and squashed the rumor.

"I'll call you when I leave the bookstore. I'm looking forward to our date tonight. I have some things I want to share with you," she said.

"Okay, I'll see you tonight, then."

Ruth started up her car and pulled from the parking lot. She groaned heavily. *I have a lot going on,* she thought.

When Daniel arrived home, he felt pleased about the way his discussion had gone with Ruth, and he wore a smug look on his face. He was pretty much convinced that she would rent him the apartment. By being that close to her, he figured, it would be only a matter of time before they reconciled. He had activated plan A of his mission to get Ruth back, beginning with phone calls seeking her advice. Plus, he knew Ruth loved children, and he felt the boys would warm to her one day.

He felt lucky that Sarah had left a couple of church bulletins at his house when she stayed with him. Sarah's leaving them helped Daniel put plan B into motion. He used the numbers listed in the bulletin to place telephone calls to several church members, expressing his displeasure to them that their pastor was dating a convicted murderer.

He checked the messages on his answering machine, and there was one from David's school. The school secretary explained that David had been fighting, and that Daniel needed to come to school to pick up his son. David was also being suspended from school for two days.

I swear that boy is hard to handle, but handle him I will, Daniel thought. He erased the message and listened to the next one. It was from Lenora. He tightened his grip on the receiver of the telephone and frowned.

"Hey, Dan, it's me, Lenora." Her voice sounded cheerful. "I'm going to be in town Friday. Trevor has a concert in Old Town. I'd like to talk to you and get some things settled. Please give me a call back at 775-555-1515."

Daniel held his breath and then exhaled noisily. He rocked back on his heels, hung up the telephone, went to the living room, and sat down on his reclining chair. He wondered what Lenora really wanted. What was she up to?

The telephone rang again. There was a scowl on Daniel's face as he stomped to the kitchen.

"Hello," he said, nearly yelling as he answered the telephone.

"Mr. Wilcox, this is Mrs. Perry again from Arcadia Elementary School. I called you earlier regarding David. I'm afraid I'm calling again with bad news. Your son Darnell was in an accident at school. We just sent him by ambulance to St. James Hospital."

"My son is on the way to the hospital and you're just now calling me?" Daniel shouted. "Why wasn't I notified earlier?"

"Sir, we tried to call you and no one answered. We have his mother's work number on file, but when we called it, the number was disconnected. We only have the home number for you," the woman quickly explained.

"Was he hurt badly?" Daniel asked anxiously.

"He fell and hit his head in the playground, so it was serious," the woman told him in a mournful tone of voice.

"Okay, I'm on my way." Daniel hung up the telephone and rushed out of the house.

As he broke the speed limit during the short ride to the hospital, he called Sarah to tell her what had happened.

"I'm sorry to hear that, Daddy. Do you want me to meet you at the hospital?" Sarah asked anxiously as well.

"Would you?" Daniel pulled into the hospital's parking lot.

"Sure, Brian and I are off work today. We'll pick up Damon and David and bring them to our house. Joshua and Maggie can watch them. Then we'll be there as soon as we can," Sarah promised.

Daniel hurriedly exited the car. He walked briskly toward the emergency room entrance. His heart thudded deeply inside his chest as the door to the hospital automatically opened. He stepped across the threshold and raced as fast as his legs would take him to the nursing station, not having a clue as to what was awaiting him.

Chapter Thirty-two

Ruth sat with Alice for a while after she returned home. She filled her friend in on the festivities from Naomi's graduation. She showed Alice the pictures Brian had taken, and played the DVD, which she had created, on the television.

"I plan to take this picture to Walgreens this week and have it enlarged for you." Ruth pointed to what she considered the best photograph of Naomi, clad in her cap and gown. "Naomi also told me to thank you for her gift. She was quite pleased. I personally think you could have given her less money," she proclaimed.

"She called and thanked me last night," Alice told Ruth. "One thing is for sure, you can't take your money with you after you're gone," she remarked sagely. She looked older and drawn, and had lost weight. The disease had taken a toll on her physically, but not mentally.

"I guess I've made that same statement so many times over the years." Ruth laughed. Then her mood became somber; she hated to hear any reference to death or dying.

"Yes, you have, and I'll do the same for Maggie when she graduates next month. Isn't D3 graduating this year too?"

"No, he comes out in two years," Ruth replied. "Sarah and I are planning to go to his graduation. I was hoping DJ would make it home for Naomi's graduation. When

I talked to him last week, he said he had put in for leave for late this summer. So he, Chelsea, and D3 should be here then."

"It will be good to see them," Alice said wistfully. "They haven't been home in a while. You've gone there, but they haven't come here."

"You know DJ, he's full of pride, like his father. He wanted to make sure he could walk properly before he took any trips. Speaking of Daniel, he came by my apartment this morning," Ruth said.

Alice's eyebrows rose questioningly. "What did Mr. Wilcox want?"

"You won't believe this; he actually wants to move into our building."

"Has he lost his mind? I know you told him no."

"Well, not quite," Ruth hedged as she clasped her hands together nervously.

"What do you mean by that?" Alice seemed infused with a burst of energy.

"I kind of told him I would discuss it with you. In my defense, I told him that his moving into the building wasn't a good idea."

"Let me guess"—Alice's lips twisted cynically—"he gave you a sob story, and you fell for it. You know that you're more than welcome to rent the apartment to whomever you choose. But I don't think it's a good idea for Daniel to move in here."

"I agree with you. But he laid it on thick about how he and his boys were going to be put out of his house, and how he didn't have anyplace else to go."

Alice made a motion with her hands, as if playing a violin. "I knew his sob story had to be good for you to even bring this up. Poor Daniel and his boys." She shook her head. "That is not your problem. Don't let Daniel suck you in. What's wrong with his finding another place to move to?"

"He claims his credit isn't good, and that if I would bypass the credit process, he'd be good for the money."

"I don't doubt that he would be able to pay us, because he has some form of income, but I just don't trust his motives. You've had a good relationship with Aron and I don't think you should jeopardize it, because of some scheme Daniel is trying to pull. Did you talk to Aron about Daniel's request?"

"Um, well, not yet."

"Why didn't you?" Alice probed.

"I don't know. . . . I guess I wanted to sort out the request in my head before I talked to anyone about it, except for you."

"You're grown, and then some. You're free to make your own decisions. All I'm going to say, and then I'll leave it alone, is don't let Daniel back into your life. At the very least, you need to give it more time to make sure that he has changed."

"Alice, we know that people can change, if they're inclined. I wouldn't say a person's character is etched in stone. You know, all things are possible with God."

"I will give you that, but I just have a feeling that is not the case with Daniel. Do what you want to do," Alice said.

Ruth sighed; then she changed the subject. "Aron wants to go with me to Courtney's book signing and I told him no. I think his feelings were hurt."

"As they should be. You've got to stop riding the fence regarding your feelings for him. I personally think you're entitled to your life, minister or not. You need to ask yourself why you would even entertain the thought of letting Daniel move in here and not accept Aron for who he is. If your members find out you're dating him—oh, well. He's a good man."

Ruth looked down at the floor, then back up at Alice. "You're right. I'm going to head home and get ready for the signing, if you don't need me to do anything else."

"I'm good for now. Fred will be by later this evening; he's off work tonight. He's been taking good care of me. He's another man who has turned his life around, and you know I give less than a darn what people say about me. I will ask him what Daniel is up to."

"Thanks, girl, that would be a great help. And I'm going to think about where things are going with Aron. It's not fair to string him along."

"Go on, Ruth, have a good time at the signing and with Aron. Tell him I said hello."

"Will do." Ruth stood up and departed to her apartment. Forty minutes later, she had bathed and changed clothes. She was standing in front of her dresser, brushing her hair, when her telephone rang. *Goodness gracious, sometimes it's like Union Station here, very busy.*

"Hi, June," she said to her secretary after peeping at the caller ID and picking up the phone. "What's up?"

Ruth's face became ashen as she listened to her secretary. Her legs felt weak, and she sat down on the side of the bed. Her hand shook as she held the receiver to her ear.

She was in shock that some of her members had called June to complain about her relationship with Aron. She thought, at the very least, they would talk to her first.

"Okay, June. Thanks for giving me a heads-up about this. I'll address the matter as soon as possible." Ruth clicked off the telephone.

Panic invaded her body. What she had feared most had happened. The church members had found out about her dating Aron and disapproved. According to

June, several congregants had requested she talk to the church about what was really going on in her personal life. She rubbed her temples and nibbled on her lower lip as she contemplated her next move.

After sitting indecisively on the side of her bed for a few minutes, Ruth called Aron. When he answered the telephone, she told him that she had to cancel their date. "Is everything okay, Ruth?" Aron asked her worriedly. "You sound upset."

She tried to interject an upbeat mood into her voice. "I'm fine. Something's come up that requires my attention. I'll try to call you later."

"If you need me for something, you know how to find me. I'm sure that whatever came up, you can resolve it. Take care."

They ended the call on a somber note. Ruth couldn't believe she was involved in a scandal at the church. She shook her head sadly, thinking, *How did it come to this? What did I do to deserve this? I've been found guilty without anyone hearing my side of the story. What a nightmare.*

Chapter Thirty-three

When Sarah and Brian arrived at the hospital, Felicia and Reggie were there. The couples exchanged greetings.

"How's Darnell? Where is Daddy?" Sarah asked Felicia. She and Brian sat down.

Felicia flung out her hand. "He's with Darnell, who is still unconscious. They want to perform surgery. Apparently, there's swelling in his brain. The doctor is talking to Daniel now."

"Lord, take care of that child." Sarah shook her head. "Do you know what happened?"

"He had fallen during recess, but the school monitor didn't think it was serious. Later he complained of a headache and then just fell out."

"Oh, my God," Sarah murmured. "I know Daddy must be beside himself with worry."

"He is upset. I don't think Darnell's life is in jeopardy, but brain surgery is always serious. I called Lenora and asked her to come home," Felicia added. "She's on her way here from Nevada now. Lenora called me a month ago. I'm thankful that I was able get ahold of her. I've tried to talk to her about the mess she left here, but Lenora kept changing the subject. I plan to read her the riot act when I see her today."

"I'm glad she's coming. She should be here during this time. I'm going to see Daddy and find out what else is going on," Sarah said.

Felicia nodded. Sarah stood up and walked to the nursing station. She explained that Darnell Wilcox was her brother, and asked if she could see him.

The nurse pointed to the double doors and informed Sarah that Darnell was in examination room three. She could go in there, but she cautioned Sarah not to stay long.

Daniel was sitting by his son's side. He looked like he had aged ten years. All the life had drained from him.

Sarah walked over and put her hand on his shoulder. "Daddy, I got here as quickly as I could. How is Darnell doing?"

Darnell looked like an infant in the large bed. IVs and tubes were connected to his small body.

"Darnell has swelling in his brain. The doctor wants to schedule surgery soon. I hope the boy isn't permanently damaged by this. I would hate for that to happen to him." Daniel looked at Sarah with anguish in his eyes.

"He's going to pull through this, Daddy. Felicia told me what happened. We're going to pray for Darnell, and I know everything will be fine." Sarah tried to console her father, although she felt devastated by what had happened to her young half brother. She rubbed her father's arm.

"He's just a little boy. He doesn't deserve this," Daniel commented, gulping helplessly.

"Now, don't assume the worst. Medicine has come a long way from a technological standpoint. Darnell is a strong little boy."

"Sarah, would you do something for me?"

"Sure, Daddy. What do you need?" Sarah was glad to do anything she could to help out during the crisis.

"Would you call your mother and ask her to come to the hospital?" Daniel looked at his daughter pleadingly.

"Yes, but whatever for? I don't know if that's a good idea. Felicia told me she called Lenora and she's on her way here. You know Lenora doesn't like Momma. I think we should just leave Momma out of this for now," Sarah said.

"I don't give a rat's . . . I don't care who Lenora likes or dislikes. She lost all privileges and her right to be called a mother when she walked out on me and the boys. Please, Sarah, call Ruth. I need her."

Sarah hadn't ever seen her father that vulnerable. Against her better judgment, she told him that she would call Ruth, and she left the room to do just that. Daniel knew that Ruth, being a minister, would never refuse to help anyone in need. Even her ex-husband.

Chapter Thirty-four

Daniel returned to the waiting room nearly an hour later. He strode over to the family. "They're taking Darnell to the pediatric wing to prep him for surgery. I just came from the lab, donating blood just in case. We need to go to the second floor and wait." He looked at Ruth, who looked at him uncomfortably. "Thank you for coming," he said gratefully.

"No problem. That's part of my job," she said. She hadn't missed the look Felicia had given her when she walked inside the waiting room. Felicia's arched eyebrows looked like question marks that seem to inquire, *"Why are you here?"*

Felicia looked at Ruth confrontationally, like she was an intruder. Reggie quickly led his wife away from the waiting room for coffee before the situation got out of hand.

"I don't understand why she's here," Felicia complained as they walked to the elevator. "I hope Sarah told Ruth that Lenora was coming here. It could get ugly. The lady minister should have stayed home."

"Now, Fee, Reverend Wilcox is correct. Ministers do come to hospitals to support people during emergencies, and this situation definitely qualifies as an emergency. Try to behave," he chided his wife.

"I can't make any promises," Felicia said. After she purchased cups of coffee for herself and Reggie, they returned to the waiting room.

Ruth was starting to feel uneasier by the moment. She wished she had followed her better judgment and gone to Courtney's book signing, and had kept her date with Aron. Sarah had to beg her to come to the hospital; Ruth's temples pounded from the onset of a stress headache.

The group was now gathered together in a private waiting room on the second floor. A nurse entered and told Daniel the doctor would be in, momentarily, to talk to him. Daniel's expression was bleak, and he held his head down as he waited for the doctor. Sarah sat on one side of him and was talking to him quietly, while Ruth sat on his other side.

When Felicia wasn't sipping from her coffee, she kept a permanent smirk on her face as she took in the scene.

The doctor entered the room and walked over to Daniel. "Mr. Wilcox, I see that Mrs. Wilcox has made it." He looked at Ruth. "My name is Dr. McManus. I'm a neurosurgeon and I will be operating on Darnell."

"No, we're not married," Ruth quickly corrected the doctor. "I'm a family friend and a minister." She and the doctor shook hands.

"Thank you for coming to be with the family, Reverend." The doctor turned his attention back to Daniel. "Mr. Wilcox, we'll be taking Darnell into surgery in about twenty minutes. The staff has nearly completed the prep phase. I wanted to reassure you that I have performed this surgery many times in the past, so your son is in good hands. He seems to be a tough little fellow. I will have one of the nurses update you as to the status of the surgery throughout the evening."

"How long will the surgery take?" Sarah asked.

"Usually three to four hours, but timing is not a perfect science. I'll have a better idea once the surgery commences. And I'll be out to talk to you when the surgery is completed."

"Thank you," Sarah said before the doctor departed.

"I think this would be a good time to pray," Ruth suggested. The group, with the exception of Felicia, who felt that Ruth as Daniel's ex-wife had no business at the hospital, stood and held hands.

"Father, God, we come before you tonight asking that you keep Darnell in your healing hands. We can take comfort in knowing that you are the one who can make a way out of no way. Father above, guide the surgeon's hands as he works to fix whatever ails Darnell."

"Amen," Sarah murmured, with her eyes closed tightly. Brian squeezed her hand.

"Father, give us strength and patience as we wait for the surgeon to come out and tell us that all is well, and your will has been done. These blessings I ask in your son's name. Amen."

Felicia's mouth dropped open as she looked at the doorway.

"Well, isn't this a cozy scene," Lenora remarked scathingly as she walked into the room, with her tall, imposing, dreadlocked boyfriend beside her. She stood a few feet from Ruth and Daniel, with her arms folded across her chest.

Ruth's eyes traveled from Daniel and then back to Lenora.

"I see Daniel didn't waste any time calling you," Lenora spat at Ruth. "That's really ironic, because he didn't even bother to call me, and I'm Darnell's mother. I had to depend on my sister to call me. What's really been going on since I've been gone? You're not a blood relative to my son, so I don't understand why you're here," she said to Ruth.

Ruth had to admit her former nemesis still looked good. Lenora's features had become a little harder; there were lines forming around her mouth. But she still retained her trim, lithe figure. Her hair was coiffed stylishly. She wore a black sable jacket over a rose-colored silk pantsuit.

"Hello, Lenora. I'm here merely to support Sarah, Brian, and Daniel. There is nothing going on between me and your husband," Ruth said piously. She truly wished she were anywhere but at St. James Hospital. She flinched slightly when she saw Lenora walking her way.

Daniel walked to Lenora and grabbed his ex-wife's arm. "We need to talk," he said curtly as he steered her out the door and down the hallway.

Trevor stood indecisively near the door, debating if he should follow Lenora. Felicia quickly walked over to him. She introduced herself and invited Trevor to sit with her and Reggie until Lenora returned. The young man did.

Outside the waiting room, Lenora pulled away from Daniel. "Hmm, it didn't take long for your ex to come running back to you. Some women will use any excuse they can to get their claws into a man. Everyone knows that she still loves you."

Daniel gave Lenora a disgusted look and shook his head. "You should know, those are your tactics. How about asking how your son is doing? That's what any normal mother would be concerned about."

"Pardon me, I talked to the doctor. I saw him as he was leaving the waiting room. I took care of my mommy business," Lenora retorted haughtily. She folded her arms across her chest.

"Why don't you act like it, then? This is not the time or place for you to bait Ruth. She came here, as she said, to support our family. She didn't have to come at all."

"What a new twist," Lenora snickered, "you defending Ruth! Times have definitely changed."

"I'm warning you, Lenora, lay off Ruth." Daniel's tone of voice had become menacing.

"Or what?" Lenora threw back at him. She tilted her head to the side. "We'll have to continue this conversation later. I'm going to the lab to donate blood for Darnell too. The doctor suggested I do that, if he needs a transfusion. When I return, I want her gone. You don't want me to have to make her leave." She turned on her heels and returned to the waiting room. A few minutes later, Lenora and Trevor went to the lab.

Shortly afterward, Ruth rose from her seat. She told Sarah that she was leaving, and that she'd call her later. She told Daniel that she would keep Darnell in her prayers.

Sarah followed her mother out of the room. Ruth walked rapidly to the elevator, while Sarah ran to catch up with her. She was out of breath by the time Ruth paused at the elevator and punched the button for the first floor.

"Momma, I'm so sorry that happened. Please believe me," Sarah blurted out, trying to make amends.

Ruth bit her lip. She silently counted to ten in her head. "You know what, Sarah, Lenora was right about one thing: I really have no business being here. Your father is not a member of my church, or my family anymore. I hope everything goes well with Darnell. I'm sure he'll pull through the surgery successfully. Call me later and let me know how he's doing."

Sarah's eyes filled with tears as she hugged her mother. Ruth held her body rigidly against Sarah's, and the young woman was all too aware of how miserable her mother felt by Lenora's callous behavior.

Sarah whispered in Ruth's ear, "Don't let Lenora get you down. She's a witch most of the time—that's just her nature. You didn't do anything wrong."

Ruth's chin jutted upward. "I'm fine, just a little tired." She tried to smile. "Keep me posted about the baby."

"I will. Momma, I love you."

The elevator doors opened and Ruth stepped inside. She waved to Sarah as the doors closed. Ruth sighed heavily. Any ideas she had regarding a future with Daniel were gone.

Poof, up in smoke, Ruth pondered. *Who in her right mind would want to deal with that "baby mama" drama? I'm too old for that, and I have someone who appreciates me for me, and who doesn't expect favors in return.* She could hardly wait to get home to talk to Aron. What a new appreciation she had for the man.

When she exited the elevator, she peered at her watch and hoped she had time to stop at Borders and support Courtney. She knew the store closed at nine o'clock. Courtney planned to stay until the store closing.

Meanwhile, upstairs, Sarah let Daniel have it. How dare he let his ex-wife talk to her mother like that. Daniel bore his daughter's umbrage stoically. He knew there wasn't anyone who could control Lenora once she got on a roll. Daniel tried to defend himself; then he looked at Brian pleadingly, asking for help.

Finally Brian stepped in. He took Sarah by the waist and led her out of the room and outside the building. "Sarah, you know how Lenora is. There wasn't anything your dad could do. He got Lenora out of the room as soon as humanly possible. Please try to concentrate on the issue at hand, your brother's health," he urged her.

"You're right." Sarah sagged against his body. "Lenora just makes me mad sometimes. She is so selfish. How dare she come here like she's the lady of the manor or something."

"And what exactly is a 'lady of the manor'?" Brian's eyebrow rose.

"I don't know . . . but I bet Naomi does. You're right. All Lenora wants to do is get a rise out of me, anyway. I should never have let her get to me. I'm going to call Nay and tell her what's going on. I'll be back in a minute," Sarah said.

"You need some time to cool off. I swear I can see steam coming from the top of your head. Since we're out here, I'll call home to check on the kids."

Daniel felt naked as he remained in the room with Felicia and Reggie. He wished there were someone sitting with him on his side of the room, who wasn't smirking at him, like they were making fun of him. As he sat on his chair, he became angrier with Lenora. He felt it was her fault that he was in the predicament he was in. He crossed and uncrossed his legs, and tapped his fingers on the arm of the chair. He wondered what was taking Sarah and Brian so long.

A nurse walked into the room and over to Daniel. "I just wanted to give you an update on your son, Mr. Wilcox," the nurse said.

"Excuse me," Lenora interjected arrogantly. "I am Mrs. Wilcox, and would prefer you address both me and my ex-husband." The only outward sign she gave of her emotions was the rapid tapping of her foot. She and Trevor had just walked into the room. Her sleeve was rolled up and she sported a bandage on her arm.

"I'm sorry, Mrs. Wilcox," the nurse apologized, "I didn't realize you had arrived. As I was about to tell Mr. Wilcox, the surgery is progressing nicely. The doctor thinks it will take another two hours. He'll be out to talk to you once he's done." The nurse left the room.

"Well, she really didn't tell us much," Lenora grumbled. She flounced to her seat and pushed her hair out of her face.

"Why don't we go get some coffee?" Felicia suggested to her sister. "We still have a long wait. I also need to call our parents and give them an update on what's happening. Momma told me to tell you that she wanted to be here, but Ernest was drunk. So we decided it was best they sit this one out. I promised to keep her posted on Darnell's condition."

"I was wondering where they were. Sure, let's go for coffee," Lenora mumbled. "I'm really not good with waiting."

Lenora and Felicia informed Trevor and Reggie that they would be back in a few minutes. The sisters left the room. When they had walked down the hall and around the corner, Lenora let loose, with an incredulous look on her face. "I can't believe Daniel had the nerve to allow Ruth Wilcox to come here. I don't know who she thinks she is."

"I agree with you on that." Felicia nodded her head. "She had no business being here. Now, you, on the other hand, what were you thinking? How could you leave Daniel and the boys without a word to anyone?"

"I was thinking that I was tired of being saddled with an old man. Daniel stopped living; he was choking the life out of me," Lenora complained, with a sneer on her face.

"I can understand your wanting to leave Daniel, but what about the boys?" Felicia asked cautiously.

"I know I was wrong to leave the boys," Lenora said; there was a remorseful look on her face. "Obviously, that was a bad decision. Look what happened to Darnell. I feel awful."

"To be honest, Lenora, Daniel and Sarah have been taking care of the boys, mostly Sarah. Daniel seemed to become paralyzed when you left. I thought for a minute that Reggie and I, or Momma and Daddy, were going to have to take care of the boys. I don't know what Sarah said to Daniel, but she was able to snap him out of the coma he seemed to be in."

They purchased coffee from a vending machine, and then they sat at a small table in the cafeteria. Lenora poured cream and two packets of sugar into her coffee, and then stirred the liquid. "Good, I'm glad someone was able to get Daniel out of his funk. I tried, but he wasn't hearing me. A woman can only take that kind of treatment for so long," Lenora said.

"What about the house? Daniel said he's on the verge of losing it. He made it sound like you cleared out all the bank accounts."

Lenora was intent on chewing a hangnail on the side of her finger. "Well, I, um, did take the majority of the money. I knew Daniel had another check coming in the following week. What does it matter, anyway? Most of the money was mine." She looked away from Felicia's disapproving eyes.

"It matters a lot, Nora. How was Daniel supposed to take care of the boys if you didn't leave him much money?"

"He's a grown man. I was sure that he'd figure it out."

Felicia was stunned by the cruelty of her sister's words and actions. She decided to change the subject for now. After Darnell's surgery, she would let her have it. "So who is the boy toy you brought with you? He looks barely legal."

"That's my man, Trevor," Lenora bragged. "He's very legal. We've been kicking it for a while. Trevor is a musician, and I just love his lifestyle. I really didn't want to drag him into all this drama, but he insisted on coming. I hope the boys will like him."

Felicia just shook her head, feeling disgusted. Her nephew was having major surgery, and all her sister seemed to be concerned about was her own self. "You didn't even ask me about the other boys."

"I meant to. I was just caught up in what's happening with Darnell."

"The boys didn't take your leaving well. Damon has been on a tear, acting out, fighting, and God knows what else. Darnell has begun wetting the bed again. David, well, he imitates Damon; so the boys have been a mess."

"I'm sorry to hear that," Lenora said meekly. "I knew the boys would miss me, but I figured in time they would get over it. Plus, they're boys. They should be with Daniel, anyway."

"They're little boys, not teenagers," Felicia corrected her sister. "They don't understand why you aren't there with them. Daniel told us you got a quickie divorce, and he has custody of the boys. To my way of thinking, you abandoned them. That's cold, even for you, Nora."

"Who do you think you are to judge me, after all the help I've given you over the years? If you don't have anything good to say, then just keep your opinions to yourself. I'll live my life the way I see fit, just like you do."

"That may be true, but I am not hurting anyone in the process. I'm taking care of my husband and children, and sometimes your children." Felicia banged her hand on the top of the table.

"Let's agree to disagree." Lenora changed the subject. "How are Momma, Daddy, the twins, Quita, and Kente doing?"

Felicia was still taken aback at her sister's behavior. But she knew it wasn't the right time or place to make her feelings known. "Jamal has made a career out of being locked up. He promised he was going to straighten himself up when he was arrested last month. He got ten years, drug related as usual. Jabari is still working at the shop with me and Reggie. Quita and Kente are doing okay. Your boys and Kente stayed at my house last weekend."

"Great. I'm glad to hear mostly everyone is doing okay. And as far as Jamal is concerned"—she shrugged her shoulders—"that boy wasn't ever any good."

"Just how long have you been kicking it with Trevor?" Felicia asked. Her eyebrow arched.

"Long enough to know he's the man I want to be with," Lenora answered evasively.

The sisters continued to talk, until Lenora said, "I guess we should go back upstairs. Maybe the nurse has some news for us. Trevor and I still need to check into our hotel."

"Where are you staying? You guys could have stayed with us," Felicia said.

"We're staying downtown at the Ritz-Carlton hotel. Trevor's people headed there to check us in, after the limo dropped us here. Girl, you know how I loved partying there. The hotel reeks of money."

"Yeah, I know. Anyway, let's head back then."

As they neared the waiting room, Daniel and Dr. McManus were standing outside the room. Judging by the look on the physician's face, they sensed the news wasn't good.

Daniel caught sight of the two women as they walked toward the room. He looked at Lenora with a bitter accusing look in his eyes.

Chapter Thirty-five

Instead of going to the book signing, Ruth had a keen longing to see Aron. She decided to obey what her spirit and heart called her to do. Thirty minutes later, she had parked in front of Aron's building. Ruth prayed it wasn't too late and that he would talk to her. She exited her car, set the alarm, and walked to the garden apartment. Ruth remembered his address from his job application. Ruth rubbed her arms and then pressed the doorbell.

Aron opened the door. If he was surprised to see Ruth, his eyes didn't portray it. They exchanged greetings; then Aron stood to the side and let her in. They walked into the living room and sat on the sofa.

"What brings you here?" he asked Ruth quietly. He couldn't keep his eyes from roaming her face.

Ruth ran her hand nervously through her hair. She exhaled loudly. "God, where should I start?"

"Wherever you want." Aron took her hand and held it tightly.

"I owe you an apology," Ruth began. Her hand felt so comfortable in Aron's, and peace filled her heart.

Aron shook his head. He put his other arm along the back of the sofa.

"Yes, I do. I really do. I have allowed people's opinion to cloud my better judgment, instead of opening up to you about my feelings for you. Please forgive me."

"Apology accepted, but not needed." Aron nodded for Ruth to continue.

"I was never what you would call an exceptional-looking woman. So when you expressed your interest in me and so did my ex-husband, I guess the attention went to my head." Ruth's eyes dropped.

"Ruth, I have told you many times, you are lovely both inside and out. And I meant that. There is nothing more precious than a woman's inner and outer beauty," Aron admonished her gently.

"I know," she answered, sighing. "I would also like to apologize for taking you for granted, and, most of all, for keeping our relationship a secret. I was groomed from an early age that whatever I do is a reflection on me and on the church. And sometimes it's hard for me to break that habit."

Aron tilted Ruth's face toward his. "I understand. Do you still have feelings for your ex-husband?" He swallowed nervously waiting for her answer.

"I can truthfully say that I don't," Ruth replied forcefully. "I guess a part of me wanted Daniel to come crawling back to me and beg me to take him back. But reality hit me in the face over the weekend, this evening, and even before then. I realize that our time is over."

Aron peered into Ruth's eyes. "Are you sure?" His grip tightened on her hand.

"Absolutely," Ruth responded, smiling. "There is no doubt whatsoever in my mind. I care deeply for the man sitting beside me." She touched Aron's chest lightly. "He leaves a rose on my desk each week. I can call him anytime, day or night. The man who lifts my spirits when I am down, and who is attuned to my feelings like no other, is you, Aron." Deep affection shone in her eyes.

Aron's face lit up like he'd won the lottery. Then he asked her, "Are you sure, Ruth? I want to claim you as my lady. Are you ready for that? I know you've heard the rumors going around the church about you and me."

"I am one hundred percent sure. And I plan to address those rumors in the immediate future." She explained how Daniel's son had become injured and how she went to the hospital to support Daniel and Sarah. Ruth told Aron about everything, including Lenora's behavior.

Aron listened intently and rubbed her back when she faltered. "If this is what it took for you to see me for the man I am, then all I can say is 'hallelujah.'"

"No, it didn't take what happened this evening; I knew it all along. I just fought my feelings because I was afraid of what other people would say," Ruth admitted.

"I am not a rich man, but all that I have is yours, if you want it," Aron told Ruth tenderly. "You have such a heavy load, trying to be all things to all people. I'll do anything that is humanly possible to lighten that load." He put his arms around Ruth's shoulders and drew her into his chest.

Ruth touched Aron's face. "Thank you. You don't know how much that means to me."

"No. Thank you, Ruth. The pleasure is all mine. I think we should continue to see each other, and see where this thing will take us." Aron gently pulled Ruth's face to his and kissed her tenderly.

The couple had shown affection toward one another before that evening. However, admitting their feelings for one another took the relationship to another level. They sat on Aron's sofa, where they talked, held hands, and cuddled. A relationship founded on friendship blossomed into a new intimacy.

By the time Ruth departed for home a few hours later, peace flooded her being. Her heart had found a home. Aron felt humbled and blessed to have been a part of the lives of two phenomenal women, first Gayvelle and now Ruth.

Meanwhile, trouble like storm clouds was brewing at the hospital.

Chapter Thirty-six

"Why don't you go back inside the waiting room, Felicia? Lenora and I need to talk to Dr. McManus alone," Daniel requested of his former sister-in-law.

Felicia went inside the room and looked back at her sister questioningly.

"Mrs. Wilcox," Dr. McManus nodded, acknowledging Lenora's presence, "I was just telling your husband that the surgery was a success. There was pressure building on your son's frontal brain lobe, and I was able to relieve the pressure."

"That's wonderful news. But why are you both looking like someone died?" Lenora asked nervously as she nibbled on her lip. She clasped her arms around her upper body.

"Well, I was telling your husband that it was a good thing we were proactive, and that you two donated blood. But, unfortunately after testing Mr. Wilcox's blood, we found that there is no possible way he could be your son's father." The doctor looked at Lenora with his head tilted to the side.

"Then your lab made a mistake." Lenora's head swiveled on her neck indignantly. "My ex-husband is the father of all my sons. How dare you upset us with this kind of news, knowing we have a gravely ill child, who just had brain surgery! I should sue you for slander," Lenora ranted. "When can we see Darnell?" she asked. Her body was overcome with tremors. She held her shaking hands together.

"He's in recovery, and you can see him soon," the doctor answered evenly. "Give us about fifteen minutes. Please limit your visit; he needs his rest. Do either one of you have any questions?"

Daniel shook his head. He was livid with anger and unable to articulate a word.

Dr. McManus cleared his throat. "Well, feel free to have the nurse come get me if you have any questions. I'll be at the hospital a little longer." He walked away from the couple and went down the hall.

"Danny, I don't know why you're acting like this," Lenora said defensively. She could feel the poisonous darts that his eyes seemed to fling at her. "Labs can make mistakes. I ought to know who my children's father is, so stop acting like that." She pulled at his arm.

Daniel wrenched away from Lenora abruptly, nearly causing her to fall. He glared at her with blazing eyes, and his voice was thick like molten lava. "You played me, Lenora. Why? I treated you like a queen. I gave you everything your heart desired, and nearly went broke in the process. I moved into that monstrosity of a house because you wanted to. Then you leave me for a boy nearly young enough to be my grandson. What kind of woman are you?" he roared.

Lenora reached for Daniel's arm again, and he moved away from her grasp once more. Her voice rose. "Daniel, you're overreacting. The lab test was wrong. Let's have another test performed, and you'll see that I'm right. I've done some things in my time, but I would never do anything like that. Let's just have another test performed, please," she begged him.

"Oh, we will have another test performed, all right; not only on Darnell, but on all three boys. I'll make the arrangements myself. I'd like the tests done as soon as possible." Daniel stomped away from Lenora, heading down the hall.

Lenora put a bright smile on her face and walked into the waiting room. She could see from the stunned expressions on everyone's faces that they had heard her and Daniel's conversation, thanks to Daniel's loud, outraged voice.

"Where is my father?" Sarah asked with rancor in her voice. She looked angrily at her former stepmother. There was loathing in Sarah's eyes. She and Brian stood up.

Lenora shrugged her shoulders helplessly. "I don't know. He looked like he was going toward the elevator." Brian and Sarah rushed out the door.

Felicia stared at her sister, openmouthed. Her expression wavered between disbelief and disgust.

Reggie tsked and shook his head; Trevor stared at Lenora with calculating eyes. He stood up. "Lenora, I've got to go. I had a call from my agent. Let me know when you're ready to go, and I'll send the car to pick you up," he said.

Lenora nodded, and Trevor hurried from the room. Reggie told the sisters he was going outside to get some air and would return shortly.

Felicia stared at her sister for a long time; then she said, "Lenora, what have you done? What in God's name were you thinking?"

"I don't know what you're talking about," she responded casually, waving her hand in the air. "I've not done anything wrong. The lab test is wrong."

"That's your story and you're sticking to it, is that it? This hospital has a state-of-the-art lab, so I doubt very seriously if any mistake was made on their part. Why did you perpetrate the lie? Is Daniel the father of any of the boys?" Lenora turned away from Felicia. Felicia grabbed her by the shoulders and spun her around. "Do you hear me talking to you?" she asked.

"How dare you ask me that question!" Lenora growled at her sister. "Yes, he's Damon's father. But I'm not sure about the twins. I mean, I'm not one hundred percent sure. They were conceived during my clubbing days, and there is a possibility they could be someone else's."

"Do you even know who?"

"Of course, I do." Lenora's chin jutted up, and she stared at her sister with her catlike eyes.

"So, not only did you leave Daniel with the boys, but you left him to raise boys who might not have even been his? That's low, Lenora."

"Look, I was tired of being cooped up in the house with a sick old man. Daniel couldn't do anything for me. He could barely support me and the lifestyle that I wanted. He didn't want to go anyplace, and he couldn't make love to me. After he had his heart attack, Daniel was impotent. I was a young woman, and I didn't know how to cope with that situation. So I wanted out, and eventually I left. Trevor fulfills all my needs."

"Why did you marry Daniel? And why didn't you take the boys with you? You're their mother. You haven't called them once since you've been gone." Felicia let Lenora have it.

Lenora didn't answer immediately. She appeared lost in thought. Finally she said, "I married Daniel because he represented everything I wanted Glenda and Ernest to be to us when we were children. He was a pillar of stability, which we never had growing up. Fee, our parents never even bothered to get married. Let's keep it real. Ernest is a drunk, who browbeats Momma. I loved Daniel and the normalcy he brought to my life. But after time, love wasn't enough."

"You should have toughed it out and made it enough, Nora," Felicia spat out at her sister. "You had a life most women dream of, and Daniel loved your dirty drawers."

"It wasn't enough. After Daniel took to his bed and wouldn't get up, I started going to the club with a few of my old girlfriends, and I saw Trevor performing. I talked to him after his set. We had a vibe and clicked. Sometimes I'd go on weekend trips with him, and I grew to love him, and I love his traveling lifestyle. I didn't think that was a good environment for the boys to be in."

"No, what you mean is that you didn't want to be bothered with the dirty work that comes with raising children." Felicia couldn't keep the disgust she felt for her sister out of her voice. Her hand itched to slap Lenora. "Being a parent is not something you put on hold because you'd rather do something else. It's a twenty-four-hour, seven-day job, three hundred sixty-five days a year. If you didn't want the work that came with the territory, why bother to have children, anyway? Daniel was pretty vocal about not wanting any more kids."

"I was the second wife," Lenora explained, "and I refused to let Ruth be the only woman that Daniel had children with."

"You're sick, you know that." Felicia looked at her sister with pity in her eyes. "If it wasn't for my nephew who just had surgery, I'd leave here. But I've got to be here for him, because God knows he has a sorry excuse for a mother." She turned away from Lenora and departed angrily from the room.

Lenora rubbed her temples vigorously. She felt unsettled. Tonight was the first time ever in her life that Felicia had turned her back on her. The sisters had shared some emotional times in their dysfunctional upbringing. Both women were embarrassed about being born out of wedlock. Their father was a drunk, who would hustle anyone, including his own mother. Lenora was still haunted by her high-school teacher being arrested for molesting her. Even though she was a minor, she was a willing participant. Then she set her sights on Daniel. Their union wouldn't have a fairy-tale ending. Daniel would have to put back the pieces of his and the boys' lives.

For the first time in her life, Lenora felt alone, and she felt unsettled. She stood motionless for a few minutes, and then she, too, left the room. She decided to go see Darnell. Everything else, including paternity tests, would be dealt with later.

Chapter Thirty-seven

Sarah and Brian went searching for Daniel, and they found him standing listlessly outside in front of the hospital. In her entire life, Sarah had never seen her father look so shell-shocked. He hadn't reacted that badly when the news was revealed that Naomi had found out the truth about her parents.

When Daniel faced Sarah and Brian, he appeared to be a broken man. He rubbed his eyes and cleared his throat. "I don't know what to think. Maybe Lenora is telling the truth." He looked at the couple, pleading for hope with his eyes.

Sarah shook her head sympathetically at her father. "I'm sorry, Daddy. I don't think so. I'm pretty sure Darnell's blood, as well as yours and Lenora's, was screened carefully before surgery. I know finding out the truth of Darnell's paternity must be a low blow to you."

"'Low blow' doesn't even come close to explaining how I'm feeling. I want tests done on all three boys, and I want them done immediately. Can you arrange that for me?"

"Of course, I will. I know you don't want to hear this, but you should be grateful that you and Lenora are divorced. You will only have to deal with her regarding the boys." Sarah twisted her lips at the inappropriateness of her words. "I'm sorry, you know what I mean."

"At this point, I don't know anything. I just want to go, leave here, and never come back," Daniel said.

"You have to put your feelings aside. There is an injured boy in there"—she pointed to the hospital—"who needs you. We know he can't depend on Lenora. I know this is a bad situation, but he's innocent in this. Please don't let him down. You will never be able to live with yourself if you do," Sarah begged her father.

"I'm sorry, Sarah, I can't do it." Regret shone in Daniel's eyes as he turned from them and walked down the street to his car.

Sarah and Brian watched him until he was no longer in sight.

"So what do you want to do?" Brian asked Sarah. "It's getting late. Maybe I should go home and check on the children. The boys can stay with us tonight."

"I wouldn't be able to live with myself if I didn't stay here, at least until Darnell regains consciousness," Sarah said.

"What a day. Your brothers might not even be related to you. How weird is that?" Brian commented.

The sun had made its descent for the night. The temperature had dropped slightly, and it had become cool. The piercing shrill tone of an ambulance could be heard a few blocks away.

"I believe Damon is Daddy's son. He has that Wilcox nose. The twins are clones of Lenora. I never saw many traits of Daddy in them. Darnell is light-skinned like Lenora, and David is darker like Daddy. Regardless, they will still be my brothers until they are old enough to learn the truth. Daddy is going to have to pull himself together and put the boys' feelings before his own. They will never understand this; they're too young," Sarah said.

"Okay, then. I'm going to head home and make sure the kids are okay. Give me a call when you're ready to come home, and I'll come back and get you. Darnell's in good hands." Brian pulled Sarah into his arms. She looked like she was in need of affection. "And don't let Lenora get to you. Oh, when this latest crisis is over, we need to talk to Maggie again. She just hasn't been herself lately."

She rested her head against his chest. "I agree. Something is bothering her. I've asked her numerous times, but she says she's okay. Brian, thanks for being here with me tonight. I know you had your meeting at the church to go to."

"Not a problem. That's what spouses are for, to support each other in emotional times. Speaking of church, I hear there's been some rumbling about your mother and Aron Reynolds. I'm really curious as to the source; because to my knowledge, they have been discreet about their relationship."

"I heard the same thing. It's probably some old biddy with nothing but time on her hands. Would you give Nay a call and give her an update? Tell her that I'll talk to her later."

"Sure thing. Take care, and call me when you're ready." Brian squeezed Sarah's hand and walked away.

Sarah waved to Brian when he turned to look at her before he was out of view. She pushed her hair off her face, sighed, and went back inside the hospital. Sarah never imagined she would keep vigil at the hospital with Lenora and her family. She never fathomed in her wildest dreams that her young half brothers might not even be related to her. Sarah whispered, "God, help us all" then she walked toward the elevator and back to Darnell.

Chapter Thirty-eight

A week later, Ruth was sitting at her desk in her home office. She had just finished checking the church's voice mail system. She had listened to the messages June had saved from more than a few church members who expressed their concern about their minister's love life.

Some of the members were supportive; others didn't think it was appropriate that Ruth consort with someone who had committed murder. She disconnected the call, then took a cup of tea from the desk and went into the kitchen. She rinsed the cup and put it into the drain, when her doorbell rang.

Ruth opened the door. A beaten-down Daniel stood at her threshold. It was his second visit in as many weeks.

"Daniel, what are you doing here?" she asked warily.

"I need to talk to you, Ruth," Daniel said morosely. "Please let me come in."

"This is really not a good time. I was in the middle of working. Can't this wait until another time?"

"If it could, trust me, I wouldn't be here. I really need to talk to you. Please, Ruth."

Ruth allowed Daniel to enter. They sat exactly where they had sat the last time Daniel had visited.

Daniel explained to Ruth what had happened at the hospital regarding Darnell's paternity. When he finished talking, he asked Ruth what she thought he should do.

"First of all, you should give praises to the Almighty that Darnell pulled through the surgery successfully. Brain surgery is a delicate procedure, and praise God for guiding the surgeon's hands. As far as the paternity tests are concerned, in the long run, it doesn't matter. You've raised all the boys as your sons, up until this point, and you're the only father figure they know. You should continue on the path you started."

"I know that's your religious mumbo jumbo you're spouting off, but it doesn't change the fact that Lenora cheated on me, and she tried to pawn off her kids on me, knowing I might not be the father," Daniel stated.

"We have all fallen short from time to time, Daniel, and that includes you and me. But it doesn't change the fact that the boys know you as their father; and from a moral standpoint, you should be there for them," Ruth advised.

"That's easy for you to say. Lenora used me, plain and simple, and I don't feel obligated to do anything for her or her children." Daniel's eyes bulged, and the vein in his neck throbbed ominously.

"Calm down." Ruth held up her hand. "First of all, you're assuming all the boys aren't yours, and you don't know that to be true yet. What if Damon is yours and not the twins? What would you do then?"

Daniel dropped his head. "I—I don't know," he stammered.

"Then you need to think the situation through and consider every aspect. If the twins aren't your biological sons, then you need to think about preserving the family unit. It wouldn't be fair to separate the boys," Ruth said.

"That's easy for you to say!" Daniel shot back.

"You're right. I'm not walking in your shoes. But I do know right from wrong, and it would be wrong of you to separate them, or make a difference in how you treat them."

Daniel laughed aloud sarcastically.

Ruth looked at him, confused. "Did I miss something?" she asked.

"I feel like God has played a big joke on me. Here I am again, possibly becoming a daddy to children who aren't mine, just like I did for Naomi."

"Maybe God is giving you another chance to get it right, Daniel." Ruth nodded wisely. "Did you ever consider that? God doesn't make mistakes. There's a reason for everything that happens, besides the obvious. Maybe He wants you to take care of those boys and raise them the right way."

"Ruth, I'm no longer a young man. I don't know if I have the time or energy for raising three boys at my age." Daniel exhaled heavily.

"I think you're selling yourself short. There are many people who have children in their older years, and they say the children help keep them young. You're going to have to search deep within yourself. God willing, you'll make the right choice, and get things right this time."

"I don't think so. Maybe discovering that the boys are not mine is my way out. Maybe Lenora will take them with her and raise them, and I can get my life back on track. Perhaps this is the Lord's way of allowing me to right some wrongs, and that includes you, Ruth. I was a fool all those years ago, but you've never been far from my heart and mind. What do you say we try making a go of things again?" Daniel spoke sincerely. The intensity in his eyes seemed to pierce Ruth's heart.

She wet her lips, shook her head, and spoke candidly. "I think our time has come and gone, Daniel. We fulfilled the destiny God had in store for us. We are the parents of three beautiful children, who've grown up to become wonderful adults. We share grandchildren, and I'm sure there will be great-grandchildren down the road. Our time has passed. I know we can be friends, and be there for each other and our children; but as far as getting back together is concerned, no."

"Is it because of that man?" Daniel asked. He felt hurt that Ruth had chosen a convict over him.

Ruth thought about her answer. "To an extent, it is. But it is also because we're in different places, and that might have been the problem with our marriage. I'm content with my life, and in this case, content isn't bad. I'm a minister. Could you see yourself as the first man?"

"Could the con . . . I mean that other man be an effective first man? I'm sure I could do better than he can. What will your members think about you dating a person with a criminal past? What if they ask you to step down as minister?"

"I would hope my congregation would understand that a person should be judged by his deeds and spirit. I admit, I went along with the program or agenda we had during our marriage. Because I was the minister's daughter, I turned a blind eye to your philandering. I knew in my heart that just accepting your actions was wrong. But, you see, it's not even about me or about you; it's about putting God first in our lives. He always comes first. When you put Him first, you cannot go wrong. God will always be on my side. As far as my members are concerned, I plan to address their concerns soon."

"We share a history, Ruth. Did you ever consider that maybe God wants us to get it right this time?" Daniel learned forward on his chair and continued to press his case.

"No, I don't think so, Daniel. We had more than enough time to get it right—over thirty years. You will always occupy a place in my heart. You were my first love." Ruth tried to soften the blows she had delivered to him.

"I guess this means, you won't rent the apartment to me," Daniel continued, though he knew the answer to that question.

"You're right. Now that Lenora is back, this would be a good time for the two of you to discuss finances. If you have custody of the boys, then she should pay you child support."

Daniel looked at Ruth regretfully. "I really messed up letting you go. My doctor warned me many years ago, and I can remember the words like yesterday. He talked about how the grass may not be greener on the other side, and he was so right. I wish we could turn back the hands of time."

"I used to think the same thing. We may be older, but we're not down-and-out. I believe the Lord has good things in store for you, if you would just open yourself up to the possibilities."

"I guess I should get out of here and check on Darnell. He will be coming home soon. Ruth, I hope you can forgive me for all the wrong I've done to you."

"Of course. That's what we do as Christians; we turn the other cheek, so to speak. When this latest dilemma has passed, you need to find a way to get through to DJ. He has mellowed somewhat after his injury in Afghanistan. Tomorrow is not promised; try to make things right with your oldest son," Ruth said.

Daniel nodded and stood up. "I guess I should be heading back to Olympia Fields."

Ruth stood up and walked Daniel to the door. As they stood in the foyer, Daniel held out his arms, and

Ruth walked into them. They stood that way for a few minutes.

"I'm so sorry for every wrong thing that I've done to you," he whispered into her ear.

"I understand," she replied. "Things will work out. Just wait on the Lord to work them out."

Ruth opened the door and Daniel walked outside. He looked at her one more time regretfully. "Be happy, Ruth. That's what I want for you," he said emotionally.

"I will." She held up two crossed fingers.

She closed and locked the door after Daniel left, and then she sat back down on the sofa. Her body trembled as she swayed back and forth. Peace washed over her soul, and soon she was content. She knew that she had done the right thing. She also realized that Daniel, in time, would be fine.

Ruth stood and walked into her home office. The envelope she'd gotten from Edwina lay on her desk. She picked it up and smiled. She held the answer to her prayers in her hand.

Chapter Thirty-nine

Three weeks later on a Thursday morning, Daniel and Lenora were seated in the waiting room of a local clinic in Olympia Fields, where the paternity tests had been performed. Daniel had gotten the call late yesterday evening that the test results were in. He had insisted all three boys be tested.

Lenora had given Daniel money, which allowed him to catch up on the mortgage. They had put the house on the market to sell, and they even had a prospective buyer. Daniel had found a house in Chicago to rent. It was big enough for all three boys, just in case. He and Lenora were still working on custodial logistics.

Darnell had been released from the hospital, and Trevor had hired a nurse to care for him. The boy's health was better, and he was receiving physical therapy. In time, he could begin to resume his normal activities. The boys had settled down somewhat, now that their mother had returned to Chicago.

A doctor came into the waiting room, introduced himself as Dr. Levy, and ushered the pair into his office.

After Lenora and Daniel sat down on the plush seats in front of his desk, the doctor opened an envelope. "Your case is most unusual," he commented as he laid the paper on his desk.

"How so?" Daniel asked, with a puzzled look on his face.

"Well, let me explain. The test results for Damon Wilcox state conclusively that you are the father, Mr. Wilcox. But you are the father of only one of the twins, David Wilcox. You are not the father of Darnell Wilcox. The test results are ninety-nine point eight percent accurate."

Lenora shook her head. "How could that be?" she asked. She knew in her heart that she'd had sexual relations with both Trevor and Daniel on the same day. She hadn't bothered to divulge to anyone that she'd been having sex with a minor. Her relationship with Trevor went back longer than Lenora chose to acknowledge to her family. She chose to engage in sexual relations with a minor. Her actions were similar to, and no better than, the teacher who had molested her.

"Well, the usual way, Mrs. Wilcox," he told Lenora solemnly. "You apparently had sexual relations with your husband and another man within your five-day ovulation period. The situation doesn't happen often, but we have seen it before in the medical community. Your body produced two eggs during ovulation, and Mr. Wilcox's sperm fertilized one of the eggs, and another party the second egg."

Lenora reeled from the latest revelation, while Daniel stared at his wife with something akin to hatred in his eyes. The drama never seemed to end with her.

He stood up and barked, "I need some air. I'll be outside."

Lenora insisted to the doctor that there had to be an error. The physician slid the paper across the desk, with the facts proving his findings.

After hemming and hawing, she eventually accepted the results and paid the hefty bill. Before she left, the doctor presented her with two copies of the tests in sealed envelopes. One copy was for Lenora; the other one was for Daniel. The physician assured Lenora the test results would be kept in strict confidence as he ushered her out of his office.

When she walked outside the building, she found Daniel sitting in his car. She walked to it, opened the door, and sat in the passenger side.

"Lady, you are truly a piece of work" flew from Daniel's mouth. "Do you even know who Damon's father is?"

"Of course, I do," Lenora shot back. "Trevor is."

Daniel quickly did the math in his head. He shook his head. "You mean you were messing around with a boy. God, Lenora, Trevor wasn't even legal back then. You're a preying cougar. I don't understand how you could have turned your back on your sons for a man." Daniel looked at her with loathing in his eyes. His hand arched upward.

She looked ashamed. "Look, Danny, I'm sorry about this. We knew David and Darnell weren't identical twins, but I never imagined they had different fathers. Trevor will be performing in Canada the week after next, and I'd like to join him. We planned to get married then."

"You mean you don't plan to stay with Darnell until he fully recuperates?" Daniel couldn't believe Lenora. She had a lot of nerve. "Did you tell Trevor that he could be Darnell's father?"

Lenora smoothed down the hem of her skirt. "I planned to talk to Trevor after we got the test results. Anyway, Darnell is doing better. He has begun therapy, and the doctor expects him to make a full recovery."

"I'm sorry that I don't measure up to your expectations, Danny, but I am who I am. I don't make any apologies to anyone for my behavior, and that definitely includes you." Lenora's perfume wafted in the air. She still wore the same perfume as when Daniel met her. She had always told him that it was her signature scent, and that she would wear it until the day she died. "So, are you going to keep the boys or what?" she questioned.

"I'm still thinking about it," Daniel responded.

"Well, don't take too long," Lenora said, with an amused glint in her eyes. "If you won't take them, then I'm sure Felicia and Reggie would, or my mother and father." She reached into her purse and took out the envelope that Dr. Levy had given her for Daniel. She gave it to him.

Daniel's stomach somersaulted at the thought of Ernest raising the boys. "I'll let you know by the end of the week," he announced. He started the car. "I need to go. I have some things I need to do."

"Aw, Danny, don't be like that," Lenora lisped. "We had some good times. Well, we did before you decided you needed Viagra to keep up with me."

"Whatever," Daniel said dismissively. He shifted the gear to drive.

Lenora leaned over and tried to kiss his cheek. Daniel pulled away from her.

"Call me." She held two fingers toward her ear. Lenora exited the vehicle and walked to her red Mercedes-Benz Roadster. Daniel watched her walk down the street. He tugged at the collar of his shirt. He sighed and pulled out into traffic.

On the same day that Daniel discovered Darnell's paternity, Sarah worked late. When she walked into the house, she knew immediately something was terribly wrong. Brian didn't greet her with a kiss, like he usually did. When she hung up her coat and slipped off her shoes, she found her husband sitting in the den, looking dejected. She walked over to the sofa and sat down next to him. "What's up? Why are you looking like you lost your best friend?"

"We have trouble," Brian said mournfully as he took her hand.

"What do you mean? Did something happen to one of the kids?" Sarah looked frightened.

"Not quite. You know how we said Maggie hadn't been herself since we returned from Edwardsville. Well, I talked to Joshua this evening, and he told me that Maggie had talked to him about what was bothering her."

"Well, what did he say?" Sarah asked impatiently.

"There's no easy way to tell you this, so I'll just say it. When we were in Edwardsville, Maggie had gone to the bathroom. Our bedroom door was slightly open, and she heard us talking about Naomi being our daughter," Brian said.

Sarah snatched her hand from his and covered her face. "Lord, God Almighty. What are we going to do?" she moaned, slumping on the sofa.

"We're going to have to talk to her and Joshua, and explain what happened," Brian answered in a shaky voice.

"How do we do that without coming off sounding like hypocrites? I really wanted to wait until they were older. This isn't a good time, with them being impressionable teenagers." Sarah felt heartbroken.

"We've raised them right, Sarah, and we have to believe that they will learn from our mistake and not repeat it. Perhaps that's the lesson to be learned with Maggie learning the truth."

Sarah sat motionless. "This is my worst nightmare come true. Well, maybe my second, after Naomi learning the truth. How did Josh react?"

"He was surprised, of course, but you know his head stays on the basketball court. Maggie, however, is a different story," he said. "She can't get past us lying to them all these years. You know how she looks up to Naomi as a big sister, anyway."

"I guess we should go talk to her," Sarah suggested. Her heart beat violently inside her chest.

"Let's pray first," Brian suggested. He took Sarah's hand, and the couple bowed their heads.

Brian sighed heavily and began speaking. "Father, God, we come before you today humbly, seeking your guidance. We have a situation here at our house. Father, help us to find the right words to say to our daughter as we explain the sins we committed as young adults. Father, please put openness and forgiveness in Maggie's heart. We don't want her to suffer from what happened years ago. Father, we're leaning on you and trusting in you. Please guide us. Amen."

"In Jesus' name," Sarah intoned.

They stood and walked up the stairs to Maggie's bedroom. Sarah knocked on the closed door.

"Maggie," she called out, "may we come in?"

"Okay," Maggie answered languidly.

Brian opened the door, and he and Sarah walked inside. Maggie was sitting in the middle of her canopy bed, legs crossed, with her schoolbooks spread unopened around her.

Sarah smiled at her daughter, but Maggie didn't smile back. She merely stacked her books on top of each other.

Brian sat on one side of the bed and Sarah on the other. Brian looked at Sarah, seeing if she would initiate the conversation. He could tell from her expression she wasn't up to it.

"Maggie, I talked to Joshua, and he told me that you overheard Mommy and me talking, back in Edwardsville, and that you're upset. Is that what's been bothering you?"

Maggie's face crumpled. She covered her face and bawled. Brian pulled her into his arms; he held her until she calmed down.

"Why didn't you and Mommy tell me and Joshua that Naomi is our sister, and not our aunt?" Maggie cried hysterically.

"We were going to tell you, just not yet," Brian said, trying to explain.

"Does everyone know except for me and Josh?" With accusing eyes, Maggie looked from Brian to Sarah.

"Well, yes, other f-family members are aware of it," Sarah stammered.

"How come they know, and Josh and I didn't? That's not fair." Maggie's lips quivered as her eyes were awash with tears.

"We planned to tell you and Josh later," Sarah tried to explain in a trembling voice. "We thought you were too young to understand what happened."

"Mommy, how could you get pregnant?" Maggie held up a shaking hand. "You were only two years older than I am now. You and Nana have preached to me, over and over, how having sexual relations outside marriage is a sin. Mommy, you're a minister's daughter and granddaughter. I don't understand."

"That's one of the reasons I wanted to wait until you two were older." As she watched Maggie's anguished face, Sarah felt like her heart was being shredded. The family could hear the back door open and then close.

Brian yelled, "Joshua, is that you?"

"Yep, it's me," he answered loudly, dribbling the basketball.

"Would you come upstairs? Your mother and I are talking to Maggie, and we'd like you to join us," Brian said.

"Sure," Joshua replied before taking a bottle of water out of the refrigerator and walking upstairs to the attic. "Wow, everybody looks so serious." He sat on Maggie's desk chair. "What's up?"

"We're trying to explain to your sister about Naomi being your sister," Sarah answered.

"That's deep. Maggie and Aunt Naomi always looked alike. I guess the truth was staring us in the face, but we didn't see it." Joshua turned up the bottle and swallowed.

"But Mommy and Daddy lied to us!" Maggie shouted indignantly. "They told us the importance of waiting for marriage to have sex, and she got pregnant when she was a teenager. That doesn't seem right to me." She collapsed against Brian's chest and sobbed.

"I apologize for not telling you sooner," Sarah told her children imploringly. "And I'm sorry about the way you found out about Naomi being your sister. Your father and I fully intended to tell you the truth when you were older. You're right, Maggie, I shouldn't have had sexual relations at an early age. And yes, I was a minister's granddaughter, but that didn't make me exempt from sin. I made a mistake, and I pay for it whenever I see Naomi." Sarah dissolved into tears.

Joshua stood up and walked to his mother. He patted her shoulder awkwardly. Sarah sniffled.

"Nana and your grandfather were having marital difficulties, and I thought they were going to get a divorce. In those days, grown folks' business was just that, grown folks' business. Problems weren't discussed with children. I turned to your father for attention and affection. Your father and I grew up in the church together. He was my boyfriend, and I loved him. We had relations and got caught. Despite everything we went through, I've never regretted giving birth to Naomi, or the two of you. I love all my children dearly," Sarah said.

"Why did Nana and Gramps raise Naomi, and say that she was their daughter? I don't understand that part," Maggie asked. Her face was moist from tearstains.

"It's a long story. The family decided I was too young to raise a child. So that the church wouldn't know that I had sinned, Momma pretended to be pregnant. I stayed with Aunt Helen in St. Louis until I had Naomi. When she was born, Momma and Daddy adopted her. Nana and Gramps adopting Naomi was good in a way, and bad in another. I was able to continue my life and be around Naomi as her sister when she was growing up. The times were good and bad. We really wanted to wait to tell you, because we didn't want you or Josh to think teenage sex is okay or allowable," Sarah said.

"But if you two had relations, how could you tell me and Josh not to? That's so hypocritical," Maggie complained, sounding like Queen.

Joshua sat quietly and listened to his sister and parents speak.

"It might be hypocritical, but all parents want their children to do things correctly, even if we fall short ourselves. We've prayed and asked God to forgive us, and He has," Brian said.

"Does Naomi know the truth?" Joshua asked.

"She does, and she took it as bad as Maggie did." Brian ruffled his daughter's hair. "She has accepted the truth, and she's content with being Nana and Gramp's daughter, as she should be. They were the ones who raised her, who stayed up with her when she was sick, and paid her expenses. That was the choice we made when Nana and Gramps adopted Naomi."

"Did you want to keep Naomi and raise her as your own daughter?" Maggie asked. She didn't look as pale and listless as she had when her parents had come into her room.

"I did, so badly, but I didn't have the means to support her," Sarah said passionately.

"Your mother and I talked about taking Naomi and running away from home," Brian added. "We wanted to raise her ourselves, but we knew that we couldn't really support her. It was a tough time, and tough decisions were made. Believe me, it really affected our marriage. God willing, though, we weathered the storm. Maggs, I don't want you beating up on your mother. We were just kids who found ourselves in a bad predicament. Your grandparents made the decisions for us, and we went along with it," Brian explained, hoping that in time his children would understand.

"I feel so mortified," Maggie moaned as she raised her arms in the air, and then she covered her face. "Oh, Lord. My mother was fast. I just can't get over that." She shook her head.

The family continued to talk as late afternoon turned into evening. Sarah and Brian allowed the children to express their feelings, get it all out. And when all was said and done, Sarah and Brian admitted to falling short. They reiterated how they didn't want the sins of the parents to fall on the children. By the time the family went downstairs for dinner, Maggie was talking to Sarah, but not as easily as she had in the past. The young girl looked at her mother many times with an accusing expression on her face. Sarah felt devastated. Her only comfort was that the talk the family shared was a start. The thought of Maggie never forgiving her seared Sarah's heart. She just couldn't bear it if she lost both her daughters.

Chapter Forty

When Sarah awakened the following morning, she immediately burst into tears. Sleep didn't come easy to her the previous night. Brian held her in his arms until she finally fell asleep. "Oh, God," she sobbed inconsolably, "I have messed up my children, all of them." She felt so distraught that Brian suggested she take the day off from work. Later, Brian brought a reluctant Maggie into the couple's bedroom before she headed off for school. The young girl refused to meet her mother's eyes before she told her good-bye.

After her family departed for school and work, Sarah called Ruth. She was sobbing, nearly hysterically, when she told her mother what had transpired the previous evening.

Ruth immediately made a beeline for Sarah's house. It took a while for Ruth to get her daughter to calm down. Later she called Naomi, explained the situation, and suggested Naomi come home as soon as she could. Sarah needed her.

Early on Saturday morning, Naomi left Edwardsville and drove nearly nonstop to her sister's house. Once Naomi arrived, Ruth opened the door and enfolded Naomi inside her arms. When Sarah saw Naomi, she began shaking and burst into tears. She moaned continuously about how Maggie hated her.

Ruth sat on one side of Sarah and Naomi on the other. They did their best to console Sarah. They planned to talk to Maggie when she arrived home from gymnastic practice.

When Maggie walked into the house, she was surprised to see her grandmother and aunt. There was a big smile on her face. It faded a second later, when she realized the reason for their visit.

Ruth patted the cushion on the sofa between her and Sarah. "Come here and sit next to Nana," she bade the girl.

Maggie dropped her gym bag on the floor and went into the living room. She sat between her mother and grandmother. She looked at Naomi, who was sitting on the chair across from the sofa.

"Nana, I just don't understand," she began saying. She turned to Ruth. "My mommy was fast! Mothers—especially mothers whose mother and grandfather are ministers—should never be fast." She looked miserable and dropped her face.

Ruth took Maggie's shaking hand in her own and clutched it firmly. "Oh, precious, I wish I could take your hurt away. I know this has been hard for you to comprehend, but please don't blame your mother and father for what happened all those years ago."

Maggie turned and looked at Ruth. "Then whose fault is it, Nana? Mommy had a baby that you and Gramps raised. And, no one bothered to tell me and Joshua." Her lips trembled as tears spilled from her eyes.

"Trust me," she told Maggie. "You know I've never lied to you. Your parents planned to tell you and Joshua, when you got older, that Naomi is your sister. Your parents were young and misguided. Your grandfather and I were having difficulties, and I wasn't there for your mother, like I should have been."

"So it was *your* fault?" Maggie asked. She sniffled as she looked from Ruth to Sarah, then at Naomi.

"In a way, it was." Ruth nodded. "In fact, blame me. Parents aren't perfect; we make mistakes too. We thought we were doing what was right at the time, to protect Sarah and Naomi."

Maggie looked thoughtful. "I feel disappointed. I thought Mommy and Daddy were perfect. I was always so proud that Josh and I have a mother and father who both live with us." She waved her hand. "So many of my friends' parents are divorced. I thought I was better than they are, I guess."

"There are only two perfect persons, and that is our Father above and Christ the Lord. Though I'm a minister, and Bishop was too, we still made mistakes. I regret now how we handled your mother's pregnancy. But I gained a daughter in return, my youngest child, just like you're Sarah's baby girl. Always love your mother, your parents, as our Father has loved us. And try to find it in your heart to forgive your parents, as He has forgiven us."

"I'll try, Nana." Maggie nodded, looking doubtful. "But, I don't know, it's still hard. Naomi is my sister, not my aunt. Should I think of her as my aunt or as my sister?" She looked across the room at Naomi.

Naomi wiped her eyes. She was moved by Maggie's emotional outburst. She was also in awe of how Ruth was handling the situation. She nodded and cleared her throat. "You can think of me any way you want. We always had a special relationship, and I don't want anything to come in the way of that. I know how you feel, Maggie. I felt the same way when I learned that Sarah and Brian were my biological parents. Hurt and betrayal had become my best friends. It took me a long time to let go of my feelings and accept my family for

who they are. So if you ever need someone to talk to—
who can relate to how you're feeling—I'd be honored if
you would talk to me."

Naomi stood up and walked to Maggie. The younger
girl stood up and hugged Naomi.

They sat back down.

"But I can't tell anyone I have a big sister, can I? I
mean, anyone except the family? Isn't that right?"

"That's true, Maggie," Naomi answered. "Nana raised
me and she'll always be my mother. Nana and Gramps
adopted me. So legally I am their child. But when we're
together, just the two of us, or around the family, I can
be your big sister."

Maggie nodded and turned toward Sarah. "Doesn't
that make you sad, Mommy? That you can never claim
your own daughter?"

Sarah wet her lips; while all waited on her to answer.
"Yes, I do feel sad at times. But I feel glad and secure in
knowing that my parents raised my child. I was blessed
that I was able to grow up in the same house with her,
and watch her grow into the beautiful woman that she
has become. Being able to be a part of her life helps to
ease the hurt. Sometimes we have to make sacrifices in
life, and Brian and I were too young to take care of a
child. Momma and Daddy would have ended up raising
and supporting Naomi, anyway."

Maggie chewed her lower lip and looked at each of
the women. "Well, if all of you are okay with what happened, then I guess I'll have to accept it. Knowing that
Naomi is really my sister is going to take some getting
used to."

Maggie turned to look at Sarah. "I'm sorry, Mommy,
for the way I've been acting. I was just so confused."

Sarah pulled her daughter into her arms. "I understand, baby. I really do. Please don't shut me out. If

you have a problem, I want you to come to me so we can discuss it."

"I will," Maggie said in a soft voice.

"That includes me and Naomi too. We're all here for you and each other. Because after all, that's what family is for," Ruth told Maggie in a gentle tone of voice.

An invisible pall was lifted from the room. After a while, everything was almost back to normal, at least for the time being. Sarah knew the crisis wasn't quite over. But with her mother and Naomi's help, she knew that in time, with help from the Lord, eventually everything would be all right.

Chapter Forty-one

Two weeks later, on a Thursday evening, Ruth called an emergency meeting with the finance committee. In the meeting, she explained how new details had come forth that affected the church's finances.

Later, after Ruth arrived home, and was relaxing on the sofa in the living room, her telephone rang. "Hi, Daniel. How are you and the boys doing?" Ruth asked after checking caller ID.

"We're doing well. Darnell is getting better every day. I'm in the process of packing up the house. I hope to move in a couple of weeks."

"Good, I'm glad everything worked out for you. God will bless you for keeping the boys together. So what's up?"

"Well, ah, um," Daniel stammered. He tugged on his shirt collar anxiously.

"Tell me," Ruth urged him.

"Well, um, Sarah was telling me about how you've been receiving calls from your church members about you dating Aron. I, uh, kind of had a role in why they've been calling."

"What do you mean?" Ruth asked, alarmed. She sat upright, clutching the receiver tightly against her ear.

"Ruthie, I was jealous of you and Aron," Daniel said humbly. "So I figured when your church got wind of you dating him, they wouldn't approve. Then you'd drop him, and you'd come back to me."

Ruth was momentarily speechless. She didn't know whether to laugh or cry.

"Are you still there?" Daniel asked uneasily. Beads of sweat dotted his forehead.

Finally Ruth answered, "Yes, I'm still here. Goodness gracious, that was the last thing I expected you to say. I can't believe you would go that far to try to win me back."

"I've been a fool about so many things, and you can add that bad decision to the list." Daniel sighed. "You've been so helpful to me, listening and guiding me. Many women in your position would have turned their back on me. My conscience wouldn't let me go another day without telling you about my part in what happened. I'm sorry, Ruth. Do you think you'll ever be able to forgive me?"

"Believe it or not, Daniel, your plan backfired. You did me a huge favor."

"What do you mean?" Daniel wasn't sure if Ruth understood what he had told her.

"Our Father works in mysterious ways, His wonders to behold. Had you not forced my hand, I may have lost out on Aron. Without your intervention—I won't call it divine, because your motives were impure—I might not have had the courage to face my congregation this coming Sunday, and set the record straight."

"Maybe if you had fought harder for me when it came to Lenora, we wouldn't be having this conversation, and we would still be together," Daniel remarked.

"I don't think so." Ruth shook her head. "If it had not been that incident, trust me, it would have been another. Daniel, thank you for calling me. Believe it or not, I appreciate it."

"You really have changed, Ruth. I think I like the new Reverend Wilcox," Daniel said admiringly, though his heart ached for what he had won and lost.

"Thank you, Daniel. Coming from you, that's high praise. I have some things to do. You take care of yourself, and I'm sure we'll see each other at family events."

"No, thank you for being so understanding."

They ended the call.

Though Daniel felt relieved that Ruth had let him off so easily, he still felt a keen sense of loss for what could have been.

Chapter Forty-two

The following Sunday morning, Ruth stood at the pulpit, preparing to deliver her sermon. She also planned to share the news of a financial windfall the church had received.

The choir had finished their B selection, "Yield Not to Temptation" and the offering had been collected. Ruth walked to the podium. She adjusted the microphone, and it made a squealing sound. She looked into the sanctuary and smiled.

"This is the day the Lord made, let us rejoice and be glad. Shall we pray?" She bowed her head and closed her eyes. "Father in heaven, we come to you this morning. Blessed that you have allowed us to see another day. We give all praises to you. Father, I ask that you lay your healing hands upon the sick and shut-in members of the church and all over the world. Someone is sad this morning. Lord, please stop by and strengthen them. Someone is worried about the loss of a job. Lord, let them know that all things are possible because only you will continue to provide for our needs. As we begin the new week, Lord, keep all of us safe from hurt, harm, and danger. These blessings in your Son's name, I ask. Amen."

Ruth then said, "I'd like those of you who have your Bibles with you to open it to the book of Matthew 7:1 through 8, and read along with me."

There was a slight rustle as the members found the section, and they read the following scripture:

Judge not, that ye be not judged. For with what judgment ye judge, ye shall be judged; and with what measure ye mete, it shall be measured to you again. And why beholdest thou the mote that is in your brother's eye, but considerest not the beam that is in thine own eye? Or how wilt thou say to thy brother, Let me pull out the mote out of thine eye; and, behold, a beam is in thine own eye? Thou hypocrite, first cast out the beam out of thine own eye; and then shalt thou see clearly to cast out the mote in thy brother's eye. Give not that which is holy unto the dogs, neither cast ye your pearls before swine, lest they trample them under their feet, and turn again and rend you.

Ask, and it shall be given you; seek, and ye shall find; knock, and it shall be opened unto you: For every one that asketh receiveth; and he that seeketh findeth; and to him that knocketh it shall be opened.

Ruth's eyes roamed the sanctuary. "I use that particular scripture we just read, along with the Golden Rule, for guidelines on how to treat our fellow man. None of us are perfect, and we have all fallen short from time to time. But if we keep in mind that we should judge people according to how we want to be judged, the world would be a better place." She looked out into the congregation. "How many of you are perfect out there and have never committed a sin?"

The church was quiet. Not one hand was raised.

"As you can see, my hand isn't raised either," Ruth joked.

The congregation responded with appreciative chuckles.

"The good thing is that God forgives our sins, even when our fellow man is unable to. And, most important, when we can't forgive ourselves, we carry around baggage sometimes until it consumes our very being. We should take comfort in knowing that Christ died on the cross for our sins, and how we carry ourselves as a child of God speaks volumes about how we appreciate and honor the sacrifice made for us.

"One of the verses talked about pulling a mote out of our brother's eye, and being mindful of the beam in our own eye. When we work on our own selves, and get our own spirit right, only then can we see clearly enough to help our fellow man.

"There is no problem too big for God to help us overcome. He tells us plainly that we only have to ask, and it shall be given."

Strident responses of "Amen" resounded in the sanctuary.

"I don't mean, ask for a new car, when you know you can't afford it." Ruth paused while several members laughed. "What I mean is, ask Him for strength, guidance, and, most of all, patience because God doesn't work on our timetable. He supplies our needs as He sees fit. He asks that we love our neighbor as ourselves, and how we are charged with doing what we can to help our fellow man."

Ruth continued preaching on the agape, loving each other unconditionally as our Father does. She urged the members to love one another, and not to be quick to judge, and to leave retribution to God. When she finished, she returned to her seat. The assistant pastor took her place at the pulpit and opened the doors of the church. A family of four, along with a woman and man, joined The Temple.

While June led the new members to her office to get their personal information, the choir sang "He's Sweet, I Know." When they finished the selection, Ruth returned to the podium.

"I'd like to address a few issues with you. We know that the grapevine of any enterprise is a powerful force, and the church is no exception. It's come to my attention that several members of the church are not happy with my dating selection."

All eyes were glued on her. Some members turned to the person sitting next to them and began whispering.

"Let me start by saying," Ruth said firmly, "that I would never do anything to dishonor God or our church. I have served you faithfully since I was ordained by my father as an associate minister. I ask that you trust in me, and respect my judgment. I have learned some life lessons. After all, I'm not exactly what you'd call a 'spring chicken.'"

The members laughed aloud, and some of the tension dissolved from the room.

"I have been seeing a member of the church socially. We're great friends, and that's what has made our relationship so unique. We are friends first, friends who share a love of God. Aron Reynolds works with Wade and Marcus, mentoring the young men of the church. We always hear about the more pleasant side of life, but sometimes we need someone who has experienced negative situations to explain to our youth the consequences of disobedience. Be mindful that everything that happens in life happens for a reason, and we have to be obedient of God's plans for us. We may not understand why sometimes, but we have to be attentive to what He wants for us, and learn from those experiences and witness about them.

"I have prayed and reflected on my relationship with Mr. Reynolds, and I can honestly say he challenges me sometimes, and I reflect on things differently that I may not have in the past. I have not always divulged my dating partners to you, but in this case, I felt compelled to discuss this matter with you and allay your doubts. I hope if any of you have any issues about my personal life, which I will always share with you if I find it detrimental to the church, will feel free to come to me and talk about it. My door is always open. Let's keep those scriptures we read together this morning in mind when we feel the need to judge our fellow man harshly," she said, completing that part of her talk.

Her throat was suddenly dry, so she picked up a bottle of water. Ruth looked up as she heard a smattering of applause that turned thunderous. A vast majority of the congregation stood on their feet.

"We love you, Pastor Ruth!" many people shouted, while some looked at her dubiously.

"Thank you." Ruth's eyes filled with tears. "I appreciate your support, and I'll never let you or my Father down, because He is the head of my life. I also have good news." She smiled brightly. "I've met with the finance committee, and we've put in place new controls to monitor our spending. We have combined some auxiliaries, and discontinued a few, but not many. We did this because it made sense from a financial standpoint. We will still be able to continue the works my father and grandfather implemented for the church. We have quite a few entrepreneurs who belong to the church, and they will donate their time and services. We will also work with local merchants to offer discounts at grocery and clothing stores. The committee did a wonderful job of helping us cut expenses, and I think we should give them a hand."

The church members nodded and clapped their hands in appreciation.

"Most of all, I'd like to give thanks to the late Eddie Duncan. Bishop has rescued us, it seems, from the grave, and has provided a cushion that should keep us financially secure for years to come. Unbeknownst to me, my father had taken out a life insurance policy for a million dollars, and Brother Duncan was the beneficiary. My father entrusted Brother Duncan to present the funds to the church when a financial crisis arose, and that's exactly what Brother Duncan did. The monies were deposited into an interest-bearing account. I marvel at the power of God. He is awesome and supplies our every need. The committee and I decided the funds will be distributed on an as-needed basis."

After the service had concluded, Ruth returned to her office. Sitting on her desk was a vase of red roses. She smiled after she opened the card and read the note from Aron. She went into the bathroom adjoining her office and refreshed herself, and then went to the church dining room to have supper with her members.

When she arrived in the dining room, the family, along with Aron, were seated at the family's designated table. Sarah hugged her mother when Ruth came to the table.

"I'm so proud of you, Momma. You are truly our family treasure," Sarah said.

Aron winked at Ruth. During the course of the meal, several members stopped by to tell Ruth that she had their support, and how proud Bishop would be of her.

She said a silent prayer of thanks inside her heart. She knew Bishop and Ezra were smiling down at her from heaven, the two men who had greatly shaped and influenced her life.

Chapter Forty-three

A month later, the Wilcox family was seated in the auditorium of McDade Elementary School for Maggie's eighth-grade graduation. Naomi and Montgomery had driven up from Edwardsville. Queen Esther, Alice, and Fred were there, along with Daniel and his sons. Fred's family was in attendance too. DJ, Chelsea, and their son, D3, had flown in from Atlanta for the ceremony. All the men in the family stood up, cheered, and whistled when the principal presented Maggie with her diploma. She blushed as she returned to her seat. She had received several awards.

Joshua took pictures of his sister and her friends, while Brian videotaped the ceremony. Sarah had a bouquet of roses in her lap to present to her daughter.

Sarah decided to hold the family dinner at the Hilton Hotel in Oak Lawn in a private dining room. After the ceremony and photo session, the family piled into their cars, left the crowded parking lot, and headed west on Ninety-fifth Street. When they arrived at the hotel, Aron, Monet, Marcus, Faith, and the twins joined them.

After the large party was seated, everyone congratulated Maggie again, and they presented her with envelopes. She eagerly tore them open.

"Wow, I feel rich," she exclaimed, riffling the dollars and checks. "Thank you, everyone. I love you!" she said, blowing kisses at her family.

"That money is going into your bank account, to be used for college," Sarah informed her daughter emphatically.

"Aw, Mommy, can't I buy a few things?" Maggie complained. She looked at her mother hopefully.

"Sure, you can," Alice told Maggie as Fred sat comfortably at her side. "If your mother won't let you use that money, I'll take you shopping."

"See, that's what I mean, Aunt Alice. You spoil her rotten." Sarah shook her head.

The wait staff brought out glasses of water and warm bread, and placed them on the table.

"That's what grand-godmothers are for," Alice told Sarah. "I swear, you sound like your mother. She used to say the same thing."

"My being like Momma is a good thing." Sarah smiled at Ruth and Aron, whose heads were bent together as they talked.

"Thank you, Aunt Alice. I'm so glad you feel better. I missed my cooking lessons," Maggie said.

"I missed them too, little girl. Cancer may have had me down, but not out," Alice lovingly told Maggie. During her last medical appointment, she heard the news she was praying to hear: her cancer was in remission.

"I feel so special. Everyone in the family is here, including Uncle DJ, Aunt Chelsea, and D3. Thank you for coming, Uncle DJ."

DJ smiled at his niece. "We wouldn't have missed it for the world. You, Joshua, and D3 are growing up so fast. It's good when we can get together as a family and celebrate happy events."

Queen Esther sat on Ruth's left and Aron on her right side. The older woman leaned over to her daughter and whispered, "Who did you say those people are again?" She gestured her head toward Aron and the Caldwell family.

"That's my friend, Aron, and his family. You remember, you met them a few months ago. Aron came with me to visit you last week," Ruth said.

"Oh, I forgot." Queen Esther looked thoughtfully at Aron's family.

The waiters returned to the table, carrying soups and salads. They quickly distributed them among the family.

Conversation flowed smoothly among the guests. Daniel and DJ spoke more cordially than they had in years. Daniel's oldest son sat on his left, while his youngest sons were on his right. Daniel had settled into the new house; and at Sarah's urging, Daniel had begun calling his oldest son on the weekends. They were on the way to mending their relationship. Ruth urged her son to bury the hatchet, since his father had taken the first step. DJ decided to heed her advice.

In thirty minutes, the entrées were placed on the table. Ruth blessed the food, while the family joined hands. "Father above, thank you for bringing my family together again as we celebrate Maggie's graduation. As Maggie's daddy said, we hope it's the first of what will be at least two or three more graduations. Continue to bless my grandbaby as she enters into yet another phase of life. Bless all of us gathered here today. Bless the cooks. Amen."

The clink of forks and knives made music upon the plates as the family partook in the scrumptious steak and seafood meals.

"So, Nay, when are you getting married? Have you and Montgomery set a date?" DJ asked. "Your ring is blinding me."

"We're thinking June of next year. That should give us enough time to plan everything." Naomi grabbed Montgomery's hand. "I like the sound of having a June wedding."

"Are you going to get married here or in Edwards-ville?" Chelsea asked.

"We haven't quite decided, and I need to start making plans soon. Momma suggested we have the wedding in the garden at our house, and I'm kind of partial to that idea. We won't have to spend time on finding a venue. That would be one thing I could scratch off our list."

"Can I be in your wedding?" Maggie shyly asked Naomi.

"Of course, you can. I have you penciled in as my junior bridesmaid. And I hope you and D3 will be ushers, Joshua."

Joshua smiled and bobbed his head, while D3 nodded excitedly and said, "I've never been in a wedding before."

"I'd also like to break with tradition and have Momma and Daddy give me away, if that's okay with you, Daddy?" Naomi asked Daniel.

"Times have sure changed. I guess I have no choice but to go along with the program. That's fine," Daniel replied affably.

"How long are you going to be here?" Daniel asked his oldest son.

"Chelsea and I have a week leave. We're close to the end of our tour, and we're considering moving back to Chicago to be close to the family. But I don't know, I've kind of gotten used to those mild winters in the South."

"I hear you on that. Well, I hope you will consider moving back to Chicago. It would be nice having you back here," Daniel told his son.

At the other end of the table, Sarah informed Naomi, "You know Monet coordinates weddings when she has time. You might want to get some pointers from her."

"Sure, I'm going to need all the help I can get. Make sure you give me your information before we leave," Naomi told Monet.

"I sure will. I worked as a nurse, but after my little ones were born, I decided to coordinate weddings, and, of course, volunteer at the church. My brother is getting married in the fall, and I'm working with him and his fiancée."

"That's sounds like fun. I know it must have been hard to leave nursing."

Monet pushed her hair back off her shoulder. "It was, and I miss it, but I'm truly enjoying my new job as a mother. When the boys start school, I may return to work."

"Great. I just began working as an actuary for the state, and so far, I'm enjoying my new job," Naomi told Monet.

Daniel held up his hand to get everyone's attention. He announced that he would retain custody of the boys, after conferring with his spiritual advisor. He looked at Ruth and smiled. "I decided that would be the best course to take. My finances have improved. It helps when your ex marries money, so I can relax a bit. We moved into the new house a few weeks ago."

"How did Lenora's boyfriend react about finding out that Darnell is his son?" Naomi whispered to her father, who was sitting on her left side.

"At first he was shocked and then he talked to me, man-to-man. He pays child support for all the boys for Lenora. We plan to tell Darnell the truth when he's older."

As the family continued to talk, Aron took Ruth's hand under the table and held it. Ruth looked out and took stock of her family. There were new faces and familiar old faces, but, most of all, the family unit had been preserved. All that really mattered in the long run was family members being there for each other, and supporting one another, in good times and in bad.

Little did Aron know, but Ruth had a rose of her own to present to him. Her color selection would be red.

God had revealed to Ruth what Aron's role in her life would be. Ruth decided she might buck tradition and ask Aron to marry her.

She took heart in knowing that Sarah, Brian, DJ, and Chelsea would become overseers of the family, when the time came, along with Naomi. She felt secure in knowing the family would be in good hands.

Thank You, Father, for the blessing you have bestowed on my family. Ruth looked upward, closed her eyes, and smiled beautifully.

Readers' Group Guide Questions

1. Do you feel Ruth had grown both spiritually and emotionally since reading about her in *Keeping Misery Company*?

2. How did you feel about Ruth putting Queen in a nursing home? Should she have allowed Queen to live with her? Did she make the correct decision, given her lifestyle?

3. Were you surprised that Alice and Fred had become a couple?

4. Should Ruth have developed a relationship with Aron, given his background?

5. Did Daniel deserve what happened with him and Lenora?

6. Should Ruth have reconciled with Daniel?

7. How did you feel about Naomi and her fiancée, Montgomery? Was she remiss in her relationship with her family?

8. Do you think Queen was lonely? Did the family do a good job with visiting her?

9. Did you feel Fred had matured? What about Daniel?

10. Should Naomi have acknowledged Sarah and Brian as her parents?

11. Should Ruth have allowed Sarah and Naomi room to develop a mother-daughter relationship?

12. What did you think about Lenora leaving Daniel for a younger man? Was that in character for her?

13. Would Daniel have been justified in allowing Felicia and Reggie to raise his children? Was he too old?

14. Did you feel Daniel had genuine feelings for Ruth? Or was he looking for financial help?

15. Were you pleased with the sequel to *Keeping Misery Company*? Why or why not?

UC HIS GLORY BOOK CLUB!

www.uchisglorybookclub.net

UC His Glory Book Club is the spirit-inspired brain-child of Joylynn Jossel, Author and Acquisitions Editor of Urban Christian, and Kendra Norman-Bellamy, Author for Urban Christian. This is an online book club that hosts authors of Urban Christian. We welcome as members all men and women who have a passion for reading Christian-based fiction.

UC His Glory Book Club pledges our commitment to provide support, positive feedback, encouragement, and a forum whereby members can openly discuss and review the literary works of Urban Christian authors.

There is no membership fee associated with UC His Glory Book Club; however, we do ask that you support the authors through purchasing, encouraging, providing book reviews, and of course, your prayers. We also ask that you respect our beliefs and follow the guidelines of the book club. We hope to receive your valuable input, opinions, and reviews that build up, rather than tear down our authors.

WHAT WE BELIEVE

—We believe that Jesus is the Christ, Son of the Living God.

—We believe the Bible is the true, living Word of God.

—We believe all Urban Christian authors should use their God-given writing abilities to honor God and share the message of the written word God has given to each of them uniquely.

—We believe in supporting Urban Christian authors in their literary endeavors by reading, purchasing and sharing their titles with our online community.

—We believe that in everything we do in our literary arena should be done in a manner that will lead to God being glorified and honored.

—We look forward to the online fellowship with you. Please visit us often at www.uchisglorybookclub.net.

Many Blessing to You!

Shelia E. Lipsey,
President, UC His Glory Book Club